X

# It Had to Be You

# Books by Janice Thompson

## WEDDINGS BY BELLA

*Fools Rush In*
*Swinging on a Star*
*It Had to Be You*

*Weddings* by *Bella*

BOOK THREE

# IT HAD *to* BE YOU

A NOVEL

## Janice Thompson

Revell

*a division of Baker Publishing Group*
Grand Rapids, Michigan

© 2010 by Janice Thompson

Published by Revell
a division of Baker Publishing Group
P.O. Box 6287, Grand Rapids, MI 49516-6287
www.revellbooks.com

Printed in the United States of America

Library of Congress Cataloging-in-Publication Data
Thompson, Janice A.
    It had to be you : a novel / Janice Thompson.
        p.    cm. — (Weddings by Bella ; bk. 3)
    ISBN 978-0-8007-3344-5 (pbk.)
    1. Weddings—Planning—Fiction. I. Title.
PS3620.H6824I8  2010
813'.6—dc22                                                    2009048667

Published in association with MacGregor Literary Agency.

10   11   12   13   14   15   16        7   6   5   4   3   2   1

To Emilio. Mama mia! You've been a wonderful addition to the family. Also, to Brenda White, Don Pope, and the other illustrious members of the swing band at my daughter's surprise birthday party. And to my four girls, who boogie-woogied the night away along with their friends. Swing's the thing!

Those from Italy send you their greetings.
Hebrews 13:24

# 1

## You Make Me Feel So Young

If Aunt Rosa and Uncle Lazarro hadn't wasted sixteen years bickering over who was the better singer—Frank Sinatra or Dean Martin—they probably would have ended up married years ago . . . and I would never have found myself trying to factor a mob boss into the wedding party. Still, I've learned not to question God's timing, particularly in matters of the heart. So what if the sixtysomething lovebirds waited until their golden years to confess their undying love for each other? The blissful couple still had plenty of days ahead to make up for lost time. And I made it my goal to give them the best possible chance at happiness by coordinating a wedding they wouldn't soon forget, even if it did include a few questionable characters from their past.

Laz and Rosa's desire for a forties-themed reception came as no surprise. They were both born during the swing era, after all. But their plan to transform our family's Galveston Island wedding facility into a big band wonderland would take some work . . . and lots of it. With only six weeks till the mid-December extravaganza, I had my hands full. Hiring a band, designing the room, helping Rosa pick out her gown and forties-themed bridesmaids' dresses. Whew! And all while planning my own wedding to D.J. Neeley, the hunkiest cowboy on the island. How could I possibly handle it all?

Ah yes, with the Lord's help. He alone would see me through this. And I might even have a little fun along the way.

I met with the happy couple on a Tuesday afternoon in late October to talk things through. We didn't have to go far to meet. After all, our family-run wedding facility was just next door to the Rossi home on Broadway, near the heart of the island.

Rosa, my mother's older sister, grinned like a Cheshire cat as she settled into her seat on the opposite side of my desk. Rosa had never been the sort to pay much attention to her hair or makeup, and her simple dresses—which were usually hidden behind a tomato-stained apron—weren't exactly couture. The sagging knee-highs were a bit of a distraction at times, as were the orthopedic shoes. Oh, but as she sat across from me now, a blushing bride-to-be, the joy of the Lord radiated from her smile and her eyes. In that moment I thought her the most beautiful bride I'd ever seen. I could hardly wait to see her walk down the aisle in her white wedding gown.

My gaze shifted to Lazarro, my father's older brother. Laz had always been the cocky, sophisticated sort with a somewhat brusque demeanor. These days, however, he was a changed man, a happier version of his old self. That's what love would do to you. This I knew from firsthand experience, having finally met the man of my dreams. Like Uncle Laz, I had been transformed.

Rosa glanced at the clock on the wall, her eyes narrowing.

"We can't stay long, Bella. Laz and I have already started dinner. We'll need to get back to the house by 5:30."

"No problem. I'll have you out of here in plenty of time." I leaned back in my chair, my gaze shifting between my aunt and uncle. "So, let's start with you. What's up? You two said you had something special to tell me. I'm dying to know."

"Bella, the most wonderful thing has happened." Rosa looked at Uncle Lazarro, then back at me. She clasped her hands together and grinned. "Laz has found the *perfect* swing band for our reception."

"Oh?" This news surprised me, particularly in light of the fact that I'd been looking for a band for over a week now and hadn't been able to locate one yet. Apparently, there was a run on swing bands during the Christmas season. Most were booked well into the New Year. How my uncle had accomplished this feat was nothing short of a miracle.

Laz leaned forward, and I could read the excitement in his eyes. "These guys are based out of Houston. They're called Band of Gold. Want to guess why?"

"Um, they have matching gold jackets?"

"Nope."

"Gold teeth?" I tried.

"No." Laz laughed. "I'll put you out of your misery. They're all in their golden years. The youngest guy in the group is sixty-seven. The oldest is eighty-four."

"Whoa." I swallowed hard, curious as to how this would work. "Laz, have you heard their music? How do you know they're any good?"

"I went to their website this morning," he said with a wave of his hand. "Heard samples of their stuff. They're amazing. And they know all of the best swing music—Glenn Miller, Benny Goodman, Tommy Dorsey, Cab Calloway, Kay Kyser,

Count Basie, Paul Whiteman, Artie Shaw." He went off on a tangent, listing bands I'd never even heard of. Apparently Band of Gold knew them all and played their tunes to perfection, at least according to Laz.

"They even feature a few Rosemary Clooney songs," Rosa threw in when Laz paused for breath. "You know how much I love her music." She began to list Rosemary's top ten songs, her eyes wide with excitement. Then she began to sing "Come On-a My House" in perfect pitch. Hmm. Maybe we could get Rosa to sing a number at her own reception. Something to think about.

My aunt finally stopped singing and flashed a girlish smile. "Great music sets the tone for a wonderful event, and we want the best." As she began to explain her passion for music, her language shifted to Italian. I had to smile. She often did this when excited, though she rarely realized it.

"Well, speaking of the best music around, what about Sinatra and Dino?" I asked the question hesitantly, predicting the answer before it was spoken. For years, Rosa had listened to nothing but Ol' Blue Eyes. And my uncle's addiction to Dean Martin had spilled over to his restaurant, Parma John's, where the daily pizza specials were named after some of Dino's most famous songs. The Mambo Italiano was still my favorite, but the Simpatico came in a close second. Just thinking about that pepperoni made my mouth water, even now.

Rosa shook her head at my question. "We've declared a truce."

"And in honor of that truce, there will be no Dean Martin tunes played at our wedding," Laz said with a nod. "I've had my fill of him."

"Or Frank Sinatra tunes," Rosa was quick to add. "I'm sick to death of Ol' Blue Eyes, if you want the truth of it."

"Gotcha." I knew they'd put their quarreling to rest, but secretly hoped they'd work in at least a few Sinatra/Martin tunes. The rest of the Rossi clan still loved the dynamic duo, even if Rosa and Laz had given up on them. "Well, tell me more about your new band, and I'll get them booked right away." Reaching for a pen and paper, I scribbled down the information Uncle Laz gave. Turned out the bandleader was a fellow named Gordy. I made a mental note to call him as soon as our little meeting ended.

"Will you still need a deejay?" I asked.

"Of course." Rosa nodded. "Someone has to run this show."

"D.J. or Armando?" I listed my fiancé first, hoping they would pick him instead of my impulsive middle brother. Thankfully, Rosa played along.

"I'd say D.J. He's got that nice bass voice that all the women love. It's like velvet."

"I'm not so sure about that," Uncle Lazarro said. "Armando knows the soundboard. And he's familiar with big band music. He might be the better choice this time around."

"Sounds like a compromise is in order," I said. "Armando can run the sound, and D.J. can schmooze the crowd with his silky voice. Agreed?"

"Agreed," Rosa said with a nod.

Uncle Laz leaned over and gave my aunt a gentle kiss on the lips. She turned several shades of red. I diverted my attention by reaching for my bottle of water and taking a swig.

"That's one of the things I love most about you, Rosa," Laz whispered. "Always ready to compromise. And so even-tempered."

The water almost came shooting out of my nose at that point. I'd heard Laz call Aunt Rosa a great many things over the years. They had, after all, been archenemies. But, even-tempered? Never had those words been used to describe her. Stifling a chuckle, I tried to imagine my volatile aunt as even-tempered.

*Time to get this train back on track, Bella.* I did my best to keep them focused on the matter at hand—their wedding. Scribbling the information down, I said, "It's settled then. D.J. and Armando will work together. And now, about the caterers . . ."

Laz put his hand up in the air. "You know me better than that, Bella. I couldn't possibly hire a caterer at my own wedding."

"I would never dream of it either," Rosa said, crossing her arms at her chest. "I will cook."

"So will I." Laz nodded.

"But how?" I asked. "I know you two are the best cooks on the island, but catering your own wedding? You'll be exhausted. It's too much to expect." I turned to Rosa. "Can't you see the dilemma? You'll be worn out by the time you get into your dress." *And you'll probably end up with tomato sauce all over the front of it.*

"Of course it's not too much to expect," Rosa exclaimed. "I cook every day of my life. I can certainly cook for my own wedding." As my eyes narrowed, she quickly added, "But don't you worry, Bella. I'll start preparing the food days ahead of time. There won't be much to do on the final day, anyway. Just getting it warmed up and onto the tables is all, really."

"Besides, Jenna and Bubba will be there to help," Laz said with a wave of his hand.

I nodded, realizing that my best friend and her boyfriend would do all they could to make the day easier on Rosa and Laz. Not that I'd seen much of Jenna lately. Now that we were both in love—she with the younger Neeley brother and I with the older—we barely saw each other any more. I'd have to remedy that, and soon.

Laz's voice jolted me back to the present. "We will have the best Italian food our friends and family have ever seen!" He and Rosa dove into a lengthy chat about the various food items, and I wrote everything down, just in case they forgot.

When Laz finally paused, I had one more question for him. "Have you two settled on your honeymoon spot yet?"

"Have we!" He grinned ear to ear.

"Why, I'm surprised you didn't figure it out, Bella," Rosa said with a smile. "It's so obvious. We're going to—"

"Napoli!" Laz joined her in shouting.

"We're going back to our roots, Bella Bambina," Rosa said with tears in her eyes. "To Naples. Do you know how many years it's been since I've seen my homeland?"

"Seven? Eight?" I said.

"Nine and a half." She dabbed at her eyes. "I miss the Italian countryside so much." She smiled. "And we've come up with the perfect plan. Did your mama tell you that our middle sisters are coming from Italy for the wedding?"

"Yes, she's thrilled."

"So am I." Rosa's eyes brimmed over. "Bertina and Bianca will stand up for me, along with your mother, of course."

"That's what Mama said. I'm so excited for you." If anyone deserved to see her family on her wedding day, it was Aunt Rosa. She'd left so many friends and loved ones behind all those years ago when she came to live with us in the States.

"My brother is coming from Italy as well." Laz nodded. "Haven't seen Emilio in ages."

"We're all flying back together," Rosa explained. "It will

be a party all the way from Houston to Rome. I can hardly wait!"

I wanted to ask how they could possibly have time to themselves on their honeymoon with this plan in motion, but didn't. Frankly, every time I thought about my elderly aunt and uncle having a honeymoon, I felt a little squeamish. There were just some things a girl didn't need to know.

One thing I knew for sure, though. As I stared at the look of love pouring out of my aunt's eyes, and when I watched the tender way Uncle Laz spoke to her, I realized they both completed each other. Oh, and if the Lord could do that for two people who had once despised one another, what wonderful things lay ahead for a couple who had gotten off to a really great start—say, a bumbling wedding planner and the sweetest cowboy in the state of Texas?

Mmm! Suddenly, I could hardly wait to see D.J.

# 2

## Come On-a My House

For years, our family has leaned heavily on the old Italian saying, *Vivi bene, ridi spesso, e ama tanto.* "Live well, laugh often, love much." I've always loved the phrase and have found it to be a great recipe for happiness and contentment.

Now, I knew the Rossis had conquered the art of living well. No doubt about that. And our ever-growing family exuded love. Laughter came naturally too. With half a dozen family members residing under one roof and so many other friends and relatives living nearby, we never suffered for company. Even our meals were traditional Italian events—long, loud, and filled with entertaining stories. I knew tonight's dinner would be no different and, as always, looked forward to spending the evening with the people I loved most. The frosting on the cake? D.J. would be seated next to me for the whole thing.

Walking across the lawn from the wedding facility after our meeting, Rosa, Laz, and I continued our conversation about their big day. Only when I saw D.J.'s black Dodge 4x4 with its oversized running boards pull up did I find my thoughts shifting elsewhere. Something about the boy's arrival always made me a little giddy. I could almost envision myself fifty years from now, still getting butterflies when he walked in the door.

I gave my aunt and uncle an apologetic look for ditching them as I sprinted toward my hunky cowboy. I arrived at the edge of the driveway just as he stepped out of the cab, his pointed leather boots leading the way. Mmm! The scent of his heavenly cologne lingered in the air as he closed the truck door. Very manly. The stuff television commercials were made of.

"Bella." He flashed a winning smile, and I responded with a happy sigh. I loved the way the boy said my name: *Bay-luh*. Made me happy my parents had moved our family to the South.

My heart caught in my throat as I slipped into his outstretched arms. What was it about this guy that took my breath away? Ah yes . . . everything! I adored every single thing about him, inside and out. His heart for God. His love for my family. His tall, broad-shouldered physique. His brawny good looks. His boyish charm. His deep bass voice with its sultry Texas twang. His pressed jeans and worn leather boots. Yummy! I could live forever with a guy like this.

And I would. If things would just slow down long enough for me to plan our Valentine's Day wedding.

I planted a tender kiss on his lips, and he held me close. When we came up for air, he gazed into my eyes, brushing a long, dark curl off my face. "Wow. If that's how I'm greeted when I come back, I'll go away more often."

"Well, you've been gone forty-eight hours," I said with a

pout. "I missed you." Not that I minded, really. My honey's trek to his hometown of Splendora, about an hour and a half north of Galveston, was a gesture of kindness. D.J. had agreed to do some construction work on his parents' church. At no charge, of course. Just one more thing I loved about him—his generous nature.

"Sorry I was gone so long." He held me close again. "But thanks for understanding. My parents send their hellos, by the way. Mama wants you to know she's already picked out her dress for our wedding. She wanted to know if you thought red would be brazen, whatever that means."

"Funny." I laughed. "She knows our wedding colors are black and red, so red makes perfect sense. I'd rather she be brazen in red than mournful in black!"

"You have a point." He gave me a smile, and my heart fluttered. "But you know how my mom is. She wants us to be happy, and if that means changing the color of her dress, she's willing to do it."

"Aw." I grinned. Earline Neeley, my soon-to-be mother-in-law, was about the sweetest person I'd ever met. She and her church friends from Splendora would likely make our wedding unforgettable. They'd already impacted our lives in so many fun and quirky ways.

"I wish you could have heard me trying to talk my dad out of wearing his motorcycle jacket to the ceremony." D.J. laughed. "He suggested we have a motorcycle-themed ceremony. He even went into detail about how we could accomplish that. I'll spare you the details."

I couldn't help but laugh at that one. "Did you tell him we're going with a traditional Valentine's wedding instead? No gimmicks?"

"Yeah, but he's determined to sneak a Harley or two in

there. If I tell him our wedding colors, he'll probably have seat covers made to match. Oh, and by the way, he specifically asked if Guido was invited to the ceremony."

I groaned as D.J. mentioned our family's adopted parrot. "No. We left him off the guest list on purpose. Remember what happened the last time he showed up at a wedding?"

"How could I forget?" D.J. chuckled. "He stole my dad's toupee."

I shook my head, trying to push the image out of my brain. Oh, what chaos had transpired that horrible, wacky night! "Guido is a reformed bird now," I said. "Well, sort of, anyway. I still don't trust him in public arenas, so I'm going to have to put my foot down on this one. No birds at the wedding."

"Except the lovebirds that happen to be flying overhead at the time." D.J. winked, and my heart jolted. Oy, what this cowboy could do to me!

I gazed into his eyes and then gave him a kiss on the cheek. "You hungry?" I asked.

"Mmm." He quirked a brow, and his blue eyes twinkled. "You have to ask?"

"Laz made his famous Caesar salad tonight, and Rosa's cooking chicken parmesan."

"With her garlic twists?" D.J. asked, his eyebrows elevating.

"Of course!" My aunt's garlic twists were famous, not just on the island, but across the country. She'd recently been featured on a Food Network special, *Italian Chefs from Coast to Coast*. The fine folks at the network had offered her a show of her very own, but she'd turned them down after Laz declared his intentions. To her way of thinking, love trumped fame. I had to agree. Not that I'd ever been offered fame. Still, I had to believe I'd pick love any day.

"What's for dessert?" D.J. asked.

"White chocolate raspberry cheesecake."

At this announcement, we both closed our eyes and breathed deeply, enjoying a spiritual moment. Aunt Rosa's cheesecake was nothing short of heavenly, after all.

After a moment, D.J. kissed my closed eyelids. "What are we doing standing out here then?" he asked.

As we walked in the front door, the pungent aroma of garlic and other spices caused us both to stop and draw in another lingering breath. Rosa's cooking could do that to you.

"I'm learning to love that smell," D.J. said with a nod.

"It ain't chicken-fried steak," I responded with a laugh. "Not exactly Texas fare. But you have to admit, Rosa's the best cook on the island, and Laz comes in a close second."

"Yeah, I don't know what everyone is going to do without them once they get married."

I shook my head, unwilling to think about that. We'd all secretly wondered if we would starve to death once Rosa and Laz found their own place to live. Rosa had always resided in the room next to mine, with Laz's room just on the other side of hers. For as long as I'd remembered, she'd been a permanent fixture in both our home and our kitchen, where the magic took place. How would we make it without her? I had no idea.

"Looks like we'll be visiting them often." D.J. offered up a wink, once again melting my heart.

At this point, my Yorkie-Poo, Precious, greeted us by springing up and down repeatedly. I finally scooped her into my arms and planted a few kisses on her little head. "Were you a good girl while Mama was next door?" I asked in baby talk.

"Good?" Mama asked, approaching us. "You might want

to check out what she did in Rosa's room. She got into the silk floral centerpieces and chewed one of them up."

"No way!" Not after all the work we'd done on them. I leaned down to scold her, then found myself captivated by her sweet little face. Maybe I could scold her tomorrow. The centerpieces were replaceable. My loveable pooch was not.

As we approached the living room, I heard Uncle Laz's adopted parrot, Guido, singing "Amazing Grace." Nothing unusual there. We paused to look at him. Though he drove me crazy at times, I was happy to see that Guido's feathers were finally growing back in. He'd lost most of them over the summer—an allergic reaction.

When the song ended, the ornery parrot hollered, "Go to the mattresses!" then lifted his leg and let out what sounded like machine-gun fire. So much for saying the bird was reformed. Laz had been working with him for months now, but Guido was apparently still waffling. Another week or two and my uncle would surely have him walking the straight and narrow. No doubt about it. If anyone could work a miracle, Laz could.

Rosa and Laz headed into the kitchen to help Mama finish up our dinner, and I washed my hands, then went into the dining room to set the table. D.J. knew the routine, so he offered to help.

"How many?" he asked, holding up the placemats.

"Hmm." I did a quick head count. "Nick, Marcella, and their boys . . ." I smiled, thinking about my oldest brother and his wife. They were expecting a baby in a few months.

"What about Joey?" D.J. asked.

"Yes." My baby brother would be there too, along with his fiancée. "Norah will be with him." I paused a moment. "Armando won't be here. He's in Houston again." I shrugged as I thought of my middle brother. He was always flitting off after some woman or another, usually on the mainland.

"Sophia?"

"Yes." I smiled as my younger sister's latest announcement resurfaced in my brain. "And here's an interesting tidbit. She and Tony are dating. As in, seriously dating."

"Wow." D.J. almost lost his grip on the placemats at that announcement. No doubt. Seeing my sister with my ex-boyfriend still took a bit of getting used to. Personally, I thought they made a great couple and hoped things worked out for them.

D.J. composed himself, and his eyes narrowed as he did the math. "So, with your parents, Rosa, and Laz, that makes fourteen, right?"

"Sounds about right." I nodded.

"Good thing you have a big table." He pointed at the family's oversized mahogany table, imported from Europe.

"I hate to break it to you, D.J., but every Italian family has a table like this. And it's always filled with food and surrounded by laughter."

"Then I wish I'd been born in Italy." He released his hold on the placemats and gave me a kiss on the forehead.

"You're marrying into a true-blue Italian family. That's close enough." I wriggled into his arms, and we enjoyed a kiss for the record books.

Just then, my pop walked into the room. He narrowed his gaze. "Hey, no PDA."

Pop was half-kidding, but I knew what he meant. No public displays of affection. Not until after marriage, of course. D.J. and I backed away from each other as my father grabbed the placemats and started putting them in place.

"Oh, to be young again." Pop sighed but continued his work.

"No one says you have to be young to be in love," Laz said, entering the room. "Look at me and Rosa! I'll be sixty-seven next month, and she's—"

"She's not keen on you telling everyone her age," I threw in.

Laz grinned. "You're probably right. But you don't have to be young to be in love."

Just then, the sound of swing music filled the room. Laz's face lit up. "Ah. Rosa must've put in the Glenn Miller CD. We're trying to get in the mood before our big day." He laughed. "Get it? 'In the mood'?"

D.J.'s bright red cheeks faded to a somewhat lighter color as Laz explained that "In the Mood" was the name of a Glenn Miller song.

We continued to set up the room for dinner, adding Aunt Rosa's hand-painted plates from her beloved Napoli, silverware that had been in the family for over fifty years, and beautiful etched glasses Mama had purchased on her last European jaunt. When it was all said and done, D.J. and I stood back and stared at the table. He let out a whistle.

"Man. Looks like something out of a magazine."

"Prettier than a magazine," I added.

Rosa entered with a serving dish in hand. Chicken parmesan. The sauce still bubbled, and the melted mozzarella on top was perfectly browned. Yum! I could hardly wait to take my first bite.

The pungent aroma of garlic now permeated the room. I drew in a long breath, savoring every second. My mouth watered as I looked down at the table. The vibrant colors of the red tomato gravy and the crisp, green Caesar salad drew my eye. These, combined with the steam coming from the buttered garlic twists, made me so hungry I could hardly wait for the others.

Still, I must wait. Probably wouldn't be very nice to dive right in ahead of the crowd. No, that sort of thing was left to Armando, who had a habit of beating the rest of us to the punch. When he bothered to show up, anyway.

By the time Rosa and Laz had the food on the table, the room was full. My brother Joey arrived first with his fiancée. Norah gave me a hug and commented on my new blouse, a silky green number I'd picked up on a recent trip to the Galleria in Houston. My older brother Nick arrived next with his boys, Deany-boy and Frankie.

"Hey, where's Marcella?" I asked, looking around.

"She's here. Just had to make a pit stop."

True enough, Marcella walked into the dining room a couple of minutes later, her protruding belly leading the way. She looked miserably uncomfortable, in spite of her stretchy maternity attire.

"How's it going at the florist shop?" I asked. "Did you get all of the flowers ordered for Rosa?"

"Yes." She nodded. "I finally found them at that great place in Houston near the medical center." She released a groan as she took a seat. "Sorry if I seem a little out of sorts. I've been on my feet all day, and this baby is giving me fits."

"Morning sickness?" I asked.

"No, that passed ages ago. I'm starting to feel him move now."

"Him?" I quirked a brow in Nick's direction, wondering if he and his wife had been keeping something from us. Marcella and Nick already had two boys. Two hyper, disobedient boys, who had now taken to fighting over where they were going to

23

sit. I was holding out for a girl this time around. Surely her timely arrival would break the evil spell.

My sister Sophia entered the room moments later with my ex-boyfriend on her heels. I'd known Tony DeLuca for years. He was, as my mother put it, practically perfect in every way. Came from just the right family line in Sicily. Spoke fluent Italian. Was shockingly handsome. Still, I'd never truly fallen for him, and in the end, I'd broken his heart with my rejection of his affections.

Funny. As he gazed into my sister's big brown eyes, he didn't look heartbroken now. Tony had always enjoyed hanging out at the Rossi home. Perhaps he'd had the right address all along, just the wrong girl.

Not that I minded. Oh no. My gaze shifted to the one person whose heartstrings were looped with my own—D.J. Neeley. The background music changed to a familiar swing number, and I wanted to grab him by the hand and ask for a spin around the dance floor. Only, not now. Those tantalizing garlic twists still called out to me. There would be plenty of time for dancing later, especially if this swing music kept up.

Within seconds, everyone in the household was gathered around the table. My gaze shifted from my perfectly made-up mother to my father, who had actually combed his hair and put on a shirt for dinner. Then I transitioned my thoughts to Laz as he pulled out a seat for Rosa. In all the years I'd known him, I'd never seen this loving, tender side of him. Ah, what love could do to a crusty old heart! It had melted Uncle Laz like the mozzarella on top of the chicken parmesan.

"Let's pray." Pop's voice rang out above the chatter of my other family members.

We all reached to take hands, though I noticed Deany-boy

and Frankie refused to touch each other. Nothing new there. They would come around in time, surely.

I closed my eyes and listened as my father's melodic voice rang out. Even after half a lifetime in the States, he still had that marvelous lyrical sound to his voice—kind of like water flowing over rocks.

When the prayer ended, everyone began to talk at once. To my left, Nick and Joey talked about something that had happened at Parma John's. Marcella and Rosa talked about flowers. Mama told Pop about a website she'd found with great deals on European vacations. Laz and D.J. talked about music for the upcoming wedding. Sophia chatted with Norah about wedding dresses. Deany-boy and Frankie argued over a video game. The only one not talking was, well, me. Not that I minded. I was having too much fun just listening.

As always, the voices overlapped. I heard snippets of a thousand conversations.

"Are you thinking of using babies' breath—"

"—to take a train to the wine country. Then we'll move on to the Vatican. After that, we'll—"

"—add a new pizza to our menu. I'm thinking it's going to be—"

"—a great swing number that the band can play. And speaking of bands, we've hired the best one in the country. Wait till you see their—"

"—new video game! It's the best. Even better than a—"

"—pink wedding dress? Are you kidding me? White is still the ideal color for a wedding dress, no matter what the bridal magazines try to tell you. Those—"

"—Double Delight roses have the prettiest petals I've ever seen in my life. Have you ever seen such a great mixture of colors and—"

"What a dish! This chicken parmesan is the best thing I've ever eaten in my life. I'd like another—"

"Garlic twist, anyone?" Rosa held up the plate, and Nick reached for it, never dropping a line in his conversation with Joey about the new pizza they planned to add to the menu at Parma John's.

Above the noise, a pinging sound rang out. I looked across the table to see Laz tapping his water glass with his spoon. "Attention, everyone. Attention. Rosa and I have an announcement to make."

"You're eloping?" Pop suggested with a smile.

"Over my dead body!" I whispered, chasing away the shudder that wiggled down my spine. They'd better not!

"I've talked about this for months, but I've finally decided to officially retire from the restaurant," Laz said. "Want to give my undivided attention to our wedding and our wedding guests."

"Isn't that wonderful?" Rosa beamed with delight.

"Nick and Joey can handle things without me," Laz said. "And if I can keep Jenna focused, I think the transition will be fine."

Keeping my best friend focused might be harder than he knew. She was, after all, in love.

Laz put his hand to his chest and spoke with a tremor in his voice. "I have more news to share. As you know, my good friend Salvadore Lucci has entrusted Guido to us for a season. I don't take that season lightly. The Lord has given us this time to minister to Guido in the hopes that he will remember what he's learned and share it with Sal when the time comes."

I sighed, thinking about my uncle's passion to reach out to his friend Sal. Call it desperation. Call it inspiration from on high. Laz had this idea that Sal would be won by the words coming from Guido's beak, so he'd been filling the bird's head with sermons, songs, and Scriptures. He called this the "Triple S" program.

I watched with tenderness wrapping my heart as Laz dabbed his eyes and whispered, *"Chi la dura la vince."* I knew the translation, of course: "He who perseveres wins at last." Laz would keep at this until the very end, if need be.

From across the table, Pop's voice rang out. "What are you saying, Laz? Is Sal coming to get Guido? To take him back to Atlantic City?"

Laz nodded and his eyes filled with tears. "Yes. I'm gonna miss the old bird." He dabbed his eyes. "Guido, I mean."

"When is Sal coming?" Sophia asked.

Laz's eyes lit with excitement. "One week before our big day. He will stay at the Tremont and help me with the wedding plans. In fact . . ." Laz's eyes brimmed over. "Sal has agreed to be my best man."

I stifled the gasp that threatened to escape at this news. Sal? Was he serious?

Nick looked at Laz in horror. "You picked someone with mob ties to stand up for you at your wedding? Are you kidding me?"

"Nicholas, please." Laz shook his head. "Sal is seventy-six years old. Whatever ties he might've had have long since been severed. And, as you know, my primary goal is to win Salvadore Lucci to the Lord while there is still time, so please do not question my motives."

The room fell silent. Rarely did we hear Laz chasten anyone in such a way. But as I looked into his tear-filled eyes, I realized the truth—he genuinely cared about Sal's relationship with the Lord and would do whatever it took to share the truth of God's love with his friend. No one could fault him for his passion. His common sense, perhaps, but not his passion.

D.J. leaned over and whispered in my ear. "I think your uncle is the most amazing man I've ever met. Next to my dad and your father, of course."

Well, there you had it. D.J. Neeley—Galveston's hunkiest cowboy—could see straight through to my uncle's heart and apparently loved what he saw. Which only made me love D.J. Neeley all the more.

# 3

# The Gang's All Here

The weeks before Rosa and Laz's big day flew by at warp speed. Before long, everything was running together in my head. And I'd never heard so much swing music in all my life! Rosa and Laz played it around the clock, listening to tunes that kept my toes tapping. Every song made me want to get up and dance. But who had time to dance? There were dresses to order, centerpieces to make, linens to press. The workload kept my fingers flying.

Exactly one week before the wedding, Pop led the way to the George Bush Intercontinental Airport on Houston's north end to pick up our relatives from Napoli. D.J. and I followed in his 4x4. From where I sat in the cab, I felt like a queen—on top of the world. I could hardly contain my excitement as we made our way north on Interstate 45.

"Thanks for doing this, D.J.," I said. "I know how busy you are at this time of year, so it means a lot to me that you would help pick up my relatives."

"Sounds like the perfect thing to do on a Saturday," he said.

"Well, I know you've got your new business and all . . ." Offering up a reassuring smile, I thought about the many possibilities his new construction business would afford.

"I've been thinking about asking Bubba to come to work for me. If I can ever find him, I mean."

"Bubba's missing?"

"Sort of." D.J. shrugged. "I tried to call him this morning and he didn't answer. He didn't respond to an email I sent yesterday either. If I don't hear from him by nightfall, I'm going to call my parents and ask about him."

"It's not barbecue cook-off season, is it?" I asked. Bubba Neeley was the brisket champion at the Houston Livestock Show and Rodeo. Not that I'd ever paid much attention to such things. Until meeting D.J., of course.

"No, it's not cook-off season." D.J. shook his head. "Not till late February."

"Well, this is really odd." I gave him a pensive look. "Laz told me that Jenna called him a couple of days ago with the most cryptic message. Said something unexpected came up and she wouldn't be in for a few days. He took it to mean she wasn't feeling so well, but I'm not sure. She's been acting so weird lately. Have you noticed?"

"They both have."

We sat in silence for a moment before one of us—me—finally broke it with a speculation. "D.J., do you think they're . . . together?"

His expression tightened. "I know my brother better than that. He's got his head on straight. He won't do anything to compromise Jenna. Besides, my mom would kill him if she got wind of the fact that he and Jenna were . . . well, you know."

I shook my head, more confused than ever. "She's not returning my calls. I wonder if she's upset at me."

30

"Why would she be?" D.J. asked.

"No idea." I offered up a shrug. "I missed a couple of calls from her last week, and I did try to call her back, I promise. I've been so busy planning two weddings at once." A sigh erupted. "I'm a terrible friend."

"No, you're not. You're just distracted. But no one can blame you. Your plate is really full right now, Bella."

As I glanced at his chiseled features and winsome smile, I had to admit, my plate wasn't the only thing that was full. Nope. My heart felt pretty full right about now too.

We continued north through Houston. I tried to push all thoughts of my best friend out of my mind to focus on the conversation with the guy I adored. This was the first time in weeks we'd really been alone. Might as well enjoy it.

"So, tell me about these folks we're picking up," D.J. said with that crooked grin I loved so much. "How many people are coming, anyway?"

"Well, let's see." I went through my mental checklist. "Mama and Rosa have two sisters between them, Bianca and Bertina. They're twins."

"I think I've heard you talk about them."

"Right. One is widowed and the other divorced. They're coming with Bertina's oldest daughter, Deanna, my cousin." I dove into a story about what fun I'd had with Deanna years ago, the last time we'd seen each other. "It's so sad that our family lives so far away. We hardly ever get to see each other, but this week is going to be a blast. The house is going to be filled to overflowing."

"Your house is already filled to overflowing." He shook his head and chuckled. "Never seen so many people under one roof in all of my life."

"But wait, there's more!" I laughed. "My pop and Uncle

31

Laz have a middle brother, Uncle Emilio, also from Napoli. He's a bachelor in his late fifties, never married. Sort of a quiet man. I never really got to know him very well."

"Maybe that will change this time around."

I shrugged. "In a family as big as mine, we're surrounded on every side by relatives. There's hardly time to get to know anyone well. Let's just say he's always had a mysterious air about him. He's a puzzle waiting to be solved."

"Intriguing."

"No kidding."

I lit into another story about something Laz and Emilio had done years ago, but I had trouble concentrating. For whatever reason, I kept thinking about Jenna. Should I call her? See why she'd skipped out on work? I pulled out my cell phone and punched in her number but got her voice mail. Very strange.

Thankfully, I didn't have long to think about it. We arrived at the airport in short order and met up with my parents in the parking garage. I hadn't seen my mother this excited in years, but who could blame her?

"We're supposed to meet everyone in baggage claim." Pop looked at his watch. "Their plane should have landed by now. Hopefully we won't have long to wait."

Unfortunately, the baggage claim area in the international terminal was a mess. I'd never seen so many people or heard so many overlapping languages at once. I somehow found myself separated from D.J. and my parents. With so many people pressing in around me, I had to wonder if I would ever see them again. A woman in a sari called out to a little girl in a language I couldn't quite make out.

Peering through the crowd, I tried to find a familiar face or two. Moments later, a suave-looking fellow in an expensive suit walked my way. He pulled off his Versace sunglasses and flashed a winning smile.

"Uncle Emilio!" I grinned as I sprinted his direction. "So happy to . . ." My words trailed off as a curvaceous young woman approached carrying a Gucci handbag. I took in the stunning brunette, overwhelmed by her full, pouty lips, her high, rose-blushed cheekbones, the whitest teeth I'd ever seen, and eyes the color of espresso under beautifully made-up eyelids. The woman was the very picture of perfection, though I had my suspicions there was a bit of collagen involved in the pouty lips.

The intriguing stranger slipped her arm through Emilio's and gave him a coy smile. "Sorry, baby," she said in Italian. "Had to make a pit stop."

*Baby?* I looked at this person—whoever she was—completely stunned. She couldn't be much older than me, if even. Did Uncle Emilio have a daughter I knew nothing about? If so, why had he kept her hidden all of these years? Stranger still, why did she call him "baby"? I shook my head, convinced I'd misunderstood.

Emilio grinned, pulling her close. "Bella, this is Francesca Adriana Rossi, my wife."

"Your . . . wife?" I could hardly formulate the words, the shock was so severe. *Just wait till Pop and Laz find out about this!* I stood there gaping for a moment, then finally came to my senses. Extending my hand, I managed, "Francesca, welcome to Texas. We're happy to have you."

"*Gratzi.*" Her voice sounded like velvet. She dove into a lengthy explanation in Italian of how she'd hoped to give us the news by phone ahead of time. Apparently Emilio had other ideas. He liked the element of surprise. I just hoped Uncle Laz's heart could take it. And what would

Rosa think about this Sophia Loren look-alike? I could only imagine!

Francesca ended with words that took awhile to absorb. "If Emilio is your uncle, I guess that would make me your aunt!" A giggle escaped her pouty lips.

"Well, I guess it does," was about all I could muster. Was it possible to have an aunt my own age? All of my others were in their fifties, at least. Still, I couldn't deny Francesca's relationship with my uncle, could I? Instead, I just smiled and nodded, something my very polite mama had taught me to do when in doubt.

D.J. miraculously appeared at that moment. Being the consummate Southern gentleman, he dove into a well-intentioned conversation with the happy couple as we fetched their bags. Looked like Francesca had great taste in luggage. I'd never seen so much Gucci in my life. Dollar signs rolled around where my eyeballs used to be as I took it all in. Mama mia! To have luggage like that . . . I could only imagine.

I heard the sound of female voices ping-ponging back and forth in Italian off in the distance. Looked like Mama had located Bertina and Bianca.

Through the crowd, I caught a glimpse of the quirky duo chatting with my parents. With D.J. and the others in tow, I made my way toward them. As I did, I took in my Italian aunties. They were an interesting mix of my mother and Rosa—not quite as thin as Mama, yet not as fluffy as Rosa. Neither wore orthopedic shoes, and I didn't notice any sagging pantyhose, so we were off to a good start. Still, I couldn't help but smile when I realized they were dressed alike from head to toe. You would think twins in their late fifties would skip the matchy-matchy stuff, but not so in this case.

As I drew near, my gaze shifted to a woman standing alongside my aunts. Surely this couldn't be my cousin Deanna! She was . . . why, she was probably thirty, at least. When did she get so . . . old?

Hmm. I'd probably aged a bit since she had seen me last as well.

Extending my hand, I offered a smile. "It's so good to see you!"

Before Deanna could respond, Bertina—at least, I think it was Bertina—threw her arms around my neck, pronouncing her well wishes in Italian. Seconds later, Bianca had her arms around my neck too. I was swallowed alive by two gushing Italian divas clearly excited to see me.

"Mama, please!" Deanna's voice rang out.

Bianca and Bertina turned their attention to the others, and Deanna reached to give me a warm hug. "I wouldn't have known you," she whispered in my ear. "You're so grown up!"

"I was thinking the same thing about you."

Deanna's gaze traveled to D.J., who had been standing in silence. She leaned in to whisper, "Mama mia, Bella. He's a real Texas cowboy. Does he belong to you?"

"Yep." I slipped my arm around D.J.'s waist, staking my claim. "Everyone, this is D.J., my fiancé." Smiling came naturally when I used the word *fiancé*. To think, I would soon be his wife! The idea still caused my heart to flutter.

Deanna didn't have the same reaction to the word, sadly. From the moment I made the introduction, her expression shifted from one of interest to a profound sadness. I'm pretty sure I even heard her sigh.

"What is it, honey?" I whispered. "Did I say something wrong?"

"No, no," she responded. "Only, I just broke up with my

boyfriend, Rocco. We dated for years, but he wouldn't commit, so I had to break it off." Tears filled her eyes, but she brushed them away. "Sorry, I don't mean to focus attention on myself." She forced a smile. "This is a happy time. A time when Aunt Rosa marries the man of her dreams."

"Well, if it's any consolation, it took Laz sixteen years to come around. Poor Rosa waited all of that time, poor thing." I paused, realizing my story probably wasn't making Deanna feel any better. "Oops. Sorry."

"It's fine." She looped her arm through mine and smiled. "No more talk about men."

D.J. cleared his throat, and I smiled, sensing his awkwardness. Thank goodness he had an easy way about him.

Off in the distance, Francesca carried on and on. Something about her need for a manicure and a pedicure.

I leaned in to Deanna, whispering, "I can't believe Emilio has a new wife. He didn't even tell us. Can you believe that?"

"They just got married a couple of months ago. We were there for the celebration, and trust me, it was a celebration." Deanna rolled her eyes. "Emilio's business is less than a mile from our home in Napoli, remember? And besides, he's very well-known in our region."

"Oh, that's right." I'd nearly forgotten that my uncle's home-building business was such a big deal in Italy. People over there saw him as quite the entrepreneur.

"You should have seen the write-up in the paper when they got engaged." Deanna sighed. "A little over-the-top, but then again, that's how Francesca likes things. And she's a woman who gets what she wants, trust me. I wish you could have heard her on the plane. I've never heard a woman complain so much in my life. And she was up and down the whole trip. Spent half of her time in the restroom, touching up her makeup."

As Francesca approached, followed by Uncle Emilio, who pulled three large Gucci suitcases, I gave Deanna a "better watch it or she might hear you" look. We would have to finish this conversation later. I had a feeling Rosa would have a lot to say about this. I could almost hear her words now: *Il buon giorno si vede dal mattino.* Roughly translated: "The good person is evident from the beginning." I wondered if she would pick up on the good in this voluptuous beauty or if she would see her as some sort of threat. Only time would tell.

We loaded up the cars, putting the luggage in the back of D.J.'s truck. Emilio and Francesca rode with us; the others climbed into my mother's SUV for the drive back to the island. I knew we had a bit of a drive ahead of us—over an hour, anyway—and wondered how long I could go on hearing about Francesca's cuticles. To make things worse, I'd opted to take the seat in back next to her so that Emilio could have more room up front.

As D.J. pulled onto the interstate, Francesca's eyes widened. "I didn't expect Texas to look like *this*." The look of disgust on her face let me know that *this* wasn't good.

"Oh?" I tried to imagine the scene through her eyes. "You were thinking wide-open plains and tumbleweeds?"

"Yes." She pointed at the businesses on the side of the highway. "The whole place is a sea of car dealerships. Where are the cattle? The ranches?"

"Well, now . . ." D.J.'s thick Texas twang reverberated across the cab of the truck. "We're crazy about our cars and trucks in Texas. No doubt about it."

"Still . . ." Francesca leaned back, looking a bit disappointed. She spoke the rest in Italian, probably trying to spare D.J.'s feelings. "This is ridiculous. Nothing like the travel brochures."

I tried to explain that Texas was filled with beautiful ranch-land and cattle, just not in this area. She rolled her eyes and leaned back against the seat, complaining of a headache.

In the rearview mirror, I caught a glimpse of D.J.'s face. God bless him. He was stifling laughter, I could tell.

"You folks hungry?" he asked. "I know a great steakhouse not too far from here."

"Steak?" Emilio sounded excited by that possibility.

Francesca's eyes fluttered open, and she gave a nod. Looked like they were both hungry. A quick phone call to my parents was all it took. They decided to stop along with us. Minutes later, we were all seated inside Texas Roadhouse at the intersection of Interstate 45 and FM 1960, ordering the biggest pieces of beef the Lone Star State had to offer. Surely this would squelch Francesca's complaints and reinforce her former beliefs about Texas.

She looked around the restaurant at the eclectic Texas decor and smiled. "Now, *this* is more like it!"

There was that word again. I'd have to be on the lookout for it in future conversations.

"Thought a real Texas steakhouse might do the trick," D.J. whispered. "Maybe we can fill 'er up and shut 'er up at the same time."

I did my best not to laugh out loud. Still, the comment seemed a little out of character for my usually soft-spoken honey. Had he reached his limit with Francesca already? If so, how would we ever survive the week ahead?

The hostess seated us at a large table and passed around the menus. At this point, everyone began to talk at once, as always. By the time we'd ordered our steaks, Mama and Francesca were deeply engaged in a conversation about nail salons. I let my mother take it from here, knowing she held a frequent-flier card at the best salon on Galveston Island. She certainly didn't need my input.

Within minutes, my mother had shifted gears and was telling Francesca all of her beauty secrets—how she used udder cream to keep her hands and feet silky smooth, and how Crisco made the best makeup remover. She went on and on about the benefits of using coffee grounds to remove cellulite and a feed-store product called Mane and Tail for soft, bouncy hair. Francesca reached into her purse and pulled out an iPod, taking quick notes. I'd never seen such excitement in a woman's eyes.

Hmm. The more I thought about that, the more I realized women were women, no matter where they came from. And nothing—I repeat, nothing—could beat a great jar of udder cream and soft, bouncy hair.

# 4

## Zip-a-Dee-Doo-Dah

We arrived back on the island just as the sun began to set. I could hardly wait to see the look on my sister's face when she laid eyes on Uncle Emilio's new wife. And what would Aunt Rosa say? I could only imagine!

As we made our way down Broadway, the island's quaint thoroughfare, Francesca pointed to a banner on the side of the road. "What is this 'Dickens on the Strand'?" she asked.

"Oh, it's a wonderful Christmas festival the island hosts every year," I explained. "People come from all over the state, dressed in Victorian costumes." I went on to explain that vendors sold their wares and folks performed music from Dickens's era.

"We can get Dickens in Europe," Francesca huffed. "Where are the cattle?"

I sighed. Surely it would take some time to convince her that Texas—at least our corner of it—wasn't exactly like the TV shows she'd seen. The closest thing she would see to anything Western this week was my fiancé. His boots and slow Southern drawl should be enough to give her hope, anyway. If I could get her quiet long enough to listen to him speak.

As we pulled the cars into the driveway, we were met by Rosa standing on the veranda, waving. Thankfully, she'd donned a fresh dress and applied a little makeup. I had a feeling she was going to need it. Laz appeared beside her, and the two of them offered joyous shouts as we exited the vehicles. At first Rosa was too excited about seeing the twins and Deanna to pay much attention to Francesca, but soon enough the young woman caught her eye.

"Who have we here?" Rosa asked in Italian, taking Francesca's hand.

"I am your future sister-in-law, Francesca Adriana Rossi." The beauty queen slipped an arm around Emilio's waist in case anyone had any further questions on the matter.

The look on Rosa's face was priceless.

"W-what?" Laz looked at his younger brother, clearly stunned. "You've married, Emilio?"

"I did." He grinned. "Several weeks ago."

"It's true, Laz," my father said, entering the veranda with Francesca's overnight bag in his hand. "Our brother is a confirmed bachelor no more. He finally did it. After all these years."

"Well, go figure." Laz raked his fingers through his thinning hair and looked at Emilio with admiration on his face.

Sophia joined us, looking back and forth between Rosa and Francesca. No doubt she had a lot of questions. So did I, actually.

"We had the most beautiful wedding in all of Napoli," Francesca crooned. She went on to describe it in great detail, leaving nothing to the imagination.

I could see Rosa's eyes narrowing and tried to imagine what she must be thinking. This was supposed to be her special week. No bride wanted to be outdone by another, even if that person happened to be a future sister-in-law. A gorgeous, young sister-in-law, to boot. Nope, this would not go over well with Rosa, I could tell.

Laz slapped Emilio on the back. "You old dog!" he cried out. "I didn't know you had it in you." He approached Francesca and gave her a warm hug. "Welcome to the family, sister!"

Francesca responded by kissing Uncle Laz on both cheeks and saying, "*Ciao!*"

At this point, I thought Rosa was going to hyperventilate. Or punch Laz. One or the other. Instead, to her credit, she ushered everyone inside with the promise of the best tiramisu in the state of Texas. I saw her strategy at once. If she couldn't win the crowd with her youth and beauty, she would get them with her cooking. Not a bad plan, really. She led the way, chattering all the while about her world-famous dessert. Sophia and I both chimed in, offering our support for Rosa's cooking.

Pop looked back at D.J. with a sigh. "Guess we'd better get busy with all that luggage."

"Oh yeah." My honey stopped short of entering the house and turned back around. "Almost forgot." He shrugged, a hint of a smile crossing his face.

"So did I," Pop said. "Looks like everyone else did too."

We headed back to D.J.'s truck and started to unload. Just as the last piece came out, a black stretch limo pulled up to the curb.

"Expecting someone?" D.J. asked, giving me a curious glance.

"Not to my knowledge. The last time I saw a limo like that was the day Guido . . ." I paused and then snapped my fingers. "The day Guido was delivered. Sal's limo driver brought him all the way from Atlantic City in a black stretch limo that looked exactly like that."

"That's gotta be Sal Lucci inside," Pop said, his brow wrinkling in concern. "Didn't think he was supposed to get here till tomorrow."

"Well, Sal was always one for surprises, right?" I elbowed my father, and he laughed.

"To put it mildly. That's what makes me nervous. We have enough to think about this week without adding fuel to the fire."

"Just don't let Laz hear you saying that," D.J. reminded him. "He's looking at this week as an opportunity to minister to his friend."

"He's right." Pop nodded, gazing at the limo. "Salvadore Lucci always did travel in style. Just wonder if he realizes you can't get through the pearly gates in a limo, even if you have your own driver."

"Speaking of drivers . . ." I nodded as the limo driver got out. He was tall and stately, dressed in a black tuxedo, white dress shirt, and black bow tie. "Yep, that's the same guy. I even remember his name. Joe Barbini."

"That's right." Pop nodded. "Joe Barbini. Nice guy."

Joe tipped his cap to us, then opened the back door of the limo to let the passenger out. What happened next will be forever seared in my memory. Uncle Laz's voice calling out from the veranda. The sight of Salvadore Lucci, five-foot-nothing, easing his weakened frame from the limousine and attempting to stand aright.

I couldn't help but gasp. The Sal I remembered was buff and

tanned with a menacing face and a thick New-Jersey-meets-Old-Italy accent. This man was . . . elderly. Frail. Walked bent over. Had thin wisps of white hair. Wore tweed.

Laz came running down the front steps of the house—*running* being a loose term, since there was a cane involved. Precious followed on his heels, yapping like a maniac. Laz drew near to Sal with tears in his eyes, greeting him in Italian. His words flowed like water. So did the tears, which stunned me. Laz planted a kiss on his old friend's cheek—*old* being the key word, now that I'd seen him face-to-face.

I could hardly believe this was the man who'd been the center of so many family stories over the past twenty-plus years. No longer did he look like the infamous tough guy I'd recalled from my childhood days. No, this guy looked more like someone you would see in a Geritol commercial. Soft wrinkles lined his eyes. Age spots covered his arms and face.

"*Salve*, Salvadore!" Laz said, wrapping him in a tight embrace. "*Come va?*"

"Hello to you too, my good friend," Sal said in a frail voice as Laz stepped back and looked him in the eye. "And to answer your question, I'm . . . I'm doing fine, thank you. Recovering nicely. H-how are you?"

"Don't worry about me," Laz said with a wave of his hand. "I am fine." He turned his attention to Sal once more. I could see the concern in my uncle's eyes as he took in his friend's appearance, but he flew into action, offering to help Joe with Sal's bags.

"No, my friend." Sal put up a hand. "Let my limo driver handle it. Besides, I'm not staying here, remember? Joe will take my things to the Tremont while I am visiting with you."

Laz nodded. "All right then." He grinned. "Come inside and meet my bride-to-be, Sal. I don't think you ever met Rosa. Two of her sisters have just arrived from Napoli, along with my brother and his new wife. She's quite a looker."

"Who's a looker?" Sal asked with a spark of interest in his eyes. "Your bride-to-be or your brother's new wife?"

I could see the wheels turning in Laz's head. To his credit, he gave just the right answer. "Both, actually."

"I remember meeting your brother briefly when you lived in Atlantic City," Sal said with a brusque nod. "And it seems I heard Rosa's name mentioned, but I don't believe I ever met her. I will come inside to see these visions of loveliness myself."

*Oh boy. This should be interesting.*

Just then, Sal looked my way. "Ah. Who have we here?" His eyes narrowed to slits, and he shook his head. "Surely this is not Bella Bambina, the little girl with the lopsided head?"

I groaned. Of all the things for him to remember!

"It's good to see you again, Mr. Lucci," I said.

"What's with this Mr. Lucci stuff?" he said. "As I recall, you Rossis always called me Sallie, did you not? And you called me Uncle Sallie, Bella Bambina."

I couldn't stop the grin. "You're right. I did. Good to see you, Uncle Sallie."

D.J. was looking at me curiously, and I felt compelled to explain Sal's earlier comment. "It's okay," I whispered. "I don't think it's hereditary, but when I was born, my head was slightly misshapen."

He laughed. "Good thing I found this out before we had kids. Should we consider adoption?"

"No. We Rossis have great hair. Covers all our imperfections." After a pause, I added, "Well, most, anyway."

45

"Let's get inside and take a load off," my uncle said, turning toward the door. "Rosa has made tiramisu. She's the best cook on the island. Just wait and see!"

D.J. turned my way again, clearly stunned at my uncle's admission. In spite of Laz's love for Rosa, we'd never actually heard him say she was the better cook. In fact, they'd feuded over who could cook the better meal for years.

"Well, there you have it," D.J. whispered.

I nodded and smiled, following on Sal's heels as we entered the house.

No sooner did we arrive inside than we were greeted by Francesca, who greeted the men with a rehearsed pose. Sal's eyes grew wide. "Mama mia is right!" He turned to Laz with a crooked grin. "Laz, your bride-to-be is exquisite. Don't know what you ever did to deserve her." He took Francesca's hand and gave the back of it a kiss.

She giggled and shared her thoughts in Italian. "I don't know who you are, but I think I like you. You've got the wrong bride, though. I'm married to Laz's brother Emilio."

"Ah, my apologies." Sal shrugged and turned to Laz. "If she's this pretty, I can hardly wait to see your Rosa!"

D.J.'s eyes grew wide, and we all held our breath as Rosa entered the foyer. She'd slipped on an apron, stained with tomato sauce, of course. I gave her a quick glance, trying to see her through Sal's eyes. Not bad. Still, not Sophia Loren.

Rosa took one look at Sal and rushed toward him, arms extended. "Oh, you must be Sal! I've heard so much about you." She began to gush over him in Italian, but the look of confusion on his face stopped her in her tracks. "Is—is everything okay, Sal?" She stared, obviously unsure of how to interpret his silence. The rest of us probably had it figured out.

"Yes." He nodded. "Yes, well, sorry. I'm just trying to figure out who you are. My first guess would be Bella's mother, but I don't think that's right."

"No." Rosa grinned. "I'm not Imelda, though I'm tickled you made that mistake. I can think of no greater compliment than to be confused with my sister."

"S-sister?" He looked more perplexed than ever.

A smile lit her face. "Of course. I'm Rosa, Sal! *Laz's* Rosa!" She leaned close to Uncle Laz, who planted a kiss on her cheek.

The look on Sal's face was Academy Award–worthy. If I had to choose three words to describe it, they would be: shocked, horrified, confused. Thank goodness, he shifted gears at once, and this look was replaced with what appeared to be a forced smile. Relief flooded over me as I realized Rosa was too busy nuzzling up to Uncle Lazarro to notice.

"Well, we meet at last." He took her hand and, with the flair of a true-blue Italian, kissed the back of it. "I've heard so many wonderful things about you."

"Oh, and I of you!" She took him by the hand and led him into the living room to meet the others. "Come. I've made tiramisu, and Laz has prepared some cappuccino. Take a seat and we'll visit." After helping Sal onto the sofa, she headed to the kitchen. As she left the room, I noticed Sal giving Laz a curious look. Likely they would talk later, but in that moment, I wanted to punch the man for the expression I'd seen on his face seconds earlier. Instead, I settled onto the loveseat, surrounded by loved ones who would kill me if I pummeled our guest in the first five minutes after his arrival, even if he didn't think my aunt was a beauty queen like Francesca.

Laz went around the room, making introductions. From the way he talked about Sal to the others, you would think the man had been canonized. By the time we got to Emilio, Sal offered an admiring nod.

"Congratulations on your marriage, Emilio. You are a lucky man."

"Don't I know it." Emilio reached over and wrapped Francesca in his arms, then kissed her soundly on the lips. D.J. rolled his eyes and Pop turned his head, his cheeks flaming red.

The womenfolk weren't so quick to respond, at least not openly. I heard Mama clear her throat, and Aunt Bianca mentioned something about the weather. Deanna reached for her cell phone, claiming she had to make a call. To Italy. Something urgent had come up.

Right.

When Emilio and Francesca finally came up for air, a sound rang out from Pop's office, just one room over. Guido. Singing "Amazing Grace." Sal turned, albeit slowly, the expression on his face something to behold. "What in the world?" He looked at Laz. "Is that . . ."

"Yes." My uncle rose and led the way to the office. "It's your old friend, Guido! Come with me."

Everyone in the room took that as a cue. The whole group of us rose and followed him into the small office, where Guido's cage stood in the corner near the window. Sal took one look at him and began to weep.

"Guido! Oh, Guido!"

He began to sing the bird's praises in fluent Italian, and Guido responded by looking his way and hollering, "Go to the mattresses!"

At this point, Bianca and Bertina stifled their laughter and disappeared back into the living room. I wanted to go with them, but Pop and Laz hung around, so I figured I should too. Thankfully, D.J. stuck by my side. I knew he was probably dying to know what Sal thought about the almost new and improved parrot he'd placed into my family's care.

Sal opened the door of the cage and extended a shaky hand inside. Guido took it as a sign and hopped aboard, squawking nonstop at his old friend. Sal stroked the bird with his free hand and then looked at my uncle, voice trembling. "Laz, I cannot thank you enough for watching Guido for me. I've missed him terribly. Guido and I are . . . well, we are old and dear friends."

The way Sal spoke about the bird, I could tell they really *were* old and dear friends. And I knew, having raised a spoiled little Yorkie-Poo, how important a pet could be in a person's life.

"We enjoyed having him," Laz said. "He kept us entertained."

"And vice versa," Pop threw in. "We kept him entertained too."

"Oh?" Sal looked at my father with a wrinkled brow. "How so?"

"We, um, well, we taught him some new songs," Laz explained. "He has quite a voice, this one."

"Yes, what was that he was singing when I came in the room?" Sal asked. "Sounded familiar."

"'Amazing Grace.'" Laz began to repeat the lyrics, and Guido, who'd remained silent for the last couple minutes, dove in again, singing at the top of his lungs. He warbled out just enough to put a look of horror on Sal's face.

"What is happening here?" Sal turned to Laz, clearly upset. "You've converted my bird?"

Laz paled but didn't say a word.

"Technically a bird doesn't have a soul," D.J. interjected. "So he's not exactly converted, per se."

49

"We just . . ." Laz fumbled around, finally coming up with, "He's just been gleaning from us. Learning a couple of songs."

At this point, Guido looked at Laz and began to quote his new favorite Scripture: "May the words of my mouth be acceptable. May the words of my mouth be acceptable."

Sal smacked himself in the head. "What next? Are you going to baptize him too?"

"He sort of did," D.J. whispered to me, then stifled a laugh.

I knew what he was talking about, of course. Laz had doused the poor bird in anointing oil a few months back—oil he'd purchased from a televangelist. The gooey stuff had only served to irritate the parrot's skin. He'd lost several feathers as a result, which Sal now seemed to notice.

"Guido looks different than the last time I saw him," Sal said, examining him from side to side, top to bottom.

"O-oh?" Laz tried to play it cool, but beads of sweat had popped out on his forehead.

"Yes. His colors were brighter," Sal said. "It's almost like something is missing."

Thank goodness, Rosa's voice rang out. "Tiramisu, everyone! And coffees." She popped her head in the door. "Laz, want to help me with the cappuccino? I know our guests are ready for a treat." She smiled as she saw Guido perched on Sal's hand. "Oh, what a happy sight! Aren't you glad to see him again, Sal? Guido has missed you terribly."

"Yes, I am happy to see him. I missed Guido too." He continued to stare at the bird, the creases between his brows deepening.

Pop convinced Sal to put the parrot back in his cage so he could enjoy some coffee and dessert. However, I had a feeling we hadn't heard the last of this. Once Sal figured out that Laz had made a concerted effort to train Guido as a missionary, he would not be happy. I could just sense it.

Not that I objected to my uncle's plan. Though it had seemed far-fetched at the time, it made sense to me now. And seeing Sal again made me realize just how much he needed the love of the Lord. At this stage of his life, he also needed the love and care of his friends. We would be those friends, even if only for a week or so. Even if his first reaction to seeing Rosa wasn't all I'd hoped it would be.

We headed back into the living room, the whole place now coming alive with laughter and the clinking of silverware as we dove into Rosa's tiramisu. I saw the look of appreciation on Francesca's face as she took her first bite.

"Rosa, this is better than my mother's."

"Thank you." My aunt's cheeks turned a pretty shade of pink. "I've had plenty of years to perfect my recipe. There's been a lot of trial and error along the way, but I finally have a recipe I'm happy with."

"I'd be happy with it too, if you don't mind sharing." Francesca gave her a warm smile. "I'm not the best cook in the world, but Emilio is very encouraging."

"We eat out a lot," Emilio said between bites. "That's how I encourage her. There's nothing like a five-star restaurant to encourage a woman who doesn't know her way around a kitchen."

This brought a chuckle from many in the room, especially D.J. He knew my cooking skills were limited at best. Not that there would be a lot of five-star restaurants in our future. No, I sincerely longed to cook like Aunt Rosa. Someday, anyway.

I looked back and forth between Francesca and Rosa, realizing they were both my aunts now—though three decades separated them. Weird. I still couldn't get over the fact that I had an aunt not much older than myself.

As I pondered this, Emilio started telling stories about the various new restaurants in Napoli, and before long, Bianca and Bertina chimed in, sharing all of the many changes that had taken place in my parents' hometown since their last visit. After that, we told stories, sang old songs, and shared in the love that only a family knows, until the clock in the front hallway struck ten. At that point, D.J. announced that he needed to get some shut-eye.

Walking him to the door, I whispered, "So, what do you think of my nutty family now that you've met the Italian contention?"

"Honestly?" he asked. "Bella, I think you're the most fortunate person on the planet. You've got great relatives. They're a blast to be around. And all of them clearly love the Lord."

"Well, all but Sal, not that he's technically a relative."

"True. But he'll come around. I've been praying for him."

"Me too."

D.J. kissed the tip of my nose as he pulled me close. "Our children are going to be so blessed, Bella. They're going to grow up surrounded by people who love them . . . and love God."

My heart swelled—not just at the idea that D.J. was already thinking ahead to the children we would one day have, but at the realization that he was right. His parents and brother were committed to the Lord, with deep abiding faith leading the way. And my family, however goofy at times, was equally as committed. Of course, there were probably times when D.J. thought we needed to *be* committed . . . but that was another story.

I gazed into his eyes, overcome with emotion. Suddenly, I didn't want to wait until February to get married. I wanted to start my happily ever after right here, right now.

On the other hand, I had no decor, no cake, and no plan of action. I'd been so busy planning for everyone else's wedding that I'd barely had time to give thought to my own. That would come in time. I hoped.

"A penny for your thoughts." D.J. gazed at me tenderly.

"Oh, just thinking how amazing it's going to be when I'm Bella Neeley."

"I can hardly wait." He leaned down and gave me a kiss . . . one that convinced me that—no matter how difficult things got—this was a guy worth waiting for.

# 5

## Moonlight Serenade

After D.J. left, I climbed the stairs, more than ready for bed. The last few days had really knocked the wind out of my sails. As I reached the top step, I was reminded of my earlier attempt to try to reach Jenna. Once I arrived in my bedroom, I fetched my phone from my purse and looked to see if she had returned the call. Confusion set in when I saw that she had not.

"What's up with you, girlfriend?" I asked, setting the phone on the bedside table. "Are you ignoring me?"

I slipped out of my clothes and into a comfortable nightie, then reached for the Crisco to remove my makeup. I'd learned a few things from my mama of late. Of course, most of her beauty secrets she'd acquired from the ladies at D.J.'s church, but she still took the credit.

The sound of laughter rang out from the guest room next to mine. Looked like Bianca and Bertina were having a high old time with Mama and Rosa. Their relationship—though tested by miles—was still going strong, even after all these years. Surely Jenna and I could make it through ours with just as much finesse, in spite of my busy schedule and her preoccupation with Bubba Neeley.

At once I thought about something I'd heard in a sermon: "It's about the people, not the project." This statement was never truer than now. Still, with two weddings to plan, keeping people front and center wasn't always easy.

A rap on my door caught my attention. I hollered, "Come in," then smiled as I saw Deanna standing there, dressed in her pj's and robe.

"Feel like having a sleepover?" she asked with a twinkle in her eye.

"Sure. Did they kick you out of Armando's room?"

"No, just thought it would be more fun this way. We have a lot of catching up to do. Unless you're too tired, that is."

"Never." *It's the people, not the project. Focus on the people, Bella!* When would I ever have another chance for a sleepover with my Italian cousin, after all?

She reached into the pocket of her robe and came out with several small chocolates. "I brought these from home. I remembered they were your favorite."

"No way!" I reached to open one of the delectable goodies and popped it in my mouth, overcome by its creamy goodness.

Deanna grinned. "Some things never change. You always did have a sweet tooth."

I nodded, my mouth too full to respond properly.

At that moment, another rap on the door sounded, and Aunt Bianca—at least, I think it was Bianca—popped her head inside. She took one look at my cousin, and her anxious expression shifted to one of relief. "There you are, Deanna. Your mama was wondering what happened to you."

*Okay, this one is Bianca.* Perhaps I would be able to tell the twins apart by week's end.

"We're having a slumber party," I said.

Deanna held up the chocolates and elevated her brows in a playful sort of way.

Bianca took that as a sign to join us. She practically sprinted to my bed and hopped aboard. I smiled as I looked at her Scooby-Doo pajamas. Who knew Scooby was popular in Italy? Seconds later, another rap sounded at the door. Bertina stuck her head inside.

"There you are!" She put her hands on her hips and stared at Bianca and Deanna. "I thought maybe the Rapture had taken place and I'd been left behind." She giggled and scurried into the room, climbing on my bed alongside her sister and daughter. Only then did I notice she also wore Scooby-Doo pajamas. Man. The twins had this matching thing down to a science. Made me wonder what the rest of the week was going to look like.

Before long, Mama joined us. Then Rosa. Then Sophia. By this point, the whole atmosphere had really shifted to a party scene. The only female missing was Francesca. I had a feeling neither she nor Emilio would be emerging anytime soon.

"Remember all of those things we used to do at slumber parties when we were kids?" Sophia said, climbing onto the bed alongside the rest of us. "Wrapping houses. Tossing water balloons at cars."

"W-what?" Mama gasped. "You threw water balloons at cars?"

Sophia clapped a hand over her mouth and laughed. "I can't believe I just confessed that."

"When I was a girl, we would call boys on the telephone."

Bertina giggled. "We were brazen." She looked at her sisters and sighed. "Mama would've had a fit."

"Back then, girls didn't call boys," Bianca explained, giving me a knowing look.

"Now they just send text messages," Sophia said. "The rules have changed, I guess."

"Whenever I went to a slumber party, we always did each other's hair and makeup," Mama said. Her face lit up. "That would be so much fun! We can practice for the wedding!"

She sprinted out of the room and came back with her humongous makeup bag. The ladies began to squeal with delight as they looked through it, and all the more as she began to explain her beauty secrets. Out came the tube of hemorrhoid cream, which she rubbed into the crow's-feet around Bianca's eyes. Out came the udder cream, which she used to soften Bertina's hands. Out came half a dozen other products, most purchased at the local feed store or Walmart. The women found these things delightful. Even Deanna went on and on about how she wished they had a Walmart in Napoli.

"Now I want to do Rosa's makeup," Mama said. "We need to practice for next Saturday."

"But it's eleven o'clock at night," Rosa argued. "And I'm in my nightgown."

"Who cares!" Bertina crossed her arms and gave Rosa a look of warning. "This is going to be fun."

Bianca reached for the makeup bag and tossed it Mama's way. "Just relax and enjoy yourself, Rosa."

I wondered if Rosa knew *how* to relax and enjoy herself, but I didn't say so.

The sisters spent the next twenty minutes meticulously applying foundation, powder, blush, lipstick, eye shadow, eyebrow pencil, and mascara. Rosa fussed and fumed, not used to sitting still for so long, and definitely not used to this amount of pampering. While Mama worked on her face, Bertina painted her fingernails and Bianca gave her a pedicure.

When they finished, Rosa stood and approached the mirror over my dressing table, gasping as she saw herself for the first time. "O-oh my." The face that stared back at her was beautifully made up—not too much, not too little. Just right.

"Rosa!" I stood beside her, gazing at her reflection. "You look like a movie star."

"Laz won't recognize me." She giggled. "And that's not necessarily a bad thing."

"Don't be so hard on yourself!" Bertina said with a wave of her hand. "You're a beautiful woman."

Rosa grimaced and shook her head.

"Of course she is. Beauty runs in our family," Bianca assured us all.

Mama dove in, going on and on about what a head-turner Rosa would be on her wedding day. Listening to my mama and aunts and their girlish chatter brought a smile to my face. Made me wonder if one day Sophia and I would have a conversation like this—say, in forty years or so. Though, of course, I wouldn't have to wait till then for my wedding day. Hopefully, she wouldn't either.

My sister approached and began to fuss with Rosa's long hair. "We need to put this in a nice updo." She turned to me. "Bella, do you have any rubber bands? Hairpins?"

Minutes later, Rosa was seated on the chair at my dressing table, having her hair done. After a bit of work on Sophia's part, it was beautifully styled. We all gasped at the change. Honestly, Rosa was right. Laz might not recognize her. The transformation was pretty amazing.

The conversation rose to a roar at this point as we all

oohed and aahed at my aunt's appearance. She stood and turned with her back to the mirror, and Sophia handed her a handheld mirror to use as well. Now seeing the whole picture, Rosa began to cry.

"It's so . . . pretty!"

"That reminds me of a song." Bertina began to sing, "I feel pretty, oh so pretty," from *West Side Story*, and within seconds, we all joined in, creating a rousing chorus.

That's pretty much where our party ended. Francesca appeared in my doorway with a sour look on her face. I found myself distracted, however, by her red negligee. So distracted, in fact, that I actually squeezed my eyes shut to force the image away. At once, everyone stopped singing, freezing in place. Bertina clamped a hand over her mouth. I couldn't be sure if she did so to stop the song from flowing out or to keep from saying anything about Francesca's attire.

"Ladies, I know you haven't seen each other in ages," Francesca said, her accent thicker than ever, "but I've *got* to get some rest, and you're making it impossible. It was a long flight. A *very* long flight." She gave my aunts a pensive look. "Surely we *all* need our beauty sleep."

You could've heard a pin drop at that proclamation. Something about the words *beauty sleep* sounded like an accusation. The slumber party ended immediately, though I had my suspicions Bianca, Bertina, and Rosa would've tossed a few eggs at Francesca's head if they'd happened to have any handy. And Sophia surely would have hurled a water balloon at her.

Francesca disappeared from view, and Bertina's eyes narrowed to slits. She whispered, "*Il pessimo vicini e il parente piu stretto.*"

For this one, I had to ask for a translation.

"The worst neighbor is the closest relation," Deanna whispered. "She's trying to say this is going to be hard for Rosa, marrying into Laz's family, especially with a woman like that in the mix."

Rosa's expression softened as she looked at her hair in the mirror once again. "Not so. Francesca just needs the love of the Lord, that's all. I'm not giving up on her. She's a sweet young thing."

"Emphasis on *young*," Bianca said as she rolled her eyes.

"There's nothing wrong with being young." Rosa nodded, rubbing at her crow's-feet as she gazed at her reflection. "We were all young once. Remember?" She turned back to her sisters with a smile.

A collective sigh went up, and the excitement fizzled out of the room. Nothing like being reminded of your age to shift things out of slumber party gear. Even Deanna—who couldn't stop yawning—decided she'd be better off sleeping in Armando's room.

After we parted ways, I settled into bed with Precious at my side. The little monster took my comforter in her teeth and began to chew with vigor. Still, I loved her. Couldn't envision things any other way. Pulling the fabric from her teeth, I scolded her, then gave her a kiss.

As I rested my head against the pillow, I thought about what had happened earlier, when Sal met Rosa for the first time. The look on his face. The judgment in his eyes. So what if she wasn't the thin, young beauty that Francesca was? Did that mean she wasn't as valuable? How dare he formulate an opinion based on appearance only. Oooh, it made my blood boil!

I found myself growing angry and decided I'd better do business with the Lord about this before it ate me alive.

My words poured out like Rosa's olive oil, and I shared my thoughts with God in rapid succession. He, in turn, calmed me down and reminded me that he saw every one of us as beautiful, no matter our appearance.

When my prayer time ended, I started thinking about Bianca and Bertina in their matching Scooby-Doo pajamas. How fun would it be to reach your fifties and still be best friends?

As the words *best friends* flitted through my mind, I thought again of Jenna. Reaching for my phone, I checked to see if, perhaps, I'd missed a call from her during our slumber party chaos. Sadly, no.

"What's up with you, girl?" I asked, putting the phone back down. "Why are you avoiding me?"

I reached to turn off my lamp, then rolled over, ready to put all thoughts of slumber parties and best friends out of my mind.

# 6

## Band of Gold

On Monday morning, I met with the members of the swing band. They wanted a look at the facility to see how and where they would set up on the big day. I couldn't help but smile as they pulled up in a renovated school bus with a large gold wedding ring painted on the side and the words BAND OF GOLD emblazoned across it. Looked like their name had a dual meaning. They must play at a lot of weddings.

I watched in surprise as the band members exited the bus. Truly, I'd never seen so many elderly men in one place before. If I had to guess, I'd say the average age was somewhere around seventy-five. One of the men appeared to be much older, and a few were probably in their late sixties. Approaching the bus, I looked around for Gordy, the leader of the band.

"Bella Rossi?" A white-haired gentleman approached and extended his hand.

"The one and only." I extended my hand and was surprised at his strength as he grasped it. Looks could be deceiving.

"I'm Gordy. These fellas are my band members. Happy to meet you. I can't tell you how excited we are about this gig."

"Same here. And I know my aunt and uncle are thrilled that you had the evening free on such short notice."

"It's a fluke, really. We were supposed to play a retirement home event that day—a Christmas banquet—but it fell through."

"Their loss is our gain." I offered him a warm smile, wondering about the fact that he still held my hand. Man, the fellow had a tight grip.

I managed to wriggle free just as I caught a glimpse of Laz and Sal approaching from our house next door. Sal took one look at the band director and nearly hyperventilated. For a minute there, I thought we were going to have to resuscitate him.

"Gordy? Gordy DiMarco?" he said as he approached. "Is that you?"

Gordy turned Sal's way, his brow wrinkled. "Yes. I'm Gordy DiMarco."

"You don't remember me . . . us?" Sal waved his arms, suddenly loaded with zeal. "Sal Lucci."

"From Atlantic City!" Gordy gasped. "How could I forget that name?"

"The one and only!" Sal grabbed him, gave him a tight squeeze, and began to speak to him in Italian, carrying on and on about the old days in New Jersey.

Laz stood off in the distance, a confused look on his face. A moment later, however, his face lit up. "Gordy DiMarco!" Laz pointed at the fellow. "I remember you now. I once sold you a vacuum cleaner when you lived in Jersey. Sal put me in contact with you. You were . . ." He paused a minute and raked his fingers through his thinning hair. I could almost see the wheels turning in his head. "You were one of Sal's, um, friends."

I knew what that meant. Sal's ties to the mob in Atlantic City—however loose—had been infamous. Had this soft-spoken man standing before me now once been a mob boss, perhaps? Surely not.

Gordy nodded. "I remember those days." He paused for a moment, the expression on his face shifting to one of chagrin. "You know, things were different back then. *I* was different back then. I'm not that Gordy DiMarco anymore."

"We got old." Sal grunted. "Nothing's the same."

"There's more to it than that." A wistful look passed over Gordy as he spoke. "I'm truly not that same man any-more."

"Ah." Laz nodded. "I think I get your point. Life has settled down?"

"*I* have settled down. Met the Lord face-to-face about ten years ago in the federal penitentiary and never looked back. The old Gordy is dead and gone. The new one is a resur-rected man."

"Well, hallelujah!" Laz practically hollered. "I had an en-counter with the Lord myself." His eyes lit up as he went on to tell Gordy about his conversion experience. "Happened in Jersey back in the seventies. I was walking home from my fa-vorite bar, drunk as a skunk, when suddenly I saw what looked like a flash of light from heaven in the road ahead of me."

"Really?" Gordy leaned in, obviously caught up in the story.

"Yep." Laz's voice grew more animated. "Then I heard a sound. Can't really do it justice, but it seemed to rise up from the bowels of hell. The most intense thing I've ever heard."

"No way." Gordy's eyes grew wider by the moment. "Then what happened?"

"Well, next thing you know, I'm belly-up on the road, my leg and shoulder aching something fierce. Turns out that flash of light was really a pair of headlights from a city bus. The screeching sound was the squealing of the tires as the driver tried to dodge me. In my drunken state, I'd apparently stumbled out into the middle of the street."

"Oh my." Gordy paled.

"He almost missed," Laz continued with a knowing look in his eye. "Clipped me and knocked me to the ground. I was unconscious for a few minutes. Next thing I remember was being in an ambulance. They took me to the Sisters of Mercy Hospital, where the nuns patched my wounds and led me to the Lord."

I remembered this story well. Laz always called it his Damascus Road experience. From everything I'd been told, he was never the same after that night.

"The Lord met me on that road . . . just like Saul of Tarsus in the book of Acts," Laz said, his voice growing more intense. "The old Lazarro Rossi died that night, and the new one was born. I've never been the same. The nuns called it a 'come to Jesus' meeting."

Sal grunted. "Never did buy into all that Jesus stuff. Makes for a great story, though. Very dramatic."

I couldn't help but sigh at Sal's words. I knew my uncle had been working for months to figure out a way to reach out to Sal with the gospel message. He'd worked double time, teaching Guido memory verses and the lyrics to "Amazing Grace," on the off chance that Sal's parrot might play an evangelistic role. So far, the bird's song choices had served only to irritate Sal.

Gordy turned to Sal, his face softening. "Well, until you've experienced it for yourself, Sallie, there's no way to do the conversion story justice." Gordy slapped him on the back. "But if you're ever interested in hearing my sordid tale, I'll tell it." He flashed a smile my way. "Just not today. Today we have a wedding to talk about. You want to take us inside and show us around, Bella?"

"Of course!"

By now, the other members of the band had gathered around us in a tight circle. A few of them held instruments. I saw a couple of trombones and a few clarinets. What really got my attention, however, were the fellows with the tubas and the French horns. Their lips were already perched and ready on the instruments, and their fingers were moving in anticipation even before we got in the building.

*Alrighty then. These folks love what they do!*

I led everyone inside, giving them a few notes about the upcoming wedding and sharing Rosa and Laz's vision for the perfect reception as we walked. When we got inside the reception hall, I finished my spiel. Only then did I realize there was a woman in the group. The silver-haired beauty came my way, tucked her clarinet under her left arm, and extended her right hand for a shake.

"I'm Lilly," she said with a smile. Her soft blue-gray eyes sparkled in anticipation, and a whiff of tea rose rushed over me.

"Lilly, good to meet you." I shook her hand. "Bella Rossi. I'm the manager of Club Wed."

"Love your place. Great name too. Club Wed. Love that." As she smiled, the crinkles around her eyes grew more pronounced. What a beautiful woman!

"Well, thanks. We like it too." I didn't tell her the name

had been my idea, or that my parents had originally named the place "Bella's Wedding Facility," after me. No, those days were long gone. So were the never-ending traditional ceremonies. These days we focused on theme weddings, and man, we'd had a few doozies!

She clutched my hand, her tender grip exuding love. "We're so happy to be here. I hope once you hear us play, you'll invite us back."

"Oh, I'm sure I will." I stared at the silver-haired darling, captivated by her winning smile. "This is a first for us," I explained. "We used a smaller group of musicians at a recent Renaissance-themed wedding, but never anything this size before." I gestured to the crowd of band members. "There are a lot of you. Good thing we have a big stage area."

"Well, we're growing every day," she said. "We started out with three clarinets, and now we have six. Started with one trombone, now we have three. God is really blessing us, I guess you'd say. Our horns runneth over."

I giggled and said, "He's blessing us too," as a ditto. As I glanced around, my curiosity set in. "Are you the only female in the group?"

"Yes." She grinned. "I weaseled my way in about four months ago. Several of the fellas still aren't keen on it, but I'd do just about anything to . . ." Her words drifted away, and she gazed at Gordy with love pouring from her eyes.

"Ah. Say no more. I get it."

She snapped to attention. "Anyway, let's just say I'm happy to be in the band. And I sing for them as well. Just wait till you hear our rendition of 'Eight to the Bar.' Gordy and I sing in perfect harmony. Every note in tune." Her cheeks blazoned red at that revelation.

"Well, maybe that's a sign." I winked and then went back

to talking about the facility, not wanting to get in over my head. I had a feeling Lilly and I would have plenty of conversations in the future. I also couldn't help but think she and Rosa would hit it off.

"Gordy, what do you think about this space?" Laz gestured to the large ballroom where the reception would be held.

"It's a great setup," Gordy said with a nod. "I can't believe this facility is so big. Looks smaller from the outside."

"Yeah, these old Victorians can be deceptive," I said. "But Pop did a lot of renovations before we opened up. Took down a few walls to make more room for the banquet hall and the little chapel. And you should see the backyard. We've got the prettiest gazebo in town. Great for outdoor ceremonies, though not at this time of year. We don't get any requests for Christmas weddings in the gazebo."

"So, the wedding will take place in the chapel?" Gordy asked.

"No, in here." I pointed to the reception hall. "The chapel won't accommodate the number of people we're expecting."

"That's right," Laz said. "The ceremony and reception are going to be in the same room. We're expecting a lot of guests and want them to be comfortable."

"Besides, Rosa wants the band to have an active role in the actual ceremony," I added.

"I think it would be a good idea to go ahead and play a couple of tunes while we're here today," Gordy said. "We need to get an idea of the acoustics, and that's really only possible if we actually play." He looked around, the worry lines between his brows now deepening. "Though, things will sound a little different when this place is full of people. It's a shame we can't test it with a crowd."

"Maybe you can." I gave a nod, convinced I could help.

"Oh?" He didn't look as sure.

If only the fellow knew we had a crowd just next door. Then he would relax.

I smiled and said, "Hold that thought," then grabbed my cell phone and called Mama. When she answered, I could hear the sound of half a dozen voices behind her.

"Bella? Everything okay?"

"Yes, but I have a favor to ask. Can you bring everyone next door to the reception hall?"

"Right now?" She didn't sound thrilled with the idea. "Why?"

"I'll explain when you get here. Just trust me. This won't take long, but we need everyone. And tell them to bring their dancing shoes and lots of smiles."

"O-okay."

As we ended the call, I turned to Gordy and grinned. "At Club Wed, you get what you ask for. You're about to get a crowd."

"*Primo.*" He gathered his troops, and they began to set up the stage. By the time Mama and the others arrived, the band members were warming up their instruments.

"What's going on, Bella?" my mother asked, drawing near.

"It's the band. They want an audience."

"Ah, I see. Well, that we've got!"

A few seconds later, the room was filled with all of the relatives, and Gordy led the band in their first number, something totally upbeat and very swinglike, though I couldn't place the melody.

"Oh, this is wonderful!" Aunts Bertina and Bianca spoke in unison. "Our very own private performance!" They stood with Deanna, clapping their hands to the beat as the swing band took to flight.

A couple dozen measures into the song, Uncle Emilio took Francesca in his arms and began to move her around the dance floor, though his movements were awkward at best. Looked like swing wasn't exactly his thing. Still, he gave it the old college try. Watching them, I lost track of the difference in their ages. He seemed to come alive again. Like a kid in a candy store. Strange that music would have such an effect.

"Wow," Mama said after listening for a while. "This band is amazing. One of the best I've heard. Where did you find them?"

"Laz found them on the Internet." I raised my voice to be heard above the horns. "Can you believe it?"

"I guess that just goes to show you, you can find anything—or anyone—on the World Wide Web. Welcome to the twenty-first century!"

I had to laugh at that one, and all the more as she lifted the hem of her jeans and showed off the cowgirl boots she was wearing. I'd accidentally purchased enough boots to outfit a contention of rodeo cowboys a few months ago while planning my first Boot-Scootin' wedding, and everyone in the family now had at least one pair to remind me of the fact. You really *could* find just about anything on the World Wide Web, even the things you weren't looking for. I'd purchased the boots on eBay.

The first song ended a few seconds later. Emilio and Francesca finally gave up on their dance and retreated to the opposite side of the dance floor, where they stood arm in arm.

"What do you think of those two?" I leaned in to whisper.

Mama's eyes narrowed. "Well, it's different. Sometimes . . ." She shrugged.

70

"What?"

"Emilio is your father's brother, and look at how young and pretty his wife is. I just . . . I don't know. I feel really old when she's around."

"Mama!" I'd never seen my mother as anything less than confident, particularly when it came to her appearance. She was the queen of makeup, after all, and had maintained a youthful figure. So this really threw me.

She shrugged. "Sorry, but it's true. And did you see her in that negligee?"

"Who didn't?" I tried to bury the sigh that rose up but found myself unable to.

Mama's gaze shifted down. "I just wonder sometimes if your pop is sorry that he doesn't have a pretty, young wife like that. Someone to show off to his friends."

"I heard that, Imelda." My father's voice rang out from behind us. "And in case you're really wondering, I have the prettiest wife on Galveston Island. I wouldn't give anyone else a second glance." He swept her into his arms and gave her a kiss on the forehead. "Besides, you look as young as you did the day I married you."

"It's the hemorrhoid cream," she said without missing a beat. "Ever since I started using it, I've lost most of the wrinkles around my eyes."

"Strange," Sal said, drawing near. "Been using it for years, and it hasn't done a thing for my wrinkles."

Mama and I erupted in laughter. Should we explain that she applied it directly to the wrinkles? Nah. Sal would never hear about her tricks of the trade, no matter how effective.

Pop snorted too, and that got us all tickled. Before long, the band took to playing again, and we all hit the floor. I had the feeling this was just the first of many dances left to come.

71

# 7

## Eight to the Bar

Life is filled with what I like to call "bada-bing, bada-boom" moments. These unexpected surprises always thrill and delight, because they are so, well, unexpected. We experienced a bada-bing, bada-boom moment as Gordy led the band in a jazzed-up version of "I Got Rhythm." No sooner had his bandmates bellowed out the first few notes on their horns than D.J. and his mother, Earline, arrived at the wedding facility, along with three of my favorite women in the world—Sister Twila, Sister Jolene, and Sister Bonnie Sue. All three "sisters" attended D.J.'s home church in Splendora, and all three had become semi-permanent fixtures in the Rossi home over the past few months.

Now, these three bodacious beauties weren't really sisters, and they *definitely* weren't nuns. But in their neck of the woods—the piney woods of Splendora, Texas—every believer went by *brother* or *sister*. I'd learned to love both the terms of endearment and the people themselves. In fact, these women not only epitomized the love of the Lord, they kept me on my toes with their humorous antics. They'd even gone so far as to bail me out of jail during my last wedding fiasco—a total misunderstanding, mind you—so I owed them. And then some.

As soon as Earline and the three sisters entered the reception hall, Mama, Rosa, and I went crazy greeting them.

"What a wonderful surprise!" I gave the women warm hugs.

The ladies responded in kind and then turned to face Gordy and the other musicians. I could see the excitement on the faces of the ladies as they took in the swing band. These three were genuine music lovers. So was Earline, who would serve as pianist for the upcoming wedding. I had a feeling that's why they'd come—to practice for the big day. Rosa and Laz must've set this up.

We managed to talk above the band, though they increased their volume as they went along. Gordy signaled for us to keep talking, probably trying to get a feel for what it would be like on the night of the wedding when the whole room was filled with talkative guests.

Sister Twila, often the ringleader of the trio, turned to Rosa with a smile and hollered out, "We're so excited about the wedding! Thank you so much for asking us to sing, hon!"

"I can't think of anyone I'd rather have," Rosa shouted in response. "You ladies are the best."

She wasn't kidding. They'd been quite a hit at the medieval wedding I'd coordinated a couple of months back, drawing rave reviews from both the crowd and a newspaper reporter who happened to be in attendance. In fact, they'd garnered such support that they had been asked to sing at Galveston's famed "Dickens on the Strand," a local Christmas event that drew tourists from all over the state. I'd seen a blip in the *Galveston Daily* about their rousing performance just this morning.

Thankfully, Gordy halted the band, and all of the men turned to look at our new guests, some with intrigue on their faces. Who could blame them? The trio of sisters always drew a crowd, especially a male crowd. I couldn't figure out why none of the sixtysomethings had ever married. Sure, they were all plus-sized—and then some—but I'd never seen such pretty faces or better personalities. And talk about wardrobe! These women added a whole new dimension to the word *sparkle*. Rhinestones and glitter abounded, as did a frequent display of sequins when the situation called for it. Today, however, they were all dressed in slacks and T-shirts that read, WHERE'S THE BEEF? I'd have to remember to ask them about the shirts later.

"We're here to run through our tunes with Earline," Bonnie Sue said, looking around. "But I see that the band's here, so maybe they could accompany us." She looked at the sea of men, and her cheeks flushed pink. Turning back to the other ladies, she whispered, "Will you look at that! I've died and gone to swing-band heaven." She began to fuss with her bouffant hairdo and pulled out a compact to touch up her already-too-pink lipstick. After a moment, she glanced down at her T-shirt and then at Twila with a horrified look on her face. She pointed down at the black-on-white tee and whispered, "I can't believe you made me wear this! Of all the times to show up underdressed!"

"It's for a good cause," Twila said with a nod. She looked at me and explained, "We're testing out these shirts for the barbecue cook-off in February." She turned around, and I read the back: SHADE TREE COOKERS: SPLENDIFEROUS BARBECUE FROM SPLENDORA, TEXAS!

It all made sense to me now. They were promoting Bubba's upcoming barbecue competition. Cute.

"What do you think, Bella?" Twila asked, turning back to face me. "Make you hungry?"

I wasn't sure I could answer that without laughing, so I just nodded. I did happen to notice, however, that a couple of the older guys in the band looked hungry as they gazed at our three new guests. Only, I had a feeling they weren't hankerin' for any barbecue. No, I saw a definite look of interest in the saxophone player's eyes as he gazed at Jolene. She smiled at him and her face turned red.

Turning back to me, she whispered, "Someone hand me an umbrella! It really is raining men, just like the song says." Reaching inside her purse, she came out with breath spray, which she used at once.

"I daresay, there are more handsome fellas in this room than we saw on our last cruise, ladies," Twila said, her eyes bright with excitement. "I like that tall one right there." She pointed to the saxophone player who'd eyed Jolene.

"I saw him first," Jolene responded with a pout. "Hands off, Twila. Besides, you've already got a boyfriend."

"You do?" I looked at Twila, stunned. Since when?

With a wave of her hand, Twila dismissed the idea. "Oh, I've been seeing Terrell Buell again. You remember him, Bella? You met him at the Fourth of July picnic, I think."

"Oh, that's right." I vaguely remembered the older man with the soft skin and vivacious twinkle in his eyes. If memory served me correctly, he was sweet on Twila back then too, but she had passed off the idea as unrealistic. I had to wonder what had changed, if anything.

"Poor Terrell's been after me for years," she explained with a shrug. "Never really spent much time thinking about the possibilities . . . till lately. There's something about almost getting swept out to sea that puts a whole new spin on things."

The Splendora trio had been on a cruise ship a couple months back when a storm hit. The event had rocked them—literally and emotionally. Looked like it had also caused Twila to rethink her love life. Only, today she seemed to have eyes for our band members. Probably not a good thing, with Lilly looking on.

"Tell the truth, hon," Bonnie Sue said with a nod. "You're just skittish because of Terrell's last name. You don't want to be Twila Buell."

"That's a bunch of Buell, Bonnie Sue!" Twila said, then slapped her knee. "Get it? A bunch of 'bull'?"

Everyone in our circle erupted in laughter. Well, all but Jolene. She sighed and closed her eyes, listening to the band play. "There's just something about the saxophone that makes me swoon," she said in a dreamy voice. "It casts a spell on me. I can't explain it."

"She's always been a sucker for the sax," Twila said. "I had to hold her back on our last cruise. Every time the band would start to play—"

Jolene's eyes popped open. "Don't you dare tell that story, Twila. It's no one's business. Besides"—her eyes narrowed—"I thought we had an understanding: 'What happens on the cruise ship stays on the cruise ship.'"

"True, true," Bonnie Sue said. "We did agree to that, didn't we." She began to sway with the rhythm of the music. "Oh dear. Oh dear."

"What is it?" I asked, looking her way.

"Sorry, Bella, but I just can't help myself." Her toes took to tapping, and her face lit into a smile. "Whenever I hear swing music, I just lose all of my inhibitions. I *have* to dance. Do you mind?"

"W-what?" I watched, mesmerized, as she headed to the dance floor and began some rather complicated dance steps.

"Bonnie Sue is the swing dance champion of Montgomery County," Twila said with a nod. "There's no stopping her when the band starts to play, trust me. She just can't seem to help herself. But, then again, that's what dancers do. They dance."

Who knew?

"I need a partner!" Bonnie Sue turned to my uncle. "Hmm."

Laz raised his cane as if to ward her off, so she shifted her attention to Emilio. Francesca took a firm hold of her husband's arm, driving her message home. At this point, a determined Bonnie Sue reached to grab Sal by the hand.

I wish I'd had a video camera in hand as she pulled him to the center of the dance floor. The expression on his face was worth a million bucks. She took him by the hands and began to move back and forth, side to side, in some snazzy swing moves.

"Come on, Sallie!" Gordy called out over the microphone. "You used to be the best dancer in Atlantic City back in the day. Remember all those nights at the Blue Velvet? Show her what you've got!"

I could hardly believe my eyes when Sal shifted into swing dance mode. Bonnie Sue let out a whoop as she turned back to her friends. "Can you believe this?" she hollered, and then went back to dancing.

Actually, I *couldn't* believe it, and I wondered if the paramedics would either, once they arrived. Ushering up a silent prayer for Sal's safety seemed the most appropriate thing to do. Sal was hardly fit to be dancing like this. The man was recovering from a stroke, for Pete's sake. I reached for my cell phone, just in case I needed to call 9-1-1.

On the other hand . . . it seemed the more Sal danced, the more his joints loosened up. Before long, he was doing a few moves that amazed me. Hmm. I relaxed a little bit and shoved my phone back in my pocket. Maybe this was just what the doctor ordered. Forget the Geritol. This guy was ready to boogie! He grabbed Bonnie Sue's hands in his own, and they picked up the pace. She squealed with delight, her feet moving faster than I'd imagined possible for someone of her age and size.

"I've died and gone to heaven," she called out, her arms now flailing. "Finally found my partner after all these years."

From the look on her face, I had a feeling she was talking about more than a dance partner. Not that Sal seemed to mind. He swept the plus-sized diva into his arms and spun her around. For a minute she looked like she might swoon, but she managed to catch her breath and keep going. Nothing a little oxygen wouldn't cure. Or another spin around the dance floor with the right partner. Looked like Sal was the Romeo to Bonnie Sue's Juliet.

The dancing went on for another ten minutes or so with all of my relatives finally joining in, even Laz and Rosa, who seemed to be having the best time of all. I found myself glancing at my watch, wondering when the party would die down. As much as I enjoyed all of this, we still had a wedding to plan. And what about the trio of sisters? Rosa had apparently called them down to the island to practice, and practice they must.

At a particular lull in the music, I approached D.J.'s mom, the most levelheaded of the bunch. "Earline, are you ready to rehearse now?"

"Sure thing." She reached into her oversized bag and came out with some sheet music. "I planned to accompany the ladies on their two songs, but as long as we have the band . . ." Her voice drifted off, but her expression remained hopeful.

"Maybe they could join you?" I suggested.

"Sure. I brought my keyboard, of course. Planned to practice."

I commissioned a couple of the fellows to help her bring it in, and before long, she was set up and ready, just to the right of the band.

"Do you know these two songs, fellas?" Bonnie Sue asked, approaching Gordy with the music.

He took one look at the music and laughed. "'Boogie Woogie Bugle Boy' and 'Eight to the Bar'? Are you kidding me? These are standards. Of course, we usually play 'Eight to the Bar' in the key of B flat, but for you pretty ladies, we'll play it in the key of L for lovely, if you like." He gave her a wink, and I swallowed hard as I caught a glimpse of Lilly glaring in the distance. *Yikes*.

Twila fluttered her eyelashes at him, which almost sent poor Lilly into a tailspin. I watched her out of the corner of my eye. Looked like she didn't take kindly to other women flirting with her man. Not that Twila took note. No, she was far too busy gazing into Gordy's eyes.

"Ladies, let's make this a real rehearsal," I suggested, trying to keep things professional. "I'll turn on the sound system, and you can use the microphones."

"Wonderful!" Twila clapped her hands together and grinned. "Let's go to town!"

79

My Italian relatives all took a seat, as if preparing for a night at the opera. The band began to play "Boogie Woogie Bugle Boy," and seconds later, Twila, Bonnie Sue, and Jolene performed a flawless rendition of the old song in perfect three-part harmony. Deanna, Bertina, and Bianca couldn't stay seated for long. They were on their feet and moving to the beat within seconds. On and on the ladies sang, amazing me with their harmony, which was tighter than their WHERE'S THE BEEF? T-shirts. I'd never heard anything finer.

Obviously, neither had Gordy. When the song ended, he turned to them, his jaw at his toes. "Ladies, where have you been all of my life?"

"I've been waiting for years to hear a fella say that," Twila said with a laugh.

Gordy's eyes sparkled with mischief, and I had a feeling he was up to something here. Wanting to hire the ladies, perhaps? Or was there more to this flirtatious wrangling?

This served only to further aggravate Lilly, who now looked like she was ready to toss her clarinet across the room. At the heads of our Splendora guests, no less.

"We've been in Splendora, Texas, sir," Twila said to Gordy, "singing on the worship team at Full Gospel Chapel in the Pines. You're welcome to come and hear us anytime. But be prepared for the Holy Ghost anointing if you do. We're a Spirit-filled church, no doubt about that."

"Sounds good to me." He grinned. "I believe in blooming where you're planted. But I'm also into evangelism, so if you ever decide you want to hit the road, we could use a few new singers."

*Bingo!*

Lilly rose from her seat and stormed from the room, clarinet in hand. Uh-oh. I could smell trouble brewing. Gordy seemed too caught up in the frenzy of the Splendora sisters to notice. He turned back to the band. "Let's try that second number, fellas!"

"Fellas" was right. Lilly was long gone. As the music to "Eight to the Bar" began, I watched her slip into the hallway. Yep. Trouble was definitely brewing.

I found her a couple of minutes later in the ladies' room, holed up in the second stall. "Lilly?"

She responded with a couple of sniffles.

"Lilly? You in there?"

"Yep."

"If you want to talk—"

"Nope."

"If you change your mind—"

"Won't."

"Okay." I leaned against the wall and sighed. What else could I do, really?

She began to play a slow, haunting piece on the clarinet, one that sent a cold chill down my spine. I'd never actually heard a heartbroken woman play the clarinet in a bathroom stall before, so this was all new to me. Still, I couldn't help but feel her pain. The man she loved had just flattered another. Actually, a trio of others. That had to sting.

The door to the ladies' room opened, and Earline walked in. I knew D.J.'s mom pretty well and figured she'd followed me in here for a reason. If anyone was sensitive to the leading of the Holy Spirit, this woman was, even if it meant giving up her position at the keyboard. She looked a little surprised as she heard the clarinet music coming from the second stall, but she didn't say a word. I know she would wait it out. Earline Neeley wasn't above ministering to a woman in need, even in the ladies' room. She gave me a knowing look, then took to washing her hands. A ruse. I knew it. But still, she had to do something while she waited for Lilly to reappear.

When the music finally stopped, Earline dove in headfirst. "Bella, I'm so thrilled for your Aunt Rosa. This wedding is going to be *glorious*. That band is the best thing I've ever heard in my life. Never seen so many talented people together in one place."

"Amen to that." I nodded, wondering where she was going with this.

"And how kind they are to play for our friends. Why, I don't know when I've ever seen such kindness."

"Right. Me either." I shrugged, trying to figure this out.

At this point, Rosa joined us. She looked under the door of the stalls, nodding as she saw Lilly's shoes.

She walked over to the sink and turned on the water, pretending to wash her hands. "How's everyone doing in here?" she asked.

"Fine." What else could I say?

"That's nice." Rosa reached for a paper towel.

Seconds later, Mama appeared. Then Bianca. Then Bertina. Deanna followed on their heels, and we all stood in quiet anticipation, just waiting for Lilly to join us.

"Oh, okay. I give up." She pushed the stall door open and stepped out, her eyes widening when she saw just how many of us there were. "Good grief. Have you staged an intervention?"

Rosa nodded, and I felt compelled to interject something. "It's okay," I assured her. "You're among friends."

"Yes, and I could tell at once that something troubled you," Earline said. "I don't know you, but I want you to know that I care about whatever you're going through, and the Lord does as well."

82

Lilly began to cry. All of the women rushed her, and she dissolved in a haze of tears, clutching her clarinet to her chest.

"I'm . . . so . . . sorry!" she blubbered. "I didn't . . . want to cause . . . a . . . scene! I'm just so jealous any time another woman looks at Gordy. I can't seem to help myself. I can try to fight it, but these feelings always come back up again."

"Which one is Gordy?" Earline whispered in my ear.

"The band director," I mouthed in response.

"Ah." Earline nodded. "I see how it is." She faced Lilly head-on. "Can I ask you a question, honey?"

"Sure." Lilly looked up, her face tear-stained.

"Are you a believer?"

"I am." Lilly nodded. "Though my faith has been sorely tried when it comes to that man, let me tell you!"

"Our faith is always tried by the men we love," Rosa threw in. "I know from whence I speak, trust me."

She did, indeed. She'd been tried by Laz for much of her life. Tried by fire, no less.

"I just don't know how much more I can take," Lilly said, sounding dejected. "I'm plum tuckered out. Exhausted. It was fun when it started, but now . . . well, now I have to wonder if I'm ever going to see the fruit of my labors. And trust me when I say I've labored over that man."

Deanna's eyes filled with tears. "I know just what you mean," she whispered. "Sometimes a man is worth waiting for, and sometimes . . ." Her voice trailed away.

"I never wanted anything so bad in my life," Lilly said, a determined look coming over her. "Just don't know if I have it in me to keep working at it."

"Well, if you are a believer, then you know that the Lord longs to give you the desires of your heart," Earline said. "So, if that man is God's best for you, we just have to pray him through the door."

"That's what I did with my Laz," Rosa said. "Prayed for fifty years."

Deanna paled, her eyes wide. "F-fifty years?" I could almost hear the wheels turning in her head and had to wonder if she'd contemplated waiting this long for Rocco—whoever and wherever he was.

Lilly burst into tears at Rosa's proclamation. "I don't *have* fifty years left in me!" she said. "Don't . . . don't you see? That's my p-problem! I'm already sixty-eight years old. I'll be a hundred and eighteen by the time he looks my way. Who has time for *that*?"

This got a bit of a chuckle from the crowd, which served to reduce the tension in the room. Even Deanna cracked a smile, though I had a feeling her upturned lips were hiding a broken heart.

In the next room, I heard the music come to its inevitable conclusion. Moments later, much to my chagrin, the trio of Splendora sisters joined us, sounding a bit breathless.

"What's happening in here?" Twila asked, pushing her way to the front of the line. "Has someone fainted or something?"

"Yes, is someone ill?" Jolene asked. "I'm ready to pray if so!"

"We *do* need to pray, ladies," Earline instructed them, gesturing for everyone to step back. "But not for healing."

"I'm not so sure about that," Lilly whispered. "Maybe I do need healing." She sniffled and hugged her clarinet. "Healing of the h-heart!" She started crying all over again.

"Oh my goodness!" Jolene rushed her way. "I see it all so clearly now. You're brokenhearted." Her face tightened.

"Which one of those fellas did this to you, sister? Give me his name and social security number, and I'll make him pay." She went off on a tangent about all of the many ways she planned to do that, her words moving faster than the beat of the music she'd just sung.

"Jolene, really." Twila shook her head. "What would Jesus do?"

"Certainly not ruin the man's reputation or his credit," Bonnie Sue said with a nod. "You've slipped out from under the anointing, Jolene. You've shifted over to the dark side. Reel it back in."

"Sorry." Jolene hung her head. "I just hate to see a fellow sister in pain. And men can be so . . ." She groaned. "Anyway, who did this to you?"

"No one did anything to me," Lilly managed. "I'm just head over heels for a man who doesn't even know that I . . . that I exist!" She dissolved into a fit of tears once more. Finally coming up for air, she turned to Twila and said, "And I don't mind admitting that seeing you flirt with him out there put a knife in my heart."

Twila's eyes filled with tears, and she began to fan herself. "Oh my. You're talking about the band leader, aren't you?"

When Lilly nodded, Bonnie Sue nudged Twila. "You *were* flirting with him."

"I suppose I was." Twila looked ashamed. "I had no business doing that. Shame on me. Of course, I didn't know he was spoken for, but still . . ."

"It's the swing music," Bonnie Sue announced. "I'm telling you, it casts a spell. I'm not sure we can pin all the fault on Twila. The Lord himself must've known when he invented music that this could happen."

"I think you're right," Lilly admitted. "There's something

about 'Eight to the Bar' that does me in. Eight beats per measure are obviously just too much for my poor heart to take." She sighed. "Swing music always gives me hope that one day I'll have a partner . . ." Here she dissolved into tears again. "L-l-like Gordy!"

"Honey, it's time for a prayer meeting." Earline held up her hand and, with no further warning, began to talk to the Lord in a voice quivering with emotion. "Father, you see us here . . . in the ladies' room. We're not ashamed to call this our prayer closet right about now."

"No, we're not, Lord," Bonnie Sue threw in. "We are not ashamed!"

"Lord, you see right into the heart of our sister Lilly here," Earline said. "You said if we asked, we would receive."

"So we're askin'!" Twila added.

"You said if we would seek, we would find," Earline continued.

"So we're seekin'!" Jolene threw in.

"And Lord, you said you would give us the desires of our heart."

"Give us our desires, Lord!" Bonnie Sue interjected.

I whispered, "Within reason," as a precaution. No point in bossing the Lord around, after all.

Earline paused for a moment, clearly picking up on the same idea. "O' course, we realize our will has to line up with yours, but Lord, only you know for sure when things are in alignment and when they're not. We just know that you've asked us to pray, so that's what we're doing. We ask that you touch our sister's heart and give her peace in the middle of this storm. And Lord, if there's any work to be done in the heart of that man out there . . ." Her voice began to tremble with emotion.

At this, all of the women in the room added a quivering, "*Yes*, Lord!"

"Well, you know how to speak to him, Father," Earline said. "So we ask you to do it in your time and in your way. In Jesus's mighty name!"

"Amen!" we all echoed.

And there you had it. The prayer meeting came to its rightful conclusion. All of the women took their turns hugging Lilly and giving her words of wisdom and advice. For the first time I noticed that Francesca had slipped into the room. When her turn came, she gazed at Lilly with tears in her eyes.

"Just keep praying," she said, albeit in Italian. "God knows what you need and when you need it."

Alrighty then. Looked like we'd all jumped the gun on Francesca. Maybe some of us needed to repent for more than just flirting with the band members. How many of us had judged her at first glance based on her outward appearance?

"So . . ." Mama looked at the bathroom door with a half-smile. "Who's going to be the first to go back out there? You know the men have got to be wondering what we're doing in here."

"Hmm." I grinned and then offered up a shrug. "Guess it should be me. I'm the leader of this merry little band, I suppose. Being the wedding coordinator and all." I drew in a deep breath, squared my shoulders, and headed for the door.

# 8

## Tuxedo Junction

Monday has always been my favorite day at Parma John's because I love the Mambo Italiano special. There's just something about it that does me in. The smell of the sizzling sausage with its spicy kick. The taste of the spicy red sauce, still bubbling, fresh from the oven. The texture of the gooey cheese atop a thick, layered crust. Mmm! I could hardly wait for Mondays!

Laz decided Monday would be the perfect day to treat the family to lunch, so we loaded up the cars with the whole gang and headed to the Strand—a historic street in the hub of the island's market district—where our family's pizza restaurant resided. I could see the look of interest in Bianca's eyes as we pulled onto the street.

"These buildings are quite old and quaint," she said, looking around. "Lovely. And they look like they've weathered the years."

"Yes, you're right on both counts. They're over a hundred years old," I explained. "In fact, they survived both the Galveston hurricane of 1900 and Hurricane Ike in 2008, so they've more than weathered the years." I went on to tell her that Ike's waters had risen along the Strand to the tune of four or even five feet.

Bertina gave me a nod. "I remember hearing all about Ike. Rosa called us as soon as your phones were turned back on. We were so worried about you."

"Well, we rode out that one in Houston," I said. "And I won't lie—that storm took quite a toll on Galveston Island. We're still working to get things rebuilt. That's why D.J. moved down here. He and hundreds of other carpenters have had their hands full putting things back together."

"You must be so proud of him, Bella!" Bianca gushed. "*È bellissimo ciò che ha fatto!* It is a wonderful thing that he did!" Her smile warmed me.

"Oh, I am proud of him, trust me. He's not just kind-hearted and wonderful to me and my family, D.J. is that way with everyone he meets. He's a good guy through and through."

"And he's getting a great girl," Bianca said, giving me a wink.

I responded with a smile, my heart so full I thought I might cry. Why oh why did I only get to see my Italian relatives every ten years or so? It hardly seemed fair! And how glorious that they loved my sweetie. What a blessed confirmation to have people from the other side of the globe give their stamp of approval.

After parking, we spent a few minutes walking down the Strand to give our guests a proper feel of the place before taking them inside our family's restaurant. Bianca especially loved the Confectionary, while Bertina had her eye on several touristy shops. She even bought a couple of trinkets, which she claimed would always remind her of her trip to the island. Should I have told her that both of the items she'd purchased were actually made in China? Nah.

Deanna trudged along behind us, looking more than a little dejected. I had a feeling her thoughts were not on Galveston Island or souvenirs. No, she was still deep in thought about what had happened this morning. Likely she was thinking about how Rosa had to wait for Laz for over fifty years. No wonder the girl looked pale. I took her by the arm and distracted her with the promise of the best pizza in the world. She finally cracked a smile, albeit a small one.

Finally we landed at the front door of Parma John's. My heart swelled with pride as we stepped inside. There was something about this place that did my heart good. Well, if you didn't count the excessive calories I consumed eating pepperoni and sausage, anyway. And the fact that Pop had to take a lactose intolerance pill before entering the premises.

Joey met us at the door and greeted us with enthusiasm, as he always did. I loved this baby brother of mine. Sure, he was different from the other guys in my family. His shorter stature and longer hair set him apart, as did the tattoos. Oh, but when it came to goodness and personality, this guy couldn't be outdone. And Joey had such a heart for the teens who frequented Parma John's. That made him the perfect candidate to work here. He'd turned the family's pizzeria into a mission field. Everyone responded to his sincerity and genuine goodness. Not that I was biased, of course. He just happened to stand heads taller than most other people I knew. Symbolically, anyway.

"I pushed several tables together so you could all eat as

one big happy family," he said, gesturing to a spot at the very back of the room.

"Of course you did." I reached to give him a hug. "You're as good as gold. Always thinking of others."

"Actually, I was thinking of sparing our customers from the noise by putting you at the back of the room," he said with a wink. "Does that make me a bad guy?"

"No, just a responsible one." I laughed.

"Hey, speaking of customers, the Burtons are here." He pointed to the left wall where my mother's best friend, Phoebe, sat with her husband and son. I gave them a little wave, and they responded in kind.

I turned my attention back to Deanna, who smiled as she looked around the eclectic restaurant with its red- and white-checkered tablecloths and drippy wine-bottle candles. Her gaze shifted to the counter, where the espresso bar was located. Above the scent of the mouth-watering pizza, you could always smell the various coffees at Parma John's. And the vibrant colors of the room were sure to tantalize as well.

"Oh, Bella! This reminds me so much of home. The colors, the smell, the decor." Deanna closed her eyes and drew in a deep breath, then opened them and reached to hug Uncle Laz, whispering, "I love it here!"

"You've done so much to the place since we were here last," Bertina said with a smile. "It's perfect. I wouldn't change a thing."

Laz responded with tears in his eyes, whispering a gentle, "Thank you, ladies." I knew they were tears of both joy and sorrow. He'd run this place like a champ for the past sixteen years. But now that he was facing retirement, it had to be tough to let go, even though the family business would be in my brothers' capable hands.

D.J. joined us, leaning down to kiss me as I took my seat. "You look great," he whispered.

I felt my cheeks warm and gave him a playful wink. "Thanks. You too." He did look great, in a hot and sweaty sort of way. I smiled as I saw the bits of sawdust in his hair. Hazards of the carpentry trade. Not that I minded. They added character and pizzazz. Nope, I wouldn't change a thing about this boy, especially not his work ethic.

D.J. grinned as he said, "Mambo Italiano!"

"Mmm," I added.

"I can almost taste that sausage now."

Emilio's voice rose above the crowd. "Laz, *qual è la specialità della casa?*"

"The specialty of the house?" Laz rose with a smile on his face and a menu in his hand, ready to explain, as always. "I'm glad you asked!" He addressed the family, describing the various pizza specials and how they were named after Dean Martin songs. The Mambo Italiano. The Pennies from Heaven. The Simpatico. All of the various themed pizzas were described in detail.

I heard Dino crooning "Mambo Italiano" off in the distance, so I knew my uncle hadn't completely lost his love for the guy. Maybe I could talk Laz into at least one Dean Martin song for the reception, for old times' sake. Surely Rosa wouldn't mind, as long as we threw in a tune by Ol' Blue Eyes just for fun.

Nick approached and took our drink orders, pausing to talk with everyone as he went. The process took awhile, what with all of the chatter, but no one seemed to mind. I couldn't help but think that Parma John's would surely be in good hands with both Nick and Joey on board.

And Jenna.

I looked up at the register, where my best friend usually stood. Hmm. No Jenna. What was up with that? And why hadn't she returned my call?

Leaning over to D.J., I whispered, "Hey, did you notice that Jenna's not here?"

"Mm-hmm. First thing I noticed, in fact."

"Still no word from Bubba?"

"Nope."

"Hmm."

After Nick took our orders, he disappeared back to the kitchen, and I decided to join him. I slipped out of my chair unnoticed by all but D.J., who likely knew what I was up to. I had some investigative work to take care of.

"Hey." My one-word opening caused Nick to look up from filling glasses with soda.

"Hey, Bella." A concerned look crossed my brother's face. "What's up? Did I miss something? Leave someone out?"

"No, I'm just curious about something. Where is Jenna?"

He shrugged and rolled his eyes. "You tell me. It's just so weird. She's been gone for three days now, you know."

"You mean she called in sick three days in a row?"

"No." Nick stopped filling the glasses and turned to face me. I could read the worry in his eyes. "She called in sick three days ago, then never came back."

Nothing about this made sense. "I saw her four or five days ago and she looked fine. We talked for a few minutes, and nothing struck me as unusual. Do you think maybe she came down with a cold or something? Maybe she's trying to spare you guys from getting it."

He shrugged. "Could be. But she's apparently been sick awhile. So sick she couldn't even pick up the phone to call me. I've had a huge workload, especially with the family in town. And I'm more concerned than ever now that I know she didn't even call you, her best friend."

"Actually, I'm hardly best friend material these days." I sighed, thinking about how I'd ignored Jenna of late. Of course, I was up to my earlobes with wedding plans, but a girl should call her best friend, especially if she was sick.

"It's just weird." Nick shrugged. "She's worked here . . . what? Five years? And rarely called in sick. She's always been a trouper."

"Right." I paused, deep in thought. "The story just keeps getting stranger," I said, feeling my nerves kick in. "Mama said that Bubba missed rehearsal a couple of days ago. For the opera, I mean. He's starring in that Christmas production—what's it called again?"

"*Ahmal and the Night Visitors?*"

"Yeah, that one. Anyway, he called in sick night before last."

"Maybe he's really sick too," Nick said with a shrug.

"I really don't think that's it." I paused to release a sigh. "D.J. said he's had trouble reaching him all weekend. No one has heard from either of them."

"Hmm."

"Exactly."

We stood in silence for a moment before Nick startled to attention. "Better get these drinks to the table before our imaginations get the best of us."

"Right. Let me help you." I slipped into gear, helping him load the drinks onto a tray, which I carried back to the table.

When I arrived, I saw that the Burtons had stopped by to meet the family. I could see the curiosity in Phoebe's eyes when she looked at Francesca and knew she'd probably have a million questions for Mama later.

94

I continued to balance the tray as they talked, nearly losing it a time or two. After they left, Deanna looked my way. "You work here too, Bella?"

I laughed, nearly dropping the tray in the process. "No, they won't let me. I tried working here the summer after my junior year, and, well . . ."

"Let's just say it's cheaper *not* to let her work here," Laz interjected.

"I, um . . . dropped a few things," I said, struggling to hang on to the tray.

Thankfully, Joey showed up and lifted the tray from my arms and began to pass around the drinks. On the other side of the table, Nick did the same. I watched as everyone settled back into the routine of talking, but then I noticed something odd out of the corner of my eye. Sal, looking back and forth between Laz and Rosa. Hmm. What was his deal, anyway? I tried to push all of the "what if's" out of my mind, focusing instead on my cousin, who peppered me with questions about Parma John's. I willingly answered, happy for the distraction.

Our spicy sausage pizzas arrived moments later, and we dove in headfirst. D.J. swallowed down his first piece, then reached for a second. He was like a track star in training, moving faster than the speed of light. Not that I blamed him. There's something about a spicy sausage pizza that causes a person to lose control of their senses. Kind of the same effect swing music had on the older generation, actually. Magical, really.

"Mmm." I took another bite, savoring the delicious flavors. This was always my favorite part. Those first few moments after a pizza arrives at the table are the very best. The gooey, melted cheese is just the right texture and taste, and the fragrant aroma of the meat as it sizzles on top of the pizza pie only adds to the adventure. Add to that Laz's spicy tomato sauce dolloped atop the best thick crust on Galveston Island, and you had a pizza lover's delight. Unless you happened to be lactose intolerant.

I heard Mama whisper, "Cosmo, take your pill!" and my pop reached into his pocket, coming up with his daily stash of tablets. Poor guy. Still, he was the only one who paused, even for a second.

All around the table, I could hear my family members voicing their enjoyment. Not in words, but in guttural sounds—the kind no one usually pays much attention to. Those "mmms" and "wows" echoed in my ears, a positive endorsement for all of the work my uncle had done over the years. He'd taken a tiny dream of a business and morphed it into the greatest pizza biz in south Texas. How could I do any less with our family's wedding facility?

*You can do this, Bella . . . with the Lord's help. Deep breath, girl.*

Surely another piece of pizza would help. I reached for a small one but then changed my mind, opting for a big slice. I still had plenty of time to watch my diet before my wedding. My dress could be altered to fit whatever size I happened to be at the time, right?

I'd just finished my second slice when Laz's voice rang out. "Attention, everyone. Attention!"

We all stopped chewing and looked his way.

"Another announcement?" Nick asked, approaching the table to refill drinks.

"Yes," Rosa said with a smile. "I think you're going to like this one."

We gave them our undivided attention.

Laz's eyes twinkled with mischief as he spoke. "I know everyone has been asking us where we're going to live after we get married."

"Ah." I sat up straight for this one. Finally! An answer to the ongoing question.

D.J. reached for my hand and gave it a squeeze. I turned to him, wondering what he was up to. *Do you know something I don't?*

"We've looked at houses all over the island," Rosa said, drawing my attention back to the head of the table. "Found a really pretty one on the west end."

"So that's it!" I whispered to D.J. "They're buying a house!"

"But it's in a low-lying area," Laz continued, oblivious to my thoughts. "And too far away from the family."

*Ah. Maybe not.*

"Then we found a great condo near the seawall," Rosa said.

*Aha. A condo would be just right for the two of them. Not too big, not too small . . .*

"But it's on the third floor, and I just don't think I can make the trip up and down all those stairs," Laz said.

"We even looked at a retirement community," Rosa said.

*Whoa. Never figured they would go that route.*

"Filled with great people and lots of planned activities, so it was a temptation," Laz said, "but it was pretty expensive. I hate to fritter away my retirement money. I'd rather spend it on my bride. And on traveling." He gave Rosa a kiss, and she responded with a flutter of eyelashes.

"So, what's the answer?" Joey asked. "Gonna stick around at our place awhile?"

"Actually, yes." Laz beamed ear to ear, and all the more

when we broke out in wild, celebratory applause, which caused several of the restaurant's patrons to turn our way.

Uncle Laz looked at Pop, who grinned. "Cosmo has agreed that we should stay. And it just makes sense. We're so at home in that big house, and we need all of our family close by."

"We need you too," Mama said, wiping the tears from her eyes. "It broke my heart to think Rosa might be moving away. And you too, of course, Laz."

Everyone chuckled.

"Well, here's what we've decided," Pop interjected. "There's just one wall separating Rosa's room from Laz's. It's not a support wall. I know, because D.J. already checked it out for me."

I turned to him, stunned. "You did? When?"

"I have my ways." He gave my hand another squeeze. So he *did* have inside information! Not that I minded. This was fabulous news!

"Anyway, that wall is coming down," Pop said. "Once and for all." He gave Rosa a wink.

"We see it as a symbolic move, anyway," Laz threw in. "After years of the walls Rosa and I had put up . . ." He reached to take her hand. "The walls have all crumbled to the ground. No more barriers between us."

She gave him a kiss on the cheek. "And with so much space, we can turn the room into a suite with a nice living area and a bath. I've always wanted my own bath." She giggled, clearly as tickled as if she'd won the Publishers Clearing House sweepstakes. "Laz says I can have a garden tub."

Her cheeks flushed pink, and Laz nodded. "Nothing is too much for my girl."

"Fabulous!" Bianca and Bertina said in tandem.

I felt compelled to throw in something. Turning to Rosa,

98

I smiled. "Rosa, if anyone deserves a nice space to kick back in, you do. You work harder than anyone I know."

"Thank you, Bella." Tears welled up in her eyes. "I'm so thrilled."

"Oh, I can hardly wait to get started!" Mama said. "When should we begin?"

"I've already got the building permits," D.J. said. "So I can have a crew at your place as soon as you say the word."

"Just need to get past the wedding first," Pop said. "Much of the work can be done while Rosa and Laz are on their monthlong honeymoon to Italy."

Now it all made perfect sense. No wonder my aunt and uncle wanted an extended honeymoon on the opposite side of the globe—so they could be away from the mess.

Hmm. One major problem with this plan. D.J. and I were still planning a wedding too. If this construction went on too long . . .

No, I wouldn't think about it. I forced a smile and rose to make a toast. "To Laz and Rosa! And to many more family dinners together in the Rossi home!"

"To many more dinners together!" Mama echoed, lifting her glass.

Out of the corner of my eye, I happened to catch a glimpse of Sal Lucci. His expression seemed tight. Maybe he was put off by our family's boisterous behavior in public. Or maybe . . . I watched his gaze shift to Rosa and wondered what he might be thinking. Hmm. Might be worth keeping an eye on him.

Everyone began to talk at once, and I turned to D.J. with a grin. "You're full of surprises."

"I am." He winked. "I hope that's a good thing."

"A very good thing." I leaned in to whisper, "Why don't

you surprise me with a night out when this is all over with? I miss you."

"I miss you too." He kissed the top of my head and drew me close.

"Rosa's planning a picnic for Wednesday afternoon at Galveston State Park. Can you take a long lunch and meet us there?" I gave him a little pout, hoping it would help convince him.

"What time?"

"Noon."

He nodded. "For you, anything. Just promise me we'll have a few minutes alone to take a walk on the beach. I want to talk to you about something."

"O-oh?" For whatever reason, my fear antennae shot straight up in the air. "Everything okay?"

"More than okay." He leaned over and kissed me. "Don't fret, Bella Bambina. All is well."

"Okay." I did my best to relax. Didn't need any extra stress right now, anyway. Surely whatever he had to talk with me about would be good. It was probably about the honeymoon. Maybe D.J. was finally going to come clean and tell me where we were going. The suspense was killing me, though I'd nearly figured it out. Someplace with the prettiest water in the world. I'd already narrowed the list of possibilities to Cancun or Grand Cayman. Either way, I could hardly wait!

After we finished our pizzas, the cappuccino and espresso flowed freely from the coffee bar. My family—though loud and crazy at times—eventually grew quiet as stomachs and hearts were filled. I even saw a couple of them yawn and realized the ladies would soon be heading home to nap. Oh, if only I had that luxury! But no. I had work to do—work that would not wait.

"Men, are you ready to leave for the tuxedo shop?" Laz asked, rising.

"Mm-hmm." Emilio stretched and rose, giving his wife a peck on the top of the head. "Come on, Cosmo. We've got to look dashing for our ladies."

My father stood up and gave my mother a kiss. My heart flip-flopped as I watched them. How wonderful to be so in love after thirty-plus years together. And how fabulous it was going to be to see them walking arm in arm down the aisle as groomsman and bridesmaid on Laz and Rosa's big day.

Thinking about Rosa and Laz reminded me of all the work I still had to do. Thinking of my workload got me to thinking of Jenna. My gaze instinctively went to the register where she usually stood, and I felt my pulse begin to quicken as I gazed at the empty spot.

*Lord, where is my friend?*

I had a feeling in my gut the answer would be a long time in coming.

# 9

## Sentimental Journey

As soon as the meal ended, the men headed off to the tuxedo shop and Mama drove the women home in her car. Deanna opted to stay with me, though she knew I had work to do. With everyone else out of the picture, she turned to me. "What do we do first?"

"You sure you want to hang out with the wedding planner?" I asked. "It's going to be all work and no play. I've got to go to the florist shop, then make a few calls. I'm double-checking a couple of things with Joey before we leave the restaurant, though. He's our photographer."

"I want to hang out with you. Of course." She gave me a funny look. Suspicious, even.

"What?"

"Well, actually . . ." Deanna smiled. "Mama and Bianca and I have been thinking of opening a wedding facility in Napoli, so they've sent me on a mission to learn all I can from you. Good, bad, and otherwise."

"W-what?" I couldn't believe it. "Really?"

"Yes. And Emilio heard us talking about it on the plane and wants to help fund it. Even Francesca liked the idea. There are no wedding facilities in our area. Most people get married at church and then celebrate after in their homes or restaurants. But we think it would be wonderful to have another Club Wed in Italy. What do you think?"

"Deanna, this is fabulous!" I grabbed her hand and gave it a squeeze. "I'm happy to share what I know about the business. And Club Wed in Italy! Oh, how wonderful that sounds!"

"I have a lot to learn, though," she said. "So, one step at a time. I especially want to hear about these themed weddings you've been doing." She laughed. "I've been trying to imagine how a Texas-themed wedding would go over in Napoli."

"Pretty well, I'd imagine." I giggled. "You have Italian cowboys too, right? Oh, but there's so much more to it than just the Texas theme. Think of the possibilities! Medieval. Tropical. Garden party. Victorian. You name it, brides want it. You'll be surprised at the response, I promise."

"Only one problem." Her eyes filled with tears.

"What is it, honey?"

"My boyfriend and I . . ." She shook her head and brushed away the tears. "From the moment Mama and I started talking about this wedding facility idea, we both imagined that I would be the first client. That Rocco and I would get married there and use the photos to help market the facility. But now . . ." She sighed. "Well, anyway, that's not going to happen. Rocco has cold feet and is clearly not interested in marriage."

"Ah." I could see the dilemma she now faced. Must be tough thinking of weddings when the one person you wanted more than anything else in the world seemed allergic to the process.

Deanna's conversation shifted to Italian, where she began to share her passionate feelings about men. I did my best not to add fuel to her fire. I was, after all, happily in love. Not all men were reluctant to commit. Take D.J., for instance. He'd made it plain from the start that he wanted a wife and family.

I made a move toward the counter where Joey stood talking to a customer. When he finished, he looked my way.

"Ready to get to work?"

"Yes." We shifted to the office in back, where we spent the next half hour talking through every phase of the wedding and reception.

"I still think it's odd that they're not getting married at St. Patrick's," Joey said. "Did you ever figure out why they changed their minds on that?"

"Yeah. The church idea was kaput the minute Father Michael found out there was a swing band involved. Rosa wants the band to play during the ceremony, and Father Michael didn't think there would be enough room for them in the church. Plus he wasn't sure it would go over very well with the bishop."

Joey laughed. "Funny, considering Father Michael's the best trumpet player on the island."

"True. But on top of everything else, St. Patrick's is having a Christmas party that same night in the fellowship hall, so that would've been tricky, juggling things—and people— around."

"I see."

I shrugged. "Besides, with it being so close to Christmas, Rosa wants to do full-out Christmas decor, and the wedding facility is perfect for that. We're going to have lots of Christmas trees and twinkling white lights—that sort of thing. So during both the ceremony and the reception, we'll turn down the overhead chandeliers, and the tiny lights from the trees will really stand out."

"This is going to be a tough one, Bella," Joey said. "Having the lights down, I mean. Makes it rough on the photographer."

"I know, but they want it to look and feel like an old swing band hall. We'll have plenty of ambient lighting from candles and Christmas lights to make up for the big lights overhead. Is that going to be a problem?"

"I just need everything set the night before, if possible. That way I can get the right settings on my camera. Don't want to be guessing on the night of the wedding."

"Hmm." I paused a moment. "I guess I could have everything done the night of the rehearsal." I sighed, and Joey smiled.

"It's okay, Bella. Look at all of the people you have to help. You won't be working alone, I'm sure." He gestured to Deanna, who grinned in response.

"Yes, please." She nodded. "I want to learn everything I can, so use me as much as you like."

"You don't hear that every day." Joey grinned.

We wrapped up our conversation and then said our good-byes. As we climbed into the car, I noticed that Deanna looked a little melancholy once again. This was getting to be quite the routine.

"Everything okay?" I asked.

"Yes. No." She shrugged. "All this talk of weddings is just making me . . ." She paused. "Making me miss Rocco."

Yikes. Better change the direction of our conversation. No point in dredging up any more tears. Instead, I pointed my car toward the center of town, ready to deal with the flowers for Rosa and Laz's big day.

We pulled up to Patti-Lou's Petals, the flower shop Marcella managed. Patti-Lou, the original owner, had recently moved to Montana, where she'd finally found the man of her dreams. I knew the sign above the store would change names as soon as Nick and Marcella could afford to buy the business. In the meantime, my sister-in-law did a fine job keeping the island in flowers. And flowers we needed, especially in the wedding biz!

I stepped inside and breathed deeply of the fragrant aromas. Marcella saw me and grinned. "Bella!"

"Marcella, you look beautiful!" Why, she was beaming! I'd never seen anything quite like the glow on her face at this very moment. Of course, she had a lot to beam about, didn't she? Her blossoming midsection spoke of exciting things to come. Hopefully exciting things with pink tutus and ballet slippers.

"Thank you." She took my hand and gave an impish smile. "I have something to tell you, but it's top secret."

"Oh?"

"First I need you to promise that what I tell you will be kept between us." She looked back and forth between Deanna and me. "Promise?"

"Of course!"

"Nick and I found out the sex of the baby this morning."

"Really?" My heart began to thump wildly. "Is it a—"

"A girl!" She clasped her hands at her chest and grinned. "Isn't that glorious? She's a girl!"

At last, the evil spell was broken! "Oh, this is wonderful!" I began to gush over her, and soon Deanna joined the celebration.

"Oh, I'm going to pay for dance lessons!" I said. "Let me

know when she's ready to start ballet. And you know Mama will want to give her singing lessons so she can stand on the stage at the opera house one day and melt the crowds. And Pop will teach her to play basketball with the boys. He won't have a clue." On and on I went, talking about how we Rossis would sweep in around this little girl and share our love with her.

Marcella laughed. "One thing at a time, Bella! First we have to move into our new place, and then I have to decorate the nursery in pink. I've never done that before, especially not while taking care of a shop and raising two rowdy boys."

Two rowdy boys was right. I wondered how Frankie and Deany-boy would take this news. Likely not very well. They were probably counting on a little brother, not a frilly girl.

We lowered our voices when a couple of customers came in and started browsing the flowers in the case. I did my best to keep things hush-hush. "So, do the boys know?"

Marcella shook her head. "No. No one knows but Nick and me. And now you two." She put her finger to her lips. "And I know you would never tell."

"Never!" Deanna and I spoke in unison.

"We're trying to figure out when and where to tell everyone," Marcella said. "We want it to be really special, but we don't want to interfere with Rosa and Laz's big day."

"Understandable."

"I'm open to suggestions," she said. "Let me know if anything comes to you."

"Hmm. Okay." I paused a moment. "Hey, how's the house hunt going? Did you and Nick find a place yet?"

"Actually, we're looking at a Victorian just a few blocks from your place." She nodded. "And speaking of houses, have you and D.J. decided where you're going to live after you get married?"

I shook my head. "He's renting a condo on the seawall, but that's not long-term. We've given some thought to getting a place on Jamaica Beach, but that's so far away."

Marcella laughed. "You're funny, Bella. My family lives in Houston, and I think that's far away. The opposite side of the island doesn't seem far at all."

"We're still praying about it," I said. "God will show us what to do."

"He always does." She paused as the other customers approached the counter, ready to place an order. Deanna and I turned to the roses in the case while Marcella shifted gears.

"Those are gorgeous." Deanna pointed to a multicolored rose, and I nodded.

"Yeah, I agree. Those are Double Delights. That's what Rosa has chosen for her wedding. Do you like the red and white mixed together?"

"Beautiful."

"And picture this," I said, growing more excited by the minute. "Once we get all of the greenery mixed in and topped off with gold ribbon, the whole place will have a Christmas feel to it. That's what Rosa wants, anyway."

Deanna nodded. "It's going to be gorgeous. And I think I heard her say something about having miniature Christmas trees on all of the tables?"

"Yes, I bought those a couple of weeks ago on the Web," I said. "They're pre-lit and work off of batteries, so we don't have to worry about plugs or anything. We'll do red bows on top of half of them and gold on the rest."

"Perfect. Are you decorating the trees?"

"I thought about putting some red and gold bows on them. Nothing too elaborate. The lights will really look pretty, even if the trees aren't too dolled up."

"I know Rosa's going to love that. She's always been crazy about Christmas, so I think it's perfect that her wedding falls during the Christmas season."

Deanna was just a few sentences into her explanation when the door to the flower shop opened and Tony DeLuca walked in.

"Tony?" I stared at my ex, curious to find him here.

"Oh, hey, Bella . . ." His words trailed off, and his gaze shifted to the flowers in the case. "What are you doing here?"

"Same thing I'm always doing here," I responded with a shrug.

He walked to the glass case and stared at the roses. "So, roses are the best, right?"

"Of course."

He began to speak in Italian, and Deanna responded.

"Do you need help, Tony?" Marcella asked, coming out of the back room.

"Well, I, uh . . ." He shrugged. "Yeah."

"Roses for Sophia?"

He looked my way, a hard-to-read expression on his face. "Yeah. Is that weird for you, Bella? I mean—"

"Say no more. It's not weird for me. I think it's wonderful. And I happen to know Sophia loves yellow roses."

"Yellow, huh?" He stared at them.

"It's that 'Yellow Rose of Texas' song," I explained. "She always used to say that she wanted to find a true-blue Texan who would give her yellow roses."

"What about a true-blue Italian who happens to live in Texas giving her yellow roses?" He quirked a brow, and we all laughed.

"That'll do." I nodded. "The point is, the roses are coming from someone who cares about her."

"I do. Very much." His eyes filled with tears, and my heart quickened. The last time I'd seen that look on his face, he'd been fighting for my attentions. Now it looked like everything had come full circle.

"I'm so glad." I reached out and touched his arm. "She's a great girl, Tony. And I think you two are a wonderful couple."

Deanna began to tell him—in Italian—all of the reasons why he and Sophia made a perfect match. Somewhere along the way she mentioned Rocco's name, going on and on about how he'd given her two dozen pink roses on her last birthday and how much they'd meant to her. How she had hoped to see the next bunch of roses in a lovely shade of red, since red symbolized love. How she'd probably never get another rose from another man as long as she lived.

"You know, it's funny," she said, peering into Tony's eyes. "You remind me so much of Rocco. You look alike, even sound alike."

Uh-oh. Better stop this train from barreling down the wrong track. "Tony is from Sicily, Deanna," I said. "No doubt he looks and sounds like your Rocco."

She sighed. "Only, he's not my Rocco anymore." She dabbed her eyes. "Of course, I once thought he really cared about me." She sniffled. "Now I know better." Her smile quickly faded, then reappeared a moment later, this time more forced. "Anyway, buy the roses. She will never forget them. Or you. Ever. For the rest of her life. No matter where she goes or how many times you forget to call. Or write."

Wow.

Tony, undeterred by Deanna's odd explanation, nodded in Marcella's direction. "I'll take two dozen yellow roses." He turned to look at me. "Bella, you're sure about the yellow?"

"Sure as I've ever been about anything in my life."

"Okay, because Brock said I should buy red. He's pretty good with the women, so I took his advice seriously."

"Wait." I stopped dead in my tracks. "Brock? As in Brock Benson?"

Deanna's eyes lit with recognition. "Brock Benson, the Hollywood superstar hottie? The guy who starred in *The Pirate's Revenge*?"

Tony nodded and then shrugged. "Yeah. We still talk sometimes."

Deanna looked my way, clearly dumbfounded. "Brock Benson? Are we talking about the same guy, Bella?"

"Yes. The same Brock Benson." A warm feeling washed over me at the mention of Brock's name. Should I tell Deanna the whole story—how Brock had played the role of best man at the recent medieval wedding I'd coordinated? How the media had shown up and we'd all ended up on the national news? How the Rossi family had taken in Brock—a lost soul— and made him part of the family?

Nah. I'd leave that for another day.

"I'll fill you in later," I whispered to Deanna. "It's kind of a long story."

"O-okay." She grinned, and we returned to helping Tony with his rose order. Still, I couldn't help but smile as I thought about Tony talking to Brock. Who would have guessed those two would turn out to be fast friends?

We spent the next few minutes finalizing plans for Rosa's wedding flowers, then Deanna and I hit the road. As we climbed into the car, my cell phone rang. I smiled as I read the words Bridal Boutique on the caller ID, then answered with a happy "Hello."

"Bella?"

111

I recognized the voice at once. Stacey O'Farrell, owner of my favorite wedding dress shop.

"Hi, Stacey. What's up?"

I could hear customers talking in the background but did my best to focus as Stacey spoke. "Your sister came in to be fitted for her bridesmaid dress this morning. She was the last one on the list, so we're good to go to place the order now. You should have the dresses in plenty of time for the big day."

"Awesome." One more thing I could check off of the list, praise the Lord!

"I just wanted to double-check something before I place the order," Stacey said. "Because one thing about it struck me as odd."

"What's that?" I reached for my keys and put them in the ignition as I waited for her reply.

"I thought you said your bridesmaids' dresses were going to be a deep red."

"Right." I turned the key in the ignition.

"Then why did you write the word *gold* on the order form?"

"W-what?" I groaned, my thoughts suddenly reeling. Finally it hit me. "Oh, Stacey, I'm sorry. My aunt's bridesmaids are wearing gold. I must've gotten confused."

She laughed. "That's what I figured. You've seemed a little scattered lately. Good thing we caught this before the order was placed. Would've been catastrophic, and I don't think there would've been time to reorder."

"No kidding. I'm indebted to you, Stacey. Please change the color to red and place the order."

"Will do."

As we ended the call, I scolded myself for having been so

careless. "I can't believe I did that," I muttered. "Guess I'm trying to handle too many things at once."

Deanna gave me a curious look, and I filled her in, telling her about the near miss.

"You poor girl!" She shook her head. "You've really got your hands full, Bella."

"Don't I know it." I shook my head, deep in thought. Pondering the color of my bridesmaids' dresses drew my thoughts to Jenna again. Thinking of Jenna caused a gripping sensation in my chest. If I didn't figure out why she'd stopped taking my calls, I was going to go crazy.

I turned to Deanna. "Hey, do you mind if I make one more quick call? Something's been bothering me all day."

"Sure." She gave me a curious look. "Everything okay?"

"I'm about to find out." I punched in Jenna's number and waited for her to pick up. Oddly, the phone went to voice mail just after the first ring. When I heard the beep, I left a long, detailed message.

"Jenna, I've been trying to reach you for days. I'm hoping you're not sick. If I don't hear from you by tomorrow, maybe I'll swing by your place to check on you. I'm a little worried because . . ." I wanted to say, "Because Bubba is missing too," but didn't. Instead, I said, "Because you never do this. You never disappear on us like this. I'm worried. So, call me. Or text, if you're too sick. Anyway, let me know you're okay."

I ended the call and tossed the phone in my purse. Deanna looked at me. "Still can't find your best friend?"

"No."

Her eyes filled with tears. "I know just what that feels like. It's so weird, not hearing from Rocco every day. He was my best friend."

"Mm-hmm." I couldn't even imagine what it must be like to lose your best friend.

On the other hand, Jenna was now my second-best friend, since D.J. was in the picture. She'd slipped out of the number one spot the minute he slipped that engagement ring on my finger. Surely she wasn't upset about that though, right? If so, she'd done a great job of hiding it till now.

More concerned than ever, I pointed the car toward home.

# 10

## You Made Me Love You

On Wednesday morning, I finished up my shopping for the wedding with Deanna at my side. She particularly enjoyed our local Walmart, still carrying on about how she wished they had one in Napoli. Francesca came with us, but she didn't look as impressed. Perhaps before all was said and done, I could take her up to Houston to see the Galleria. It was always so beautiful at this time of the year. Likely she'd be more at home there, with the high-end shops and large ice-skating rink in the hub of it all. And the Christmas tree in the center of the ice always made it very conversational.

I pressed back the smile as I tried to imagine Francesca and Emilio ice-skating together. What would it be like to marry a man twenty-five-plus years your senior?

No time to dwell on that right now, not with so much to do. I had some last-minute purchases to make for Rosa's reception, including several bolts of fabric to use as a backdrop and gold lamé to use under the centerpieces.

I headed off to the fabric department with Deanna in tow. Francesca settled into a booth at the nail salon, thrilled to finally get her mani and pedi. As I left her, she was trying to converse with a woman whose English was limited at best. Funny, watching a woman from Italy trying to talk to a woman from Asia using the English language as a middle ground. Somehow they made it work.

Deanna and I arrived in the fabric department a couple of minutes later. "I don't want to spend much time in here," I explained. "We've got to get over to the state park to meet the others in forty-five minutes."

"Do you think Francesca's nails will be dry by then?" Deanna asked, grinning.

"Who knows? But we don't want to miss this."

"I think a picnic at the beach is a great idea," Deanna said. "There's something about the water that's very healing."

That stopped me in my tracks. I turned to her. "I feel exactly the same way. Whenever I get really down, I go to the water's edge and just sit in the sand and pray. Or walk. I can't explain it, but the rise and fall of the waves . . . well, it does something to me."

"Me too." She nodded and gave me a funny look. "You know, Bella, for two people who've hardly ever seen each other, we sure have a lot in common."

"Yeah, we do." I smiled at her, not wanting to let the moment slip away from me. "And in case I haven't said it, I'm so glad you were able to come for Rosa's wedding. It means the world to her . . . and to me."

"You'll have to come see me next time," Deanna said. "I can introduce you to—" She stopped herself short of saying Rocco's name, her eyes filling with tears. She put a hand over her mouth, then pulled it away. "I'm so sorry. I keep forgetting. I'm not dating Rocco anymore, so I can't introduce you to him."

"Still . . ." I tried to make the best of this. "Maybe someday I'll come to see you and you can show me all of your favorite stores." I gestured to the women's underwear department. "Like I'm doing for you. Treating you to the local culture."

She laughed. "It's a deal."

I found the gold lamé at once. I was eyeing the shimmering fabric as Deanna turned my way, her brow wrinkled.

"What's up?" I asked. "Something wrong?"

"Well, not really. I've wanted to ask you something for a couple of days, but I keep forgetting."

I reached for the bolt of fabric and picked it up. "What is it?"

"Have you noticed something a little . . . I don't know . . . odd going on at the house?"

"What do you mean?" I shifted the bolt to the basket and wheeled it toward the cutting table. "Something to do with Francesca?"

"No. Sal."

"Sal?" I carried the bolt of fabric to the counter and plopped it down. "What about him?"

Deanna's brow furrowed. "I don't think he cares much for Rosa, and I get the feeling Emilio doesn't either."

"Funny." I paused, remembering the look I'd seen on Sal's face Monday at the restaurant. It had raised red flags, but I couldn't say why for sure. If Sal didn't care for Rosa, it couldn't be blamed on anything she had done. She'd been nothing but kind to him. I hadn't really noticed anything obvious—other than their initial greeting—but maybe Deanna was onto something here. Sal had seemed a little cold at the restaurant, hadn't he? And he hadn't exactly warmed up to Rosa, no matter how hard she'd tried.

I looked Deanna in the eye. "Tell me what you know."

"Well . . ." She paused, and her gaze shifted to the ground. "Maybe I'm betraying a confidence here . . . I don't know. I just heard Mama and Aunt Bianca talking, and they mentioned Sal saying something inappropriate when Rosa was in the kitchen."

"Inappropriate how?"

Just then, the woman who cut the fabric returned to the table. "Sorry," she said breathlessly. "They needed me for a price check. How many yards?"

"Hmm. Ten, I think. No, fifteen." I paused. "Better make that eighteen."

"Honey, I doubt there's that much on the bolt."

"Well, whatever you have, then."

She went to work measuring, and I turned back to Deanna, who pursed her lips.

"I hate to even repeat this," she whispered. "Since I didn't hear it for myself."

"Didn't hear what?"

For a moment I thought she wouldn't say, but she finally coughed it up. "Mama said that Sal called Rosa a heifer."

"W-what?" I stared at her, shocked. "You don't mean that."

"I know, it's awful." She shifted to Italian as a family with young children passed by. "I asked Mama twice, just to make sure I heard right. She said it could have been taken a couple of different ways, but there was no doubting his meaning. He thinks Rosa is all wrong for Laz."

"How dare he!" I went into a tirade—right there in the fabric department in Walmart—about how Sal Lucci had no business butting into my family's affairs. How Rosa had waited for Laz's affections for fifty years. How she'd finally won his heart, not with her outer beauty, but her inner beauty. And her cooking, of course.

The lady cutting my fabric looked up, concerned. Maybe she thought I was having it out with Deanna or something. I lowered my voice but continued to rant, hardly pausing to take a breath.

Deanna listened to all of this in silence. When I stopped, she nodded. "I know, Bella. I feel the same way. And you should've heard Mama. She was beside herself. And Aunt Bianca wanted to tell Rosa what they'd heard."

"No!" I shook my head. "Never!"

"That's what I said. So Mama and Bianca didn't breathe a word." Deanna paused a moment. "I've been worried they might tell your mama."

"Man, I hope not." I knew my mother to be one of the godliest women ever, but when it came to her family, sometimes her claws came out. She was sure to do Sal mortal harm once she heard this news. No, we couldn't let her know. Or Pop. He would forbid Sal from entering our home.

I stopped to think about what a conundrum that would be, what with Sal being the best man and all. I also had to wonder—if Pop resorted to such tactics—if Sal would pull from his list of former mob buddies to retaliate.

A shiver ran down my spine.

Just as quickly, the fear passed. Sal Lucci was just a shell of his former self. Surely most of his former acquaintances were long gone. This wasn't a physical battle, it was a spiritual battle, and it needed to be fought on my knees, not in back alleys with former mob bosses.

"I don't like any of this," I said, looking Deanna in the eye.

"But I'm going to keep it to myself. Well, I might tell D.J. I'm not sure. But no one else." Right then and there, I decided to pray about this. Surely, if David could take down Goliath with five smooth stones, I could deal with Sal Lucci.

I glanced at my watch and gasped. "Deanna, it's 11:45. I wasted too much time ranting and raving. We need to get on the road."

"Okay. Hope Francesca's toenails are dry."

We found her in the nail salon, conversing with a woman I'd never seen before. She introduced herself as Kathy Francis, from the west end of the island. Between Francesca's thick Italian accent, the manicurist's fast-moving Asian dialogue, and Kathy's slow-moving twang, they were really something to hear. Talk about multicultural!

Thankfully, it took only a few minutes for Francesca to slip on her sandals and pay. I noticed that she left a hefty tip—twenty dollars. Man. I would have offered to do her nails myself for that kind of money.

We quickly paid for our purchases and set off on our way. As I drove up the seawall, I found myself lost in thoughts about Sal Lucci. Much as I wanted to be angry with him, I realized his opinions—however wrong—were not Laz's. And surely Laz was man enough to stand up to him, should the need arise. Not that I expected anything from Sal. Not really. Surely he wouldn't stir up trouble this close to my aunt and uncle's big day. Right?

My cell phone rang, and I glanced down, happy to see D.J.'s number.

"You on your way?" he asked when I answered.

"Yeah, we just left Walmart."

Something in the tone of my voice must've tipped him off. "Everything okay, Bella? You sound kind of . . . mad."

"I'm mad all right, but I'll calm down by the time I get there."

"Not mad at me, I hope."

At once my voice softened. "No, not at all. Sorry to scare you. I'm just upset at something Sal did." I lowered my voice, not wanting to raise suspicions. Francesca was happily chatting with Deanna in Italian about her cuticles, so I was safe.

"Ah. Well, you want to tell me about it?" D.J. asked.

"Maybe at the park. I'm hoping to have some alone time with you." Not that I wanted to spend my few minutes of alone time with my sweetie pouring out my heart about Sal Lucci. No, I needed my private time with D.J. just to be with him. Nothing more.

"We'll still take that walk on the beach. Sound good?"

"Perfect." I ended the call, feeling better about things. D.J. always had that effect on me.

Deanna, Francesca, and I arrived at the park at 12:05, just as the Rossi caravan pulled in. As we got out of the car, I noticed Deanna had brought her bathing suit.

"Girl, it's fifty-four degrees outside," I said. "No one swims in December!"

"Well, I do." She laughed. "Besides, fifty-four degrees isn't cold. We swim in much colder water than that sometimes."

We joined the others, and Francesca looked at Deanna with a horrified expression on her face. "You're actually going to get in that disgusting water? Have you looked at it?"

"Hey, now . . ." I turned to her, wondering at her outburst. What was it with this woman? One minute she was happily conversing with strangers, the next she was insulting the Gulf of Mexico? *Make up your mind, sister. Either you're nice or you're not.*

121

I sucked in a deep breath, trying to calm down. Likely this thing about Sal had me more worked up than I needed to be. Maybe I thought—based on the little bit Deanna had said back there at the store—that Emilio and Francesca were somehow in on this too. Were they all conspiring against Rosa? If so, I really might come out swinging.

*Lord, calm me down. I'm like Sister Jolene—I've slipped out from under the anointing.*

Francesca crossed her arms at her chest and stared me down. "Bella, how long has it been since you've been to Italy?"

I shrugged. "Hmm. I think my only trip was in fifth grade. So, maybe nineteen years?"

"Do you remember the Mediterranean at all?"

"Vaguely."

Francesca's eyes took on a dreamy look. "Well, most never forget it. The water is ice blue. And the colors of the buildings along the shoreline are magnificent in comparison. There's nothing like it."

I sighed, knowing she was right but not willing to concede. "The Gulf of Mexico might not be the Mediterranean," I said, "but if you take a boat out a few miles, the water gets bluer as you go. And where the gulf merges with the Caribbean . . . well, you've never seen waters that color. Indigo. And warm as sunshine, even in December."

"Humph." She went back to examining her nails.

Laz slipped his arm around Rosa's waist and gave her a kiss in her hair. I happened to catch a glimpse of Sal just a few feet away, taking this in. His jawline was tight, but he said nothing. *That's right, mister. You'd better keep your thoughts to yourself.*

D.J. arrived at 12:30, just as we set up the food on a couple of the carefully chosen picnic tables. Mama and Rosa had prepared meatball sandwiches along with some pasta salad. Yum. We drank sweet tea with our meal, and I smiled as I watched Deanna react to it.

"Whoa!" She held up the glass, a stunned look on her face.

"Yeah, I know." I laughed. "D.J.'s mama calls that glucose tea. Don't drink it if you have a blood sugar problem."

"I might if I drink this whole glass." Deanna grinned, then took another swig. "We sure don't drink it like this in Napoli."

We enjoyed a wonderful lunch together, but I found myself distracted, wondering what D.J. wanted to talk to me about. After we ate, I gave him one of those "let's sneak away from the crowd" looks, and he responded by rising from the table and stretching. He winked, then spoke to anyone who might be listening. "I'd like to see the water before I have to go back."

"Good idea," I echoed, grabbing him by the hand. "See you guys later."

And we were off to the sand, where I pulled off my shoes and ran my toes along the edge of the cold water. Then I stopped and turned to face the mighty Gulf of Mexico, breathing in the salty air. D.J. came up behind me and wrapped his arms around my shoulders, leaning his head against mine. We stood frozen in time and space, just staring. The waves pulled in and out, doing their usual thing. I found myself caught up in the rhythm of it all, thinking about how much our lives were like that—ins and outs, goods and bads. Thankfully, more good than bad.

After a few moments, D.J. broke the silence. "I have something to tell you," he said. "Something I hope you're going to like."

"Oh?" I turned to face him, and the wind whipped a loose hair into my face.

D.J. brushed it aside, his fingertips lingering against my cheek. "You know I have a lot of friends in the construction business."

"Sure." I gazed at him, more curious than ever.

"Well, one of them—a guy named John—told me a couple of months ago about this old house in town, just a few blocks from your parents."

This certainly got my attention. "Yeah?"

"Bella, when I say old, I mean old. It survived the hurricane of 1900."

"Hmm." I hated to speculate. I'd seen several of those older homes, and they rarely impressed me. Well, except the ones that had been overhauled.

"Anyway, it's been vacant ever since Hurricane Ike hit. The owners abandoned it, and the county took it over once back taxes became an issue. So I found out that I could get it for a song."

"Really? You think it's right for us?"

"I don't think I'd let my dog live there right now, to be honest," he said. "I won't lie to you, Bella. It's really bad. And not terribly big. But the lot is huge, so it has lots of possibilities."

"Hmm." Another long pause on my end must've clued him in to my discomfort.

"I want to take you by to see it," he said, "but I'm afraid it'll scare you off. When I look at it . . ." He smiled. "Well, when I look at it, I see it completely renovated. I see hardwood floors and ten-foot ceilings. I see a modern kitchen and a new stairway. I see huge windows and a wide veranda where we can hang a porch swing like your parents have."

124

"Mmm. Sounds yummy. What else?"

"I see a big living room where our families can get together and an even bigger dining room with one of those huge tables like y'all have in your dining room. I see a large master bedroom where we can . . ." His face turned red. "Turn in after a long day."

"Mm-hmm. I like what you see." Reaching up, I gave him a kiss on the cheek.

"Unfortunately, you probably won't have the same view of things if I actually take you to see the place."

"Ah." I paused, deep in thought. "How do we move forward if I don't see it?"

"Well, I had this idea." He offered up a crooked grin. "I was thinking maybe you wouldn't see it at all. Until it's done, I mean."

"W-what?" I stared at him, completely dumbfounded. "You want to buy a house and not let me see it until it's done?"

"Right. That's exactly what I want to do. And I want you to trust me."

"I do trust you, but . . ." Shaking my head, I tried to make sense of this. "Are you really serious?"

"Never more so."

"Aren't you going to be busy doing the work on Rosa and Laz's suite?" I asked him.

"I'll contract it out, mostly," he said. "Probably oversee it. That's part of what it's like to be your own boss. You don't always do the grunt work."

"Right, but still, you're going to be plenty busy with that."

"And several other projects too, if things go well," he said. "Getting this business up and running means dedicating a lot of time to a lot of different jobs. But one of the benefits

125

is knowing how to renovate an old home, which is what I'm itching to do for the two of us."

"So, how will you have time to work on a house that we would need to live in by February?"

He shrugged. "When you want something bad enough, you make it happen."

"Mmm." I slipped my arms around his waist, convinced he was right. I'd wanted D.J. Neeley, and—with a lot of help from above—had made it happen. Okay, so I'd had very little to do with it. Our happily ever after was all the Lord's doing, not my own. Still, I knew how to fight for something I wanted.

Obviously, so did D.J. From the look on his face, I could tell he wanted this house—and bad.

I reached for my shoes and slid them back on, feeling the grainy sand underneath my feet. I turned back to my sweetie. "I'll make you a deal. If you pray about this and feel like it's really a God-idea, then go for it. Your house is my house. I completely trust you."

He grinned. "And think of the stories we'll have to tell our kids one day about how Daddy wouldn't let Mommy see her house until it was finished."

I couldn't help but smile as he talked about our children yet to come. What would it be like to have children with D.J.? Would they turn out like Frankie and Deany-boy—rotten to the core but loveable when the situation called for it? Or would I one day have a beautiful, doe-eyed daughter with frilly pink dresses and bows in her hair?

Looking at D.J., I suddenly realized the house didn't matter. Sure, we needed a place to live, but who cared if it was an older, renovated house or a new one? As long as we were close to the people we loved, any house he built would be a home.

# 11

## Don't Fence Me In

I spent Wednesday afternoon tying up loose ends at the wedding facility. Time to check and double-check everything. Candelabras. Tablecloths. Silverware. Serving dishes. I certainly had my work cut out for me. Armando had always accused me of being obsessive-compulsive, and I couldn't deny it. Still, there were some advantages to being a list maker. You could check things off one at a time. And that's what I spent the afternoon doing.

At 3:00 I received a visit from Aunt Rosa, who looked a little flustered. She sat across from me, fanning herself.

"Problem?" I asked.

"Bella, remember how I asked you to drop off Laz's ring at the jeweler last week to be sized?"

"Sure." I nodded. "I did that. Dropped it off, just like you asked."

"Right." She fanned herself again. "Well, I picked it up

today and they sized it wrong. Laz wears a nine. They sized it an eleven."

"Oh no." I slapped myself in the head, realizing what must've happened. "Rosa, I'm so sorry. D.J. wears an eleven. I must've gotten confused when I filled out the paperwork. Can they fix it?"

"Yes." She sighed. "I can pick it up tomorrow. But talk about cutting it close!"

"I'm so sorry." I gave her my best pout, and she grinned.

"Who could be angry with you, Bella Bambina? I love you, my girl."

"I love you too." I stood and gave her a hug.

As she left the room, I shook my head, perplexed by how many things I'd gotten confused about lately. First the brides-maids' dresses, now the rings? Man! I'd better start paying attention.

At 4:45 D.J. showed up. I watched from my office window as his Dodge 4x4 pulled up in the driveway of Club Wed and thought back on that first day I'd seen him. Nothing much had changed. He still drew my eye and caused me to lose my breath. A couple of things were different now, though. Now—as I watched him amble up the drive with those pointed cowboy boots leading the way—I knew he was mine. Knew I'd spend forever with him.

Hmm. My mind reeled backward in time, not to the day we'd met, but to our conversation about the house. I knew he probably wanted to talk more about it. Hopefully things would slow down long enough to do that after Rosa and Laz's wedding. In the meantime, I needed to put all thoughts of home renovation out of my mind and focus on the up-coming wedding. Just three days! Saturday was going to be glorious—perfect in every way. The reception hall at Club

Wed was coming along nicely, and with the addition of the swing band, we would have the party of the century!

D.J. and I walked arm in arm to my house next door, our conversation easy. Oh, how I loved this guy. I loved the way his eyes lit up when he got excited about something. I loved the way he prayed with me when things got tough. And I especially loved the fact that he loved not just me but my family as well. Anyone who could fall in love with the Rossi clan was all right in my book.

I paused on the veranda and gazed into his eyes. "Have I told you today how much I adore you?"

"Hmm, let me think." After a second's pause, he said, "Nope," with that long Texas drawl of his.

"Well then, I'm long overdue. I love you, Dwayne Neeley Jr. And I can't wait till Rosa and Laz's big day is behind me so I can give our wedding my undivided attention. It's going to be so wonderful, merging our two families together. Can you even imagine?"

"Nope."

"It's going to be glorious."

He held me close and kissed me. Waves of joy—stronger than the pull of the gulf—washed over me. What had I ever done to deserve this guy? I whispered up a prayer of thanks, opening my eyes only when I heard D.J. speak.

"Bella, I'm crazy about you. Whenever I think about where I'd be without you . . ." He paused, and his eyes filled with tears. "Well, I can't imagine it. Being with you has been the best decision of my life, next to choosing to walk with the Lord. And I thank him every day for you. Every minute of every day. I honestly believe he brought us together, and he's going to keep us going for years and years to come."

Now who had tears in her eyes? I brushed them away and

kissed him soundly, then lingered in his arms a minute or two.

"When we're Rosa and Laz's age, we'll have been married thirty-plus years," D.J. said.

"Crazy." I shook my head. "But at least we'll have spent those years together, instead of bickering like they did!"

"No kidding. Thank goodness those days are behind them now. People spend entirely too much time not getting along when they could be doing this." D.J. kissed the tip of my nose. "And this." He kissed each cheek. "And this." He gave me a passionate kiss on the lips I wouldn't soon forget, then released his hold on me. He opened the front door, and we stepped inside the foyer. As we passed my father's office, D.J. put a finger to his lips and leaned close to the door to listen to something.

"What?" I asked.

"Maybe I spoke too soon. Sounds like someone's arguing," he whispered.

I strained to hear where the voices were coming from. Sure enough, it sounded like two grown men going at it. Not physically fighting, but sparring with their words. No doubt about that.

I leaned against the office door, trying to make sense of the conversation inside. Was Pop on the phone with someone, maybe?

Nope. It became abundantly clear within seconds what I was hearing . . . and whom. Sal and Laz. Fighting.

Sal's words came through all too clear. "I can't let you marry that woman, Lazarro."

"And why not?" My uncle's voice trembled with anger.

"Look at her. She's . . ."

My jaw dropped open. So did D.J.'s. I could see the anger in his eyes.

"She's *what*, Sallie?" Laz's voice again, this time shaking more than ever.

"Old. And not . . . well, there's no nice way to say it, Lazarro. She's not pretty. There's no amount of makeup to do the trick with someone as plain as Rosa. Her figure is . . . well, you have eyes. Surely you can see. She has no figure. Nothing to capture a man's imagination. And at this age, you need something to capture the imagination. Am I right or am I wrong?" A nervous laugh followed, but I didn't feel like laughing right now. Oh no. I felt like taking someone's head off.

"For your information, I *like* what I see." Laz's voice came through loud and clear. "And my imagination works overtime when I look at Rosa. She's captured me, heart and soul."

*You go, Laz!*

"C'mon, Lazarro. Think big. You deserve someone special. You've waited a long time since your wife died—God rest her soul." I could hear the staged sympathy in Sal's voice, but he wasn't fooling me. Hopefully, he wasn't fooling Laz either.

Oooh! I wanted to swing wide the door and take Sal down. How dare he say such horrible things about Rosa? Beautiful, sweet, precious Rosa! And how dare he bring Laz's deceased wife into this? What a low blow!

At this point, I heard Guido holler out, "Wise guy!" followed by a string of curse words. So much for a life change. Something about being in the presence of his owner apparently brought out the worst in the old bird—Guido, not Sal. Though Sal didn't appear to be doing very well either.

The ornery parrot continued to curse, then gave a rousing rendition of "Ninety-Nine Bottles of Beer on the Wall," one of his favorite tunes. I took a step toward the door, reaching for the knob. D.J. shook his head and put a finger to his lips again, obviously sensing my desire to stop this in its tracks.

Thankfully, I heard my uncle's voice again. "How dare you speak to me like this! And in my own home!" Laz went into a detailed explanation of how much he loved Rosa, how he didn't give a whit about her personal appearance—good, bad, or otherwise. On and on he went, singing her praises, focusing on the beauty in her heart, in her character. Then he shifted gears and went into a dissertation about her cooking skills and her stint—however short—with the Food Network.

If all of this was meant to impress Sal, it didn't work. He countered with a doozy. "Don't you want a wife who's young? Someone like Francesca? Your brother found someone young and pretty. Surely you can too. You've just been looking in the wrong places, old man. But there are plenty of fish in the sea."

Okay, those were most assuredly fighting words. I'd just rolled up my sleeves to do battle when Rosa appeared, a look of concern on her face. "What's going on in there?" she whispered. "They're going to stir up everyone in the neighborhood."

D.J.—God bless him—took my aunt by the arm and guided her back into the hallway toward the kitchen, chatting about the dinner menu. I followed along on their heels, determined to get my whipped-up emotions under control before she realized I was ready to blow. What happened between Laz and Sal would stay between Laz and Sal. Rosa would never know.

Or so I thought.

Sal's booming voice rang out across the house just before we entered the kitchen: *"Il bene del matrimonio dura tre die—il male dura fino a la morte."*

I'd have to give D.J. the interpretation later: "The good marriage lasts three days—and the bad lasts till death."

I got Sal's meaning. He went on to say something about Emilio feeling the same way about the situation, and that was all she wrote for Laz. I'd never heard him this angry before. I actually feared he might do Sal mortal harm. I could almost see the headlines now: FORMER MOB BOSS MURDERED WHEN LOCAL MAN SNAPS. CRAZED PARROT SERVES AS WITNESS.

I looked into my aunt's wide eyes, sickened by the fact that she'd heard this. So much for protecting her feelings. She clamped a hand over her mouth, and tears rose to cover her lashes. I didn't know which I wanted to do first—punch Sal's lights out or throw my arms around her and tell her she'd somehow misunderstood.

Hmm. Punching his lights out sounded like the more logical choice. Of course, the Lord frowned on such things. Turn the other cheek and all that. Still, even the Almighty knew when to take action. Right?

At this point, Laz came storming out of the office with Sal on his heels. I knew they hadn't seen us. I'd done a pretty good job of keeping Rosa in the hallway, out of sight. But we were still very much within hearing distance, much to my chagrin.

"Laz, just think about it!" Sal implored. "You've got a lot of good years left in you. Do you really want to spend them with a woman who looks like that?"

I squeezed my eyes shut, immediately praying Rosa hadn't heard. But I knew better. Still, a little prayer never hurt. As I turned toward her, my heart dropped to my toes. Her mouth rounded into a perfect "O" shape, and her big brown eyes filled with tears again. I rushed her way and slipped an arm over her shoulder.

"Just pretend you didn't hear that," I said. "He's a stupid

man who still thinks he's a young playboy. You know he doesn't speak for Laz, so don't believe a word of it."

Rosa drew in a deep breath and tried to compose herself. With the hem of her apron, she dabbed the moisture from her eyes, then marched into the kitchen under the guise of cooking. She began to reach for several pots and pans, making a tremendous amount of noise as she went. Relieving stress, no doubt. Getting some of her emotions out in the open. Beating them to death with a frying pan.

"A-are you okay?" I asked as she swung a skillet around and then put it on the counter.

"Mm-hmm." More clanging and banging took place as she reached for the large silver mixing bowl. "I have work to do. I will cook now. It's best if you give me some time alone, Bella. I need to think."

"No! That's exactly what you *don't* need to do," I said. "Don't give a second's thought to what Sal said. It's not true, anyway. You're the most beautiful woman I know."

"Humph." She began to sift flour over the bowl, her hands moving so erratically that the white powder went flying all over the countertop.

"It's true, Rosa. You are."

She stopped sifting and pushed her work aside, staring me in the eye. "Look, Bella, I'm not blind, and I don't like to lie to myself. I know I'm not a pretty woman, and I know I'm not young. So you don't need to lie to me about either."

"I . . . I'm not lying."

She wiped the flour off her hands. "I consider myself fortunate that a man like Lazarro would look twice at me, let alone want to marry me. And I know him well enough to know he genuinely loves me, despite my appearance. He loves me . . . for me. And vice versa."

"Well then—"

"But I also know that this has to be difficult, seeing Emilio marry such a beautiful young woman. Maybe Laz is having second thoughts about marrying a woman his own age. Maybe he thinks he deserves better. Younger. Prettier. It's possible Sal is just voicing what Laz was already thinking."

"Rosa!" I stared at her, unsure of what to say next. None of this made sense. If she really knew Laz like she said she did, she would have to know this was ludicrous.

I took a couple of deep breaths, determined to cool down. Surely this would all fade away once we got our emotions under control. In the meantime, I just had to check for collateral damage. Had to make sure Rosa wasn't permanently wounded.

If she would let me.

"I really need some space, Bella," she said with a wave of her hand. "You go spend some time with Deanna. Or Jenna."

"I can't find Jenna. She's been missing for days."

Rosa's eyes narrowed to slits at this news. Not that she looked at me for long. Instead, she opened the pantry door and came out with some Crisco. I didn't know if she planned to use it to remove her makeup or to make a piecrust. Rosa pulled off the top and measured out a half cup, then tossed it in the mixing bowl. Okay, so she was baking. At least she hadn't lost all control of her senses. And surely, if I gave her the space she craved, she would calm down. Eventually. In the meantime, I had a little talking to do . . . with Sal.

As I headed to the front hallway in search of the man in question, the front doorbell rang. I could hear Aunt Rosa crying off in the distance. No wonder she wanted to be alone. On the other side of the house, Laz started yelling at someone again. Likely Sal. Guido bellowed, "Wise guy!" then shouted, "Go to the mattresses!" over and over, occasionally interjecting a few lines of "Ninety-Nine Bottles of Beer on the Wall." Francesca and Emilio made their entrance at this point, hollering at both Sal and Laz to calm down. All of this in Italian, of course.

The doorbell continued to ring. I heard Precious yapping upstairs. She came bounding down the steps in attack mode. I reached to pick her up, trying to quiet her down, but she would not be stilled. I'd never seen her quite this worked up, but who could blame her? The whole house had gone crazy, after all. After a few words of reassurance from me, the frantic pup finally settled down.

With my nerves completely frayed, I yanked the door open, ready to snap off the head of whoever happened to be standing on the other side. Strangely, there was a man about my own age dressed in an amazing Italian suit and holding a bunch of red roses in his hand—a shockingly handsome man with chocolate brown eyes and rich, tanned skin. *Mama mia.*

"*Ciao!*" He nodded and offered a welcoming smile.

Precious let out a low growl and tried to lurch forward. My guest—whoever he was—took a step backward.

"*Ciao.*" I managed one word but didn't know what to do next because I was distracted by Rosa's wails, which now shook the house. Out of the corner of my eye I caught a glimpse of Mama running down the stairs with a panicked look on her face. She paused at the door, probably curious about the young man standing in front of me. When she realized she didn't know him, she hollered, "We gave at the office!" then went tearing toward the kitchen. She was met by Rosa, who came barreling out of the kitchen with a fry-

136

ing pan in her hand and tears streaming down her face. The half-crazed look on her face did little to calm my nerves.

Or our guest's. The poor fellow—who reminded me for all the world of Tony DeLuca—took a giant step backward. I didn't blame him. He probably thought Rosa was coming after him, the way she carried on.

"It's okay," I assured him, stepping out onto the veranda and shutting the door behind me. "She's harmless."

A shattering of glass from inside the house spoke otherwise. Precious continued to growl, now baring her teeth. I could see the fear in the young man's eyes, and he hugged his roses tight. Had he come to deliver those flowers, perhaps? To Rosa, the happy bride-to-be? If Marcella had hired a new delivery guy, he sure was worth whatever she happened to be paying him.

Nope. The poor fellow began to pour out his heart—in Italian—about someone altogether different. Only when I heard the name "Deanna" did I realize who I was dealing with.

"Rocco?"

"*Si!*" He nodded, his eyes filling with tears. Another long string of words in Italian followed. I couldn't exactly make out the translation, what with the words flowing faster than water, but I gave it my best shot. Something about being in love. Something about making a fool of himself for taking so long to admit it. Something about how love conquered all.

*Welcome to America!*

A shout from Uncle Laz in the front hall let me know that the party inside hadn't yet come to its fateful conclusion. Poor Rocco! He'd come halfway across the globe to make his peace with Deanna and had landed in the middle of a major world war.

"Excuse me," I said, stepping back inside.

I caught a glimpse of Mama trying to reason with Rosa, who stood with the frying pan waving in her hand. Mama tried valiantly to wrestle it away from my aunt, but Rosa would not be reasoned with. What she planned to do with that skillet was anyone's guess. Mama looked my way, wide-eyed and clearly terrified. I tried to mouth the word, "Rocco," but she didn't get it. Not at first, anyway.

At this point, Bianca came bounding down the stairs with Bertina on her heels. By now, Rocco had stepped inside. When he saw the twins, his face lit into a smile.

"Mama!" He threw his arms open wide and raced to Bertina's side, giving her a warm hug.

"Rocco?" She gazed at him, clearly bumfuzzled. "What are you doing here?" She welcomed him in Italian, then promptly burst into tears. Bianca reacted by wrapping her arms around both Rocco and Bertina, and together the three of them celebrated with tears and shouting.

At this point, Sal made an unfortunate entrance, stage left. Rosa caught a glimpse of him and began to run, waving the skillet. So, this was her plan of action. If she couldn't win him over with her stunning looks, she'd do so with her effervescent personality. Nice choice.

Rocco's eyes grew wider still, and he took a giant step backward from the twins. "I come at bad time?" he asked.

"*Si.*" I nodded. "But don't go anywhere." I knew at least one person who would be deliriously happy to see him, and I wouldn't ruin this for her for anything in the world. Even if it meant putting my life at risk by crossing the battle lines.

I gazed at him with a sigh, wishing he'd shown up at any other time than this. On the other hand, was there ever really a bad time to tell a woman that you loved her? Probably not.

I set Precious down on the entryway floor and hollered out Deanna's name, hoping she would hear me above the chaos. She appeared at the top of the stairs, her hair pulled back in a headband and Pepto Bismol hardened all over her face. Through the paste, I saw two dark brown eyes popping out. I glanced down at her feet, swallowing hard as I saw the little toe separators we girls use when painting our toenails.

"What is it, B—" She never got my name out. The minute she saw Rocco standing next to me, she came tearing down the stairs, heel-and-toe, shouting her greetings in Italian.

To his credit, he didn't run for the hills. I half expected him to, what with the chaos and the Pepto Bismol. No, Rocco stood firm, holding his roses in one hand. As she ran into his arms, everyone in the house came to a halt. The screaming stopped. The arguing ended. Everyone gathered in the front hallway to watch this go down, including Rosa, who still gripped the frying pan as if her life depended on it.

Mama appeared with a washcloth, passing it off to Deanna, who looked for a moment like she didn't know what to do with it. She must've forgotten about the thick pink paste all over her face. As the realization kicked in, Deanna covered her face with her hands and let out a scream that almost frightened Aunt Rosa right out of her teeth. The bloodcurdling yell continued as Mama grabbed the washcloth and wiped off all—well, most—of the Pepto Bismol. Then, pasting on a smile as bright as sunshine, Deanna flung herself into Rocco's arms and kissed him a thousand times. Approximately.

When she finally came up for air, he handed her the roses, gushing in Italian about how much he'd missed her. How he loved her more than life itself. How he'd been a jerk for not seeing it sooner. She clutched the roses, lifting them into the air with a victory chant. I got the meaning. Red roses, not pink. She and Rocco had officially crossed the line into true love, and they took to smooching once again. Precious responded by taking Rocco's pants leg in her teeth and pulling on it, still making a growling noise.

Yep. These two were on a roll, but they didn't need a houseful of folks looking on while they got reacquainted. I nodded at Mama, and we gestured for the audience to seek entertainment elsewhere.

Rosa slipped off to the kitchen, and the ladies headed that way too. Grabbing the roses from Deanna's outstretched hand, I passed them off to Bertina, who carried them into the kitchen, chattering the whole way in Italian. Laz stormed into Pop's office and slammed the door. Sal pulled a cell phone out of his pocket and made a call as he headed toward the door. I couldn't help but wonder who he was calling. A hit man, perhaps? As he walked out onto the veranda, he passed Phoebe Burton, my mother's best friend, who gave him a curious look. At my bidding, she entered the house. I pointed her in the direction of the kitchen, hoping she could be of help.

Emilio and Francesca decided this would be a good time to take a walk around the block. And Pop—poor Pop—stood in the middle of the hallway, looking to the right and the left, as if trying to figure out where to go. Thankfully, Joey happened in at that same time and asked him if he wanted to shoot a few hoops. I'd never seen my father so relieved.

Only at the end of all of this did I realize I'd lost D.J. I looked around, wondering where he'd gone. I found him seated in the dining room at the big family table. I walked in the room, overcome with emotion. Plopping down in a chair, I leaned my elbows on the table and sighed.

D.J. looked my way with a crooked smile and a completely relaxed expression on his face. Either he'd gotten used to my family or he'd slipped off into some sort of parallel universe. Surely he had heard all of the chaos just a few feet away. Still, he looked calm, cool, and collected, staring around the dining room as if he had nothing else to do.

"Um, D.J.?"

"Yeah?"

"W-what are you doing in here?"

"Oh." He smiled as he gestured toward the table. "Just thinking about how I want to design the dining room in our new house. If we're going to have a table this size, we'll need a pretty big room."

"And we need a table this size because . . . ?"

"Because, Bella." He reached for my hand and gave it a kiss. "Your family will be coming over for dinner a lot."

I heard Aunt Rosa wailing again, followed by Mama's voice trying to comfort her. Precious started yapping again, and Laz hollered, "Somebody calm that animal down!"

I wasn't sure if he was referring to the dog or one of the people.

I looked at D.J. once again, shaking my head. "My family? Coming over for dinner? You sure you're up for that?"

"Well, sure." D.J. looked at me and shrugged. "Why not? I love your family."

From Pop's office across the hall, Guido continued to sing. He was down to eighty-seven bottles of beer on the wall and still going strong.

And me? Well, I was up to about ninety-nine reasons why I couldn't wait to put this chaotic week behind me and get busy planning for my own big day!

# 12

## Praise the Lord
## and Pass the Ammunition

There's an old Italian saying: *Dai nemici mi guardo io, dagli amici mi guardi Iddio!* "I can protect myself from my enemies; may God protect me from my friends." The same is true of families. Sometimes we just need to protect ourselves from them. But who do we run to when folks inside our own household snap?

The Lord, of course.

I spent Thursday morning doing just that. The Lord alone knew how to solve this conundrum with my aunt and uncle. I had tried . . . to no avail. Rosa and Laz had spent last night in strained silence. Sal had made a hasty departure for the Tremont after his battle with my uncle and hadn't been seen or heard from since. I had to wonder if he'd skipped town.

No, I realized as I heard the sound of Guido's voice ringing out across the Rossi household, Sal would never have left the island without his precious bird. His precious, unruly bird.

And so I spent Thursday morning pleading with the Lord to somehow take this mess and mold it into something usable. I couldn't picture Rosa coming down the aisle with a scowl on her face, swinging pots and pans. And I certainly couldn't picture Laz standing in front of the crowd with despair written all over him. Perhaps, with a little persuasion, I could talk them through this. Not until after I showered, though. I needed the hot water running over my head to calm my troubled thoughts.

An hour later—showered, dressed, and made up—I sucked in a deep breath and headed for the stairs. Mama passed me, coming up as I went down.

"Have you seen Rosa and Laz this morning?" I asked.

She nodded and sighed. "Yes. Rosa's in the kitchen. Laz is trying to talk to her."

"Good! Is he making headway?"

Mama grunted, then continued up the stairs.

Alrighty then.

I made my way down the stairs and entered the foyer, hearing voices in the distance. At least they weren't shouting. That had to be a good sign. I stopped short of the entrance to the kitchen, not wanting to interrupt if they were in the middle of something—say, reconciliation.

Laz's voice caught my attention. "Rosa, listen to me. Rosa. Please."

Silence from her end.

"Rosa, you know that Sal does not speak for me. I am a grown man. I speak for myself. And I love you, Rosa. I am a blessed man now that you have agreed to be my wife."

"Humph."

I sighed, wishing she would play along. *Come on, Rosa. You've already spent years fighting with this man. Don't make him fight for you now.* I heard the sounds of pots and pans again. Surely she wasn't thinking of using them as weapons. Right?

All of my wedding plans—every bit of work—slipped right through my fingers as I listened to the two of them go at it. He tried to convince her to listen to reason. She slammed things around, making more than a little noise.

*Rosa, what is your problem? This isn't Uncle Laz's doing! Listen to him!*

Thankfully, my cell phone rang, distracting me from the conversation inside the kitchen. I answered the call, thrilled to hear D.J.'s voice.

"Things any better on the home front today?" he asked.

"Nope. Worse." I made my way into the living room and plopped down on the sofa.

D.J. sighed, and I could almost envision the look on his face. "What's going to happen next?"

"I have no idea. But the world has gone crazy."

"More so than usual?" he asked.

"Yes." I lowered my voice, not wanting to be overheard. "I saw Uncle Laz swinging a baseball bat out in his garden this morning. Watched him from my bedroom window."

"What's wrong with that?"

"He doesn't play baseball. I think he's practicing taking a swing at Sal. If Sal ever shows up again, that is. And you're not going to believe this . . ."

"Try me."

"He ripped up all of the tomatoes in his garden. Threw them all over the place. I've never seen such a mess."

This got a gasp and a "You've got to be kidding!" from D.J. But I wasn't kidding. Oh no. The backyard was awash in Romas, their red juice now turning putrid and drawing flies.

Pop—who had finally talked Laz into calming down—was fit to be tied.

"So, is the wedding up in the air?"

I contemplated my answer, finally coming up with, "Yeah. That's the understatement of the year."

"I thought this would blow over."

"Me too." My emotions suddenly got the better of me. Not wanting to be seen or heard by any of the others in my household, I walked out to the veranda and took a seat on the swing. Maybe if I sat, I could think clearly. Make sense of all this. Instead, I found a lump growing in my throat, and before long, I was crying like a baby. For a while, I couldn't manage a word. When I finally did, "W-what's happening to my family?" were the only words that made sense.

"This can't last forever, Bella. It's going to pass. So take a deep breath."

"I'm doing my best." I tried to catch my breath to tell the rest of the story. "Oh, but it gets worse. Emilio isn't speaking to Laz. And vice versa."

"Why?"

"It's c-c-complicated!" A couple of tears worked their way down my cheek. "The way things are going, my parents are going to end up not speaking!"

"Your parents? Never. They're the most solid couple I know, next to my own parents." I could tell from the stunned sound of his voice that D.J. thought I'd lost my mind. Maybe I had. I sucked in a deep breath and tried to compose myself. Surely I could get through this, and once I did, D.J. would make sense of it. Tell me what to do. Give me a plan of action.

"Even Bertina and Bianca had a quarrel this morning before they left for town," I said at last. "Something about shoes. Shoes! Can you believe it?"

145

"Um, no. Not really."

"Deanna says they never argue. Never. And it's all my fault!"

"Their argument over shoes?"

"No, I'm just saying I should have protected Rosa. That's what started all of this. If I hadn't been standing there when Sal and Laz had their argument yesterday, none of this would have happened."

"Say what?" D.J. said. "You're blaming yourself for this?"

"Sort of." I sniffled.

"I'm having a hard time figuring out how any of this could be your fault, Bella. And by the way, you blame yourself for things a lot. Things that have nothing to do with you."

"I—I do?"

"Yep. This is more observation than criticism, by the way. Don't want to hurt your feelings, but you're always so quick to admit fault, even when you're not at fault."

"My generous nature?" I tried.

"Sounds more like false guilt to me," D.J. said. "But you've got to let go of that, Bella. First of all, it's not exactly honest to take credit—or blame—for something that's not your fault. And I can absolutely assure you, you just happened to be standing in the right place at the right time last night. If you hadn't been in front of that door, Rosa probably would've stormed inside. Then we might've seen bloodshed. Your presence probably kept things from being worse than they already were."

"I guess." I sighed. "All I know is everyone in this household has gone nuts. Rosa's flipping out—and who can blame her? She turns on Laz, who turns on Sal, who involves Emilio. Before you know it, Emilio is insulted, thinking somehow everyone hates Francesca."

D.J. cleared his throat. "Well, let's face it, no one is very fond of her."

"It's not for lack of trying," I said. "We've all tried . . . but she makes it so difficult. One minute she's as sweet as sugar, the next she's as abrasive as sandpaper. I can't figure her out."

"Maybe she doesn't want you to," he said. "Maybe she's this way on purpose. I think she's probably afraid of being vulnerable. Maybe she's been hurt in the past."

Another sigh escaped. How dare D.J. say something that nice about Francesca right now, when I was mad at her?

*Why am I mad at her again, Lord? Ah yes, because she's practically perfect in every way.*

Shame washed over me at that revelation. Honestly, I couldn't think of one reason to dislike Francesca. Being beautiful didn't exactly prohibit you from leading a normal, healthy life.

D.J. interrupted my thoughts. "So, why are Bianca and Bertina fighting? And why are your parents going to end up not speaking?"

"They're not. I mean, I don't know if they are. I just know that Mama had a meltdown when she heard what Sal said. It just confirmed something she'd already voiced to me earlier."

"And what is that?"

I exhaled, unsure of how to proceed. "She's got this idea in her head that Pop sees his brother's pretty young wife and wishes he had one for himself," I finally said.

"Are you kidding me? Your mom is smarter than that."

"I know. It makes no sense. I've never known Mama to be insecure. But the world has tilted off its axis, and my mama is going right along with it. And me . . . I feel like I'm about to fall off. There's nothing left to hang on to."

"There is," D.J. said. "God hasn't fallen off his throne just because the Rossis have declared war on one another."

"I know, but he's been pretty silent so far."

D.J. paused, and his voice took on a deeper tone as he finally spoke once again. "What did your father have to say about all of this?"

"He flipped. The minute he heard my mother's accusation, he went storming out of the house. Drove down to the restaurant, where he found Bianca and Bertina having lunch. They made up, by the way. Bianca and Bertina, I mean. Looks like they settled their shoe issue."

"That's good. So, your father talked to them?"

"Yes. From what Deanna told me, he went a little crazy, saying all sorts of nutty things. Bianca tried to calm him down, but Bertina lit into him."

"Why?"

"No idea. I guess she just voiced what every woman in the house was already thinking—that an older man with a pretty young wife posed a threat to the whole makeup of our family."

D.J. sighed. "This is better than a soap opera, Bella. Or worse, depending on how you look at it."

"Well, things are just going to get worse if we don't do something. Emilio is really hot. And Laz is ready to take someone's head off. And here's the worst part of all—this is ruining everyone's testimony. Completely ruining it!"

"What do you mean?"

"We've waited for months for Sal to arrive so we could show him how Christians live. How they act. How the salvation experience transforms lives. All in the hopes that he would see the love of the Lord in us—and in that goofy bird—and find it irresistible. So far, all he's seen is a bunch of maniacs ready to kill one other. There's nothing irresist-ible about that."

"But technically, he started all of this with what he said to Laz about Rosa, right?"

"Yeah, I know." I groaned. "And I'm so mad at him for saying all of that stuff about Rosa not being pretty. He has no idea what pretty is—or isn't—because he's never expe-rienced the love of the Lord. Until God touches his heart, he's going to see things only as the world sees them. He's not going to get it."

"You're a smart girl, Bella Rossi," D.J. said. "You're spot-on about all of this."

"This is one time I don't want to be right. I just want some-one to tell me how to fix this." Leaning my head back against the swing, I closed my eyes and tried to will it all away.

"Unfortunately, this one's pretty big. Fortunately, we serve a really big God. But he's only going to move if you take your hands off and let him."

I released a slow, steady breath, trying to calm my nerves. At that moment, Bianca and Bertina pulled up in Mama's car.

"I have to go, D.J. Can I call you later?"

"Of course. And Bella . . . I love you."

"I love you too."

My sigh lingered in the air as I rose from the porch swing and approached my aunts, who walked alongside a giddy Rocco and Deanna, who were both in a dreamy-eyed state. At least the whole world hadn't gone crazy. These two were so in love, they couldn't see beyond it to the chaos.

"How are things?" Aunt Bianca asked as she climbed the stairs to the veranda. "Any better?"

I shook my head. "No, things are terrible." I brushed away

the tears that now stung my eyes. "Everything seems . . . hopeless."

"Oh, never hopeless, Bella," Deanna said with a wink. Rocco slipped his arm around her waist and drew her close, kissing the tip of her nose. "Sometimes life surprises you."

"Well, I could stand to be surprised right about now." I had that same feeling I once had in sixth grade when my teacher announced she was giving a pop quiz on Edgar Allan Poe. I felt doomed.

Instead of going inside, the ladies and Rocco joined me on the veranda, where I poured out my heart about anything and everything related to the wedding. On and on I went, telling them about my fears and frustrations.

"What am I supposed to do?" I asked when I finally slowed down. "The band will be here in a few minutes to practice for the reception. They wanted Rosa and Laz around to hear them rehearse so they can put their stamp of approval on the songs for Saturday night. How can they pull things together when the bride and groom aren't even speaking?"

"That is a problem," Bianca said.

"What if things don't get better?" I asked. "What if Rosa and Laz really decide to call off . . ." My words drifted off, too painful to even speak aloud.

"They won't. They will get married." Bianca turned to face me. "You know that old theater expression, 'The show must go on'?"

"Sure."

"This show will go on, Bella. They will work this out. We just have to trust the Lord to do it in his time and his way."

"I sure hope he remembers that we've got a wedding the day after tomorrow. And a rehearsal dinner tomorrow night."

"He remembers."

Bianca began to explain—in Italian, with great passion—how the true lovers of the world loved deeply and argued deeply. How, in the end, they always made up deeply. Oh, I hoped she was right!

For whatever reason, my gaze shifted to Deanna and Rocco, who'd slipped off into a world of their own once again. As they stared into each other's eyes, one thing became abundantly clear. Love really could win out in the end, especially if I factored the Lord into things.

Somehow that lit a spark of hope inside me. Maybe, just maybe, he would come through in a mighty way where Rosa and Laz were concerned.

A shattering of glass inside the house roused me to attention, and I realized Rosa and Laz were at it again. I whispered up a prayer that God would intervene. Bring down the walls of Jericho. Part the Red Sea.

Yes, the Lord had performed mighty miracles in the days of old. Surely he could do it again. He could—and would—bring two stubborn senior citizens together . . . hopefully before they killed each other!

# 13

## Ac-Cent-Tchu-Ate the Positive

World War III was well under way when Gordy and the band showed up. I met them at the wedding facility and tried my best to explain what was happening next door. Gordy's eyes widened as he heard the particulars.

"Tell you what, Bella. Let's do this. I'll get the band together, and we'll start to play."

"Even if the rehearsal's off?" Didn't make much sense to me, but I was willing to listen to his idea regardless.

"Yes. There's nothing like a little music to bring people together. *Nella vita, chi non risica, non rosica*, Bella, my dear."

"Beg your pardon?"

"'In life, he who risks nothing, gains nothing.' Nothing ventured, nothing gained, as it were."

"Ah, I see."

"Yes, you *will* see." Gordy winked. "Just do me a favor and open the windows so that everyone can hear us playing from next door. Agreed?"

"It's worth a try." At this point, I would've attempted just about anything.

"Don't worry, honey," Lilly said as some of the other band members warmed up to the tune of "In the Mood." "I've seen this with my own eyes. God can work through music just as easily as he can through preaching."

"Swing music?" I tried to picture such a thing. I mean, c'mon . . . worship music, maybe. Hymns, sure. But, "In the Mood"? How could the Lord possibly use that to bring healing and hope?

"Get ready," Gordy said with a smile. "You're about to witness a miracle of biblical proportions."

"Um, okay."

"And just so you know," Gordy called out above the clamor of the band, "the Lord has often used swing music to perform miracles."

"He has?" I must've missed the memo.

"Sure." Gordy reached for his trumpet, then turned back to me. "Think back to the 1940s, Bella."

"That's going to be a little difficult." I hid the smile that threatened to creep up. "Long before my time, you see."

"Oh yeah." He grinned. "Well, anyway, in the forties, our country was facing an unbelievable season of war, both in Europe and in Japan. People were spent, emotionally and physically. The war was really taking its toll. Musicians knew it, and they responded with some of the most amazing, upbeat music you ever heard."

"Wow, I never thought about that. I guess it makes sense, though."

"Of course it does." Gordy nodded. "In a way, they were ministering to the people to keep their spirits up. To keep people's minds off what was happening in Europe and Japan. It was a holy diversion, if you will."

"That's what we need today."

"Mm-hmm. Sounds like it. And hopefully it will be just as effective." He gave me a pensive look. "You know, this reminds me of a story in the Old Testament."

"O-oh?"

"Yes, from the book of 2 Chronicles, chapter twenty. Jehoshaphat was facing several enemies, and the Lord told him to send the Levites—the musicians—to the front lines. I'm sure those fellas were scared spitless, but they went, and you know what happened?"

"They won the battle?"

"Yep. Those musicians were real heroes that day." He laughed. "Worshiped their way through, and the enemy was confused. In the end, God's people went on to win the war. Great message for today, eh?"

"No kidding." Suddenly it made perfect sense. Maybe it wouldn't matter what songs were playing, as long as the hearts of the warriors were in the right place. Any song could be an offering of praise, right? And praise was powerful, no doubt about that!

The groove between Gordy's eyebrows deepened as he continued. "I'm of the opinion we should hand out warnings when we place an instrument in a believer's hand. Let them know that they'll eventually end up on the battlefield." He lifted his horn triumphantly and grinned.

"Yeah, I guess so." I sighed. "I'm glad you're willing to go to battle for my family, Gordy. You hardly know us."

"I'm getting to know you better every day, and I've fallen

in love with your family, Bella." He grinned. "I'm ready to lift the morale of the fighting men."

"That's what we need—a morale lift. For the fighting men. And women." Another sigh escaped. Boy, were they ever fighting.

Gordy turned back to the band with a nod and gestured for them to stop playing. "Fellas—and Lilly—we've got a situation on our hands. Folks next door are in dire need of a morale boost. We're talking a case of life or death here."

Several of the older guys nodded, gripping their horns. Lilly lifted her clarinet heavenward and hollered out a prayer for the Lord to lead the way, and a rousing "Amen!" went up from the rest. Apparently, they were accustomed to saving lives through music, though this was all new to me.

"I love it when the Lord calls us to action," Lilly said with a giggle as the prayer ended. "Heavenly swing!" A couple of seconds later, Gordy tapped his director's stick against the music stand and said, "Let's take that song from the beginning, folks. This time play it like you mean it! People are counting on you!"

Seconds later, the Glenn Miller tune filled the room once again, this time more powerful than before. All of the instruments rang out in perfect harmony. I could almost see the warriors marching off to battle.

"Louder!" Gordy called out. "Play louder, men! The troops can't hear us from here!"

I opened every window and waited. The band grew louder, then louder still. I wondered how long it would take for my relatives to respond. Or the police, asking us to turn the volume down.

Ironically, the first people to enter the room were Twila, Bonnie Sue, and Jolene, who stared at me, dumbfounded.

"Someone lose their hearing aid?" Twila shouted above the beat of the band.

"No," I hollered back. Pulling them into the next room, I did my best to explain, telling them not only what had happened between Rosa and Laz but also about Gordy's impassioned response.

Bonnie Sue's eyes grew wide. "Is my Sal involved in this?"

*My Sal?* "Well, he's involved, yes."

"Hmm."

Jolene elbowed her. "That's what you get for hanging your heart on a man who hasn't come to know the Lord yet, Bonnie Sue. We tried to warn you. Look at the trouble he's caused. And you were willing to walk along the garden path with him, simply because he showed you a little interest."

Bonnie Sue groaned. "I know you're right. Should've listened to you. But I was just so swept away by his dancing skills. Besides, he paid me more than a little interest." Her cheeks turned pink, and she stifled a grin.

"Back to the matter at hand." Jolene looked me squarely in the eye, shouting to be heard above the band as they played merrily in the other room. "That Jehoshaphat story Gordy told you was right on, Bella. But there's more to it than just worshiping your way through a battle. You've got to have prayer warriors in place. Guess that's why we're here." She linked arms with the other two. "We'll hit our knees. Won't stop till the Spirit moves."

I nodded and led the trio of praying women back into the reception hall, where Gordy and the band ended "In the Mood." The music began again, this song a slightly different tempo from the one before.

"Perfect!" Bonnie Sue said with a wink. "'Ac-Cent-Tchu-Ate the Positive'!"

"Beg your pardon?" I said.

"It's the name of the song," Twila explained. "Perfect backdrop, trust me."

"Keep praying, sisters!" Jolene called out. She and the other women knelt at the edge of the stage, making it an altar. Well, all but Bonnie Sue, who apparently prayed best while dancing.

When these women prayed . . . they prayed. I could hear their spiritual warfare above the sound of the band. Twila called out for the devil to flee in Jesus's name, and Jolene hollered out something about bringing down the walls of Jericho. We didn't see a lot of prayer meetings like this in our local Methodist church, but I didn't argue with the fact that these ladies were storming the gates of hell on my family's behalf. And Gordy seemed to be taking his cues from their words, the crescendos of the band matching the intensity of the prayers. Up and down the music moved, in steady rhythm with the women's cries on my family's behalf.

I watched all of this, mesmerized, wondering if anyone next door had a clue.

Mama showed up with her fingers in her ears. "Bella?" she hollered. "What in the world is going on? Why are they playing so loud?"

"It's a case of life or death, Mama," I explained. "They're here to do battle, just like the Levites in the Old Testament."

"Beg your pardon?" Her gaze shifted to the women gathered at the edge of the stage on their knees. "What in the world?"

At this point, Phoebe Burton showed up. "I can hear the music all the way across the street at our place, Bella," she shouted. "What in the world is going on here?"

I did my best to explain, and her eyes widened. Mama signaled for Phoebe to join her, and I turned my attention to the door once again.

Rosa came next, her eyes growing wide as she took in the music and the prayer warriors. She glanced my way with a thousand questions in her eyes, but I shifted my gaze, not wanting to interfere with whatever the Lord might do next.

Joy flooded over me when I saw the door to the reception hall open and Laz step inside. He took in the ladies at the edge of the stage, watching them in shocked silence. Then he turned to look at Rosa, who had taken to tapping her foot in sync with the music. Who could blame her, really? This stuff was contagious. Gordy turned to face Laz with tears in his eyes, which caused my uncle to do the strangest thing. He began to weep. I had to admit, I didn't see that one coming. Still, I couldn't be sure what he would do next.

Before long, the room was filled with people. The women—all but Francesca—stood on one side of the reception hall, and the men stood on the other. In between them all, the trio of Splendora sisters continued to pray.

Against that backdrop, the craziest thing happened. The door opened one final time, and Sal eased his way inside, shoulders slumped forward in defeat—or was that humility?—and a look of genuine pain on his face. I could see the tightness in Laz's expression, but to his credit, he did not reach for his bat. Even Rosa was strangely still. No pots and pans swinging now. Instead, she looked over at Sal with a hint of compassion in her eyes.

Gordy—probably realizing the gang was all here—lowered the volume to a reasonable level. I shivered against the cold pouring in from outside and decided to close the windows. The trio of sisters seemed to take this as their cue to rise and address the crowd. I wasn't sure who was going to speak first or what she would say, but I looked forward to someone breaking the ice.

Ironically, no one said a word. Instead, I watched in awe as the strangest thing happened. Twila and Jolene did a couple of funny dance moves in the middle of the floor. Bonnie Sue headed over to take Laz by the hand. Though he resisted at first, he finally cratered and joined her on the floor.

Jolene took Rosa's hand, guiding her out onto the floor. Before long, Bianca and Bertina were all smiles as they joined in. Even Rocco and Deanna decided to play along, trying their hand at some of the moves.

"What do you think?" my pop asked, approaching with a grin on his face. "Want to dance, Bella Bambina?"

"Don't think I know how to swing dance," I admitted, "but it's worth a shot, especially if it has this kind of power." As my father swept me into his loving arms, I thought back to what Gordy had said about music lifting the morale of the troops. Oh, if only Laz would look Rosa's way!

I found myself so caught up in dancing with my father that I almost missed the magical moment when it finally happened. Out of the corner of my eye, I watched the Splendora sisters ease Laz and Rosa together. As the music reached a crescendo, Laz extended his hand in my aunt's direction, and that was all she wrote. Rosa melted into Laz's arms, tears streaming down her face. She didn't say a word. She didn't have to. He pulled her close and planted a hundred kisses on her flushed, tear-stained cheeks.

At this point, I thought the band was going to have to stop playing. Everyone in the room reacted with either tears or shouts of joy. Thankfully, Gordy kept the musicians on track. I grinned as I watched Uncle Laz, who, with the skill of a pro, took to swing dancing. The others gathered around in a circle, clapping their hands to the beat.

Well, all but Sal. For a minute, he stood shell-shocked. Then the fellow's hands began to tremble, and before long, his eyes were filled with tears. I would never have believed it if I hadn't witnessed it firsthand. The former mob boss was . . . crying. No, not just crying. Weeping.

Laz boogie-woogied in Sal's direction and swept him in his arms, then led a broken Sal to the center of the floor to join him and Rosa in their dance of celebration. To my aunt's credit, she graciously extended her arms, welcoming Sal to the circle. Gordy took this as his cue to change songs. He led the band in a swingin' version of "Amazing Grace." There wasn't a dry eye in the house, and I couldn't help but think that Guido—had he been here—would've burst into song.

As I watched my aunt and uncle mend fences with swing music blazing in the background, my thoughts shifted back to Jehoshaphat and those Levites. Looked like Gordy had been right all along. No doubt about it—the musicians had led the way once again . . . and the battle had been won!

# 14

## 'S Wonderful!

That same day, after the Lord tore down the walls of Jericho, I finally came face-to-face with my missing best friend. It happened at Parma John's of all places. Jenna breezed through the door with Bubba on her heels as if nothing had ever happened, greeting us all with a carefree "Hello, everyone." She rushed behind the counter and put her purse away, then smiled at anyone who happened to glance her way.

I wanted to respond but couldn't seem to once I noticed her sunburn. The tip of her nose was blistered, and so were the tops of her ears.

"Well, hello to you too," I finally managed. "We were starting to think we needed to check the hospitals for you."

"Oh, yeah, about that . . ." She paused and shrugged. "I'm not really sick. A little sunburned, maybe, but definitely *not* sick." A suspicious smile lit her face. Very interesting.

Nick drew near, his brow wrinkled in concern. "But you said you needed a few sick days. What's up with that? I've never known you to be dishonest, Jenna." He gave her a suspicious look.

"I guess I should've called it vacation time. That's what it was." She leaned back against Bubba and grinned. "We had a great time, didn't we, baby?"

"Wait." My heart flip-flopped at this revelation. "You two went on a trip . . . together?"

"Mm-hmm." She grinned. "A cruise. To Cancun. Royal Caribbean cruise line. Great ship." She gazed into Bubba's eyes, and he gave her a kiss on the tip of her sunburned nose. She flinched at the pain but then gave him a playful wink.

"Our room was amazing," he said. "Had a balcony and everything."

"We, um, spent a lot of time on that balcony." Jenna giggled, then turned even redder.

"Yeah, pretty much the only time we left our room was for dinner," Bubba said, his eyes never leaving hers.

This was getting weirder by the minute. Since when did my friend go on an overnight trip with her boyfriend, then talk about it openly in front of a roomful of people? And Bubba had a strong walk with the Lord. Surely he wouldn't consider an overnight stay in a cruise ship room with his girlfriend appropriate. Would he?

I shook my head and stared at them both, unsure of what to say next. Thankfully, Nick intervened.

"Bubba." He grabbed Bubba's left hand and held it up. "Is that a wedding ring you're wearing?"

"Yep." Just one word from the slow-drawlin' Neeley brother said it all.

"You're . . . you're married?" When Jenna nodded, I let out a squeal. "You eloped?"

"Well, sort of." She laughed. "We got married on the

cruise ship before we left port, then we honeymooned in Cancun."

She went off on a tangent about the beautiful little wedding chapel on the ship and how much she'd loved holding the ceremony there, but I didn't hear much of what she said. My thoughts were elsewhere. So were my emotions. I didn't know if I wanted to celebrate or give Jenna a verbal lashing. How could she keep a secret like this from her best friend? "You promised I could coordinate your wedding," I said with a pout. "What happened to that?"

"Well, here's the thing." She looked at Bubba, who gave her an encouraging nod. "You've been so busy, Bella. And the wedding facility is booked up through the winter. We couldn't wait till spring."

"Nope. Couldn't wait." Bubba nodded, then quirked a brow.

Nick laughed. "So that's how it is."

"Yep. Didn't see the point," Bubba said. "So Mom and Dad came down to the ship and acted as witnesses, then headed home before the ship sailed."

"Wait." I stared at them both. "You're telling me Dwayne and Earline Neeley knew about this and said nothing?"

"Yep." Jenna nodded. "They were sworn to secrecy." She gave me a sympathetic look. "I hope you're not too mad at me, Bella. We're thinking about having a small ceremony for family and friends in three or four months, after you get all of these other weddings behind you. What do you think of that idea?"

"Makes me feel a little better. I can't imagine my best friend getting married without me there, though." I felt tears well up, and she reached to give me a hug.

"Oh, I'm so sorry, Bella. I should have called you, but I

knew it would be such a shock. We wanted to tell everyone in person. Forgive me?"

"Of course." I took her by the hand, then looked at the guys. "You fellas are going to have to excuse us for a minute, though." I pulled her into the ladies' room, then asked for details, not just about the wedding ceremony, but, well, everything. "You're really married. Married."

"I am." She giggled.

I leaned against the sink, my curiosity taking over. "What's it like?"

"Oh, Bella, it's wonderful." She paused a minute. "Well, mostly wonderful. I mean, it's great that he's there with me all the time, but . . . he's there with me. All. The. Time."

I laughed. "You're funny."

"Oh, you'll see what I mean soon. Once you get married, everything changes, including your privacy level."

"You're not sorry, are you?" I asked.

"Sorry? Never!" She laughed. "Bubba Neeley is the best thing that ever happened to me. And I'm the happiest girl on Planet Earth. Just have to figure out how to live with a man in my house."

I paused, giving her a curious look. "Are you both living at your place?"

"Yeah, it just made sense. Bubba's down here on the island a lot of the time anyway. He's going to be working with D.J. now, so it just makes sense. And besides, he's in the Christmas production at the opera house, did you know?"

"Of course." I nodded. "Are you kidding? My mama tells me everything that goes on at that opera house. I don't miss a beat." After a pause, I added, "However, she didn't mention the part about Bubba being married."

"She doesn't know. No one but Dwayne and Earline know.

And my parents, of course. They were there too, and they're tickled pink. They just love Bubba."

"Well, what's not to love about Bubba? About either of the Neeley boys, for that matter! And I'm sure Dwayne and Earline are just as excited as your parents. Earline adores you."

Jenna took my hands and gave them a squeeze. "Oh, Bella, don't you see? They're my in-laws now, and they're about to be your in-laws too. We're not just best friends anymore. We're sisters!"

"Looks like the family is growing," I said with a wink. "Not that I mind one little bit. There's always room in my world for another sister." I wrapped her in a warm embrace, and before long, we were both giggling. Suddenly, a realization hit me. I stepped back and stared at her. "You've already had your honeymoon night."

She nodded, and her whole face turned red again. "Mm-hmm." Her eyebrows elevated mischievously. "I have, indeed."

"Wow." I shook my head, unable to make sense of this. For years, Jenna and I had talked about—and wondered about—the whole wedding night thing. Now she had information that I was not yet privy to. I suddenly felt like a runner coming up for a close second in the race of the century. Close, but no cigar.

"Your day is coming, Bella," she said with a nod. "But until then, just know that it's definitely sweeter than tiramisu. You were right about that . . . and a lot more."

She waggled her brows, and I doubled over with laughter. In fact, we both laughed long and loud. So loud, in fact, that Nick rapped on the bathroom door and hollered, "You're scaring the customers!"

"Sorry!" we said in unison.

I turned back to her, anxious to play catch-up. She'd missed a lot, after all.

"Well, you've come back just in time," I said, suddenly growing serious. "Did you hear about Rosa and Laz? They almost canceled their wedding."

"W-what?" Jenna's smile faded at once. "When did this happen? And why?"

"Happened yesterday. My uncle's best friend almost talked him out of marrying Rosa."

"But why?"

"Long story. Whatever you do, don't bring it up. It's all over now. But Sal was conspiring against Rosa. I guess he thought Laz could do better—end up with a beautiful young bride like Francesca. True, Rosa's not the beauty queen that Francesca is, but still . . ."

"Wait. Francesca? Who's Francesca? And Sal is here? The same Sal you've talked about for years? The mob guy? The one who sent the parrot?"

I laughed, realizing just how much Jenna had missed while away on her honeymoon. "Oh, girl! We've got some catching up to do. What are you doing for the next hour or so?"

"Listening to your stories," she said with a smile. "And telling you a few of my own." This announcement was followed by a playful wink.

"You've got a deal," I said.

We shifted to a table in the restaurant, where Bubba joined us.

"You mad at me, Bella?" he asked with a sheepish look on his face.

"No, but I'll bet your brother is going to be. Have you told D.J. yet?"

166

"Nope." Bubba grinned. "He always thought he'd be the first to get married, but I beat him to the punch. No telling how he's going to take that news."

"Oh, I'm sure he'll manage just fine. Why don't you give him a call and see for yourself?"

Bubba nodded. "I guess so. I'll put it on speaker phone so I'll have witnesses if he flips out on me." He whipped out his cell phone and punched in D.J.'s number. The three of us sat in quiet anticipation, waiting as the phone rang once. Twice. Three times. I'd just about given up, thinking D.J.'s voice mail would kick in, when that thick Texas drawl came on the line.

"Hello?"

"D.J.?" Bubba didn't say anything for a second. Probably trying to formulate the words.

"Bubba? That you?" I could hear the sound of power tools off in the background. Sounded like my honey was still at his latest construction site.

"Yep." Bubba's lips curled up in a grin.

"You've had us scared spitless. Listen, if I hear you did anything to compromise Jenna—"

"Nope." Bubba interrupted him. "She's not, um, compromised." He looked at her and winked.

Jenna giggled, her cheeks turning crimson.

Now D.J. sounded irritated. "Well, what in blue blazes were you up to? Where have you two been for the past few days? Cough it up, Bubba, or I'm going to Mama. She'll take you down. You know she will."

Bubba laughed. "Go right ahead. She'll be happy to tell you where I was."

"Wait." D.J. paused. "I called her a couple of days ago, worried sick. Are you telling me she knew where you were and didn't tell me?"

"Yep."

"Bubba, you are a man of few words, and right now that's about to drive me out of my gourd. Are you going to cough it up, or am I going to have to come over there and drag it out of you?"

"I'd say come on over and drag it out of me." Bubba grinned again. "I'm at Parma John's with your fiancée and my—" He paused for a minute, looking at Jenna. I had the funniest feeling he'd almost let the word "wife" slip. "With Jenna," he said finally.

D.J. grunted. "Fine. I'm on my way."

Bubba ended the call and looked at Jenna and me with a shrug as he shoved his phone back in his shirt pocket. "Might as well drag out the suspense. This is getting fun."

Jenna shook her head. "I don't know, Bubba. He might come in here and take your head off. I don't think I want to lose my husband the first week of our marriage."

"Nah." I smiled, knowing D.J. better than that. "He's been worried, but he's not the type to get angry, even if he feels someone's pulled the wool over his eyes."

We continued our conversation for a few more minutes until D.J. arrived. I couldn't help but notice the look of relief that passed over him as he took in Bubba and Jenna. Still, it was mingled with a hint of frustration. He reached over and gave me a kiss on the forehead before taking a seat. Then he glared at his brother.

"You gonna tell me, or am I gonna drag it out of you?"

Jenna and Bubba held up their left hands in tandem, wiggling their ring fingers. D.J. stared, not saying a word for a moment. He finally managed a flimsy "W-what?" at which point we all laughed.

"We got married last week," Jenna said with a giggle. "Just got back from our honeymoon cruise."

"To *Cancun*," Bubba said. "Had a great time."

"Does Mama know about this?" The tips of D.J.'s ears turned red. Not a good sign.

"Yep." Good old Bubba. Giving one of those one-word answers again. They went over so well.

I wasn't sure if D.J. was going to blow like Spindletop or respond in his usual gracious manner. I watched, mesmerized, as my honey's face contorted. I could almost read the expressions as they shifted. Disbelief. Frustration. Relief. Joy.

He ended with joy, praise the Lord. Then, being the guy I knew he was, D.J. bolted from his chair and threw his arms around Bubba, proclaiming all sorts of well wishes at the top of his lungs. Afterward he turned his attention to Jenna, who beamed from ear to ear as he gushed over her as well. At the end of it all, he looked my way.

"They beat us to the punch, Bella."

"I know." Shrugging, I offered up a smile. "But it's okay. They're going to have a real wedding ceremony in the spring after we get settled into our new place."

D.J. took his seat, shaking his head. "Still, I can't believe it. My baby brother is . . . married." A moment's pause, and then D.J. grinned. "Guess that just about locks it up. You're moving to Galveston?"

"I am."

The twinkle in D.J.'s eye let me know how he felt about that. "Then you can come to work for me."

Bubba nodded. "Been thinking a lot about that offer you made, big brother, and I think I'm ready to take you up on it. Besides, I have a feeling I'm going to be a permanent fixture at the opera house. Can't believe I'm saying this, but I've fallen in love with opera." Bubba grinned, then turned to Jenna. "And I've fallen head over heels for a certain young woman here. So I think I'll stay put, thank you very much."

D.J. let out a whoop and rose once again, celebrating for everyone in the place to see and hear.

"How did your father take the news?" I asked, finally snagging a moment's quiet between D.J.'s shouts of joy. After all, Bubba had worked as a mechanic at his father's business for years. Dwayne Sr. was likely not as happy as the boys about this. What would it feel like, to have both of your boys move off and abandon the family business? Not good, I would imagine.

"Better than you know," Bubba said with a nod. "He said my decision was an answer to prayer. He and Mom want to go into full-time ministry with the motorcycle club."

"No way." D.J. looked at him, clearly stunned.

"Yeah, go figure. Remember Terrell Buell?"

"From church? Sure."

"Well, he's been talking to Pop for years about buying the business, so I think they've come to some sort of understanding."

"Wait." I shook my head, trying to sort this out. "Terrell Buell . . . the same Terrell Buell who is sweet on Twila?"

"Yep. Same one. He's been working on cars for years but never really had a place to do it proper." Bubba arched his brows. "Mama suspects he's doing this to snag Twila. He thinks if he buys the business and gets our clientele, she'll finally see him as responsible and marry him."

"Well, go figure." I had to grin at that idea. Twila Buell. I could almost see it now.

D.J. sat once again, this time ordering a round of cappuccinos for everyone at the table. "We've got some celebrating to do!" he exclaimed. "Neeley Brothers Construction has just officially opened its doors for business!" He dove into a lengthy conversation with Bubba about the renovations at my house, then shifted gears to talk about the home he was renovating for the two of us. All the while, I kept looking at Jenna. Her eyes never left Bubba. I'd never seen my best friend happier. Of course, she had every reason to be. She was married to the man of her dreams now.

Jenna. Married. Wow.

I pushed any and all thoughts of jealousy from my mind. Soon enough it would be my turn. In the meantime, I'd better stay focused on Rosa and Laz. After all, their big day was only forty-eight hours away!

# 15

## Seems Like Old Times

From the time I was a little girl, I'd always loved Mama's favorite expression: *Finché c'è vita, c'è speranza.* "As long as there is life, there is hope." For the first time in my life, I truly understood those words at their core. As a result of what I was now calling the swing-band miracle, hope had infused my family, invigorating us for the task ahead.

Friday—the day before Rosa and Laz's big day—was spent in celebration and preparation mode. I'd never seen so many people moving in so many directions at one time, nor had I heard the Italian language bantered about at such speed. The house smelled of garlic—always a good sign—and Laz had brought in a new shipment of tomatoes from the restaurant to make up for the ones he'd tossed in the backyard. Yep, things were really moving along.

Mama and I were in full-out "Let's get this show on the road!" gear, and the Italian aunts joined it. So did Sophia, Deanna, and Rocco, who all seemed happy to help. Even

Phoebe showed up to offer assistance. Only one person was noticeably absent. Francesca. Emilio explained that she was napping. I tried not to roll my eyes at that announcement, but . . . really. Napping? On a day like today?

By late afternoon Friday, we had completely transformed the reception hall. I'd never seen so much gold fabric in all my life. And the deep red tablecloths were just the right contrast.

I put the tiny Christmas trees in place, checking the lights on each one to make sure they worked. Off in the distance, Pop hung strands of small white Christmas lights, draping them along the upper edge of the grand ballroom. Oh, how beautiful this place was starting to look! The perfect blend of 1940s ballroom and quaint Italian Christmas.

Rosa and Laz tried to stop by to help, but we shooed them away. No point in working them to death the day before their wedding. Besides, they still had plenty of cooking to do next door. I had it on good authority—Bertina—that Rosa had already started the chicken cacciatore and Laz was hard at work on the meats and the appetizers. Bubba and Jenna were on their way to assist my aunt and uncle with the food prep, and the rest of us were left alone to tend to the decor.

While we worked, Mama played Band of Gold's greatest hits CD to get us all in the mood. I had to chuckle when the song "Praise the Lord and Pass the Ammunition" came on. Reminded me of where we'd been just a couple of short days ago. Oh, what a little prayer and praise could do! I thought about Jehoshaphat and couldn't help but smile.

Bianca and Bertina helped out by placing the little decorative boxes filled with sugar almonds at each place setting. I'd heard all about the tradition—how true Italian weddings always featured the tasty almonds to symbolize the union of bitter and sweet. Thinking of bitter reminded me of Sal. I glanced his way, watching as he helped Pop with the lights.

Suddenly, my heart was filled with compassion for the man. Sure, he'd said some pretty harsh things about Rosa—bitterness had ruled the day—but all of that was behind us now. He seemed genuinely repentant. I smiled again as I thought about how he and Laz had made up over cups of cappuccino, weeping all over each other and listening to Guido sing ten or twenty rounds of "Amazing Grace" in the background. Ironic. Looking again at the almonds, I could see so clearly how the Lord could take someone as bitter as Sal and sweeten him up. With time. And love.

As I set up the plates and chafing dishes on the buffet table, a familiar voice rang out. I turned to see my brother Armando entering the room. He let out a whistle.

"Man. Never seen the place look like this before. Very nice, Sis."

I sprinted his way, happy to see him. "Welcome home."

"Thanks." He looked around, noticing the aunts and Deanna. He elbowed me when he saw Rocco. "Who's the Fabio character?"

I laughed. Rocco did look a bit like a cover model. "That's our cousin's boyfriend from Napoli. Just arrived a couple days ago. Maybe you'd better go say hello."

"Okay, but . . ." He looked at Sal, confused. "Who's the old guy?"

"Armando!" Now I elbowed him. "That's Uncle Sallie."

"W-what?" His eyes narrowed, and he shook his head. "Impossible. Uncle Sal is a big guy. Tough. Broad shoulders. This guy is . . ."

"I know."

We both paused in quiet reflection.

174

"Wow." Armando's one-word response to Sal's condition spoke volumes.

"Better go say hello to Bianca and Bertina," I whispered. "They'll think you're ignoring them. And I have it on good authority Deanna and Rocco have been dying to see you."

"You've got it."

He sprinted across the room and went into a lengthy "How do you do?" with the relatives while I stood back and observed their interaction. I was especially intrigued by Sal's response to Armando. He patted him on the back and commented on what a big boy Armando was getting to be. I paused to think about that for a moment. Armando was a strapping, muscular sort of guy. A lot like Sal used to be . . . back in the day. Strange how time could transform a man. Age had softened Sal, but I had a feeling that wasn't all bad. Gave me hope that Armando—our family prodigal—could be softened by time as well.

I shifted back into wedding-planning gear and finished up the buffet tables, then checked on the silverware and fixed a couple of the gold bows on the backs of the white chair covers. Sure, it took a lot of work to make the room look great, but it would be worth it. I glanced up to the empty stage area, now framed in gold lamé, and tried to envision it with the band spread out across it. Oh, how wonderful tomorrow night was going to be!

When we finished with the reception hall, we all stood back, and Pop let out a whistle. "Bella Bambina, I've seen this place done up for a hundred weddings, but never one this beautiful. You've outdone yourself this time."

"Nothing but the best for Rosa and Laz." My eyes filled with tears, and a lump rose up in my throat. I did my best to press it down but found myself unable to as I glanced at the mist of tears in Sal's eyes.

I moved his way. "You okay, Uncle Sallie?"

"Mm-hmm." He nodded and looked around. "I'm just happy for my friend. And happy . . ." He shook his head and cleared his throat. "Happy an old fool didn't stand in the way of his friend's true happiness."

"Aw, Sal." I threw my arms around his neck and gave him a warm hug. He smelled like Old Spice and peppermint as he hugged me back. Then Mama, Pop, and the Italian aunties joined in. Before long, we were one big, sappy circle of people, gushing over Rosa and Laz's big day and how wonderful it was all going to be.

When we released our hold on each other, we all gazed one last time at the room. The others headed next door to get cleaned up and dressed for the rehearsal and rehearsal dinner, but I lingered behind to give the room a final once-over. A few seconds later, I heard Sal's voice.

"Bella?"

I turned to him, curious that he'd lagged behind the others. Must have something on his mind. "What is it, Uncle Sallie?"

He hemmed and hawed for a minute or so before responding. "Bella, I will tell you the truth." He raked his fingers through thinning hair. "I've never met a family quite like yours."

"Oh?" I wasn't sure if that was a good thing or a bad thing.

"Yes." He paused, and tears filled his eyes. "I was an old fool the other day. Almost ruined my best friend's chance at happiness." He shook his head. "Still not sure why I said all of that stuff about Rosa. Laz was right—she's a beautiful woman. Don't know why I didn't see it before."

"She's a true beauty," I said with a nod. "Inside and out."

"I think I've just been blind. Kind of like the words in that dumb song Guido keeps singing."

"Oh?"

"Yes. I once was blind, but now I see." He grinned. "I suppose that song was meant for me. Couldn't see Rosa's beauty or Laz's happiness. And the only thing standing in the way, if you want me to be brutally honest, was my own jealousy."

"Jealousy?" This certainly got my attention. What did Sal have to be jealous about?

"Yes." He nodded, then eased his way down into a chair at one of the tables. "These past few months have been the hardest of my life, Bella. Whenever you go through a stroke, you lose all control. And, um, you would have to know what a control freak I am to understand why that was so hard."

"Ah."

He shook his head, a look of disgust passing over his wrinkled face. "And I don't mind admitting I've been a stubborn old fool. Didn't want people around me. Even sent the bird away, so I wouldn't be reminded that life was going on without me."

This was starting to make sense now. Sal had attempted to sabotage Laz and Rosa's upcoming nuptials because of his own unhappiness and pain.

"The day of the stroke . . ." He shook his head. "Well, I don't actually remember a lot about that day, but I know it changed me."

"For the better, Sal," I said, taking the seat beside him. "It softened you. Opened you up."

"Like an old war wound." He sighed. "And I'll tell you what, opening up an old fool like me means there's a lot of stuff to leak out. Not necessarily good stuff either." He pursed his lips, and his jaw grew tight. "Bella, there's a lot about me you don't know."

"Don't *need* to know," I said. "But that's another reason you need Guido's favorite song."

"What do you mean?" The lines in Sal's brow intensified as he looked my way.

"Grace. We all need it. It's the very thing God offers us when we deserve it least. That's why it's so . . . amazing."

He huffed. "Look, I still don't understand all of this religious jargon. I'm just here to tell you that something happened to me after having that stroke. I pushed people away, then felt lonely as a result. So when I showed up at your house, maybe I overcompensated. I said some horrible things to Laz, and I think it was because I was secretly jealous of what he had with your Aunt Rosa." Sal paused. "What he *has* with your Aunt Rosa."

"Yes, they're a pretty special couple, no doubt about that. And I agree that they have a love much deeper than the physical. That's what makes me know it's going to last forever." I flashed Sal a grin. "But who knows, Uncle Sallie. It's possible the Lord will bring a special woman into your life too." I offered up a wink.

Sal laughed, dismissing the idea with a wave of his hand. "She'd have to be something special to see past this crusty old fool."

"Not as crusty as you think," I whispered, wrapping him in my arms. "And this gal, for one, sees you as very special." After a moment's pause, I added, "And just so you know, God thinks you're pretty amazing too, Sal. You might not see it now, but he does."

Sal's expression tightened once again, and he shook his head. "Well, enough chitchat. I appreciate your kindness,

Bella. All of you." He glanced out the window at my house next door. "A man could get used to a family like this."

"Yes, he could." I gave him another wink, then rose and glanced at my watch, gasping. "Sal! It's 5:00!"

He nodded. "Yes. Rehearsal's in one hour, right?"

"Right. And I still have to shower and dress and make a couple of calls and track down D.J. and see how Rosa's coming on the food and—"

"Bella." Sal grabbed my hands and gave them a squeeze. "Slow down a minute."

I exhaled. Loudly. "Okay."

"You're doing a fine job, and all of this is going to come off without a hitch." He gave me a playful wink. "Maybe you're the one who needs that song, not me."

"O-oh?"

"Yes. Sounds like you could use a little grace yourself right about now. Take a deep breath, Bella. Pace yourself. Or would that be *grace* yourself?"

I grinned. Leave it to a former mobster to tell a girl she needs grace.

We made our way home, and I thought about Sal's words as I showered. Maybe I did need to "grace" myself a little. Hadn't D.J. said as much? I tended to be a little hard on myself sometimes, after all.

But not tonight! No, tonight was all about celebrating. As I slipped on my favorite little black dress, I prepared for an evening of pure enjoyment.

By 6:00 the entire Rossi clan had gathered in the reception hall once again, this time dressed to the nines. Laz looked smashing in his suit, and Rosa looked exquisite in her black evening dress. Mama had done her makeup—I could tell by the perfectly placed eyeliner. And Sophia had obviously played a role in the updo. I'd never seen Rosa look prettier. Or happier. Why, even Sal took notice of her, whistling as he saw her. Rosa blushed, obviously not used to such flattery.

The wedding rehearsal was simple but fun. Father Michael seemed to have the best time of all, sharing a couple of funny stories and keeping everyone in line. I stood off in the distance, wondering how to balance my role as wedding planner with that of family member. Something about watching all of this go down just made me want to cry. In a good way, of course. I somehow managed to hold it together.

Father Michael walked everyone through the ceremony, but I found myself captivated by D.J., who stood at the sound booth alongside Armando. Several times he looked my way and grinned. I knew what he was thinking—in just two short months, we would stand in front of our families and share this same experience.

Two months! Suddenly, my breath caught in my throat. I'd handled weddings on short order before, but never my own. Did I really have only two months to completely pull together the details of my big day? How would I manage?

*Don't panic. Just get past this wedding first.*

I drew in several calculated breaths, trying to stay focused and calm. Sal's words washed over me: *Sounds like you could use a little grace yourself right about now. Take a deep breath, Bella. Pace yourself. Grace yourself.*

He was right. There would be plenty of time to think of myself later. Right now, Rosa was front and center. Literally.

After the makeshift ceremony, she and Laz practiced their wedding kiss—something that took much longer than expected—then turned to face the congregation and grinned. I had to laugh as they sprinted up the aisle. Well, sprinting

180

being a relative term, what with Uncle Laz moving so slow these days.

As they passed by me, Rosa winked, and my heart soared. I could read so much in her playful gesture. She was thanking me for all I'd done. And she was thanking God for giving her the desires of her heart.

On the other hand, she might just be signaling me to gather the troops and point them all toward Parma John's, where the rehearsal dinner would take place.

My gaze shifted to Sal. I couldn't help but think about our earlier conversation. He had admitted to being a little jealous of Uncle Laz and Aunt Rosa, and I understood it. They had a love unlike any I'd ever seen—the kind that surpassed time and circumstances. Surely he longed for such a love himself.

In that moment, I whispered a quiet prayer that the Lord would show him just that—the Love of his life. And that Sal Lucci would, after all these years, come to know just what it meant to both love and be loved by the very one who'd given him that desire in the first place.

# 16

## I Get a Kick Out of You

Saturday dawned clear and perfect with crisp, cold weather. We couldn't have asked for more. And if anyone deserved perfect weather on her wedding day, it was Aunt Rosa. I slipped into my jeans and sweater, so many memories rolling through my brain . . . The day she arrived in Texas, straight off the plane from Napoli. The look in her eye the first time she cooked a meal for our family. The constant quarreling between Rosa and Laz. The day the folks from the Food Network showed up to film her in the Rossi family kitchen. The moment Laz finally confessed his love. The thousand kisses he gave her seconds later. Oh, how that tickled my fancy, both then and now.

As these memories flooded over me, a rush of emotion gripped my heart. All good, of course, though a little sad too. Seemed odd that life was changing so much. All for the better, but still . . .

I lingered a moment, thinking about how fast the world

was spinning of late. Oh, but it was worth it when you were in love. Falling in love made everything—even the passage of time—sweeter. My thoughts drifted once again to Laz and Rosa, and I whispered a prayer that every desire of their hearts would come true. How fun to think they were finally going to be husband and wife.

I made my way down the stairs with a panting Yorkie-Poo at my heels. I'd almost reached the bottom step when my cell phone rang. I looked down at it, noticing the word PRIVATE where a number should have been. Hmm. A telemarketer, perhaps? I usually just let those go to voice mail, but today it seemed important to answer. I clicked TALK with a hesitant "Hello?"

"Bella? Is that you?"

I stopped in my tracks when I heard Brock Benson's hypnotic voice come on the line. "Brock!"

"The one and only."

I heard children's voices off in the distance, so I had to ask. "Where are you?"

"It's Saturday. I'm volunteering at the center." He turned away from the phone to say something to someone else, which took several seconds. I sat down on one of the stairs, and Precious nuzzled into my lap. Brock finally came back on the line. "Sorry. Lots going on here today. We're feeding several of the single moms and their kids a huge Christmas dinner. You should see the crowd. It's pretty amazing, Bella."

"No way." I could still hardly imagine Brock Benson—Hollywood's hottest hunk—working with Los Angeles's inner-city children. And feeding them, no less! "Serve an extra helping of goodies for me," I said with a smile.

"Will do. Hey, Rosa and Laz are getting married today, right?" His question jarred me back to attention. "I'm pretty sure I wrote down the date when we talked last."

183

"Yes. They're getting married tonight at 7:00, and the reception is after." I went on to describe the whole big band theme, which got a chuckle out of Brock.

"Sounds right up their alley." He paused. "Well, listen, I was calling for a reason. I wanted to do something special for the happy couple on their wedding day."

"Oh?"

"Yes. Or, rather, the day after their wedding. They fly out tomorrow, right?"

"Yes, but how do you know all of this?"

He laughed. "Bella, I talk to your Aunt Rosa at least once a week. She keeps me updated, trust me."

My mouth flew open at that revelation. Who knew Rosa had a private weekly chat with the Hollywood megastar? "Wow. Well, to answer your question, yes. They fly out tomorrow. They're spending tonight at the Tremont."

"I'm trying not to think about their wedding night, thank you very much," Brock said, followed by a nervous chuckle.

"Um, yeah. Same here." I swallowed my laughter and forged ahead. "So, what's up? What are you thinking?"

"Well, they have to get to the airport tomorrow morning in record time, right?"

"Yes. Their flight leaves at noon, and they have to be there two hours early since it's an international flight."

"Right. So getting them up to Houston in a hurry is key."

"I suppose. Never thought about it."

"I did." He chuckled. "I, um, well, I happen to have a friend who owns a helicopter."

"W-what?"

"Yeah." He laughed. "A guy I met out here a couple of years ago doing a shoot. He's moved off to Texas. Lives in Austin."

"Austin is hardly Galveston."

"Still, as the crow flies, it's not far. Won't take Zach long to get there in the helicopter, and he owes me. So, he's going to sweep in tomorrow morning around eight and fly them to their destination."

"Italy?" I teased.

"Um, no. The George Bush Intercontinental Airport. They're going to ride in style to the airport. What do you think of that?"

"Well . . ." I paused, thinking about Rosa's reaction to all of this. "Rosa will think she's died and gone to heaven, especially when she hears that you arranged it all."

"Well, I didn't exactly do all of it myself," he admitted.

"Oh?"

"Yeah, I've been talking to your fiancé. D.J. helped me find a place on the island for the helicopter to land. He has some connections at a local helipad, I think."

"Right. He worked on a house for a guy who—" Wait a minute. D.J. was involved in this? That stinker! He hadn't said a word! Looked like he was pretty good with secrets. First the renovations to Rosa and Laz's bedrooms. Then the home he wanted to purchase for the two of us. Now this?

"D.J. is going to the Tremont tomorrow morning at 7:45 to pick up Rosa and Laz to get them to the helipad on time."

"Wow. Maybe I could go with him. Sounds like fun."

Brock sighed. "My only regret is that I won't be there. You don't know how hard I worked, trying to get back to Galveston for the wedding."

"Really?" I had no idea, but the thought of Brock returning for Rosa's big day warmed my heart.

"Yes, but I'm in the middle of a movie right now, and the

center is so new and all. I really need to devote my time here."
His voice grew animated. "Bella, your family means the world
to me. When I think about—" He choked up. "When I think
about how much my life has changed since I met all of you,
I . . ." He paused. "I'm just so grateful to the Lord. He really
used you Rossis to, well, there's no better way to say it—to
save a wretch like me."

"Sounds like Guido."

"How is that goofy parrot, anyway?" Brock asked. "Still
singing?"

"Um, yeah. Only, now his owner has come to take him back
to New Jersey." The oddest sensation took over as I spoke
those words. Was it really possible that I might actually miss
Guido? And Sal?

"Oh, wow, that's right. I heard that Sal was coming to
the wedding."

"He's here." I lit into a full explanation of all that had
happened over the past few days, honing in on the part where
he tried to ruin the wedding.

"Well, I'll tell you this, Bella," Brock said as I wrapped up
the dramatic tale, "Sal is in the best possible place for the
Lord to grab hold of his heart. Ask me how I know."

I smiled, knowing all too well. God had really used my
family to reach Brock. Surely he would do the same for Sal,
even if we dropped the ball at times.

"Just be patient with him. I have a feeling God isn't finished
. . . with Sal or with Guido."

"Hope you're right."

Brock laughed. "Funny you should say that. I used to major
on being right. Now I just major on . . . well, on helping
others."

The sound of children's laughter in the background caught

my attention, and he began to talk to someone on his end once again.

"Listen, Bella, I've gotta go," he said at last. "I'm praying you guys have a great day today. And talk to D.J. about the details for the helicopter tomorrow, okay? But don't let Rosa and Laz know till the very last minute. I want it to be a surprise."

"Gotcha. Oh, and Brock . . . thank you."

"You're welcome, Bella. It's the least I can do."

We said our good-byes, and he disappeared off the line. For a moment I sat with the phone in my hand, deep in thought. Brock Benson, Hollywood's own, had arranged for my aunt to be escorted to the airport in style. And D.J. Neeley, the world's sweetest construction guy, had played a role in the big secret. Thinking of D.J. made me smile. I closed my eyes and thought about how he'd kissed me good night just last night, the promise of many more kisses to come lingering in the air.

"Bella?"

I opened my eyes when I heard my father's voice. "O-oh, hey, Pop."

"Everything okay?" He gave me a curious look, and I nodded.

"Yeah. Just got off the phone. Deep in thought."

"Obviously." He grinned. "Must be thinking of something nice."

"I was. I was thinking about D.J."

My father's smile broadened. "I see how it is. Getting excited about your big day?"

"Yes." I nodded and rose, putting Precious on the step beside me. "But today I need to be focused on someone else's wedding. It's Rosa's big day. There will be plenty of time for my own stuff later."

Pop wrapped me in his arms. "You're a good girl, Bella. Always thinking of others before yourself. I'm so proud of you. Don't know if I say that enough. And you've done such a good job with the wedding facility. We couldn't have chosen a better person for the job."

I gasped at this revelation. Sure, I received plenty of encouragement from my parents, but this one hit from out of the blue. "Thank you!" I threw my arms around his neck and planted a kiss on his cheek. "I needed that today, Pop." With a spring in my step, I headed down the stairs to get busy.

I found Rosa in the kitchen, of course. Cooking. She looked up with a smile when I entered. "Good morning, Bella Bambina. How are you today?"

"I'm fine. But, Rosa! It's your wedding day. You're not supposed to be working, remember?"

"I know, but there's still so much to do. Your mama and Laz just took the cake next door, so at least that's done."

"Really? Should I go over there and help them set it up? It's not put together yet, right?"

"Right. I still need to do that, and then trim off the edges and put the topper on. I'll come with you." She dried her hands on her apron, pushing her food preparations aside.

"Wait. What about that old tradition of the bride and groom not seeing each other on their wedding day? Laz is over there, right?"

Rosa laughed. "We haven't seen each other, trust me. Your mama won't allow it. She pushed me out of the room when he came in, and I'm sure she'll send him packing when we show up to put the cake together."

"Well, I'm coming with you, just to make sure." I gazed into her twinkling eyes. "And Rosa, when we get back, let

Jenna and Bubba finish up the food. They should be here any minute."

"I will." She shrugged. "I would've asked Bianca and Bertina, but I can't find them. They disappeared early this morning." She shook her head. "I have a suspicion they're up to something . . . and I don't mean something good."

"Oh?"

"Yes." My aunt's cheeks flashed pink. "They wanted to throw me one of those . . . what do you call them? Lingerie showers?"

"Ah. Yes."

"Well, of course I said no. I mean, can you imagine?" Rosa's face got redder by the minute. "But Bianca was determined to find me something special to wear tonight. Um, *after* the wedding, I mean." She coughed, and her gaze shifted down. I could read the embarrassment in her stance.

"I see." I tried to push down the edges of my lips, but they refused to cooperate. As much as I'd tried not to think about my aunt's wedding night, it seemed unavoidable, especially now.

"Anyway, I have a sneaking suspicion they've gone to town to do some last-minute shopping. I'm sure they'll come back with something, well . . ."

"Sexy?" I offered.

"Yes." Rosa grinned, then wiped her hands on her apron. "Anyway, it's silly, but I just might play along." Her eyebrows elevated mischievously. "Whatever they buy will certainly beat my flannel nightshirts, that's for sure. And who knows . . . Laz might get a kick out of it."

"I daresay. He is a man, you know." I gave her a wink.

"He is, at that." She winked back.

I took Rosa by the arm, and we walked next door to the wedding facility. When we arrived, I went inside first, ushering

Laz out of the reception hall the back way. He promised to steer clear of Rosa for the rest of the day. Not an easy task since they shared the same house. But I knew he would honor Mama's wishes. No doubt about that. If he wanted to live to see the ceremony, anyway.

Once Laz was gone, I opened the door for Rosa to enter. She looked around the reception hall and grinned. Shaking her head, she said, "It seems even prettier today than it did last night. I still can't believe the transformation. This room is beyond anything I could have expected, Bella. Looks just like a banquet hall from days gone by."

"I'm so glad you like it."

"I love it. And it's going to be wonderful tonight, once the band is in place." She closed her eyes and began to sing "Some Enchanted Evening," swaying back and forth with her imaginary dance partner. When she finished, her eyes popped open. "Oh, it's going to be glorious!"

"It sure is," Mama said as she approached. "And you deserve it, Rosa. You're going to be the happiest bride in the state of Texas if Bella and I have anything to do with it."

"Thank you." Rosa's eyes filled with tears, which she brushed away. Her gaze shifted to the cake. "Hmm. Looks like we need to get busy putting this thing together."

"It's bad luck for a bride to work on her own wedding cake, Rosa," Mama said. "Maybe you should let me do this."

"Pooh. I don't believe in luck, good or bad. You know that." Rosa reached for the oversized bottom layer and centered it on the table. "Besides, I love decorating cakes. Always have and always will. Especially wedding cakes. And I wouldn't be able to rest if I handed this project off to someone else." She grinned at Mama. "No offense intended, Imelda, but I really want to do this."

"Of course." My mother stepped back and let her.

When the bottom cake was in place, Rosa put the tiny wooden dowels in and set another layer on top of it. Once it was situated, a third smaller cake went above that. Rosa stood back at a distance to give it a thorough examination. "Is it crooked?"

"Hmm." I narrowed my gaze. "It's leaning a little to the front."

She did a bit of maneuvering, then stepped back and smiled as she looked at it once again. "There. That should do the trick." Rosa took a spool of gold ribbon about an inch and a half wide and wrapped the bottom of each cake layer. Reaching for the bag of frosting, she began to trim off the edges of the cake. I'd never seen anyone move with such speed. Less than ten minutes later, the little scalloped edges were complete. Then she added several red silk roses, cascading from the top and spilling down the front in colorful array. Stepping back once again, Rosa expressed her contentment with a sigh.

"It's beautiful," Mama said. "Absolutely perfect."

"Yes, it is," I echoed. "The prettiest one you've made so far, Rosa."

"Thank you." She nodded but never took her eyes off that cake.

For a moment, none of us said a word. We all just stared at the three-tiered beauty.

"I just had the most interesting thought," Rosa said at last. "It occurs to me that our family is like this cake."

"What do you mean? Because we're so sweet?" I offered up a playful grin.

"Well, that too." She smiled. "But I was thinking of something else. We come to the Lord as individuals. Each one spe-

191

cial and unique. Different sizes and shapes. Like the different layers of this cake. But when you put us all together . . ." She gestured to the whole of it and sighed. "Well, it's something magnificent to see, isn't it?"

"Yes, it is." I totally got it. We were different, each from the other. But the whole was certainly greater than the sum of its parts, no doubt about that.

"That's the Rossi clan," Rosa whispered. "Tall. Strong. Beautiful." She lifted the edge of her tomato-stained apron and dabbed at her eyes, finally startling back to attention. "Help me with one more thing, Bella. I've got to put the dowel rod down through the center so the cake doesn't fall over."

As we pressed the long wooden dowel down through the center of the cake, another thought hit me. What made the Rossi family so strong, so beautiful, was the one thing at the center of it all. The Lord. Without him, we would have toppled long ago.

With the dowel in place, there was really only one thing left to do. Rosa took the topper—a glorious bride and groom— and placed it on top of the cake. She grinned as she looked at it. "You know, I feel like that right now," she said, pointing.

"Oh?"

"Yes." She giggled. "I'm on top of the world."

I reached to give her a warm hug. "I have a feeling you're going to be there for a long, long time, Rosa. Tonight is just the beginning of your happily ever after."

Rosa gave my hand a squeeze. "*Finché c'è vita, c'è speranza*, Bella Bambina."

Mama and I grinned, then spoke the words in unison: "As long as there is life, there is hope!"

# 17

## Stardust

About an hour before Laz and Rosa's wedding, I slipped into my evening gown, ready for what would surely turn out to be one of the most spectacular nights of my life. I stood in front of the full-length mirror, mesmerized by the way the black satin gown made me feel. I couldn't be sure if it was the forties theme or the dress itself, but I genuinely felt like I'd stepped into a Hollywood movie set.

The flowing dress had a dramatic draped back and the prettiest rhinestone bow a girl could ask for. The front boasted a V-neck with princess seaming. My favorite part, though, was the skirt with its flared hem. I loved the fact that it was longer in back than front. Very elegant, especially with the lightweight satin swishing around my ankles. And there was something about a dress that had to be zipped up on the side that just made me feel like a Hollywood princess. Yep. I was a sucker for playing dress-up, even as an adult.

I touched up my lipstick and pressed my feet into the black

pumps I'd chosen just for tonight—a pretty number with an elegant but sensible heel—and headed to the wedding facility in plenty of time to give the room a final look before the crowd arrived.

Once inside, I found Father Michael warming up on his trumpet with the band. Looked like Gordy had talked him into playing a number during the reception. Go figure.

I noticed Gordy and Lilly slip in from the hallway with suspicious smiles on their faces. *Hmm. I wonder what's up with that.*

Gordy walked to the stage, turning back to catch Lilly's eye. She gave him a little wave, then took a few steps in my direction. "Bella!"

"Lilly, what's up?" I asked.

"I have news." She pulled me to the side of the room. "It's about Gordy," she whispered.

"What about him?"

"We had a long talk the day Laz and Rosa were fighting, Bella, and he finally admitted that he's been in love with me for months."

"Oh, Lilly!" I reached to give her hands a squeeze. "This is wonderful news. I'm thrilled for you."

"Not half as thrilled as I am." She giggled, suddenly looking and sounding about forty years younger. "I asked him what took so long, and you know what he said?"

"No."

"Fear. He was scared."

"Of what?"

"Well . . ." She sighed. "He was married to his first wife for thirty-nine years, and she passed away after a long battle with cancer. Turns out he was afraid to love again, scared he might lose that person too."

194

"Oh wow. Well, I guess that makes sense."

"Yes," she said. "But you know what makes even more sense, especially at our age?" When I shook my head, she said, "To risk it. To put everything on the line and take a chance. For love's sake."

"Wow. That's brilliant, Lilly."

She smiled. "I think so too, to be honest. And I'm willing to risk it all for love, Bella." Her gaze traveled to the stage, and she gave Gordy a flirtatious wave. "He's worth it. *We're* worth it."

I threw my arms around her neck, overcome with joy. "You are!" I said. "And I know God is in this, Lilly. He is!"

"Amen to that!" She giggled as she released her hold on me. Turning toward the stage, she wrapped up the conversation. "Of course, if I want to keep that man happy, I'd better get back to my seat. He's never happy when a musician goes missing."

"You go on then," I said with a reassuring smile. "I need to go check on the bride, anyway. But keep me posted, okay?"

"You got it."

I took note of the time—6:30. By now Sal would be at the door, greeting guests. I still smiled as I thought about his insistence to do things the way they would be done in the Old Country. Making my way to the door, I saw him at work, handing out drinks to the men and women. For toasting, of course.

Sal raised his glass and shouted, "*Per cent'anni!* For a hundred years!" and Phoebe and Bart Burton raised their glasses and shouted, "For a hundred years!"

Sal followed this with "*Evviva gli sposi!* Hurray for the newlyweds!" Bubba, who happened to be coming through the door with a stack of cloth napkins in his hands, shouted,

"Hurray for the newlyweds!" Ironic, in light of the fact that he was one.

Watching Sal at work was a mixed bag. I was so proud of him for playing the role of host. But I was also a little sad knowing he would be leaving us soon, heading back to Atlantic City. He'd truly become part of the family over the past few days.

Glancing at my watch, I realized I needed to get moving. With only twenty minutes till start time, I still needed to check on the bride and groom. I entered the bride's room to check on Rosa just a few seconds later. I gasped when I saw her, and tears sprang to my eyes. Talk about a transformation. I had seen her in her wedding dress a few weeks ago, but back then it had required alterations. Today, as I looked at her adorned in white, it occurred to me—she was truly pure in every sense of the word. Sixty-plus years old, and never married. She could wear that white dress and wear it proudly. I didn't know many twenty-year-olds who could do that, let alone a woman in her golden years.

"What do you think, Bella?" She turned my way with a grin. "Do I look like I'm from the forties?"

"Man, do you ever." The sweetheart neckline on the lace gown was amazing. And those full-length point sleeves were divine. My favorite part, however, was the darling forties-style white hat with veil attached. I could almost hear "Boogie Woogie Bugle Boy" playing in the background now. Rosa certainly looked the part, and then some.

"What about us?" I turned at Aunt Bertina's cheerful voice. Mama, Bianca, and Bertina took my breath away. They all wore their hair in typical forties updos, curled around the edges, near to the face. Very Betty Grable–like. Or would it be Rita Hayworth? And those dresses! The gold gowns were reminiscent of days gone by, all glitz and glam. Straight off of a Hollywood set. I could hardly wait to see the ladies marching down the aisle with their respective groomsmen.

And speaking of groomsmen . . . from what I'd been told, Pop, Emilio, and Sal would all be wearing double-breasted suits and fedoras. This I could hardly wait to see. In fact, I'd check on them right now.

"Be back in a few minutes." I offered Rosa a reassuring smile.

She waved me off, and I ventured down the hall to the groom's room. Rapping on the door, my anticipation mounted. Pop swung it wide, and I gasped as I saw the men. I wasn't sure whether to laugh or stare in stunned silence. Mama mia! Did these fellows look the part, or what? Their suits were fabulous from top to bottom and definitely put me in mind of a different era, one where men didn't mind a little flash and shine.

Speaking of flashes, Joey was hard at work, snapping photos of the guys. "Perfect timing!" he said. "I was just wrapping up in here. I'm headed over to get some pictures of the ladies now. Are they ready for me?"

I nodded and gave him a quick hug, never leaving my spot in the doorway. I wouldn't dare enter the men's sanctuary without invitation. "Thanks for all your hard work, Joey," I whispered. "I'm sure the pictures are going to be amazing."

"Thanks, Bella." He nodded toward me. "You look like you stepped out of a movie."

"Why, thank you!" I curtsied. "That's the idea."

After Joey left, my father drew near. "Is it almost time?"

"No, we've still got fifteen minutes. I just had to see them with my own eyes. The suits, I mean. And the shoes."

Pop turned in a circle, and I whistled as I took in the high-waisted, wide-legged trousers and the long coat with its broad lapels. What got me most, however, was the fedora. He looked smashing.

"Oh, take a look at these." Pop pointed down to the black and white shoes on his feet. "Spats. Just for fun. And you've got to see Laz. You're not going to believe it. He looks pretty dashing."

"Is it okay to come inside?" I asked.

"Sure. We've been dressed for a long time. C'mon in."

I stepped inside, gasping when I laid eyes on Laz, who was dressed in a getup similar to the others, with the addition of a feather in his fedora. Did he look like a dandy, or what? He wore a watch chain that dangled from his belt down to the knee, then draped back to his side pocket. Unbelievable—he looked like something straight from a photograph! Clearly, the man had done his homework on the forties. Or maybe he just remembered them firsthand. At any rate, he had it right.

"Laz, you look like a million bucks."

"Wish I *had* a million bucks," he said with a smile. "Rosa and I would stay in Italy much longer than planned."

"Don't you dare!" I said. "You've got to come back home to us. It's going to be hard enough to do without you for a few weeks. A few months would kill us!"

"True." He shook his head. "I haven't got a clue how you folks are going to survive without your favorite aunt and uncle. For one thing, what will you eat?"

I gave him my best offended look. "Hey now. I'll have you know that Rosa has been teaching me to cook over the past few months. I'm getting better all the time."

He quirked a brow, and we all laughed.

"Well, I'm getting better, anyway," I said. "So we won't

starve. And Mama can cook. She just rarely gets the chance to prove it."

"Good point. She will certainly have the chance now." He turned once more, looking in the mirror. "You don't think folks will mind that I'm not wearing a tux and tails? That was an option too. We just thought this would be more fun."

"Fun is good," I said with a smile. "It's your wedding, Laz. You make it what you want it to be. If I've learned anything during my time in this business, it's that the bride and groom get what they want, not what others want for them."

"Another good point, my dear." He gave me a tender look. "That's why you're the wedding planner and I'm not."

I spent a few more minutes giving instructions, then headed into the reception hall to check on the band and the singers. When I found Twila, Jolene, and Bonnie Sue, I couldn't help but gasp. "Ladies!" I gestured for them to turn around, and they did, but not without setting off a shimmer that almost blinded me. I'd never seen so many sequins. And those little hats. Darling!

"I saw this outfit in a movie once," Twila said, gesturing to her dress. "Ingrid Bergman. *Casablanca*." She fussed with her waistline and groaned. "Of course, hers was a size 2 and mine is a 22, but never mind all that."

I stifled a laugh.

"My dress is cut from the same pattern as Ginger Rogers's in *Top Hat*," Bonnie Sue said. "I've always loved that movie." She giggled. "Makes me wonder what my Fred Astaire is up to right about now."

"Fred Astaire?" I gave her a curious look.

"She's talking about Sal," Jolene said, rolling her eyes. "We keep telling her he's off limits, but she thinks she's going to win him to the Lord by slipping on her dancing shoes and taking him for a spin around the dance floor. Tell her it's senseless, Bella. Missionary dating is never a good idea, especially at a wedding."

I turned to Bonnie Sue, unsure of what to say. With a wave of her hand, she dismissed the idea altogether. "Oh, c'mon, ladies. I'm just having fun. I'll behave myself, whether Fred and Ginger trip the light fantastic or not."

"What about you?" I asked, turning to Jolene.

"Oh, Bette Davis wore this dress in *The Man Who Came to Dinner*." She ran her hands along the edges of her broad hips. "Of course, some of us have had a little *too* much dinner, thereby leading to a larger dress size, but I don't suppose it matters, do you? I mean, glamour is glamour, no matter a lady's size."

"Amen to that," Bonnie Sue and Twila threw in.

"Well, you look gorgeous." I gave them an encouraging smile. "And you're going to blow the crowd away with your songs too. I can hardly wait for the reception."

"Same here!" Twila lit into the chorus of "Eight to the Bar," and within seconds the women were singing in perfect harmony. I gestured for them to take their rehearsal into the hallway since guests were arriving. I slipped to the back of the room and adjusted the overhead lights, turning them down a bit. The twinkling Christmas lights gave the room a heavenly glow. Perfect.

I happened to glance across the room, taking note of Earline. Excusing myself, I took a few steps in her direction. As I approached, she looked up from her music with a joyous expression on her face.

"Bella!" She took my hand. "You look fabulous."

"Do you like my dress?" I spun around, showing it off.

"Do I!" She smiled. "That boy of mine is going to flip

when he sees you." Her brows elevated. "And I have a feeling you're going to flip when you see him too. In fact . . ." She gestured for me to turn around, so I did. My heart leaped to my throat when I saw D.J. in his tuxedo. Wowza! I'd seen the boy in a suit before, but never anything like this. The black tuxedo and tails made me giddy. I felt like I'd walked straight onto a movie set. I wanted to rush to his side to tell him just how dashing he looked. To let him know he took my breath away. Unfortunately, the room was rapidly filling with guests. I barely had enough time to slip over for a moment or two.

"Bella!" He whistled, and I felt my cheeks turn warm. "We're gonna have a little chat about this getup you're wearing when the night is through. You're raising my blood pressure."

"Mine's through the roof too," I said, gesturing to his tux. "But I don't have time for a medical condition tonight. Too much to do."

He gave me a gentle kiss on the lips, and I nestled against him, happy for even a few seconds alone with my leading man. The spell was broken when Sophia rushed my way to let me know that Jenna needed me in the kitchen. D.J. and I talked through a few last-minute instructions, and then I headed off to the kitchen to calm Jenna down. Turned out she'd misplaced one of the large salad bowls. I found it in a jiffy, and she dove into action, filling it with the luscious Caesar salad. Man, were the guests ever going to love this meal!

Speaking of guests, I gave the hall another quick glance and realized they were arriving in force now. Glancing at my watch, I took note of the time—6:55. Wouldn't be long now till we could get this show on the road.

After tying up a couple more loose ends, I raced to the bride room to prepare the ladies. We could hear the strains of "It Had to Be You" playing in the reception hall. Gordy and the band sounded great. I could almost envision Jehoshaphat and those Levites now, leading the way. Only this time, there were no enemies to fight. No, only friends and loved ones tonight. And a theatrical entrance for the world's most anticipated bride.

"You ready, Rosa?" I asked.

She turned to me with a twinkle in her eye. "Oh, honey, you have no idea how ready. I dare you to try and hold me back!"

"I wouldn't think of it!" With that proclamation, I led our merry little band into the hallway. When we reached the entrance to the reception hall, I paused to make sure Laz was at the front of the room next to Father Michael. Talk about perfect timing.

The groomsmen joined us in the hallway, and I could read the anticipation in their eyes. When I gave the signal, Sal and Bianca made their way down the aisle first, taking slow, calculated steps. They were followed by Emilio and Bertina. I had to wonder what Francesca was thinking right about now. I caught a glimpse of her seated near the front. She dabbed at her eyes.

When Emilio and Bertina reached the halfway point, Pop took Mama's arm, and they made their way down the long aisle. For whatever reason, seeing my parents walk the aisle together almost did me in. I tried to imagine what they must be feeling, walking the aisle again after so many years as husband and wife. Were they reflecting on their own wedding day all those years ago?

As the last couple of measures of "It Had to Be You" lingered over us, I happened to notice D.J. at the sound table. He gave me a little wink, and my heart fluttered. I found the moment strangely prophetic, almost as if God had arranged all of this just for the two of us. That song, with its near-perfect lyrics. The ambient lighting. That miraculous band. Yes, surely the Lord had gifted us with a moment of privacy in the midst of this very public celebration.

I didn't have time to ponder this for long. The song came to its rightful conclusion, and Earline joined with the band to play a forties swing-style version of "The Wedding March." I'd never heard this particular rendition, but it certainly fit the theme of the night.

I reached to give my precious aunt a kiss on the cheek before releasing her to make the walk down the aisle. The crowd rose and turned to face the back of the room, clearly anxious to see the bride in all of her glory. Rosa gave me a little nod and then took her first step. And her second. I smiled as I watched her make this journey alone. She had her reasons. This I knew from a prior conversation. In fact, I could almost hear her words as they replayed in my mind now: *This is going to be my last walk without a man leading the way, Bella Bambina. Let me enjoy it.*

Oh, but Someone was leading the way. In fact, he'd led the way from the beginning till now. Tears sprang to my eyes as that truth nuzzled its way into my spirit. He had led Rosa to America. Led her to our hearts. Led her to Lazarro Rossi. And he would continue leading her into a thousand dazzling tomorrows.

Funny. Call me a romantic fool, but through my tears, the twinkling Christmas lights overhead almost looked like stars. And the man and woman standing in front of the crowd—my beautiful aunt and my dashing uncle? Why, they were the sun and the moon, merging to put on the most spectacular light display this family had ever seen.

Now that was what I called ambient lighting.

# 18

## Puttin' on the Ritz

Standing at the back of the reception hall, I had the best seat in the house. Father Michael led Rosa and Laz through the tender ceremony, and the crowd came alive with excitement as they shared their first sweet kiss as a married couple, a handful of us even clapping and cheering.

Husband and wife. Could it really be? After all the years of quarreling and squabbling, they had laid down their swords and picked up their hearts instead. As I looked into their smiling faces, I realized the Lord had performed nothing short of a miracle.

Rosa and Laz turned to face the congregation—if that's what one could call a swing-band hall filled with guests— as Father Michael pronounced them Mr. and Mrs. Lazarro Rossi. At this point, cheers went up around the room, and several people—Sal included—shouted, "*Evviva gli sposi!* Hurray for the newlyweds!"

Rosa and Laz practically sprinted up the aisle, clearly ready to face the rest of their life together. Who could blame them? I glanced through the now-standing congregation to seek out D.J. He looked up from the sound booth as the band began to play "Puttin' on the Ritz." I gave a shy little wave, suddenly very aware of the fact that our wedding was next. Now that Laz and Rosa were truly man and wife, I could focus—at last—on my own big day. And focus I would . . . just as soon as we made it through the reception.

Father Michael gave the guests their instructions, letting everyone know they could help themselves to appetizers while photos were taken. I had no time to dally. Not with so much left to do!

The guests headed to the appetizer table, and Nick, Sophia, Jenna, Bubba, and I flew into high gear, getting the rest of the food ready to be placed on the table.

Off in the distance, Joey snapped photos of the wedding party, and guests nibbled on tasty hors d'oeuvres. Looked like everything was coming together, right down to the fabulous decor on the tables. Marcella had done a fine job with that. In fact, she'd done a fine job with everything.

Marcella! For the first time in days, I remembered her news. We were having a baby girl! There were still plenty of surprises ahead for the Rossi clan, no doubt about that. I had to wonder how—and where—Marcella and Nick would spring the good news.

Hmm. Obviously not tonight. No, we clearly had other things to deal with tonight. Like getting these guests fed and making sure the bridal party was served.

I'd learned from the master—Rosa—that most true Italian weddings have at least thirteen courses. We'd managed to convince her to trim back a bit and to offer the food buffet style, and she and Laz had done a superb job preparing all of our favorites. As the buffet table was filled, the tantalizing scent of garlic filled the air, getting all of our guests stirred up. I'd never seen so much food in my life or so many happy, hungry souls.

The guests mingled until photographs were taken, and I gave the buffet table a final sweep with my eyes. First up was the antipasto. The stuffed mushrooms, olives, salami, and prosciutto made my mouth water. Yum! I glanced at the next spot on the buffet table, where a large pot of Italian wedding soup still bubbled. The savory meatballs and rice were topped off with more than adequate amounts of Parmesan cheese. I could almost taste it now.

Beyond the wedding soup, large bowls of Caesar salad beckoned, the crisp green romaine practically begging to be eaten. I could smell the tangy dressing from here—Rosa's homemade, of course. Nothing from a bottle for her wedding day! She wouldn't dream of it.

After the salad came my favorite part—the bread. I wasn't sure how or when Jenna and Bubba had done it, but they'd arranged a variety of breads—sliced sourdough, rolls, flaky croissants, and more—on the table in true Italian style. The colorful bread baskets were tipped up on their sides with bread spilling out onto red-checkered cloths. I smiled as I saw dozens of Rosa's garlic twists on display, the buttery garlic oozing onto the pieces below. Guests were sure to love those. They were the stuff Food Network specials were made of, after all.

I paused to think about that. Rosa had turned down a weekly show on the Food Network to marry Laz. Not because he'd asked her to, but because she couldn't picture taking time away from him to pursue the life of a celebrity. How different things might have turned out if Laz had never declared his love. Perhaps Rosa would already be living elsewhere, her weekly television show beamed out to would-be chefs across the country. Instead, she was right here, where she belonged. With her family. Her husband.

*Husband.* Oh, what a glorious word! Soon enough, I would have one of my very own, one I'd gladly trade fame and fortune for. Well, fame, anyway. Hopefully, I could still make a profit from the wedding facility. Before long, this place would be overwhelmed with weddings; I could just feel it. After my own wedding, of course. Right now, that was the most important thing—to give myself plenty of undivided time preparing for my own big day!

My gaze went back to the table, and I took in the bubbling chicken cacciatore, the fettuccini with its creamy Alfredo sauce, and the large platter of cannelloni. After that came the meats—beef, chicken, and fish. Salmon, to be precise—my personal favorite, especially Laz's version, with basil crust and ratatouille salsa.

By the time I got to the end of the table, my head was swimming. In a good way. And this didn't even include the many desserts. I turned my attention to the sweets table, looking at the fresh berries and pastries. I smiled as I took in the little twists of fried dough powdered with sugar. Rosa had called them *wandas*, explaining that they symbolized good tidings for the bride and groom. They were the perfect complement to the Italian wedding cookies on the next tray and the tiramisu just beyond that. We couldn't have a party without Rosa's tiramisu!

Topping everything off, however, was the wedding candy— my absolute favorite. The yummy sweetness of the candy-covered almonds carried me away to another time, another place. I could almost see myself in Old Italy now. My mouth watered just thinking about it.

"It's a shame there's nothing to eat," D.J. said, scooting up behind me.

I turned to face him with a smile. "Have you ever seen anything like this?"

"Um, no." He grinned, and my heart melted. "Up in Splendora we usually just have a beef brisket after the wedding with some beans and potato salad. Or, if we want to be fancy, one of the ladies will make up some of those little sandwiches on croissants. Maybe a few cold veggies, cut up with ranch dip. But this . . ." He gestured. "This is really more of a feast. For the eyes and the stomach."

"All Italian weddings are like this," I said. "Some have as many as fourteen courses."

"No way."

"Yep. And some are even more elaborate, with all sorts of exotic and unusual foods."

"I'd say this is pretty elaborate." He pointed to the coffee bar. "But I have to say, that's my favorite part. Uncle Laz's espresso is the best on the island. Can't wait to get me some of that." D.J. gave me a wink.

I reached up to give him a kiss on the cheek. "Soon it will be our turn," I whispered.

"We gonna have this much food at our wedding?" he asked.

"Probably about half this much, which will be about double what we need." I laughed, and he joined me. Oh, how I loved this boy! How I wanted to stand here all night and talk about our big day!

Hmm. One glance at the front of the room convinced me I couldn't do that. Not just yet, anyway. Looked like Joey had finished taking pictures of the wedding party.

"Time to swing into action?" D.J. asked.

When I nodded, he moved back over to the sound booth and took the microphone in hand.

"Folks, could I have your attention, please."

The room grew quiet—with the exception of Twila, Bonnie Sue, and Jolene, who still carried on about Rosa's beautiful wedding dress. Mama finally gave them a nod, and they realized they were the center of attention.

"Let's pray over the meal," D.J. said. He passed off the microphone to Father Michael, who led us in a glorious—albeit long—prayer over the food.

When the "Amen" sounded, folks made their way to the buffet. All but the wedding party, that is. Bubba and Jenna would serve them at the head table, giving them the choicest food in the house.

Within minutes, people were eating some of the best Italian food ever cooked. I'd never heard so many compliments in my life. Most of them belonged to Rosa, though Laz had played a hand in the food prep as well. The guests raved over the bread especially. No doubt they would leave full and happy.

The band members scarfed down the delectable goodies while D.J. and Armando played a few piped-in favorites from the forties. Still, I could see the gleam in Gordy's eye. He was anxious to get back up on that stage and get this party rolling. Who could blame him? This was going to be a reception no one would soon forget!

I squeezed through the crowd, approaching the head table where Rosa and Laz sat with their wedding party. I couldn't wait to tell her how much people loved the food. After gushing over how beautiful the ceremony had been, I raved over her food, which brought the biggest smile to her face.

"Bless you for saying that, Bella Bambina," she said, gesturing for me to lean down. When I did, she kissed my cheek.

"You're welcome. It's the truth." I glanced at the table, horrified to see her water glass empty. I signaled for Bubba, who filled it at once. "Do you need anything else?" I asked. "More food? Drinks? Would you like some punch?"

Rosa smiled and placed a hand on my arm. "Relax, Bella. All is well. You have done a beautiful job, giving me the wedding of my dreams. Now enjoy the evening. Promise me you'll try, anyway."

I nodded but realized that there was plenty of evening ahead and I needed to stay focused. Why, the bride and groom still had to have their first dance. There was a cake to cut, toasts to make, more photographs to shoot. Who had time to relax?

After the meal, the fun began. D.J. took the microphone in hand and, with Armando's help at the soundboard, slipped into deejay gear. For a moment I closed my eyes, just listening to the hypnotic sound of his voice. Had it really been only six months since I'd heard that voice for the first time? Oh, what it had done to me then . . . and oh, what it was doing to me now!

I could tell he was taking this gig very seriously. Not that I blamed him. Rosa had kept his stomach full for the last six months. He probably figured the least he could do was to give her the reception she deserved.

My handsome cowboy introduced Gordy and the band as they took their places up front. Then, at D.J.'s prompting, Rosa and Laz danced their first dance as husband and wife. Their song of choice? "It Had to Be You." Watching them circle the dance floor, I couldn't stop the tears from flowing, and all the more when I looked up and saw Father Michael playing the trumpet solo mid-song in perfect duet with Earline on the piano. Talk about harmony!

Thinking of harmony got me to thinking about Rosa and

Laz and how much time they'd wasted quarreling over the years. My thoughts shifted to one of Pop's favorite sayings: *Quel che non ammazza ingrassa.* "That which doesn't kill you makes you stronger." Funny. If you'd asked me several months ago, I would've said it was more likely my aunt and uncle would have ended up killing each other. Now they would be spending the rest of their lives swing dancing and traveling the continents. Go figure.

The bride and groom finished their first dance, and Sal hollered out, "*Bacio, bacio!* We want a kiss!" The guests echoed his words, "*Bacio, bacio!*" Laz, likely feeling a little heady, tipped Rosa backward and planted a smooch on her lips that would've made for a great Hollywood close-up. To Aunt Rosa's credit, she didn't even blush. Instead, she tipped Laz back and returned the favor.

D.J. then announced the money dance. Mama handed Rosa a satin purse, which guests would fill with money as they danced with her. The band played a lively version of "Sing, Sing, Sing" while people—male and female—stood in line for their turn to dance with Rosa.

"Look at that, Bella," Mama said, drawing near. "Rosa's dance card is full tonight."

"No kidding."

Mama shook her head. "She has always deserved this. Always. It's such a shame—" She stopped mid-sentence, but I knew what she wanted to say. Rosa had spent most of her life without a dance partner. The lone wallflower in a room filled with roses. But no more! Now she could dance every day if she liked.

When the money dance ended, D.J. opened the dance floor to all of the guests, and the party really took off. The band began to play, and the guests—many of whom seemed well

211

rehearsed—slipped on their dancing shoes. I'd never seen so many skilled dancers in my life, particularly in this age group.

I caught a glimpse of Sal eyeing Bonnie Sue, and she eyed him back, though I knew the other ladies were keeping a watch on her. Their words about missionary dating stayed at the front of my mind. Surely Bonnie Sue wouldn't give her heart to someone who didn't know the Lord.

Or maybe she would. When Sal asked her to dance—his invitation being an extended hand—she accepted. Within seconds they were the couple to beat on the dance floor. On and on they went, song after song. They got the crowd so worked up that a dozen or more couples joined them, following their moves. Before long, the whole place was on fire with the swing.

The music paused, and Gordy introduced the Splendora sisters. I watched as Bonnie Sue caught her breath before heading up to the stage. She gave Sal's hand a squeeze. "Hang on, honey," she said with a wink. "Don't you go anywhere, you hear? I've got to sing a couple of songs, but I'll be back."

She followed Twila and Jolene onto the stage, and the music began for "Boogie Woogie Bugle Boy." As the words rollicked forth, the audience really came alive. Folks came from out of the woodwork to dance.

Now me, I'd never danced the swing in my life. Neither had D.J., to my knowledge. But he took the boogie-woogie beat as his cue to try. Taking my hand in his, he headed to the center of the dance floor. The first few steps were awkward, but by the halfway point in the song, we had almost gotten the hang of it. By the time "Eight to the Bar" began, D.J. and I were on a roll, jiving like crazy. Who knew we were born to swing?

Sal got so excited by my apparent abilities that he cut in. D.J. graciously allowed him to do so, taking a few steps back. Sal then led me on a whirlwind trek around the dance floor. By the time the song ended, my breath was coming faster and harder. Oh, but it was worth it!

When the song ended, I realized that D.J. had drifted back over to the sound booth. He announced that Rosa and Laz were going to cut the cake. I flew back into wedding-planner gear and was at Rosa's side in less than twenty seconds. Not bad, considering the fact that I couldn't breathe.

As they took their place behind the beautiful wedding cake, I saw a glimmer in Rosa's eyes. Perhaps she planned to take full advantage of the situation and smear cake all over Laz's face. Or maybe . . .

I watched with relief as she fed him a small piece, taking great care not to mess up his suit. Maybe she was just going to show us how much she cared for him. As Laz took a small piece in hand to feed to Rosa, I had that same quickening. For a moment, he looked as if he might smear the cake all over her face. Instead, he lovingly fed it to her, then reached down to kiss the sweetness away.

Sal called out, "*Evviva gli sposi!* Hurray for the newly-weds!" Everyone joined in, and the cheering began. It carried on as Rosa and Laz shared glasses of punch. Then the room grew silent as Sal took the microphone to lead the guests in a toast. With tears in his eyes, he shared the story of how he and Laz had met in Atlantic City. On and on he went, finally getting around to the matter at hand—Laz's marriage to Rosa. With tears in his eyes, Sal blessed the happy couple, lifting his glass and crying, "*Salude!*"

After the toast, Gordy and the band began to play the familiar tarantella. Mama's face lit in a smile. So did Pop's.

And Bianca's. And Bertina's. In fact, everyone in the place came alive as the lively music rang out across the room, especially Rocco, who gathered us all into a large circle and began the dance.

We worked in tandem to the beat of the music, moving clockwise at first. Then, as the music sped up, we switched directions. Each time the tempo changed, we moved the opposite direction, moving faster, faster, faster. Finally, when I thought we would collapse, Gordy and the band brought the song to its rightful conclusion.

I paused to catch my breath, then looked up as Gordy and the band led the crowd in one final number. I don't know how or when she'd done it, but Rosa had somehow managed to slip a Frank Sinatra song in the mix after all. When the melody for "Strangers in the Night" began to play, Laz turned to his new bride with a suspicious look on his face.

"Tell me you didn't!" he said.

She shrugged, and a penitent look crossed her face. "How could I help myself, Lazarro? When I hear the words, they make me think of you."

"Well, in that case . . ." He swept her into his arms and did a couple of slow turns around the dance floor.

I marveled at my aunt's ability to pull this off. She was a wonder woman, no doubt about that. She had won not only Laz's heart but his musical ear as well.

Oh, but Laz had the last word. As the couple prepared to say their good-byes, the band lit into a rousing version of Dean Martin's famed song "That's Amore." Rosa stopped cold, then turned to look at her new husband. For a moment there, I wasn't sure if she planned to take his head off or give him a big smooch. Thankfully, it turned out to be the latter.

"You know," she said after the kiss, "I always did love this song."

"Really?"

"Yes." She giggled. "Just didn't want you to know. It was more fun sparring with you, letting you think I didn't care for Dino, when in fact I did. Isn't that silly?"

"Yes, you funny girl." He kissed the tip of Rosa's nose. "But don't worry about it! I have a feeling there are going to be plenty of sparring days ahead."

"Probably." She paused, then began to sing at the top of her lungs. "When the moon hits your eye like a big pizza pie . . ."

Laz joined in with a warbling voice. "That's amore!"

Before long, everyone in the room was gathered in a circle once again, all of us singing at the top of our lungs. I felt the sting of tears in my eyes, realizing just how far we'd all come over the past several months. Laz and Rosa had mended fences, Sal was walking the straight and narrow, and Guido . . . well, our ornery little parrot would've loved this version of the song.

When the music ended, Sal took a glass and shattered it into pieces on the floor. Each piece represented one happy year of marriage. From the mess on my floor, it looked like Rosa and Laz had about a hundred years to go.

Finally the moment came to wave good-bye to the newly-weds. D.J. and I managed to get their attention long enough to tell them about Brock's gift—the helicopter ride to the airport tomorrow morning. I could see the disbelief in Laz's eyes.

"Really? A helicopter?"

When I nodded, Rosa reached to give me a hug. "Oh, Bella! That's the icing on the cake! What a wonderful gift."

"I'll tell Brock you said so. Now you two go on and—"

Hmm. I didn't really want to finish that sentence, did I? After a moment's thought, I said, "Have a great honeymoon. Oh, and don't forget to call when you get to the airport tomorrow. We want to know you made it safely."

"And call the minute you get to Napoli," my mama said. She pressed her older sister into a tight hug, tears now streaming. "Oh, I'm so jealous that you get to go home, Rosa, but I'm so thrilled for you too. Visit all of our old places, promise?"

"I promise." Rosa nodded, tears now brimming. She turned back to me, a smile on her face as she leaned in to whisper, "Bianca and Bertina bought me the prettiest white negligee, Bella." Her eyebrows elevated mischievously. "Can't wait to show it off."

I smiled and gave her a thumbs-up, then turned to my aunts, who were nudging each other. Off in the distance, Twila, Jolene, and Bonnie Sue grinned ear to ear. I had it on good authority—Mama—that the playful trio had put a couple of sexy nightgowns in Rosa's suitcase as well. Looked like everyone had a hand in making this honeymoon special.

Not that Rosa and Laz needed any help. No, as I watched them slip into the limo and pondered the lingering kiss my uncle placed on my aunt's lips before they drove away, it was abundantly clear to me. They were going to do just fine—with or without the rest of us. Talk about a bittersweet revelation.

# 19

## In the Mood

As soon as Rosa and Laz left for the Tremont, Mama and Pop pulled me to the side. I could tell they had something serious on their minds because of the look of concern in my mother's eyes.

"Bella, we have something to talk to you about." She took my hand and gave it a squeeze. Never a good sign. My mind reeled as I tried to guess what she might say. They'd sold the wedding facility? They thought I was a failure as a wedding planner? They'd decided to pass the business off to Nick and Marcella instead?

"What's up?" My pulse quickened.

"Oh, it's nothing bad." My mother dismissed that idea with a wave of her hand. She paused, then looked at Pop. "We, um . . . well, your father and I just had a really wonderful idea, but we're not sure you're going to think it's so wonderful."

"You're finally going on that European vacation? Had enough with all of these weddings?"

She laughed. "Well, maybe someday soon. But that's not what we're talking about. We've been thinking about this construction that's about to take place over at the house."

At once my anxiety lifted. This had nothing to do with the wedding facility. Thank goodness! "What about it?" I asked.

"Well, you know your room butts up against Rosa's. And you know how small her space is."

"Yeah." I felt the blood drain from my face. "Don't tell me you're thinking of—"

"Well, it was just an idea, of course. Nothing set in stone. But her existing room is so small, and so is Laz's. Even combining the two, we're really not talking a huge room, especially if the new bathroom eats up so much of the space."

"Uh-huh." I nodded, praying she wouldn't say what I knew she was going to say.

"So, Pop and I got to thinking . . ."

"Actually, this was your mother's idea," my father said, "but I think it's a good one."

"We were thinking that you won't need your room anymore in another couple of months. You'll be married, after all."

"Well, yes, but—"

"And wouldn't it be such a lovely surprise to create a full suite for Rosa and Laz? Sort of their own apartment?" Mama lit into a lengthy description of her plans to add the square footage of my room to their original plan, creating a special place just for them. I applauded my mother's efforts to give the newlyweds something special, but she was leaving one important thing out of the equation. Where would I stay once the construction began? Was I really being booted out of my own space?

218

"Mama." I paused to stare at her, convinced she wasn't thinking clearly. "I don't get married until February. February. It's just now Christmas. I thought you were wanting to start the construction on the house while Rosa and Laz were on their honeymoon."

"Right." She nodded. "The construction begins on Monday. That's why we're talking to you now."

I felt a wave of nausea pass over me. How in the world could I plan my own wedding if I didn't even have a bed to sleep in at night? I voiced the question to Pop, who had a ready answer.

"We thought about giving you Armando's room," he said. "It made sense."

"But we need that space for the workers to create a little office," Mama explained. "It's perfect for them because it's just across the hall from where they'll be working."

"So we decided you should bunk with Sophia for the next couple of months, until your wedding." Pop crossed his arms at his chest, looking mighty proud of himself at that suggestion. "What do you think?"

"What do I think?" My mind reeled. "What do I think? I'm already going to be trying to balance my workload against the construction. When am I going to have time to focus on my own wedding?"

Mama dismissed that fear with a wave of her hand. "Bella, we're just asking you to move across the hall for a few weeks. What difference does it matter where you sleep? You don't plan weddings in your bedroom, anyway."

How could I explain this in a way that made sense to her? I'd slept in the same room for most of my life. And now my life was changing—drastically. I wanted to spend my last couple months at home with things just as they'd always been. Nothing more and nothing less. Surely they could see that. Right? And besides, I did plan weddings in my bedroom. Some of my best ideas came when I rested my head against the pillow at night.

Still, as I looked into my mother's hopeful eyes, I knew she would win this battle. Knew it was the best thing—for everyone. I released a slow breath, mentally counting to ten.

What would it hurt, really, to sleep in Sophia's room over the next few weeks? I tried to envision what that would be like. She was my baby sister, and we'd certainly spent more than a few nights bunking together over the years when the situation called for it. Maybe it would even be fun.

"I . . ." Hmm. "I guess it would be okay. But what are we going to do with my things?"

"There's plenty of room to store your furniture in the garage," Pop said. "I'll take care of that myself." He reached to give me a hug. "That's my good girl. I knew you would play along. You've got such a generous heart, Bella. Always have."

"Th-thanks."

Forcing back the sigh that threatened to erupt, I plastered on a smile. Not a very convincing one, I felt sure, but a smile nonetheless.

"We can talk more about all of this later," Mama said, joining in the embrace. "Oh, it's going to be so wonderful. Can you even imagine?" She released her hold on me and began to share all of her decorating ideas.

"One thing at a time, Imelda," Pop said, taking her by the arm. "First we have to get this place cleaned up. Then we can talk about decorating the new space."

They walked away together, arm in arm. I sighed, doing

my best to think about something else. Looking around the messy room, I realized there was plenty to keep me occupied. I headed over to the storage closet to fetch some boxes for the centerpieces.

As I made my way into the hallway, D.J. approached, wrapping me in his arms. "Hey, you."

"Hey."

"My parents are leaving soon and wanted to say good night. Mama has something to ask you."

"Okay."

He gave me an inquisitive look. "You okay? You look kind of depressed."

"Yeah." I sighed.

He gave me one of those "I don't believe you" looks. "Yeah, you're okay?" he asked. "Or, yeah, you're depressed?"

"Yeah." Another sigh escaped, this one a bit louder than the first.

"Is it that letdown thing?" D.J. gave me a pensive look.

"Letdown thing?"

"You know—after-wedding blues. You always seem to get them after a wedding is over."

"Do I?"

"Mm-hmm."

"Maybe it's partly that," I said. "I always crater when these big events are behind me. But there's something else too. Did you hear what my parents are going to do?"

"Oh, that thing about stealing your bedroom to make more space for Rosa and Laz? Converting it into an apartment with a beautiful Mediterranean theme and expensive decor?"

I groaned. "You knew?"

"Well, only since this morning. I didn't want to bother you with the news on a day like today. You had enough on your mind without thinking about that." He paused and pulled me close. "So, what's the verdict?"

"I'm moving in with Sophia."

He grinned. "That'll be fun."

"Maybe." I shrugged and forced a smile. "I'll be fine. Really. And I promise, I won't let anything get in the way of our big day, D.J. From this moment on, every thought will be about our wedding."

"Every thought?" He gestured to the messy reception hall.

"Hmm. Starting tomorrow," I said. Drawing in a deep breath, I looked at my sweet fiancé. "I'd better say good night to your parents. Where are they again?"

"Putting Mama's keyboard in the truck. They've got an early day tomorrow, so they're leaving soon."

"Okay." We walked outside, joining Earline and Dwayne Sr. for a few minutes.

"I'm sorry to leave so early, Bella," Earline said. "Twila, Bonnie Sue, and Jolene are going to stay and help, but I have to be at church by 8:30 tomorrow morning for choir practice, and I'm exhausted." At the word *exhausted*, I stifled a yawn, and Earline smiled.

"Sorry," I said with a shrug. "Guess I'm tired too."

"Well, if anyone deserves some rest, you do." She took my hand in hers and gazed into my eyes. "Listen to me, Bella. You're a wonderful girl. So giving. But you've got to take care of yourself. These next few weeks are going to be very hectic. Promise me you'll get the sleep you need and eat right?"

I nodded and then hugged her. "Thank you so much for loving me."

"Oh, honey. How could I do anything but?"

"D.J. said you wanted to talk to me about something," I said. "Was it about that?"

222

"No." She shook her head. "Dwayne and I wanted to talk to you about Christmas plans. We're having a group of people over on Christmas Day, and we were hoping your family could join us. I've already talked to your parents, and they love the idea, especially with Rosa and Laz gone."

"No doubt." I laughed. Mama hadn't cooked a Christmas dinner in sixteen years. "And with the construction going on, the house will be a mess. Sounds ideal to eat elsewhere."

D.J. slipped his arm around my waist, and I nestled against him, more exhausted than ever.

"Yes, I heard all about the construction," Earline said. "And with all your family has been through lately, I just thought it was fitting that I host Christmas this year. I'll be thrilled to have you. And of course Twila, Bonnie Sue, and Jolene will be there, along with a handful of others from our church. Hope that's okay."

"Okay? I can't think of a better way to spend Christmas."

"Wonderful. We're going to have the best time ever! And some amazing food to boot."

We spent a couple more minutes wrapping up the conversation and saying our good-byes. Their truck pulled away, and D.J. turned to face me. "I want to ditto what Mom said. You need to take care of yourself."

"I will." Another yawn escaped. "But first we have to whip this building into shape."

He kissed the tip of my nose and whispered some of the sweetest words of encouragement I'd ever heard. Then, with his hand in mine, we made our way back inside to face the chaos of the reception hall.

One thing I love about the Rossi family—we all know what it means to pitch in. Over the next few minutes we worked in

223

tandem, hauling dirty dishes to the kitchen and pulling table-cloths from the tables. I knew everyone was exhausted, especially Bubba and Jenna, but they worked like champs in spite of it. Twila offered the services of the Splendora trio but insisted they couldn't work in their fancy dresses. The three ladies headed off to the restroom to change into their regular clothes.

I took note of the band. I'd paid them in advance, and they hadn't asked for any overtime, even though the evening ran late. Looked like they were staying of their own accord. But who could blame them? They'd obviously fallen in love with the Rossi family, and vice versa. And I knew that Gordy and Sal had a lot to talk about.

Hmm. Thinking of Sal reminded me that he would be leaving soon, and knowing that broke my heart. I had a feeling it was breaking Bonnie Sue's heart too. Despite the admonitions of the other ladies, she had already given at least a small piece of her heart to Sal. I'd been watching her for much of the night, and her feelings for him were undeniable.

Oh well. No time to worry about that right now, not with so much work to be done.

I pulled out the trash cans and started tossing things. Mama took the wedding cake—what was left of it, anyway—into the kitchen and returned to deal with the near-empty punch bowl and utensils. Bianca and Bertina offered to help. Sal, looking a little weary, settled into a chair at one of the tables and began to box up the salt and pepper shakers.

As he reached for the broom, Pop took to grumbling, his usual post-wedding activity. Armando slipped out the back door, insisting he had other plans. *Sure you do. Sure you do.* Joey and Norah hung around, as always. Thankfully, Nick and Marcella were here too, working harder than the rest of us put together. What troupers!

Then I realized someone was missing. Two someones, actually. Sophia and Tony. Come to think of it, I hadn't seen them since Rosa and Laz pulled away in the limousine. Sneaky, for the two of them to disappear with so much work to be done! On the other hand, with Sophia gone, I didn't have the ever-present reminder that we were now roommates.

I caught a glimpse of Nick and Marcella approaching Gordy and the band. They spoke quietly together, and then my brother took the microphone. I looked his way, intrigued.

"Could we have everyone's attention?" Nick called out to anyone who would listen. "Mama. Pop. Everyone. We'd like to have you come back in the room for a minute, if you would."

"What is it, Nicholas?" Mama asked, the worry lines becoming evident.

"We've asked Gordy and the band to play a song," he said. "Just thought it might be something nice to listen to while everyone works, that's all."

The band began to play, and everyone got back to work. For a moment. A few measures into the song, I realized what I was hearing. "My Girl."

I turned to Marcella with a grin, realizing what they were up to. The music continued, and a couple of people in the room began to sing the words as they worked. When we got to the words, "I guess you'll say, what can make me feel this way," everyone in the place sang the words, "My girl!" in rousing chorus.

It took a minute, but Mama finally snapped to attention. She turned to Nick and Marcella, who worked alongside the rest of us, faces completely straight. "Wait a minute," Mama said, her eyes narrowing into slits. "Is there some reason you asked the band to play this particular song?"

Marcella shrugged, and a hint of a smile graced her lips. "Maybe."

Nick didn't look up; he just kept working.

"Are you trying to tell us—" Mama's hand flew to her mouth. "Are we . . . I mean, are we having a baby girl?"

When Marcella nodded, the whole place came alive with joyous shouts. I thought my mother was going to faint, but she managed to hold it together. Pop raced to Nick's side, wrapping him in a tight embrace. Joey and Norah drew near, as did the Italian aunties. I saw Deanna and Rocco smiling off in the distance. I felt sure the trio of Splendora sisters would be along shortly, once they heard all of the shouts and well wishes.

A few minutes into our celebration, Gordy took the microphone. "Um, ladies and gentlemen, I guess this would be as good a time as any to do this, since we're all celebrating anyway."

Several of us paused from our chatter to look his way.

A smile lit the band director's face. "I've got something I need to say, and I can't think of a finer time or place to say it."

At this, the room grew completely silent.

He extended his hand in Lilly's direction and asked her to join him in front of the band, which she did. Her eyes sparkled with excitement.

Gordy took her hand, gazing into her eyes. "Lilly, the boys and I have planned something special just for you."

"O-oh?"

"Yes." His cheeks turned red. "We've been so busy playing tonight that I didn't have an opportunity to ask you to dance. So I'm doing that now. Will you dance with me, Lilly?"

"Well, sure, Gordy." Her cheeks turned pink as she took his arm, and they made their way to the dance floor. The band began a slow melody. Gordy wasn't the dancer Sal was, but he wasn't half bad either. And with Lilly in his arms, he looked completely happy. The first few measures of the song drifted by, the melody strangely familiar. Odd. Didn't sound like a big-band tune. Sounded more like . . . what was that? Oh yes. A slightly jazzed-up version of "Could I Have This Dance for the Rest of My Life?"

Wait a minute . . .

My breath caught in my throat as I realized what we were watching. It didn't take Lilly long to realize it either. She halted, looking more than a little startled. At this point, Gordy knelt on one knee—not an easy task at his age—and took her hand. Her other hand flew up to her mouth, and she gasped. The band took this as the cue to lower their volume. Likely they wanted to hear this as much as the rest of us did.

Joey immediately reached for his camera. I had a feeling Lilly would be thanking him later.

"Lilly, I have something to ask you." Gordy's eyes twinkled. "Something I should've asked a long time ago. I would have too, but I'm an old fool."

"Oh no you're not," she said, putting her free hand on her hip and gazing into his eyes. "There's nothing foolish about you, Gordy."

"I'm asking you to marry me, Lilly." His eyes filled with tears, and Mama reached for a tissue—not for Gordy, but herself. And me. And Aunt Bianca.

The song reached its crescendo, and Gordy reached into his pocket, coming out with a small box. The ring inside must've been a real dazzler because Lilly took to squealing, which got all of us tickled. Seconds later, the ring was on her finger and Gordy was on his feet with his fiancée in his arms.

At this point, Twila, Bonnie Sue, and Jolene emerged from the restroom wearing their WHERE'S THE BEEF? T-shirts. Bonnie Sue took one look at the couple in the middle of the dance floor and gasped. "What did we miss?"

"Everything!" Mama said, dabbing at her eyes. "We're having a baby girl . . . and Gordy just proposed to Lilly!"

"Wait. You're having a baby?" Bonnie Sue gave my mother a look of true disbelief.

"No, silly. Marcella. She's having a girl."

"And Gordy asked Lilly to marry him," I repeated.

"We missed all the good stuff." Jolene pouted. "Do you think they'd do a repeat, just for us?"

"I don't think it would have the same punch," I said, "but Joey took pictures, and I'm sure he'd be happy to show them to you."

The ladies gathered around my brother and his camera, vying for a look at what they'd missed.

"It figures I'd miss something this big while I'm in the john," Bonnie Sue said with a pout. "Flush the toilet once, and look what happens!"

"You're not the only one who missed it." I swept the room with a glance, still looking for Sophia and Tony. My baby sister had missed the big moment too. I turned back to the ladies with a sigh. "Haven't seen my sister in a while."

"Oh, we saw her with that handsome hunk-a-boy, Tony," Jolene said. "I noticed them walking out to the gazebo just as we hit the restroom to change clothes. They had stars in their eyes."

As if to ditto her words, Sophia and Tony rushed into the room, their faces lit with joy. My sister approached Mama and Pop, babbling a hundred miles an hour. I could hardly make sense of her words. Only when she extended her left hand to show off the mega-diamond did it hit me.

Tony had proposed.

# 20

## Jingle Jangle

I call it the white zone—that place you slip into when you're in shock. The room starts spinning, and you wonder if perhaps you're dreaming. The moment I saw that monstrous ring on my little sister's finger, I slipped off into the white zone. Surely this couldn't be happening. Not . . . not now!

My sister's squeals brought me out of my fog, and I leaned forward to take another look. Yep. It was a ring, all right. At least a two-karat, marquise setting, white gold. A real dazzler, no doubt about it. Tony always did know how to shop. I had to give him that. He'd probably spent a fortune on this little number. He stood alongside Sophia, a crooked grin on his face, clearly happy with both the attention and the woman on his arm.

My sister dove into the story of how he had proposed in the gazebo. I could read the excitement in her eyes, her voice, and her stance. I'd seen Sophia happy before, of course. There was that time in tenth grade when she'd made the cheerleading squad. And then there was the time about a year ago when she discovered a local dermatologist was offering a special on tattooed eyeliner. That had really been cause for celebration. But nothing—repeat, nothing—could top the look of wonder in her eyes at this very moment.

Mama reacted swiftly and surely, erupting into tears. She threw her arms around Tony and welcomed him to the family. Ironic. She'd always known he was going to be her son-in-law someday. Hadn't I heard as much hundreds of times over in the three years when Tony was dating me? Turned out he did have the right address after all. And he'd finally come to his senses, landing the right girl.

Everyone gathered around the couple, offering well wishes. Pop, clearly thrilled, hollered out his feelings for all to hear. "Tonight the news is all good!" He slapped Tony on the back— a little too hard, which sent the poor guy jolting a couple of feet forward. "Welcome to the family, Son!" Pop hollered.

Gordy and Lilly, consummate pros that they were, headed back up to the stage, and the band lit into a celebratory tarantella once again. The family gathered around, pressing Sophia and Tony to the middle of the group, and danced in a circle around them, tears flowing like wine.

Mine flowed too, but for a completely different reason. Sure, I was thrilled for Sophia and Tony. Who wouldn't be? The news *was* all good, just like Pop said. But it was ill-timed at best. *Lord, what happened to my wedding? Is it going to get lost in the chaos of everyone else's good news?*

Just as quickly, I chided myself. If anyone deserved to fall in love, it was my precious younger sister.

When the dance ended, congratulations poured forth. Nick lifted a glass and offered a toast to the happy couples. We all joined in with a vibrant, *"Salude!"*

Out of the corner of my eye, I caught a glimpse of Emilio, who looked like he might cry at any second. I'd never figured him to be the emotional sort, but he just might prove me wrong. He headed to the microphone and lifted his glass. I raised mine again, sure he was about to toast the happy couples. Instead, he floored me with his words.

"I am so happy to be here with my family on this special night." Emilio's voice cracked on the word *night*, and I gave him an encouraging smile. "Francesca and I have had a wonderful time here, and we are so delighted to share our news."

*Your news?* My mind reeled. I turned to look at Francesca, who beamed, her eyes now filled with tears.

"Francesca told me this morning that I am going to be a papa!"

For a second, no one moved. Then D.J.—God bless him—lifted his glass and hollered, "To the newest Rossi!"

We all echoed, "To the newest Rossi," then the stampede began. Mama, Bianca, Bertina, Sophia, and I rushed Francesca, whose eyes were filled with tears. At this point, Emilio was a blubbering mess.

"How did you find out?" Mama asked Francesca. "Tell me everything."

"I suspected as much on the plane ride from Napoli," she said. "I spent half of the flight in the restroom feeling sick to my stomach. But I wasn't sure. Yesterday Marcella brought me one of those little . . ." She spoke a few words in Italian, which Mama translated.

"Home pregnancy tests?"

"Yes." Francesca nodded. "I took the test this morning and showed it to Emilio. He was so happy." A lone tear made its way down her cheek. "And I am so happy too! I have wanted to be a mama for years!"

231

"This is wonderful news!" Bertina said. "And you must let us host a shower once our new wedding facility is built. What a party we will have!"

"I must apologize," Francesca said with a sigh. "I have not been myself this week. I've been having . . ." She shifted into Italian again, but I got the gist of it. Morning sickness. Turned out she'd been sick all week. What we'd taken for standoffishness was really morning sickness. Who knew?

The congratulations continued for a good long while. I'd never seen so many happy people. Nick and Marcella. Gordy and Lilly. Sophia and Tony. Emilio and Francesca. The Rossi clan was in celebration overload.

After a few more toasts, Sophia headed my way with tears in her eyes. "Oh, Bella! Can you believe it? I'm engaged!"

"I'll admit, I'm surprised." I took her hand and gave it a squeeze. "But probably not as surprised as you are. Did you expect it?"

"No." She giggled. "He caught me completely off guard." She leaned in to whisper, "Oh, but if you could have heard the things he said just before he proposed. No one has ever said such sweet things to me before. He's the one, Bella. I don't know what took me so long to figure it out!"

*Possibly the fact that he was dating your sister until seven months ago?*

"I'm actually getting *married*." Sophia's look of bliss quickly shifted to one of terror. "Oh no!"

"What?"

"I'm getting *married*, and I don't have a clue what I want my wedding to be like." She sighed. "You've had yours planned since you were little, but me . . ." She shrugged. "I never really thought much about it."

"Have you two discussed a date?"

232

"Not really." She chewed her lip, finally looking at me with a shrug. "Summer?"

"Okay. Sounds good." This idea settled well with me, since it gave me more time to focus on my own wedding first. "You've always been nuts about the beach. Have you ever given any thought to getting married there?"

"Oh, wow." She grinned. "I have always loved the beach. Might be fun. I'll have to talk to Tony, of course. He might have something else in mind. I don't know."

"Well, Rome wasn't built in a day," I reminded her. "And you don't have to decide everything right away. Take a few days to enjoy being engaged. And remember, you're not just planning for one day. You're planning for a lifetime together."

She reached over to give me a hug. "That's why you're the wedding coordinator, Bella. You always know just what to say. Me? I would botch everything up. I . . . I'm so glad I have you." Her face lit into a smile. "And I'm so happy we're going to be roommates! I'll have you to myself night and day. We can work on my wedding together around the clock!"

Apparently my parents had already talked to her about sharing rooms. Wonderful. I stifled a groan and diverted my gaze. How in the world would I ever get my own wedding planned now? Her enthusiasm would surely keep me scattered for days—or even weeks—to come.

*Stay calm, Bella. Let your sister have her moment. Remember how excited you were the night you got engaged. How excited you still are.* I chided myself for any and all selfish thoughts.

"Oh, Bella . . ." Sophia reached to hug me, and I felt her shoulders heaving in and out as she began to cry. "I'm so happy. So completely, deliriously happy."

At once she began to talk about her wedding. On and on

she went, telling me about the colors, the food, the music, the bridesmaids' dresses, and her gown. So much for not having given it a thought till now. Sounded like the girl had all sorts of ideas, most of them pretty grandiose. Maybe a little too grandiose for a beach theme.

I wanted to focus, I really did. But everything was running together in my head. My wedding. Hers. Lilly and Gordy's engagement. Rosa and Laz's ceremony.

I needed to rest. To lay my head on my pillow in my room and gather my thoughts. Perhaps then I could make sense of all this. After I cleaned up this reception hall, anyway.

Sophia went off on her merry way, chatting with the others about her big day. I went back to my work but was interrupted by a familiar voice. Lilly. I turned to face her, unable to hide my smile.

"Congratulations!" I gave her a hug.

"Bella, it looks like we have another wedding to plan! I'm so excited about my big day!"

"Well, of course!" I tried to collect my thoughts, but they wouldn't cooperate.

"I was thinking of a fifties soda shop theme," she said with a grin. "How does that sound? With all of the bells and whistles. Or rather, all of the sodas and cheeseburgers!" She laughed and then leaned in to whisper, "Gordy said cost was no object, so let's do this up big. I want it to be the wedding of the century."

Funny. I'd used the same words to describe my own wedding. The one that was rapidly slipping through my fingers.

"Can we go ahead and set a date?" Lilly asked. "That way I can start making plans."

"Um, sure. What were you thinking?"

She pursed her lips, apparently deep in thought. "March

would be good. In the little chapel. How many people does it seat?"

"A hundred and fifty. Maybe one seventy-five, but it's a tight squeeze."

"One fifty is great. We won't have that many, anyway. Do you have your calendar?"

"Come with me to my office, and we'll get this taken care of." Though my feet ached and my brain reeled, I led the way into my office. Switching on the light, I gestured for Lilly to take a seat. I opened my calendar and thumbed through it, skipping right past my own wedding date in mid-February to the beginning of March.

"I have a Saturday evening available in mid-March," I said. "Would that work?"

"Sounds lovely. A March bride." She giggled. "I'm thinking about having the bridesmaids wear poodle skirts. What do you think of that idea? Fun, right? And when I say soda shop, I'm thinking of the real deal—we'll have hot fudge sundaes and chocolate malts and hamburgers and—" She shook her head, tears filling her eyes. "Oh, Bella! It's going to be so wonderful! I can hardly wait."

"M-me either." I braved a smile.

"We'll decorate the room and have some of the guys in the band serve as soda jerks. They'll be so cute, don't you think?"

"I do."

"And Gordy. Maybe I can talk him into wearing something fiftyish." She giggled. "Oh, we're gonna have so much fun!"

As she lit into a lengthy discussion about her plans, the door swung open and Norah entered. I looked up at my future sister-in-law, relieved for the interruption. I'd have to remember to thank her later.

"Bella! There you are." Norah took a few steps into the room and then paused. "Oh, sorry. I interrupted your meeting."

"No." With a wave of her hand, Lilly dismissed that idea and stood. "We were just wrapping up. I've worn Bella out with my ideas."

"No, it's fine." I gave her what I hoped was a comforting smile.

Norah approached Lilly and gave her a hug. "Congratulations, Lilly. I'm so thrilled for you. Now we're both engaged."

"Oh, that's right." Lilly's face lit up even more than before—if that was possible. "I totally forgot you and Joey are engaged. When is your big day?"

"Well, actually . . ." Norah paused and looked my way. "That's what I wanted to talk to Bella about."

*Yikes!*

"Bella, I know you've been really busy," Norah said.

"Yes." I pushed my calendar aside and nodded. "But it's all good."

"Okay. Well, we haven't really talked about this, but Joey and I have been engaged for a while now." She paused. "I'm ready to start thinking ahead, and I want you to plan the wedding for me." She smiled. "I want to have it here, of course."

"Of course!" I grinned and reached for my calendar once again. "When?"

"Early spring? Will that give you enough time after your big day?'

"Why, that's when Gordy and I are getting married too," Lilly said, taking a seat once again. "How fun that we're both getting married so close together." She looked at me and smiled. "All three of us, I mean!"

"S-sure," I managed. "Did you have a theme in mind, Norah, or were you planning to do a traditional wedding?"

She pursed her lips. "Hmm. Haven't given that a lot of thought. I guess something with a Victorian garden party theme would be nice, since it's springtime. And outdoors. Maybe in April?"

"April showers bring May flowers," I reminded her. "You might want to shoot for May." Hopefully she'd push this back a bit. Give me some breathing room.

"I'll talk to Joey and we'll decide. In the meantime, I'll put my thoughts down on paper. Just wanted to let you know."

"I think the Victorian theme will be so pretty, don't you?" Lilly said. "I can just picture it now. For you, not me. I'm going a completely different direction."

"Yes, I can see it now," Norah said. "We'll have those little cucumber sandwiches and scones and lemon curd and all sorts of yummy delights. An honest-to-goodness garden party. We can decorate the gazebo with flowers. It's going to be so pretty."

"Sounds amazing." My stomach grumbled, and I realized that somehow, in the chaos of the night, I'd forgotten to eat. How did I manage that with the best food in the world at my disposal? Hmm. Maybe I could grab a sandwich when I got home. If I ever got home.

My discussion with Norah and Lilly ended a few minutes later. I'm pretty sure they noticed the constant yawning on my end. At any rate, Norah finally headed off to find Joey, and Lilly bounced out of the room, filled with zeal. I turned off the light in my office and sighed, completely exhausted— mind, body, and spirit.

D.J. met me at the door of my office, sweeping me into his arms. "I had a feeling I might find you in here."

"Yeah. Still working." I yawned. "What time is it?"

"Midnight. Your coach has turned back into a pumpkin. And the prince . . ." He gestured to himself. "Well, he's on the lookout for glass slippers."

"I love you, D.J." Giving him a tender kiss seemed the only appropriate thing to do. I lingered in his arms.

"You doing okay tonight, Bella Bambina?" he asked.

"I'm exhausted. And I'm worried."

"About . . . ?"

"All of these weddings!" I told him everything—about Lilly and her soda shop dreams. Sophia and her beach-themed extravaganza. Norah and her Victorian tea party.

He brushed a loose hair from my face, still holding me close. "Well, my mom always said there was only one way to handle several things at once. You've got to decide what's most important and do that first. Then choose the next most important thing and do that."

"Our wedding is the most important thing," I assured him. "I'm not going to let anything get in the way of that, I promise. Nothing."

"I'm not worried about it, Bella. We're going to have a great wedding. But even if you come down the aisle in jeans and a T-shirt, I'm still marrying you. Well, if you promise to wear your boots, I mean. For me, it's not about the frills. It's about the woman I'm marrying. I hope you know that."

Holy Toledo. If that didn't stop my heart from beating, I didn't know what would. Where did I find this guy again, anyway? Oh yeah. On sunny Galveston Island.

"Don't forget, babe, God never gives you more than you can bear. He trusts you with all of this, and I don't blame him. You've got the goods to see this through. You're a wonder."

"Th-thanks." I blinked back tears, overcome at his compliments.

After a few more consoling words from the man I loved, I felt strengthened from the inside out. We walked through the wedding facility, turned out lights, and met up with the rest of my family in the reception hall.

Minutes later, I kissed my honey good-bye. He headed back to his condo, reminding me that we would see each other in the morning at church. I stifled a yawn and headed toward home with my family members on my heels.

Deanna caught me as we walked back to the house. "I hate to do this to you tonight, Bella, with all you're going through. But we leave in the morning, and I really need to pick your brain about the wedding facility we're going to open in Napoli. Do you think we could talk? Early tomorrow morning, maybe? I have so many ideas, but I want to run them by you first. Oh, and I want to talk to you about my own wedding."

I looked at her and gasped. "Deanna! Did Rocco propose?"

"No." She shook her head. "But tonight, when he saw Gordy on his knees, he told me I would be next." Her smile quickly faded. "Of course, we had no way of knowing Sophia was receiving a proposal at that very moment, so I suppose technically she was next. But you get the idea. He's going to propose very soon. And ours will be the first wedding in our new facility—if things go as planned, anyway." She began to describe the type of wedding she wanted to have. Traditional Italian fare, of course. I could only imagine getting married in Napoli. How wonderful would that be?

We continued our conversation all the way home. When we opened the door to the house, the sound of Guido's voice rang out. "When the moon hits your eye like a big pizza pie!" We all laughed, wondering if perhaps he'd heard us from next door.

After saying our good nights, I dragged my way up the stairs, wondering if I would make it without collapsing. My feet ached. My back didn't want to straighten. And I had a whopper headache. The worst I'd had in months, actually.

Nothing a hot bath wouldn't cure. I ran the tub and settled into the bubbles, deep in thought. I relived the moment where Father Michael pronounced Laz and Rosa husband and wife. Then I jolted, realizing they were now enjoying their first night together at the Tremont. I quickly shifted my thoughts to Lilly and Gordy, smiling as I remembered the way he had proposed—through a dance. Talk about unique. And then there was Sophia. The look of delight on her face would remain with me for some time. In spite of my knee-jerk reaction, I was truly thrilled for her.

Deep in thought, I almost dozed off in the tub. Only when the bubbles tickled my chin did I realize I'd almost gone under. Time to dry off and hit the hay.

Hit the hay. Hmm. Just thinking about sleeping in my bed made me a little sad. Would this be the last time? Unfortunately, I was too tired to really enjoy it.

I'd just settled into bed when my phone rang. I recognized Jenna's number. I answered with the words, "Everything okay?" After all, she rarely called in the middle of the night.

"Yeah, I guess."

"What is it?" I asked.

"I don't mind saying I'm a little jealous."

"What do you mean?"

She sighed. "Bubba and I got married on a cruise ship.

What I witnessed tonight was a real wedding. A real, honest-to-goodness"—she sniffled—"wedding."

"Oh, Jenna! You're wishing you hadn't eloped?"

"Oh, I'm glad I'm married," she said through her tears. "I just wish Bubba and I had shared our big day with friends. I still want to have a real wedding, Bella. More so now than ever!"

"Of course! When I get back from my honeymoon, let's start making plans. That's what I was trying to say the other day. You need a special day. Every bride does."

"You don't think people will think that's weird? Or pre-sumptuous?"

"Of course not. You can renew your wedding vows. People do it all the time. Maybe, if the weather cooperates, you can get married in the gazebo and we'll have a beautiful afternoon event. Maybe even a Hawaiian luau. Anything you like."

"Mmm. A luau sounds perfect! Just what the doctor or-dered. But you know Bubba. He'll want a roasted pig at the reception. I can just see it now."

I laughed. "If I know Bubba, he'll be the one roasting the pig himself. But it doesn't matter. Whatever the two of you want, you will have. I'll make it happen."

"I love you, Bella."

"I love you too."

We ended the call, and I rested my head against the pillow, smiling as I thought of my friend's desire for a real wedding. Who could blame her? Every girl wanted to have her big day. To wear the white dress. To walk the aisle.

I know I did. In fact, I'd wanted that from the time I was a little girl, and now that I'd found Prince Charming, I wanted it more than ever!

With my eyes squeezed shut, I tried to focus on my upcoming wedding. It was going to be perfect. Beautiful! Beachy and light.

No, that was Sophia's plan, not mine. Mine was going to be a fifties-themed event, with soda jerks and chocolate malts.

No, wait. That was Lilly and Gordy. They wanted the fifties wedding.

Again I tried to focus on my wedding, dreaming of scones and lemon curd, served up with tiny cups of tea in a vintage setting. But I had the wrong wedding once again. That was Norah's, not mine. D.J. and I were the ones with the roasted pig. The luau. What a great night that was going to be!

No, wait. That didn't sound right either.

I slugged my pillow, determined to reel in my wayward thoughts, but they all tumbled madly through my brain.

The Boot-Scootin' wedding I'd coordinated this summer.

The medieval extravaganza I'd hosted over the fall.

Tonight's forties swing event.

Sophia's beach-themed wedding.

Lilly's soda shop wedding.

Norah's Victorian garden party.

Deanna's Napoli nuptials.

Jenna's tropical luau.

On and on my thoughts churned, everything overlapping in my brain. For whatever reason, I couldn't seem to get things straight, especially when I thought about the plans for my own wedding. I'd planned to have roses, right? And a Valentine's theme? We were going to get married indoors, not outdoors. At the wedding facility, not the beach.

Right?

Exhaustion kicked in, and I just wanted to sleep. Surely all of this would make more sense in the morning. I rolled over in the bed and punched the pillow one final time. A thousand emotions rushed over me at once.

Sitting up, I looked at my four-poster bed, contemplating the fact that this could very well be the last time I ever slept in it.

Suddenly, I was overcome with emotion. A lump the size of a baseball rose in my throat, and tears quickly followed. In spite of my promise to D.J. that my every thought would be about our wedding, I found myself thinking about everything . . . but that.

# 21

## Am I Blue?

Sunday morning was bittersweet. After a rushed conversation with Deanna about the Italian Club Wed, we had just enough time for a quick breakfast with the family before they caravanned back to the airport. I capitalized on my time with Francesca, feeling pretty bad about how I'd judged her. Her cheeks glowed with anticipation this morning, and I could read the excitement in her eyes.

"Oh, Bella, when will I see you again?" she asked, gripping my hand.

I shrugged. "I don't know." I offered a little pout. "I wish you could come back for my wedding, but I know it's a lot to ask."

"Oh, we would come in a heartbeat, but I think we'd better limit our travels, now that I'm . . ." Her cheeks flushed again. "Now that we have a little bambina coming."

"Bambina?" Mama looked her way. "Are you hoping for a girl?"

"Oh, a girl would be wonderful," Francesca said with a smile. "But a son would be wonderful too." She gazed at Emilio with love pouring from her eyes. "If he's anything like his papa, he will be a wonderful man someday."

A sigh went up from the women, and Pop slapped his brother on the back. "You will make a fine father, Emilio Rossi!"

We ate our breakfast at the dining room table, voices overlapping as always. I couldn't help but wonder how things were going for Rosa and Laz. Had they boarded the helicopter yet? Were they on their way to the airport in style? I felt sure we would hear all about it later.

When our meal ended, a flurry of activity began. Pop and Emilio had the vehicles loaded in no time, and we all stood on the veranda, saying our good-byes. Because the week had been so chaotic, I really didn't feel like I'd had enough time with Bianca and Bertina, but nothing could be done about that now. I offered warm hugs and plenty of thanks for their help.

Turning to Deanna, I found myself getting emotional. "I'm going to miss you most of all," I whispered.

"Same here." She gave me a hug. "But I'm going to call you—a lot! We have so much to talk about now."

"Yes, we do. Promise me you'll give Rosa my love when you see her at the airport."

"Of course!" Deanna headed off to my father's car with Rocco's arm looped through hers.

My aunts lingered on the veranda, dabbing tears from their eyes and gushing over Mama in Italian. Finally, the moment arrived. The Italian contention had to leave, and the Texas contention had to get dressed for church.

Less than an hour after the relatives headed off, Mama and I walked through the door of our church, ready for a great worship service. I smiled as I saw D.J. talking to the pastor in the foyer. What little I overheard was about our new house. Funny. I'd hardly given it a second thought since D.J. had brought it up on Wednesday. Surely he hadn't started working on it yet, right? From the sound of things, he was getting close. Good thing I'd left that situation to him. I had enough on my mind already.

After a great church service, we spent Sunday afternoon gathered together in the living room watching football. Well, most of us were watching the game. I drifted off, unable to fight the weight of my eyelids any longer. I was awakened by Pop's firm voice.

"Bella Bambina, it's time to start clearing out your room. The workers are coming first thing tomorrow morning, and I'd like to have the big stuff out of there by then."

I looked at him with panic setting in. Surely he would give me one more night. The construction guys could help tomorrow.

On the other hand, we would have to pay them for their time. No point in paying them to move my furniture into the garage when we could handle it ourselves.

D.J. reached for my hand and gave it a squeeze. "Don't worry, baby," he whispered. "I'm going to walk you through this. It'll be a piece of cake, I promise."

I trudged up the stairs on Pop's heels, D.J. following close behind me. When we reached my room, I opened the door and paused for a moment to take it all in. I didn't want to miss a thing. This was the last time I would see my bedroom in its normal, natural state. Next time it would be a shell—empty of all furniture. After that, it would be a part of Rosa and Laz's new suite. Swallowing the lump in my throat, I forged ahead.

D.J., Pop, and Joey spent the next hour taking my bed apart and moving it into the garage. After that, they moved my dresser and night tables. I took the clothes—the ones from my dresser and the ones in my closet—into Sophia's room. Unfortunately, I caught her napping. She awoke with a start.

"B-Bella?"

"It's me, hon. Don't panic. I'm just bringing in my things."

"Already?"

"Yes."

She sat up in bed and looked at the clock. "Wow, it's after five?"

"Yeah, you've been asleep for hours."

"I was tired." She yawned. "Planning a wedding takes a lot out of a girl."

"Tell me about it." I bit my tongue, determined not to say any more.

I roused her from the bed with the promise of hot coffee, and she joined us, carrying my things from my room to hers. Well, most of my things, anyway. Many of them were going to the garage, for lack of a better place.

"This is going to be so much fun, Bella," she said with a giggle. "Like when we were little girls in Atlantic City. Remember, we shared a room?"

"Yes." I smiled at the memory of our pink bedroom with its twin beds.

"Having a roomie is going to make me feel young again." Sophia gave me a look of wide-eyed wonder, a child once more. I smiled in response, convinced we could make a go of this. In fact, we would probably look back on this season of our lives with great fondness. Once we were old and gray, anyway. In the meantime, we still had a lot of work left to do.

By the time the sun set, my room was empty. Well, all but a few dust bunnies, which D.J. told me not to worry about.

"The construction guys will be blowing up all sorts of dust," he said.

"Okay." I paused, looking around at the shell of a room, my heart in my throat. Squeezing my eyes shut helped ease the pain. When I opened them, I decided a little action was in order. "Is anyone hungry?" I asked, my stomach grumbling.

"Starving," Pop said.

We all looked at each other, unsure of what to do next. This was the point in the day when Rosa would call us all down to dinner, after all. I looked at Mama, hopeful. She stifled a yawn.

"Sorry." After a pause, she said, "We have plenty of leftovers from the wedding. Want to help me in the kitchen, girls?"

Sophia and I headed downstairs on our mother's heels. This would be the first time in years the three of us had entered the Rossi kitchen alone to prepare a meal. We were entering hallowed territory. I could almost sense Rosa's essence in the place. Looking over at the hook on the wall, I saw her tomato-stained aprons. I reached for one and handed it to Mama.

"Just isn't the same without Rosa here, is it?" my mother said, slipping the apron on.

"No, not the same at all."

Having Rosa gone for this month wasn't the only change. It felt like the whole house was in a state of flux right now.

"Where do you suppose they are right now?" I asked.

"They should be in Rome in a few hours. And then on to Napoli." She reached for a tray of leftovers and placed it on the countertop.

I heard Guido singing "Amazing Grace" off in the distance. For whatever reason, I felt a little emotional, thinking of how Laz would have enjoyed that. My thoughts were interrupted by the phone ringing in Pop's office. A couple of minutes later, my father entered the kitchen. He reached to grab a piece of bread.

"Who was it, Cosmo?" Mama asked.

"Sal. He's on his way over to talk to us about Guido."

"To talk about Guido, or to take Guido back to Atlantic City?"

"Not sure." Pop shrugged. "He just said he wanted to talk."

We all grew strangely silent. Looked like the moment had finally arrived. A few months ago, we would have taken the news of Guido's leaving with a sense of relief, but now . . . well, now the goofy parrot was part of the family.

"Maybe we can talk Sal into leaving him here for further rehabilitation," I said. "It could happen."

"No, Bella." Mama gave me a sympathetic look. "Sal needs that bird too much for us to be selfish. And besides, we trained Guido up in the way he should go so that he could actually . . . well, you know . . . go."

"I suppose."

"He will have an impact on Sal's life, I just feel it," Pop said. "We'll trust God. He knows what's ahead far better than we do."

By the time Sal arrived a few minutes later, we had almost finished preparing the food. Mama carried it into the dining room, and we all gathered around the table.

"Sorry to come so late," Sal said. "Didn't mean to intrude on your dinnertime."

"Not at all," Mama said. "We hope you will stay, of course. Join us, Sal."

He smiled. "Don't mind if I do. A family dinner sounds good." He pushed back a yawn as he took his seat. "Sorry. I've been resting today. It's been a long week."

"No doubt about that." Pop took his seat at the head of the table, and we all followed suit. From the serious look on Sal's face, I knew I'd want to hear what he had to say. D.J. took a seat next to me.

Guido's voice rang out from the next room, a warbling version of "Amazing Grace," but a powerful one nonetheless. In fact, I wasn't sure when I'd ever heard anything sweeter.

"Sounds like Guido really likes it here," Sal commented, placing his napkin in his lap.

"He does," Mama said, gesturing for all of us to fill our plates. "He fits right in."

"Yes, he fits right in." Sal paused, and the strangest look came over him. "I like it here too."

"Oh?" Pop looked at him with a smile. "You mean, on Galveston Island, or you like being with the Rossi family?"

"Both." A hint of a smile graced Sal's lips. "I like the island. No doubt about that. And you Rossis are, well . . ." He paused and shook his head. "You're different, that's for sure." He took the bowl of chicken cacciatore and began to dish up a healthy serving.

"Different?" I asked, reaching for the fettuccini.

"Well, different from a lot of people I've known. In a good way." Sal offered a somber smile. "Let's just leave it at that."

"What are you saying, Sallie?" Mama asked, cutting to the chase. "Are you thinking about staying?"

When he nodded, the whole room came alive with opinions on the matter. All good, of course.

Sal smiled at our enthusiastic response. "I think I would like to stay, at least for a few months. Ride out the winter. It's warmer here."

"We'll help you find a place near the water," I said with a smile. "That way you'll feel like you're in Atlantic City again."

"No need for that." Sal's smile widened. "I've got a place, at least a temporary one. Might end up being permanent. We'll see."

"You do?" we all said in unison. Well, all but D.J., who just offered a suspicious grin. Why did I get the feeling he knew exactly what Sal was talking about?

"Yes, my friend here"—Sal pointed to D.J.—"has offered to let me share his condo for a few weeks."

"It's the perfect solution," D.J. said, looking my way. "When we get married, Sal can buy the condo from me. I won't need it anymore. Until then, he can stay in my room and I'll bunk on the couch."

"Wow." I shook my head. "When was all of this decided?"

"Last night, just before the wedding. We had a long talk."

"Does Laz know?" I asked.

"No. I wanted to surprise him," Sal said. "I hope he likes the idea."

"Are you kidding?" Pop grinned. "He's going to think this is the best news in the world. Ah, Sal, you have no idea how much Laz loves you. He always has. You're like a brother to him."

"I . . . I feel the same." Sal's eyes filled with tears. "I don't know what it is about you people." He gestured to the whole group of us. "There's something different about you Rossis, as I said. Whatever it is, it's contagious. And I have to admit . . ." He choked back a few tears and forged ahead. "I have to admit, you're the only family I've got. Without all of you, I'm just a lonely old man."

"Oh, Sal!" I rose from my seat and gave him a warm hug. Mama and Pop gathered around us, and before long, we were one sappy mess.

Pop finally took his seat and continued filling his plate, his eyes brimming over with tears. "Sal, I want you to know something," he said. "You are family. And you are welcome in this house anytime." He shifted to Italian. I couldn't make out all of the words, but the intent was clear. They were welcoming words. Words of love. No doubt Sal found our family irresistible. The former mobster had stumbled into a place where people loved genuinely, gave freely, and extended a helping hand when needed.

Speaking of extending a helping hand . . . I looked at D.J., who watched over Sal like a mother hen. Looked like the Lord was truly up to something here. I could almost read the love for this older man in D.J.'s expression. No doubt my fiancé would be the perfect antidote for Sal's loneliness. I could also see something else good coming of this. D.J. had that sweet, gentle kind of faith, the kind that drew people to him and to the Lord. If Sal moved into D.J.'s place, even for a few weeks, the possibilities were endless. Not only would Sal get a genuine friend, he would have a daily dose of D.J.'s quiet yet consistent faith. He would learn what it meant to walk with the Lord.

"What about Guido?" Mama asked, interrupting my thoughts. "Will you take him to the condo, or will he be staying with us?"

"Never really thought about it," Sal said with a shrug. "What do you think?"

"Well, if you were going back to Atlantic City, I would say take him with you. But since you're staying on the island . . ." Mama grinned, offering a shrug. "Well, he does seem to like it here, Sallie."

Off in the next room, Guido shifted to "Ninety-Nine Bottles of Beer on the Wall." We all responded with laughter.

"He's definitely entertaining," Pop threw in.

"*And* you can see that we've been a great influence on him," I added as the bird lit into another verse.

We all shared another laugh at that one. Still, in my heart, I knew we had been a good influence, not just on Guido, but on Sal as well. He saw something in the Rossi family, something that drew him to us. And, in some strange way, we were drawn to him as well. It wasn't just the fact that he was Uncle Laz's friend. No, there was something deeper going on here. Something more profound. I had the keenest sense that God was about to do something big in Sal Lucci's life—and in the lives of the Rossi family.

Somehow, just knowing that gave me the energy I needed to face the next few weeks.

# 22

## String of Pearls

That night I slept in Sophia's room for the first time. I tried to be a good sport about it—on many different levels and in many different ways. Her double bed was a lot harder than mine. I didn't mind that part so much. What really got to me was fitting the dog in between us and listening to Sophia complain about it. Precious didn't take kindly to this new setup either, even going so far as to growl at my sister on at least one occasion. Okay, two occasions. She was a creature of habit. So was I, actually. We finally settled into semi-reasonable positions—Precious and I both shoved to one side—when my eyelids grew heavy.

I was almost asleep when Sophia nudged me. "Bella, you awake?"

"Hmm?" I rolled over and looked at her through squinted eyes, trying to make out her face in the darkness. "W-what?"

"Oh good, you're awake." She giggled. "I've been thinking about my wedding and I'm ready to start making plans."

*Oh, honey . . . please not now!*

"Tony and I talked today," she said. "He doesn't like the beach idea. You know him, Bella. He's so . . . high-class. He wants all the bells and whistles. Something people will talk about for years to come."

"Mm-hmm." I closed my eyes, hoping she would take the hint. No such luck.

"Anyway, he's thinking we should get married at the church. I like that idea. Then we want to do a huge reception at the wedding facility. Nothing quirky or odd. No themes. Just really, really elegant."

*Kind of like my wedding, you mean?*

"So, when were you thinking?" I did my best to keep my voice steady but could hear the nervous vibrato.

"We talked about that part a lot," she said. "And we've decided we can't wait till summer. We're hoping to pull this off by early March."

"Early March?" My eyes popped open, and I sat straight up in bed. Was she kidding? No, from the look of confidence in her expression, she honestly believed it possible.

"I know you, Bella," she said. "You're so fast. And thorough. You can pull off a great wedding in just a few weeks. I watched you do it with that Boot-Scootin' wedding this summer. And the medieval one too. You're a pro. So I'm counting on you."

"Well, yes, but—"

"Tony says you're the best in the business and we're blessed to have you. I told him he's right. Who else gets the very best?" She sighed, and I tried to think of something to say in response. Instead, I only managed a yawn. Sophia finally took the hint. "You're sleepy. We can talk more about this tomorrow. Sweet dreams, big sister."

"Sweet dreams, little sister."

I rolled back over, thinking through what she'd said. In spite of her glowing comments, I still didn't think I could pull off a high-end wedding less than a month after my own. However, this wasn't the right time to tell her so. I would save that for tomorrow. Or the next day. Surely all of this would make more sense after I'd slept on it.

With Precious curled up at my legs, I found myself hovering at the edge of the bed, truly uncomfortable—on many levels. I managed to stay put, finally dozing off.

Perhaps Sophia's words of encouragement stuck with me through the night. I awoke the next morning, convinced I could handle the ever-growing influx of weddings as long as I kept myself on a practical schedule. Anxious to implement a plan, I dressed and headed next door, going straight to my office. Once there, I turned on my computer and faced it with a brave smile, offering up a quick prayer to the Lord for his intervention and guidance. If I ever needed his help, it was now.

"You can do this, Bella," I chided myself. "People do it every day."

By 10:00 I had run through the checklist for my wedding and had made a couple of corresponding calls. At 11:00 I called for Sophia to join me, and we put together a plan of action for her big day. With Tony now running the show on that one, I had my work cut out for me. Only the best for my former boyfriend and his fiancée.

By the time Sophia left my office, I felt strong. Invincible. Capable of just about anything. Within reason, of course.

At 12:00 straight up, D.J. called. His words, "Hey, you,

I'm next door," caught me off guard until I remembered that construction—or rather, destruction—was set to begin today. I rose and looked out of the window. Sure enough, his Dodge 4x4 sat in the driveway of my house, along with several other work vehicles.

"Can you come over for a few minutes and take a look at our plans?" he asked. "I think you'll be impressed."

Feeling confident about my workload, I agreed. "Sure. Give me five minutes and I'll be there."

After tidying up a couple of loose ends—putting away the punch bowl and starting a load of tablecloths in the commercial washer—I walked through the front door of the house, overwhelmed by people and stuff. I'd never heard so much noise in all of my life. Saws. Hammers. And the people! Men trudged up and down the stairs at will, carrying the dust of their labors with them. Man. Looked like these guys didn't waste any time. When they got to work, they got to work.

D.J. was in the thick of it. So was Bubba, who shuffled back and forth between the various workers and the makeshift office. He and D.J. had transformed Armando's room into a hub of sorts and gave their instructions from there.

As I made my way through the crowd toward D.J., an unusual pain gripped my upper abdomen, and I leaned forward, trying to catch my breath.

"You okay, Bella?" Mama said, passing by. "You don't look like you feel well."

"I . . . I guess I'm okay." Straightening up, I rubbed my stomach. "That was the weirdest sensation. For a minute I couldn't catch my breath."

"Better keep an eye on that." She gave me a pensive look, then trudged up the stairs behind a couple of guys wearing tool belts.

I entered Armando's room to spend a few minutes with D.J. Unfortunately, I caught him in the middle of a conversation with a guy wearing a very large tool belt and a construction hat. I stood at a distance, marveling at how professional D.J. sounded.

"Finish taking down those two walls," he said, pointing at the plans. "And clear the debris. Then we'll talk plumbing. Just be careful. Make sure the main is turned off so we don't have any floods."

"Floods, eh?" I said after the construction worker left. "Should I build an ark?"

"Nah. We've got this under control." He pulled me into his arms. "I'm glad you're here. I wanted to talk to you about—"

He never had an opportunity to finish his sentence because we were interrupted by my father, who came in the room wearing a pair of jeans, an undershirt, and an impressive tool belt. Now, I'd known my father all my life, obviously, but had never seen him lift a tool. Well, other than, say, a screwdriver or a pair of pliers. Did he really think he would be helping these guys?

"Pop?" I gave him an inquisitive look. "What are you doing?"

"I figured, if you can't beat 'em, join 'em!" He lifted the hanger in his hand. "I always did like tearing things down, and this is the perfect opportunity." His gaze narrowed. "The walls are coming down, Bella Bambina! The walls are coming down."

An older man wearing overalls came in the room and distracted D.J. The two dove into a conversation about plumbing, and I stood in the background, not wanting to interrupt. Still, I wondered what had D.J. so excited. I could tell from the look on his face he had something exciting to tell me.

Finally, the moment arrived. He looked my way with that crooked grin of his, the one I loved so much. "Bella, I bought the house."

"W-what?"

"The house I told you about last week at the beach. The one just a few blocks from here. I closed on it this morning."

"But . . ." I shook my head. "How did you go to closing without me? I'm not going to be on the mortgage."

"There's no mortgage." He shrugged. "I'm telling you, Bella, I got the house for a song. I'd been saving up for years to buy my own place, so the money was there, with enough left over for the renovations."

"Wow."

He grinned. "There's even a little left over for that honeymoon I'm going to take you on."

"The one to Cancun?" I asked. D.J. kept his poker face, so I tried again. "Cozumel? Grand Cayman?"

He laughed. "You can try all day, but I'm not breathing a word about the honeymoon. It's going to be a surprise. So is the house. So no more questions, all right? I really want all of this to be an adventure for both of us."

"An adventure. Hmm. Okay." I pondered his words as I followed him into the space that had been my bedroom. My heart gravitated to my throat when I saw that the wall separating my old space from Rosa's was already in the process of coming down. Memories washed over me, and I squeezed my eyes shut to keep from crying. Well, that, and to keep the dust out of my eyes.

"If you're going to be up here, wear this." D.J. handed me a face mask, which I put on. After swallowing a mouthful of sawdust, anyway. I looked around the space, trying to envision it decked out with Rosa and Laz's new furniture. The furniture Mama planned to shop for tomorrow as a surprise for the honeymooners. Still, I couldn't imagine anything new or different in this space. No, I could only envision what had always been, not what could be. And the thought of change brought a substantial lump to my throat.

After a few minutes, one of the workers approached with several questions for D.J. I was happy for the excuse to slip downstairs once again, where life—and my home—were normal. Unchanged. I found Pop in his office, having a chat with Guido.

"Hey." I walked in and took a seat in the wingback chair.

"Well, hi, Bella. Guido and I were just talking."

"Oh?"

"Yes. He's telling me all about how happy he is to be staying in Texas, and I was explaining that we're equally as happy to have Sal here."

"I am glad about that." A smile followed as I thought about Uncle Sallie becoming a Texan. Pretty soon we'd have him wearing cowboy boots and singing sappy country tunes. Maybe, anyway. At any rate, I could hardly believe he'd decided to stay on in Galveston.

"Do you ever think about what Sal was like . . . before?" I asked my father.

"Oh, sure." Pop nodded. "I remember him from the eighties back in Atlantic City."

"Do you really think he was a mob boss?" I asked. "Or was that just some story Laz made up?"

Pop shook his head. "You know, Bella, I'm not sure. I do think he had some unsavory companions. Gordy's story about doing time in the penitentiary confirms that, I suppose. We'll just leave it at that. But who they were—or what they were—I never really knew for sure."

I paused, deep in thought. "I guess what I'm getting at," I said finally, "is this—I'm wondering if anyone in New Jersey is looking for Sal."

"You mean, like the police?" Pop asked.

"Well, yeah. Or worse. The bad guys."

My father shrugged. "That's something to pray about. But Bella, I honestly think Sal is old enough now that his past is truly behind him. And if the police were looking for Sal, chances are they would've found him years ago. He was never difficult to find. I think it's much more likely he was on the outer fringes." He paused, then gave me a winsome smile. "I'm sure God knows what he's doing. I have to believe he brought Sal here."

"Same here." I smiled. "And I know Laz is going to be thrilled to hear that his best friend is staying."

The words *best friend* triggered something in me. In the chaos of the morning, I'd forgotten to call Jenna. We needed to lock in a date for her Hawaiian-themed wedding. I trudged back over to Club Wed, entered my office once more, and made the call. Jenna settled on a date in July, which brought some comfort, since July was awhile away.

After talking to Jenna, I telephoned Marcella to talk flowers—not just for my own event, but Sophia's and Jenna's too. Then I called Lilly to ask for her wedding colors. She'd settled on pink, black, and white. I asked her opinion on centerpieces, then shifted gears, listening as she talked about her upcoming honeymoon to Key West.

Thinking of honeymoons made me wonder what D.J. had up his sleeve. The more I thought about it, the more I realized he must be planning to take me to Grand Cayman. He'd hinted at beautiful indigo waters, right? And swimming. The Cayman Islands were known for their indigo waters. That had to be it.

261

I signed on to the Internet, lost in my daydreams about all things honeymoon. A phone call startled me back to reality. Glancing at the phone, I realized the afternoon had slipped over to evening. Mama was calling to let me know that she and Pop had decided to take the family out to dinner.

An hour later, the whole family—plus Sal—gathered around a large table at the Prime Cut, a great steakhouse on the seawall, enjoying lively conversation with Sal about his future adventures on Galveston Isle. I couldn't remember the last time our family had gathered around any table other than the one in our dining room or one of the many at Parma John's.

In the middle of the meal, Sal's cell phone rang, and his cheeks flamed red as he looked at the number. "Excuse me, folks," he said. "I need to take this." He offered a quick "hello" as he rose. The tone of his voice changed immediately, becoming almost flirtatious. Someone had his full attention, no doubt about that.

"Who do you think that is?" I asked, turning to Mama.

"If I had to guess . . . Bonnie Sue."

"Really?" I said. "Why would she call him? Twila and Jolene would have a fit if they knew."

We got the answer to that question moments later when Sal returned. He took his seat, pressing the phone back into his pocket. We all stared at him in silence until he finally fessed up.

"That was, um . . . well, that was Bonnie Sue."

"Oh?" Pop's eyebrows shot straight up.

"Yes, she was calling with some news. Something she thought you all would want to know. She said she tried to call your phone, Imelda, but it went straight to voice mail."

"Oh, for heaven's sake," Mama said, reaching for her phone. "I turned it off earlier and forgot to turn it back on."

"She tried you too, Bella, but you didn't answer."

I glanced at my phone. Sure enough, I'd missed a call from her. No wonder she'd finally telephoned Sal.

"So, what's the news?" I asked.

He smiled. "Twila is engaged."

"W-what?"

"Happened yesterday in church. This fellow—I think she said his name was Terrell—proposed in front of the whole congregation. Pretty risky, I'd say."

"No kidding." Pop laughed. "But apparently she said yes."

"Apparently. Bonnie Sue wanted you to know so you could call Twila tomorrow and help her with wedding plans."

I was thrilled for Twila, of course. Still, I looked at D.J. and sighed, wondering how I could possibly add another wedding to my ever-growing list. Hadn't I just promised him on Saturday night that all of my attention would be focused on our wedding?

Mama shifted gears, talking about the upcoming performance at the opera house and how proud she was of Bubba for his role as the lead. That led to a discussion about Bubba and Jenna's elopement, which led to a conversation about their upcoming ceremony. Talking about their ceremony shifted our attentions to Lilly and Gordy, and before long, we were enmeshed in a rousing chorus about their soda shop plans, which Pop loved.

In all, we had a fabulous time. And even though we talked about the upcoming weddings, I didn't feel pressure. No, today things were moving along in an easygoing sort of way. I felt confident in the fact that God would help me with the details, down to the very last one.

That night as we settled into bed, Sophia turned to me

with a suspicious smile. "Oh, Bella! I have the most wonderful news. I wanted to tell you at dinner, but Tony and I didn't think the timing was right."

"What's up?"

"We've changed our minds about not having a themed wedding."

"Really? Which one are you going with?"

"Well, it's one we've made up ourselves."

"Oh?"

"Yes, we still want it to be high-end, just like I said before. Very Rodeo Drive. But get this." She giggled. "I had the most wonderful idea, and Tony thought it was divine. Tiffany's!"

"Tiffany's?" I asked. "As in, the store?"

"Yes, we want a Tiffany's-themed wedding."

"O-okay." I shrugged, not sure what she meant by that.

"You know the Tiffany's boxes, right? They're a soft powder blue, almost teal?"

"Sure."

"Well, that will be my primary wedding color. And we'll have Tiffany's boxes on the tables for centerpieces. And all of the bridesmaids will be decked out in diamonds."

"Um, diamonds?"

"Well . . ." She shrugged. "I'll be wearing diamonds, anyway. You and the others can wear costume jewelry. But the jewelry itself will be part of the theme. Isn't that brilliant? Can you even imagine how pretty everything will be?"

"It does sound beautiful," I agreed. "I love that idea." Of course, it sounded like a lot of work, but I could handle that. Right?

"And the cake is going to be gorgeous. I can hardly wait for Rosa to get home from her honeymoon so I can describe it to her. Very chic. Expensive-looking. Every layer is going to look like a Tiffany's box. And the flowers are all going to be that same soft blue."

"Speaking of cakes . . . Have you seen those really cool cake toppers that look like engagement rings?" I asked. "That would be perfect."

"Sounds great." My sister grabbed my hand. "See, Bella? This is all coming together so nicely. We make a great team, you and me. Don't you think?"

I nodded, my confidence mounting. Yes, today was a very good day. And I had a feeling the next few weeks would bring smooth sailing for all of the many, many brides.

# 23

## This Changing World

Over the next couple of weeks, I watched in awe as D.J. guided the workers through the process of installing plumbing and putting up new walls in my parents' house. He somehow found time to let me cry on his shoulder as I mourned the loss of my bedroom. Oh, if only he could do something about the onslaught of work I'd received from Sophia, who had slipped into full-out wedding-planning gear. Sadly, D.J. could do nothing about that.

On Christmas morning, I stood in the empty shell of a room that would become Rosa and Laz's suite. I had to admit, the place was going to be fabulous. And how fun that they didn't know about the extra space. There was some satisfaction in knowing we were putting one over on them. I could almost see the look on my aunt's face when she laid eyes on the room for the first time. Add to that the fact that Laz had commissioned Mama to buy a new king-size bed to put in the room, and she would be in hog heaven.

Not that I had time to really give this much thought today. No, the Rossi family had plans. Big plans. We were headed north, to Splendora, to spend the day with D.J.'s family.

It didn't really feel like Christmas, what with the temperatures in the high seventies. Sal—a true New Jersey native—seemed perplexed by this turn of events, and went on and on about how he should have packed his bathing suit. We got a kick out of that.

After loading the cars with gifts, the whole Rossi clan caravanned up to Splendora for Christmas with the Neeleys. D.J. and I led the way in his truck, with Sal riding in the backseat. Mama and Pop followed in the Lexus with Sophia and Tony, and Nick, Marcella, and the boys came behind them in their minivan. Even Armando had come along for the day, riding with Joey and Norah in her Mini Cooper. We were set for a fantabulous day in Splendora with our friends and my soon-to-be in-laws.

With Christmas carols playing on the radio, the trip north seemed to take less time than usual. Part of the time was spent listening to Sal talk on the phone with Bonnie Sue, assuring her he was on his way. I had my doubts about those two but didn't voice them.

As we pulled up to the double-wide, Sal let out a whistle. "Well now, look at that. That's a doozy of a trailer home if I ever saw one."

"It's really big on the inside too," D.J. said, unsnapping his seat belt. "I think you'll be surprised."

"Might have to get me one of those if this condo thing doesn't work out," Sal said.

We waited for the others to pull in behind us, and I double-checked my appearance in the rearview mirror. "Do I look okay?" I asked, turning to D.J.

"You're kidding, right?" He grinned. "You're a beauty queen, Bella."

I felt my cheeks turn warm as I whispered a quiet "Thanks." Funny. I didn't feel like a beauty queen lately. No, these days I felt like a real frump. Who had time for a beauty regimen while planning so many weddings?

I also felt something else. Occasionally, I had moments of chest pain and breathlessness. I'd mentioned it to Sophia in passing, but the others were unaware. Just anxiety, likely. Still, I had my antennae up just in case. No time for sickness now, not with so much going on.

"You okay?" D.J.'s voice jarred me back to attention, and I turned his way with a smile.

"Yeah, just thinking about stuff."

"No work today, Bella. It's Christmas. Only one person works on Christmas."

"Santa?" I guessed.

"Um, no. I was thinking of the Lord. He's in the business of working overtime on Christmas, wooing people in with the story of the baby in the manger."

I nodded, suddenly feeling very much in the Christmas spirit. And D.J. was right. No work today. Not even if one of the brides took to begging. Surely they wouldn't stoop that low on Christmas Day.

Minutes later, D.J. led the way and we climbed the steps to the front porch, then entered the double-wide to the most delicious smell on Planet Earth. It was sort of a turkey-meets-honey-glazed-ham-meets-stuffing-meets-sweet-potato-pie sort of smell. And then some. I stood in the doorway, drawing in a deep breath. Man. A girl could put on a few pounds just sniffing.

Wouldn't hurt me, not with the recent weight loss. With

Rosa gone and the house under construction, we'd been existing on snatches of fast food over the past couple weeks. I could hardly wait for my aunt to get home so life could get back to normal. Not that I would be living in the Rossi home much longer.

A weighty sensation passed over me at that revelation, and I pushed it aside. There would be plenty of time to think about that later. Right now I needed to eat.

When we got inside, I realized Earline had adequately prepared the house for her guests. The dining room table was set for eight, but she'd also set up two card tables. And man, did it ever look like Christmas in here. Twinkling lights adorned the faux mantle, and the colorful tree beckoned with its homemade ornaments.

"Remind me to show you some of those ornaments later," D.J. said with a smile. "Bubba and I made most of them."

"Will do." I looked around. "Hey, speaking of Bubba, where is he? I thought you said he and Jenna were going to be here."

"They are. But he had a performance last night at the opera house, and they overslept. He sent me a text a couple of hours ago saying they would be behind us."

"Gotcha."

Mama and Pop carried in presents for Earline and Dwayne Sr. I knew, having watched my mother wrap them, that they'd spared no expense. I also knew Mama loved Earline like a sister. The two now had another common bond—their children were getting married. By doing so, D.J. and I were merging more than just our lives—we were merging two families. Just the thought of that warmed my heart.

From across the room, Earline headed my way, her apron covered in gravy stains, à la Rosa. "You're here!" She reached for me first, her large, bosomy frame swallowing me whole. Not that I minded. No, I'd grown rather used to her warm embrace. Dwayne Sr. was slightly more reserved, giving me a side hug.

One by one, we were greeted with Christmas cheer. Mama handed Earline the gifts, and they were placed under the oversized tree in the corner. Then my mother passed off a package of frozen dinner rolls with a shrug. "So sorry," she said. "With Rosa gone, we couldn't count on the garlic twists. I know it won't be the same, but I wanted to bring something."

"Well, honey, this is the brand I buy." Earline grinned as she took the bag of rolls. "They cook up nice and fluffy and taste as good as the ones made from scratch, I promise."

We followed her into the kitchen, where a lively conversation took place, much of it centered on the opera performance we'd all seen a couple of nights prior.

"That boy of yours is a wonder on the big stage," Mama said with a nod. "It's rare to find someone with such a gift."

"Both of my boys are gifted," Earline said. "I truly believe D.J. has a real knack for construction work."

"And he makes a pretty good supervisor too," Mama threw in. "I've watched him with those workers, and he knows just how to handle them—with grace and finesse."

D.J. looked our way with a smile, and I could almost read his mind. The conversation both flattered and embarrassed him. He quickly turned the tables, going back to Bubba and the opera. On and on he went, singing his brother's praises to all who would listen.

Twila, Bonnie Sue, and Jolene arrived in short order, bearing gifts. Many, many gifts. Looked like they'd done a little shopping. Make that a lot of shopping. As soon as Bonnie Sue brushed through the door, Sal gravitated her way, a smile lighting his face.

"Here, let me help you with that." He took some of the packages and carried them to the tree, putting them down with great care.

"Why, thank you, kind sir." Bonnie Sue gave him a flirtatious smile, and Twila and Jolene groaned.

An older man I recognized as Terrell Buell entered the room, carrying several pie containers.

"Terrell, have you been baking again?" Earline offered him a warm smile.

"Yes'm. Love to make those pecan pies. They're my favorite."

"Mine too!" Earline and I said at the same time. We looked at each other and laughed.

"Well, just set 'em on the table, hon," Earline said, gesturing.

I watched as Twila made her way to the table, helping Terrell with the pies. Their interaction was sweet. Innocent. In fact, they reminded me of schoolkids with crushes. I wondered what had taken her so long to see the good in this man. They were polar opposites, sure, but D.J. and I were proof that opposites did indeed attract.

Seconds later, Bubba and Jenna burst through the door, arms loaded.

"Sorry we're late," he said. "We were up half the night wrapping presents."

"We got it done," Jenna said with a smile. She rushed to Earline's side and wrapped her arms around her. "Merry Christmas, Mama Neeley."

"Merry Christmas to you too, sweet girl," Earline echoed.

Less than fifteen minutes later, we all sat down to share Christmas dinner. Dwayne Sr. led out in prayer, though Earline made him take off his baseball cap to do so. At the sound of the "Amen," we all dove in spoon first. I scooped up mashed potatoes as creamy as velvet. Then I turned my attention to the honey-baked ham and the turkey breast. Before long, my plate was filled with colorful goodies, bits and pieces of food toppling over the edges.

I caught a glimpse of Sal, his eyes wide. "Never seen this much food in one place before," he said. "Except at the wedding, I mean. Never really had a Christmas like this one."

Bonnie Sue gave him a wink. "Well, honey, here in Texas, we know how to make our guests feel welcome. We give 'em so much food they can't leave afterward!"

"Not sure I'd want to leave anyway," he said, diverting his gaze to the ham and sweet potatoes. "Haven't seen anything this tasty in a while."

I prayed he referred to the food, but Bonnie Sue's cheeks flamed pink.

"Stick around and you can eat like this anytime," Earline said with a welcoming smile.

Before long, the room was filled with the usual amount of noise—voices overlapping and laughter leading the way. I loved that sound more than almost anything else.

Out of the corner of my eye, I noticed D.J. leaning over to talk to Sal. I paused, noticing what a kind way he had about him. Somehow D.J. always made everyone feel welcome. Like they'd come home. From the look of contentment on Sal's face, I knew he wouldn't be leaving anytime soon.

As several people loaded up their plates with seconds, the conversation took an interesting turn.

"Did my dad tell you what he got for Christmas?" D.J. asked. When I shook my head, he responded. "A four-wheeler."

"What?" I looked at Dwayne Sr. "Really?"

"Sure." He shrugged. "I'm just a big kid at heart. This isn't my first one, but it's the nicest. Earline went all out." He smiled. "O' course, it cost me a pretty penny. I had to match her, gift for gift. She got that new computerized piano over there." He pointed to the large keyboard in the corner of the living room. "It records music digitally, and she can upload to her computer too. Pretty snazzy."

"Wow." I gave her an admiring look.

"Yep. Before you know it, she'll be recording movie sound-tracks—that sort of thing," Dwayne Sr. said.

I looked at Earline, stunned. "Really?"

She shrugged. "I'd like that. I'll have to pray and see what the Lord says about it. He's the one who gives the gifts, you know."

"Sorry to interrupt, but could we go back to the part about the four-wheeler?" Sal asked. "I've never been on one. Always wondered what it would be like."

"You've never been on a four-wheeler?" Bonnie Sue turned to him, a look of shock on her face. I could almost hear the wheels clicking in her head, and she finally confirmed my suspicions with four words: "I'll go with you."

You could've heard a pin drop at that announcement. Dwayne Sr. looked her way, clearly perplexed.

"You don't mind if we ride off into the sunset on your four-wheeler, do you, honey?" she asked him.

"Well, I—"

"Thanks! We'll go just as quick as we finish eating." Bonnie Sue dove into her food, cleaning her plate in no time. Sal

273

moved almost as quickly. We all followed suit, a new sense of anticipation taking over.

When we finished eating, Bonnie Sue reached for her napkin and dabbed her lips, then extended her hand in Sal's direction. He took a final bite of ham, then pushed his chair back.

D.J.'s dad rose and followed them to the front door, looking back at all of us with a panicked expression on his face. I wasn't sure if he was worried they might wreck his new toy or, as Bonnie Sue had suggested, ride off into the sunset, never to return again. Regardless, I wanted to witness it firsthand.

"Can we watch?" I whispered to D.J.

"Wouldn't miss it."

Minutes later, the whole group was standing on the front porch, watching as Bonnie Sue—all two-hundred-plus pounds of her—took her seat on the four-wheeler, with Sal taking the spot behind her. Well, what was left of the spot behind her, anyway. They made quite a pair, no doubt about that. Dwayne Sr. gave them a few instructions, and they shot off down the driveway, headed for the clearing beyond the house.

"Do you think we'll ever see them again?" Mama asked, her brow wrinkled.

"Heavens, yes," Twila said, dismissing that idea with a wave of her hand. "We haven't had dessert yet, you know. There's pecan pie inside this house. Bonnie Sue never could pass up pecan pie, even for a man."

At this revelation, we all breathed a sigh of relief and headed back indoors. Earline started a pot of coffee and sliced up the pies. I took a sampling of two kinds—pecan and chocolate. Then D.J. and I retreated to the living room, where everyone had congregated.

Twila settled onto the sofa with Terrell at her side. They held hands, gazing at each other periodically with sparks exuding. I'd seen her happy before, of course—the woman radiated joy—but the expression on her face today was different than in days past. She had that "I've been bitten by the love bug and I'm under its spell" look. Terrell had the same expression on his face.

"Oh, Bella!" She looked my way with passion in her eyes. "I still can't believe Terrell and I are getting married. Isn't it the most glorious news in the world?"

"Well, of course. Falling in love is wonderful."

"If anyone knows that, you do." She offered a wink. "Now look, honey, we're planning to get married at our own church. Pastor Higley would never forgive me if I up and married anyplace else. And we'll have a little reception in the fellowship hall too. But Terrell and I were thinking of taking a cruise for our honeymoon, so we'd be heading down to Galveston the morning after the wedding, anyway. He came up with this idea that we could have a glorious reception at your wedding facility on that day."

"W-what day?"

"Well, the cruise leaves on January 18 at five o'clock. Now, that's a Sunday, I know. But we're not asking folks to leave their church service or anything. We're thinking a one o'clock party, lasting only a couple of hours. Sort of a bon voyage as we head off on our way."

"But . . . January 18?" Did she not realize I was getting married on February 14? That I hadn't finished my own plans yet?

"We picked that day because Rosa and Laz will be back by then," she said. "I want Rosa to celebrate with me."

"Of course."

"I'm going to be her maid of honor," Jolene bragged. "But don't tell Bonnie Sue. She gets jealous."

"I heard that, Jolene," Bonnie Sue said, entering the front door. "And just so you know, I'm not jealous. Not at all." She looked at me with a brusque nod. "We drew straws. It was the only fair thing to do."

"Yes, how could I choose just one?" Twila asked.

At this point in the conversation, I took note of Sal, who came through the front door on Bonnie Sue's heels. His hair stood atop his head and his cheeks blazed red. Talk about windblown.

"Well?" Pop asked.

"It was different," Sal said, hobbling across the room in a bowlegged sort of way. "I'm not sure certain parts of me are going to recover." He rubbed his backside, then gingerly took a seat in the recliner. We all laughed, but he seemed to take our reaction in stride.

"Welcome to Texas, Uncle Sallie," I said with a wink. "You've been initiated. And on Christmas Day, no less."

"Yep. Initiated." He nodded, a look of pain on his face. "That's the word I was looking for."

Earline handed him a cup of coffee, and he took a sip and leaned back with a contented look on his face.

Before long, he and Bonnie Sue were eating pecan pie and talking about their adventures in the piney woods on the four-wheeler. I listened with a smile, convinced God was up to something here, though I couldn't be sure what. When we finished our pie, Earline announced the time had come to open presents. I'd been looking forward to this all day. I had purchased the perfect gift for D.J.—an expensive pair of Lanciotti boots. I could hardly wait to see the look on his face when he opened the package.

He insisted I open his gift first, though. When I peeled back the paper on the small box, I found a key inside.

"What is this?" I asked.

"The key to our house, of course. I figured it was about time you had one of your own."

"Does that mean . . . I can see it?"

"In a few weeks. Maybe a month or so. I'm going to have to ask you to keep trusting me till then." After a moment's pause, he added, "I want you to know I've been working hard to make that house our home, Bella," he said. "I've got a lot of work ahead of me, but don't you worry about that. Sometimes all the hard work is truly worth it."

"Yes, it is." I leaned over and gave him a kiss, and he grinned.

He walked back over to the tree, reaching down for another small box. "But just so you know, that's not the only present. I thought you might like these too." He handed me the box, which I opened at once. I found the prettiest diamond earrings inside. Real show-stoppers, shaped like teardrops.

"Wow." It was really the only word that would do. They took my breath away.

"Look, Bella!" Sophia said, her eyes wide. "I don't believe it! That's a Tiffany's box!"

Sure enough, the earrings were from Tiffany's. I looked at D.J., perplexed. "How did you know?"

He looked confused. "Know what?"

"To order them from Tiffany's?"

He shrugged. "Actually, I bought them online. Ordered them from the store after they sent an ad to my email. Didn't realize the store had some special significance."

"Well, of course it does!" Sophia went into a lengthy story about her wedding plans, and I shook my head. Seemed no matter how hard I tried to avoid thinking about all of these other weddings, they followed me.

Still, I wouldn't let it bother me. Not today. It was Christmas, after all. A day for giving.

And receiving.

I looked at the tiny key, realizing its significance. In a sense, I was holding the future in my hand. Mine and D.J.'s. Somehow, knowing that made all of Sophia's ramblings worthwhile.

Now, if only I could get this strange sensation in my chest to pass, I would be just fine.

# 24

## As Time Goes By

On January 16—just two days after D.J. and his crew put the finishing touches on the new suite—Rosa and Laz arrived home from Italy. Mama and I had worked overtime in the week leading up to their arrival, shopping for furniture and buying artwork. Everything in the room screamed Italy, right down to the terra-cotta color on the walls. We'd gone with a true Mediterranean theme, making most of our purchases from a well-known furniture shop in Houston. I had enjoyed picking out the furniture with my mother. Doing so had filled my head with all sorts of ideas for my own home. The one I hadn't seen yet.

When Pop pulled up to the house with Rosa and Laz in the car, my heart leaped for joy. Then again, my heart had been leaping a lot lately, and not just out of joy. I'd developed an erratic heartbeat, one that kept me awake at night and scared the daylights out of me at times. I would've talked to

Mama about it, or even D.J., but they were both so busy, I hated to bother them.

I took a few deep breaths and willed my heart to slow down. Then, with a smile on my face, I greeted my aunt and uncle. I could hardly believe the transformation in Rosa. It wasn't just the broad smile on her face or her tan. She'd been shopping. And had her hair done. I'd never seen her look so young—or fashionable.

"Rosa, you look amazing!" Sophia said with a smile. "I love the outfit."

"Thank you." Rosa blushed. "Turns out I like to shop. Who knew?"

After greeting us all with kisses, she went at once to her kitchen, gushing over how much she had missed it during their month away. "Laz bought me the most amazing set of pots and pans," she said. "We brought them on the plane. I hope they're not damaged."

She talked at length about their many purchases—everything from clothes to shoes to kitchenware—but pointed down at her feet for the best purchase of all. "Look, Bella! Cowboy boots!"

I had to laugh. Of all the things to buy in Italy. Only after a second glance did I realize what I was looking at. Lanciotti's. I let out a slow whistle, admiring the beautiful boots with their exquisite detailed work. If anyone deserved them, Rosa did.

Laz entered the kitchen with the box of pots and pans, which he put on the counter. Then he lifted his pants leg, showing off his own Lanciotti's.

"Christmas presents," he explained. "We couldn't resist."

"I don't blame you! I bought some for D.J. as a Christmas gift too."

This started a lengthy conversation about Christmas at the

double-wide, which led to the story of Sal riding the four-wheeler, which led to the crux of the matter—Sal's decision to stay in Texas. The minute he heard the news, Laz let out a whoop. "Praise the Lord! God is really at work here. I can feel it."

"Well, he's at work, all right," Mama said. "There's a little romance blooming between Sal and Bonnie Sue. We're praying that one through, though. Don't want to see her matched up with someone who doesn't know the Lord."

"We'll see what he does," Laz said with a nod. "You never know."

"He's in the miracle-working business, you know," Rosa added. She looked at Laz and winked. "We're proof of that, I guess."

"Well, speaking of miracles, are you ready to see your new room?" Mama clasped her hands together at her chest, ready to get on with this.

When Rosa and Laz nodded, we led them upstairs to see their new suite. Now, granted, they knew we'd been working on their room. But they had no idea how much space they had or that my parents had sprung for all new furnishings. So I anticipated quite a few tears.

What I got, however, was a gusher. Rosa stood in the doorway of her new space and wailed like a baby. Even Laz teared up, though he didn't speak a word. I had a feeling it would be some time before he could formulate words.

Rosa took a few ginger steps into her new room, not saying a word as she made her way from the bed to the tall chest of drawers with its magnificent mirror. She ran her hand along the painted walls and stood in front of the painting of her beloved Napoli, shaking her head. I had a feeling it was a good shaking, not a bad one.

"This is my home," she whispered at last. "I've come home." She turned to face us with tears streaming. "Don't misunderstand me. I loved visiting Italy. It felt wonderful to go back to the place where I grew up. But Galveston Island is my home. The people I love are here. I wouldn't trade this for anything—or anyplace—in the world."

Mama, Sophia, and I rushed her way, ending up in a holy huddle, as Pop was prone to call it. At this point—probably sensing an estrogen overload—the men headed off to Armando's room to look at the original drawings. Not that we minded. Rosa gestured to her new bed, and she, Mama, Sophia, and I climbed aboard for some serious girl time. Sophia held out her hand to show off her engagement ring, which got a whistle from Rosa. She gave Sophia a hug and whispered, "You two are going to be so happy, sweet girl."

"I can't wait." Sophia's cheeks turned pink. "It's all so wonderful."

"So, catch me up," Rosa said, turning my way. "I heard through the grapevine that everyone in the state of Texas got engaged on our wedding night. Who all's getting married, and in what order?"

"Twila and Terrell are first. Day after tomorrow." I smiled. "Then D.J. and me. Then Sophia and Tony. That leaves Joey and Norah, Lilly and Gordy, and . . ." I squinted, deep in thought. "Who else? Oh yeah—Bubba and Jenna. They're renewing their vows." I ran my fingers through my hair. "Not sure I got those last few in order, to be honest. I'll have to check my calendar."

"Can't blame you there," Rosa said with a shake of her head. "I guess I'd better write all of this down. How many of these weddings am I baking cakes for?"

I gave her a knowing look, and she nodded. "Aha. I see. Including the one in two days?"

"Well, that one's up in the air. Twila knows you're just getting back in town, so she has a bakery on speed dial, just in case."

"A bakery?" Rosa looked horrified at that suggestion. "We will have no bakery cakes at Club Wed. Not for a friend's wedding, anyway. I will call her this afternoon and get to work."

"Speaking of cakes . . ." Sophia's eyes sparkled, and she clutched Rosa's hand. "Wait till you hear my plan for our Tiffany's-themed cake. Each level is going to look like a present, Rosa. A gift box. Can you do that?"

"Well, sure. I'm getting pretty good with fondant, and I have square baking pans."

"It's going to be glorious," Sophia said. "Oh, I just know you'll make it so pretty, Rosa. You're the best!"

Sophia lit into a conversation about the design of her cake, which led to a conversation about the food at her and Tony's wedding, which led to a lengthy dissertation about the need for better serving utensils. While I found all of this enlightening, I had other things to take care of. At the appropriate moment, I dismissed myself and headed next door.

As I made my way across the lawn, I dealt with that same strange sensation in my chest. It wasn't pain, really. More of a gripping feeling followed by an erratic heartbeat. Though I did my best to dismiss it, it would not be dismissed. So I worked around it. Spent a lot of time praying through it. Surely God was big enough to handle a little erratic heartbeat, right?

That evening my symptoms intensified, and by the time I awoke the next morning, I felt a little breathless. Still, I pushed things off. Who had time to fret over the physical right now?

I had a wedding reception to coordinate! And hopefully, once Twila and Terrell boarded the cruise ship afterward, I could get back to planning for my own big day.

The morning of January 18 dawned cold and clear. After attending the morning service at church, Mama and Rosa worked with me to prepare the reception hall for Twila's reception.

"What did you think of that ceremony up in Splendora last night?" Mama asked.

I couldn't help but smile as I reflected on Twila's emotional wedding. "I thought it was beautiful. It was so sweet to see all of the tears from the bride and groom. And didn't you think the ladies did a fabulous job with that trio?"

"No kidding." Mama nodded. "The audience was speechless."

"I talked them into repeating the song today," I said. "Just had to hear it one more time."

"You know, Bella," Rosa interjected, "I really love those ladies. I find it interesting since we're all so different."

"Yes, I know what you mean. I've thought about that a lot over the past few months. God has really broadened our family circle, physically and culturally."

"I love Twila's beauty secrets," Mama said, showing off her soft hands and silky smooth elbows.

"And I love Earline's chicken-fried steak," Rosa said. "Might have to learn to make it myself."

"I can't believe I'm saying this, but I love cowboys." I giggled at this confession. "And cowboy boots." I lifted the hem of my pants and showed off my latest pair.

"We're just a bunch of Tex-Italians, I guess." Rosa nodded. "It's about time. Only took us sixteen years to make the jump."

Her words led to a conversation about how we'd all come to live in Texas, which led to a bittersweet talk about family members who had walked the road before us. As Rosa and Mama talked about their parents, I listened closely. As much as I hated to see the passage of time, I knew there would come a day—hopefully years and years from now—when Sophia and I might gather in a room just like this one to talk about the good old days, the days when our family members were gathered around us and we felt sure that life as we knew it would go on forever.

Blinking away tears, I decided not to let my mind go there. Not today, anyway. No, today I had an incoming bride. And caring for her needs was all that mattered. Tomorrow I could think about other things.

The next several hours passed in a blur. The reception hall filled with friends from both Splendora and Galveston, and though the event was simple—no band, no over-the-top decor—everyone in attendance had a lovely time. Twila looked glorious in her soft pink dress and heels. And as she and Terrell danced to a familiar country tune, I felt that same lurching in my heart. Maybe I was just emotional. I had a lot to be happy about. And now that this wedding was behind me, I could truly focus on the one that mattered most—my own.

# 25

## Always in My Heart

I somehow made it through the end of January, though my workload increased daily. Finding myself overwhelmed more often than not wasn't unusual. Still, I convinced myself it would all be worth it once Valentine's Day approached. On that wonderful Saturday night, D.J. and I would link hands and hearts.

If I made it that long. Every day I grew more exhausted and frazzled than the day before, and though I loved my sister, she was getting on my last nerve. Who had thought bunking together would be a good idea? I never had a moment to myself, never got to talk about my wedding without the discussion shifting to hers. Still, I did my best to plaster on a smile and keep going—for all of our sakes.

On the morning of February 9, Mama and I met with Marcella at the flower shop. She seemed a little out of sorts this morning, but who could blame her? Now a full eight months pregnant, she was carrying around a tummy for the record books. She'd also put on a few extra pounds in some strange places. Her ankles, for instance. I'd never seen ankles like that before. And her face looked puffy. I hadn't noticed the phenomenon with her other two pregnancies, but I didn't want to mention it in case she hadn't noticed.

We met at 10:00 in the morning to talk through the bouquets she would be making for my wedding. The roses had been ordered weeks ago, but I had special plans for how they would be pieced together. As we met in her back office, I noticed a strange look cross her face.

"What is it, Marcella?" I asked, worry setting in.

"Oh, nothing, I—"

I looked over, stunned, as she doubled over in pain. "Oh no!" I rushed her way, trying to offer assistance. She held up her hand, likely trying to allay my fears.

"It's okay, Bella," she said, making a curious panting noise. "Don't worry. I've been down this road before. These are just Braxton Hicks contractions. Nothing—" Her face tightened for a moment, then relaxed. "Nothing to worry about."

"O-okay." I nodded, unsure of what to do next. Sure enough, she straightened her posture a minute or so later and smiled broadly. "There. That wasn't so bad."

"Don't you think you should go to the hospital or something?" I asked. "Just to be safe?"

"No, I'm sure I'll be fine. Besides, I've got work to do. Can't stop just yet." She offered a reassuring smile. "Nothing is going to stop me."

"Mm-hmm." I led her over to a seat, and she eased herself down into it. "You sound just like me."

"Oh, I'll be fine. No worries." With a wave of her hand, she dismissed any concerns.

Half an hour later, however, things were not fine. Oh,

sure, we had a plan for the bouquets and boutonnieres, but I could tell from the look on Marcella's face that she was still struggling.

"I'd feel better if you called your doctor," Mama said at last. "He will know best what to do."

"Might not hurt." Marcella rose and reached for the phone. Minutes later—under doctor's orders—we drove her to the hospital. Just a precautionary thing, of course.

How would we know the next two hours would be spent in all-out chaos mode? That the doctor would admit her, no questions asked?

Turned out Marcella's blood pressure was elevated. Extremely elevated. And blood work revealed protein in her urine—never a good thing, as the nurse explained. When the doctor arrived at last, we received an official diagnosis.

"Preeclampsia," he said. "You've got to be on complete bed rest until this baby comes."

"Oh, no, no," she argued. "You don't understand. This baby isn't due for another month, and I've got work to do. I can't possibly stay in bed that long." She swung her legs over the edge of the hospital bed and reached for her purse.

"Marcella." Mama gave her a stern look. "You are going to do what the doctor says."

"But it's so silly." She shook her head. "I worked up till the minute both of the boys were born."

"You didn't have preeclampsia with those two," the doctor reminded her. "And not only that, these contractions are concerning me. I want to check you to make sure you're not dilated."

Mama and I scooted out of the room, praying all the way. A few minutes later we were ushered back in. I could tell from the look on Marcella's face that the news wasn't good.

288

"I'm dilated three centimeters." Her words were followed by a groan. "It's true. I have to be on complete bed rest. Can't even get up to go to the bathroom. How humiliating is that?" She pointed to the bedpan and grimaced.

My mind reeled at this news. "So you're staying here? At the hospital?" Somehow I'd envisioned her lounging around her own house in her pajamas, not strapped to a bunch of machines with a bedpan tucked underneath her.

"Yes, it's the safest thing for Marcella and the baby," the doctor said. "Preeclampsia can be very dangerous. We take it seriously."

I chided myself at once for being so selfish. Of course Marcella would stay. She would do whatever it took to ensure a healthy delivery—which was weeks from now.

I pulled in a few deep, cleansing breaths, trying to put this in perspective. Marcella needed us right now, and we would be here for her. No questions asked.

Surely a few days in bed would do her good. Besides, arranging flowers was easy-breezy work. Maybe she could put them together here in the hospital. Might give her something to do to pass the time. We weren't talking hard labor here. *Hard labor. Funny.*

The doctor scribbled some things on Marcella's chart, then turned to face her. "I'm going to start you on magnesium sulfate. Sometimes it can give moms-to-be flulike symptoms, but we find it does a great job of slowing down contractions."

"Lovely." Marcella did not look pleased.

"And we'll monitor these contractions around the clock," the doctor continued. "You'll be in good hands if this baby decides to come early. And just in case, we're going to give you an injection of steroids to beef up the baby's lungs."

For whatever reason, his words reminded me of Twila,

Bonnie Sue, and Jolene and their WHERE'S THE BEEF? T-shirts. Thinking about them reminded me to call Bonnie Sue and ask her to pray. Surely the prayers of the righteous would avail much, as Jolene always said. Yes, we would pray our way through this. God would bring everything into alignment in his time and his way.

I rubbed my brow, feeling a headache coming on, and my stomach felt a little funny. Glancing at the clock on the wall, I realized I hadn't eaten.

Standing at the end of Marcella's bed, I did my best to listen as the doctor went on and on about his plan to keep her quiet and still over the next few weeks until the baby arrived. I heard the words, sure, but they didn't register. No, I was too distracted by the strange fluttering sensation in my chest. And the weird whooshing sound in my ears. Why did the doctor's voice sound so loud? Was he amplified? And why was he speaking in slow motion?

Suddenly I was overly aware of the smells in the room. The alcohol swabs the nurse had used. The disinfectant. And the noise! The ticking of the clock nearly drove me mad, as did the booming words coming from the doctor.

My queasiness increased, and I wondered if I might throw up. Beads of sweat popped out on my upper lip, and I gripped the railing on the end of the bed, feeling a little wobbly. *Lord, what is going on here?*

The doctor droned on—something about the risks associated with early delivery. How Marcella needed to follow his orders to a T. How her sole job from this day forth was to rest.

I reasoned this out in my mind. The wedding could move forward without a florist. Sure it could. Norah was pretty good with flowers, right? And Rosa. We could still manage, even without Marcella in the picture.

As the doctor continued to talk, my sister-in-law cast a terrified glance my way. "Bella?"

"Y-yeah?" I held the railing of the bed even tighter, the room now spinning out of control and the crazy cacophony of sounds pitting themselves against each other.

"Bella, are you okay? You look as white as a ghost."

I shook my head in slow motion—my only option, since it suddenly felt like it weighed a hundred pounds. A fog wrapped me in its embrace, a strange, gray fog. Terrifying but inviting. It beckoned, and I gave myself over to it.

Very strange. I seemed to be falling asleep standing up. *Don't go down, Bella. Don't go down.*

Funny how I couldn't seem to convince my legs to co-operate. Gravity caught up with me, and as the room spun out of control, I found myself dropping down, down, down . . . to the cold, hard floor.

# 26

## Begin the Beguine

There's something about waking up in a hospital bed with hysterical family members gathered around that makes a girl wonder what she ever did to deserve such attention.

Apparently I had been out long enough for Mama to call the rest of the family. When I came to—a slow and weighty process—all of the Rossi women were clustered around me, wrapping me in a cocoonlike embrace of love and attention.

I tried to bring their faces into focus but could not. One blurred into the next. And that crazy whooshing sound in my ears continued, as did the sensation in my chest.

"W-what . . . happened?" I finally managed, trying to sit up in the bed. The last thing I remembered was standing at the foot of Marcella's bed. Now I was in a strange, unrecognizable room with the scent of hospital disinfectant overwhelming my senses.

Mama began to cry, a slow, pitiful cry. "Oh, my Bella. You scared us to death!"

Good grief. Couldn't a girl even faint without getting in trouble? "I'm sorry, Mama. I didn't plan for it in advance."

The pounding in my head continued, and I felt nauseated.

Marcella's doctor gave me a brusque nod. "It's not unusual for people to faint in hospitals. We see it all the time."

"Ah. See there?" I looked at Mama and shrugged. "It happens all the time."

The doctor drew near. "How have you been feeling? Before this fainting spell, I mean."

"Pretty overwhelmed," I admitted. "And I've been having some strange, well, chest pains."

"Chest pains?" He gave me a pensive look. So did my mother, who let out another cry.

"You've been in pain and didn't tell me?"

"Who had time?"

"Tell me about these pains," the doctor prompted. "When did they start? How long do they last?"

I tried to explain—though my words didn't make sense, even to my own ears—that it wasn't really pain I was feeling, but more of a gripping sensation. That my heart flip-flopped. Regularly. It drove me nuts.

The doctor reached for the blood pressure cuff and wrapped it around my arm as I continued to explain. "What else?" he asked.

"Sometimes I get a little short of breath. And queasy."

He continued to take my blood pressure, his eyes widening as the numbers came up on the screen: 152/102.

The doctor gave me a thoughtful look. "When a person faints, it's usually because their blood pressure or blood sugar is low. You've got the opposite problem, at least with your blood pressure. It's much higher than it should be, and I plan to take that very seriously. We're going to draw some blood. Run a few tests. I think it would be wise to keep you for a couple of days to see if we can figure out what's going on."

"A couple of days? But . . . I'm getting married on Saturday."

"You'll be out in plenty of time for that," he said, waving his hand. "I'm going to check your blood sugar and your thyroid levels. How has your diet been these past few weeks?"

"Diet?" I shook my head. Who had time to eat? I was a busy woman, after all. Eating would come after the wedding, not before.

"Mm-hmm." He wrote something on my chart. "I suspected as much. "And I assume you haven't been sleeping, since you've got a wedding coming up."

"She keeps me up all night," Sophia said, crossing her arms at her chest and locking me with her gaze. "I never get any rest."

"W-what?" The other way around was more like it. Still, I didn't argue. What good would it do at this point?

"Well, as I said, I will give you a few days for some R & R, and I'll run tests while you're resting." The doctor stopped writing in my file long enough to offer a weak smile, his first attempt at being personable.

"Impossible." I shook my head. "You don't understand. I'm a wedding planner. It's what I do. Half the battle—half the joy—is in the *planning*, not just the actual day. And the week before the big day is when everything gets done. Surely you can see that." I repeated myself, just in case he hadn't fully understood. "I'm. Getting. Married. On. Saturday."

He shook his head. "I'm assuming you want to live to see your first anniversary, right?"

"Well, of course." I leaned back against the pillow, finding little or no strength to argue anymore.

"Then let me run the tests. I can't have a patient complaining of chest pains and then do nothing about it. We'll do a full workup on your heart—EKG, echocardiogram, nuclear stress test . . ."

On and on he went, describing the various tests he would perform over the next few days. I heard him, of course. Saw his lips moving. Tried to make sense of the words. But I could not. Had the man not heard me say I was getting married on Saturday?

When he finished, Mama looked my way and clucked her tongue. "You don't take care of yourself, Bella. This isn't good."

"I've just been so overwhelmed with work. I . . . I've tried to do too much."

"I know, but we'd like to keep you around awhile." Her expression softened. "And not so you can work, baby. You are my girl. I need you to be healthy and strong." Her eyes filled with tears, and she looked away.

Rosa took a more practical stance. "You haven't eaten a decent meal in weeks. It's affecting your blood sugar. I'm going home to make some real food. Some pasta and gravy will be just the ticket. And protein. You need protein. I'm making salmon."

"Rosa, that's a wonderful idea," Mama said, clasping her hands together. "A good meal will work wonders. So will a good night's sleep. I'm convinced that Bella needs rest." She looked at me with tenderness in her eyes. "We're going to leave you alone for a few hours, and I hope you'll sleep.

Don't think about anything. Don't plan anything. Just rest. Promise?"

A sigh escaped. "I'll try. I don't know if that's possible, though. I really need to be printing the programs for the ceremony today. And my dress! I'm supposed to pick it up from the alterations lady. I still owe her a hundred and fifty dollars. If I don't take care of that today, she's going to hold my dress hostage!"

"Bella, you're not making sense," Sophia said, patting my arm in a mother-hen sort of way. "Don't worry about the dress. I'll swing by and pick it up."

"You just rest easy, Bella," Mama said as she headed for the door with Rosa on her heels.

"Oh, wait!" I called out. "I forgot something."

"What's that?" Mama asked, turning back to face me.

"How is Marcella? In all of the craziness, I forgot to ask."

"She's resting. Doctor's orders." Mama gave me a pensive look. "So, it looks like you're both in the same boat."

"Okay, okay."

"Don't worry, Mama," Sophia called out. "I'll stay here with her and make sure she rests."

*Sure you will.*

I leaned my head against the pillow and closed my eyes, but my thoughts tumbled madly through my head. If Sophia was staying here, I needed to call the alterations lady to check on my dress. Maybe Norah could swing by and pick it up later. Oh, and D.J.! How could I have forgotten to call him? He needed to know I was in the hospital.

Turned out my family had already taken care of that little detail. By the time I reached D.J. on his cell, he was already in the hospital parking lot. He arrived in my room a few minutes later, and I could read the worry in his eyes.

"I'm fine," I assured him. "Nothing to worry about. The wedding will go on, I promise."

"Bella, the wedding isn't what matters to me." His eyes filled with tears, and he took a seat on the edge of my bed. "You're all that matters. Getting you well. Making sure you're okay." He got choked up, and I had trouble making out his next words. "I-I don't know w-what I'd d-do if a-anything ever h-happened to you!"

Then the tears flowed freely from both of us. I'd never seen D.J. so worked up before. Unfortunately, the automatic blood pressure machine kicked in, puffing up around my upper arm and eventually registering 155/104. Seconds later a nurse appeared with an IV in her hand. "We've got to get you hooked up, sweetie. Need to get that blood pressure down ASAP."

The insertion of the IV was enough to send Sophia running from the room with the comment that she needed to spend some time with Marcella. D.J. offered to stay, of course.

The next few minutes were a blur of activity. Whatever they gave me for my blood pressure made me groggy. I found myself dozing off. Several times I awoke, finding D.J. in the chair next to my bed. Each time, he offered a reassuring smile and squeezed my hand. A couple of times, I even heard him praying, asking the Lord to bring healing and peace to my body. I felt so safe with D.J. nearby. Safe enough to drift back off to sleep once again.

Evening shadows were just falling when I heard a noise at the door. Looking up, I saw Rosa with her arms full. I could smell the garlic across the room. "Bella Bambina, wake up," she said. "I've come bringing medicine from the Old Country." A smile lit her face, and I sat up.

"What did you bring?"

"Garlic twists, of course. They're just what the doctor

ordered. And fettuccini Alfredo. I know it's your favorite. And salmon, just like I promised. Grilled just the way you like it. Well, minus the salt. The doctor said you need to be on a salt-free diet for a while." She put the food down on the table and began to open the Tupperware containers. The smell danced across the room, bringing hope.

Within minutes, the room was full of people once again. Mama. Pop. Sophia. Tony. Joey. Norah. Phoebe. They fed me, coddled me, prayed over me, and made me promise I would take care of myself. In short, they promised to love me back to health. All the while, I kept a watchful eye on D.J., who hovered over me like a mama hen, making sure I had the space I needed. God bless that cowboy of mine. He'd boot-scooted his way into my life, changing everything.

"More garlic twists, Bella?" Rosa called out, interrupting my thoughts.

When I nodded, she refilled my plate, not just with bread, but with every good thing. I couldn't possibly eat it all. Still, with so many people looking on, I would give it my best shot.

I would give something else my best shot too. Whatever the doctor said, I would do. If it meant resting a few days, fine. If it meant eating more, fine. If it meant putting off the wedding . . .

Hmm. I had to admit—that one *wasn't* so fine.

# 27

# Bewitched, Bothered, and Bewildered

I spent my second day in the hospital trying to stay calm—not an easy task with wires and tubes constricting my every movement. The morning started with a nuclear stress test. That was a blast. From there I had an echocardiogram—a somewhat easier process. After that, the bloodthirsty tech people came and drained me of every ounce of blood for more tests. Hadn't they taken enough yesterday?

I tried not to think about the wedding. Tried not to let it bother me. After all, I still had three and a half days. Surely they would spring me from this place later today or tomorrow, right?

Finally back in my room, I closed my eyes and tried to rest before the next group of guests showed up. Most everyone in the family had been suspiciously absent this morning. Of course, they'd spent half the night trucking back and forth between my room and Marcella's. I'd nearly dozed off when a soft voice roused me.

"Bella?" Mama entered, along with Aunt Rosa. "How are you feeling this morning?"

"Tired. But a little better, actually."

"Any test results yet?"

"No. Tomorrow, maybe."

Another voice sounded from the doorway. "Knock knock!"

I looked up to see Twila entering the room with Terrell alongside her. I had to smile when I read her T-shirt advertising the Royal Caribbean cruise line.

"Twila! How are the honeymooners?"

She came toward the bed with a concerned look on her face. "The honeymooners are fine. The bigger question is, how are you? I had no idea my little Bella was sick!"

"Oh, I'm not sick. Not really."

"Well, when I heard my girl was in the hospital, I couldn't stay away." Tears filled her eyes, and she reached for my hand, giving it a squeeze.

"Wild dogs couldn't keep us from coming," Jolene said, entering the room behind her.

"The minute I heard you were sick, I packed up my dancing shoes and came with," Bonnie Sue added. "I thought maybe a little entertainment would lift your spirits."

"She's teasing about the dancing shoes," Twila whispered. "Bonnie Sue thinks she's funny."

"I *am* funny." Bonnie Sue winked, and I smiled in response. "But seriously, we just came to see you. To lift your spirits. And to bring you a few goodies."

"Goodies?" I sat up a little straighter.

Earline entered the room behind Bonnie Sue, her arms full. "I've made chicken-fried steak with mashed potatoes and gravy, Bella. I know you love that! 'Course, I had to leave out the salt, but that's okay. Figured you could use a good meal right about now. Get you up and running again."

The delicious smell of fried steak permeated the room, overwhelming my senses. Still, my stomach was pretty full from all of Rosa's offerings last night. Could I really risk another huge meal?

Staring into my future mother-in-law's face, I realized I must. Besides, I could probably use the calories. And I sure didn't need to worry about my wedding dress not fitting. The alterations lady had chastised me because of my weight loss. How often did a girl get that kind of critique?

*Oh, the wedding dress! Did Sophia pick it up?* I would have to remember to ask her later.

Within minutes, we were all eating. Earline had packed enough for the crowd. By the time Jenna showed up, the room was filled to the brim with chattering guests. I enjoyed the diversion. There was something familiar and comforting about the sound of their voices.

The conversation started out light, but it quickly turned heavy when Twila asked a hard question. "Bella, I can see how you're doing physically, but how are you doing spiritually?"

I paused for a moment, not wanting to make a liar out of myself. I'd been doing pretty well, right? I still read my Bible on occasion and prayed. On the run, mostly. But surely the Lord could see that I needed to stay busy. Otherwise, why would he have given me so much to do?

Looking into Twila's eyes, I knew I had to tell the truth. "I've been struggling, to be honest. I don't feel like I'm where I need to be right now. If things would just slow down, maybe I could get back to that place where everything made sense. Where I felt really close to God. But it feels like everything

in my life is moving in fast-forward and I can't seem to slow
it down."

"This whole thing reminds me of the twenty-third psalm,"
Earline said. "You know that part about how God makes us
lie down in green pastures? That's where you are right now,
Bella. In green pastures."

"Are you saying the Lord caused me to get sick to slow me
down?" I asked.

"No." She shook her head. "That's not what I'm saying at
all. I'm just saying that while you're here, you might as well
take advantage of the quiet time to get back to that place
with the Lord where you want to be. The Bible is pretty clear
that the Lord can take what the enemy meant for evil and use
it for our good. So why not let God do that? While you're
resting—even if it's in a hospital room—think of yourself
as lying in green pastures beside still waters. When you're
in that place—truly in that place—God promises to restore
your soul."

"And I have a feeling he'll restore your body too," Twila
added. "If you get the rest and nutrition you need."

I felt the sting of tears and brushed them away. "Do . . . do
you ever feel like you have to work overtime to prove yourself?
Like, maybe people won't see your value or worth unless you
prove yourself to them?" My heart began to pound at this
confession, and I could feel my blood pressure rising. Still,
it was worth it to get this off my chest.

"I think we've all felt that way at times," Earline said. "But
I have a feeling you're getting to something specific."

I paused, willing the lump in my throat to go away. If I
opened this can of worms, there might be no turning back.
Oh, but how I needed to!

When I finally spoke, my words were shaky. Broken. Like

me. "All of my life, I've wanted to feel needed, to feel like I had something to contribute." I paused, hoping my mother wouldn't take this the wrong way. "In a family the size of mine, especially when you're a middle child like I am, you sometimes feel a little . . ."

"Overlooked?" Twila, Bonnie Sue, and Jolene said in unison.

I shrugged. "I guess that would be the word, though I'm really thinking more along the lines of feeling like I don't have as much to offer. I was a lousy waitress at Parma John's. I think we've established that. And I wasn't very good at cheerleading in high school. I was always one of those people who had to work twice as hard to do something even moderately well."

"Oh, but Bella," Mama said, "don't you see? You've done wonders with the wedding facility. Brought in a whole new clientele. You took our family business—which was struggling at best—and turned it into a five-star wedding facility."

"We've even been on the Food Network," Rosa threw in.

I laughed. "I can't take the credit for that one, Rosa. That was your gig."

"Still." She waved her hand. "Bella, you're exactly the right person for this job."

"And God knew it all along," Mama added. "You've got nothing to prove—to us or anyone else."

"If not for you, I wouldn't be married right now," Rosa said with a nod. "You pulled off the wedding of the century, Bella."

"I daresay we're all happy," Twila said with a grin. "And you've played a role in that. You listened to the Lord. You put legs underneath the wedding facility, and now people's lives are being transformed."

"Still, there's this part of me—way down deep—that feels like I have to work harder to feel valuable. Isn't that . . . silly?"

"It's normal," Earline said. "And it's something we all struggle with, if we're honest with ourselves. But honey, you've got to remember that your worth isn't found in anything you do. Even if you didn't succeed as a wedding planner—which I can't imagine, by the way—you would still be valuable to God. You never have to work overtime to prove yourself to him. Never. He loves you just as you are. No strings attached."

I sighed and leaned back against my pillow.

"Why not let him spend a couple of days convincing you of that?" Twila asked. "A few hours in his presence will be just the ticket to heal both body and soul."

"It's just that the timing of all this really stinks," I said. "I'm getting married on Saturday, and I can't even coordinate my own wedding."

"You don't have to, honey," Mama said. "This is the time to delegate."

"What?" *Delegate?*

"Give me a job," Twila said. "I'm in."

"Me too," Jolene added. "I'm pretty good with flowers. Want me to take a shot at those wedding bouquets? I heard Marcella's out of the loop."

"And I'm a whiz on the computer," Bonnie Sue said with a nod. "D.J. tells me you need someone to finalize the programs and then print them up."

"Well, that's really nice of you, but . . ." I couldn't think of anything to add after the "but." I'd always been the go-to girl, the one in charge. Was the Lord really asking me to hand over my wedding to the women in my life? Did he want some one-on-one time with me during this very critical week? If so, would I—could I—cooperate?

"Bella, we've got the reception food under control," Rosa said. "Bubba and Jenna have already said they will do anything we ask. And you know I'm on the ball when it comes to the cake. I can't wait."

"You're all so great." I sighed, realizing just how many wonderful people God had placed in my life. Surely he knew just how desperately I needed them all—not just this week, but always.

"You know I'm going to whip that reception hall into shape," Mama said with a twinkle in her eye.

"Oh, and I love to decorate. I'll help with that," Bonnie Sue added.

On and on they went, talking about the various roles they were going to play in my wedding. After a while I stopped arguing and just listened. Sounded like they were going to give me the wedding of my dreams . . . and I wouldn't have to do anything but show up. Was such a thing really possible?

Peace wrapped me in its cozy embrace, and I relaxed. For once, I didn't have to be the one in charge.

What would that feel like?

The automatic blood pressure machine kicked in, puffing up around my arm. I rested easy, listening to the ladies talk, but happened to glance over when the machine released its grip: 125/88. Interesting.

My eyes grew heavy, but the words Earline had quoted earlier ran through my brain. *He makes me lie down in green pastures. He leads me beside the still waters.*

If I closed my eyes, I could almost see those green pastures now.

# 28

## For You, for Me, for Evermore

I spent the next couple of days in the hospital, taking and retaking tests. Instead of fighting the process, I gave myself over to it, happy to finally get the rest I'd been lacking over the prior weeks. By the third day, I had the entire twenty-third psalm memorized, and I replayed the words in my head a dozen times a day, at least. I could feel the effects on both my body and my mind. My thoughts—usually in a whirlwind— finally calmed down.

In the quieter moments, I found myself humming "Amazing Grace" and wondering what Guido was up to. I missed the little guy. Missed his ever-present reminder that God's grace truly was amazing, and that people—and birds—could be transformed.

On Thursday morning, the doctor came for a visit.

"Bella." He pulled up a chair and sat next to my bed with his clipboard in hand. "All of your results are in."

"Oh?" I'd been waiting for this moment for days.

"The echocardiogram was clear," he said with a smile. "No sign of heart disease."

*Praise the Lord!*

"The stress test was negative too. Thyroid tests were normal." He looked up from his papers. "This is all very good news, young lady."

"No kidding." Relief washed over me. "So, what's wrong with me?"

He thumbed through the pages once again. "Well, your blood pressure was too high, but your blood sugar was too low. I think we've already established that could be diet-related. From what I hear, you've been eating like a champ since you got here. Yesterday's blood work showed that your blood sugar is back up in the normal range. And here's the kicker. Your blood pressure is back in the normal range too. The meds are helping, but so is the rest."

"I'm learning how to rest." I offered a weak smile after those words, hoping they made sense to him. "It's like a job for me. I'm in training."

"I know what it is to run yourself ragged," he said. "Trust me. But I also know there's only so much the body can take before you finally crater. Rest is good. Balancing your work hours against times of relaxation is critical."

"So, what's my official diagnosis?" I asked. "What do I tell people when they ask why I was in the hospital?"

"You tell them you needed a break." He smiled. "But if you're looking for an official diagnosis—other than the low blood sugar—I would have to say that you've been struggling from a classic case of anxiety. Stress, which led to the hypertension."

I sighed. For this, I had to pay thousands of dollars in medical bills?

The doctor released me from the hospital that same morning. I'd never been so happy to leave a place in my life. Well, other than that one night I'd spent in jail. Still, there was a small part of me that had enjoyed my "green pastures" time while it lasted. Who got to lounge around in bed all day and have people bring her food, after all?

D.J. came to pick me up, and we stopped off at Marcella's room on our way. As I came through the door, she offered a smile.

"You're up and running again, I see," she said.

"Up, but not running. From now on, everything slows down for me. No more burning the candle at both ends. It was taking a toll on my body."

"I hear ya." She sighed. "I'm guilty of the same thing." Marcella paused for a minute, putting her hand on her stomach. "Oh, that was a hard one."

"W-what?"

She pointed to the monitor, and I gasped as I saw the contraction show up on-screen.

"You're in labor?"

From behind me, I heard D.J. let out a little gasp. I turned with a smile, surprised to see how pale he looked. Stifling a grin, I turned back to Marcella.

"It started about an hour ago," she said. "I just called Nick. The doctor said he could try to stop it, but at this point they're pretty sure Anna Rosa's lungs are developed enough to do okay."

"Wait. Anna Rosa? Is that what you're naming the baby?"

"Mm-hmm." Marcella smiled. "Anna after my grandmother. And Rosa after, well, Rosa."

"Does she know?"

Marcella shook her head. "No. It's going to be a surprise.

308

But I don't mind telling you. You've already proven that you can be trusted with secrets."

"You know you can trust me," D.J. said.

"But, is the fact that you're in labor a secret, or should I call Mama?" I asked.

"I already did. Called my mother too. They should both be here soon. I would ask you to stick around, but you've got a wedding to plan." She grinned, then gripped her tummy once more. "Oh, wow. They're getting stronger."

When she finally stopped panting, I put my purse and bag on the windowsill and took a seat in the rocker at the foot of her bed. "You know what, Marcella? I can stay right here with you. The wedding . . . well, from what I hear, it's under control. The women . . ." I looked at D.J. and smiled. "Well, the women and this awesome fiancé of mine swept in and took the reins. If I go home, there won't be much to do but sit around and eat bonbons. I can assure you, Mama won't let me work."

"Mmm. Bonbons sound pretty good right about now."

"I know, right?"

We both laughed.

Minutes later, the room came alive with people. Both families—ours and Marcella's—flooded in. By 1:00 Marcella had dilated to seven centimeters. D.J., Joey, Pop, and Sal went down the hall to the waiting area. The women stayed in the room for as long as the doctor would allow us to. Nick paced back and forth, the typical worried papa.

At 4:00 little Anna Rosa made her entrance into the world, screaming all the way. She was born with a full shock of dark hair and the prettiest eyes I'd ever seen. We celebrated with tears and laughter at the new arrival, and the room filled with people once again, each there to offer joyous tidings.

Oh, how I loved this family! We loved with passion. We celebrated with passion. We looked at life with passion. And we welcomed new members with equally as much passion.

By 4:30 my passion was waning. Exhaustion set in. D.J. offered to drive me home, and I quickly accepted. He pointed the car toward the Rossi home, but then took an unexpected turn off Broadway onto a side street.

"What are you doing?" I looked his way, trying to make sense of this.

"Oh, just needed to make a stop. Sorry."

"Oh, okay."

He took another turn, which brought us to a tree-lined street. I'd been down it many times over the years, but I didn't remember the house in front of us now. It was a soft blue Victorian with a wide porch and broad windows.

"D.J.?" I looked at him, realization setting in. "Is this . . ."

He looked my way, his eyes filled with tears. "Do you still have that key I gave you on Christmas Day?"

"I . . . I think so." Scrambling around in my purse, I finally came up with it. I held it up in the air, and he grinned.

"You're gonna need that, Bella Bambina."

Suddenly, I could hardly move fast enough. I scrambled out of the cab and practically ran to the front door. But when I got to the porch, I stopped, taking in the wonder of it all. The porch swing caught my eye at once, as did the pristine white railings surrounding the porch. And the windows! They were spectacular.

D.J. gestured for me to use the key in the door, which I did. My first step inside took my breath away.

"Oh, D.J.!" The expansive foyer had ceilings ten feet high at least. Maybe higher. And the stained-glass piece in the

310

front door was breathtaking. Not to mention the polished wood floors. "How in the world did you . . ." I couldn't finish the sentence over the lump in my throat. I wanted to take in the rest, but the tears in my eyes prevented me from seeing everything at once.

First he showed me the downstairs powder room just off the foyer. I especially loved the pedestal sink and the mirror above it. Next D.J. showed me the dining room—a large expanse of a room with the biggest table I'd ever seen, next to the one at my parents' house, of course. I shook my head, unable to speak. We rounded the corner into the living room completely decked out with Mediterranean furniture.

"How did you know that I wanted . . ." Again I couldn't say the rest because of the catch in my throat.

"I've been paying attention to everything you've ever said about home decor, Bella," he said. "Right down to colors and styles. I hope you like it."

Like it? I loved it! But how—and when—did he accomplish this? He must've worked through the night for weeks to get this done so quickly.

We turned down a small hall, finally landing in the kitchen. It took my breath away. There was a large island in the center, and the tiled backsplash was perfect. Very Italian.

"I actually have a real Italian kitchen," I said with awe. "Now I just have to figure out what to do in it."

"We'll figure it out together. I'm not bad with a spatula myself." He winked, and my heart fluttered—this time in a good way. "Ready to look upstairs?"

I wanted to say yes but still found myself speechless, so a nod would have to do. I followed him up the stairs, marveling at the smooth railing on the banister. Surely he had done this work himself. *Primo!*

311

At the top of the stairs we entered a wide hallway. Typical Victorian layout. He showed off the guest room first, and I was stunned to see my old bedroom furniture inside, along with the same comforter I'd slept under for years. The tears started in earnest at this point. Next came the hall bath, a nice-size room for an older home. Newly renovated, clearly. Then we moved on to the room I felt sure would be my favorite—the master bedroom.

I gasped as I saw the spacious room with its king-size bed and rich Mediterranean dresser. No wonder Mama had spent so much time asking my opinion when we went furniture shopping for Laz and Rosa—she'd had a few tricks up her sleeve. Why, this was the very bedroom suite I'd picked out for them!

D.J. led me into the master bath, and I almost cried tears of joy and relief when I saw the garden tub. Was it possible all of this was really mine? I could almost envision myself in that tub now. Put a whole new meaning to the words "beside the still waters."

"Now, I have one more room to show you." D.J.'s eyes twinkled. "I think it's going to be your favorite. I hope so, anyway."

"How anything could top this is beyond me," I said, still captivated by the room we were in.

"Just wait and see, Bella."

Down the hallway we went, to a door at the end. As he pushed it open, my gaze landed on a fabulous desk and a wall filled with bookshelves and built-in cabinets.

"What in the world?" I stepped inside this wonderland, smiling as I read the sign on the desk: CLUB WED. BELLA NEELEY, WEDDING COORDINATOR.

"I know you have your office at the wedding facility," he

312

said. "But I thought it might help to have an office at home too."

"What about you?" I asked. "You need an office more than I do."

"I'll get around to that," he said. "There's a room over the garage I plan to renovate. Till then, maybe you could share your space with me."

"Oh, honey, I'm happy to share my space—and my life— with you."

I looked in the corner of the room, noticing for the first time the little dog bed, just right for Precious. D.J. had thought of everything. Absolutely everything.

He pulled me into his arms and kissed the top of my head. "So, here's the deal. We moved all of your stuff over here. Your clothes. Everything."

"What? Already?"

"Yep. This is your home now. Jenna is coming over when she gets off of work to spend the night with you. Tomorrow night—after the rehearsal—Sophia and Norah want to have a slumber party here. They thought you might like that."

"Of course! They're my bridesmaids!"

"I'll be at the condo with Sal from now till the wedding day. You, um, you heard about Sal, right?"

"No. What about him?"

D.J. smiled. "He's been talking with me about the Lord. A lot. Started with something Guido said and went from there."

"No way."

"Yep. He's had a lot of questions, but I've done a fair job of keeping up with them, I think. He's making progress, Bella. I totally see that God is doing something amazing in his life."

"D.J., that's awesome!"

"Interesting that the Lord could use a bird to evangelize his owner," he said. "Makes you believe anything's possible."

"Oh, trust me, I do believe we have a lot to learn from Guido. These past few days, I've been singing 'Amazing Grace' over and over again, realizing for the first time in years just how much I need that grace he's been singing about. Never realized how much till the past few days."

"Oh?" D.J. stepped back and gave me a curious look.

"Yes. I need God's grace, but I need to grace myself sometimes too. I think I've been too hard on myself. Been running in performance mode to prove my worth—to myself and others. But this week I had a reality check. God wants me to stop and smell the roses. To enjoy the people in my world and to remember how much more important they are than the projects. To thank him every day for my health and to take better care of myself."

"You learned all of that from a bird?" D.J. asked, drawing me close once again.

"Well, not all." I laughed. "But I don't think it would be a stretch to say that Guido reminded me that I once was blind, but now I see. God has given me a lot of insight over the past couple of days. A whole new way of looking at things."

"And what do you see?" he whispered.

"I see potential for a true happily ever after, as long as we keep him at the center of our relationship and keep our lives in balance. Not too much work. Not too much play. Lots of family time. Lots of joy. Lots of swing dancing. Great food." I threw in the food as an afterthought, but I realized just how important it was, at least in the life of the Rossi family. Food was the uniting factor. That thing that drew us to a common table for genuine fellowship.

"So, you're saying I have to swing dance to be in a good relationship with the Lord?" D.J. gave me a dubious look.

"Well, it doesn't hurt." I laughed, and he took my hands in his, then spun me around in dramatic fashion.

"All right, then," D.J. said. "Put on your dancing shoes and let's get going."

With his hand in mine, we did just that.

# 29

# It Had to Be You

For years, I'd heard brides say that their wedding day was a blur. That it seemed to pass in the blink of an eye. That all of the prep work, no matter how difficult or cumbersome, faded to the background as the whole thing whizzed by.

I found every word of that to be true.

On Saturday, the 14th of February, I married the love of my life, D.J. Neeley.

The whole thing was a whirlwind. I vaguely remembered how beautiful Sophia, Jenna, and Norah looked in their bridesmaids' dresses. How handsome my brothers and Bubba looked in their groomsmen attire. I noticed the bouquets of red roses that Norah and Jolene had put together. The fabulous buffet, a wonderland of foods prepared by Rosa, Laz, Jenna, and Bubba. The exquisite reception hall, decorated by Mama and her team of ladies. The gorgeous programs, printed by Bonnie Sue. The sound of Gordy's band, playing some of our favorite country and Italian tunes. I had some memory of Joey taking pictures and the taste of Rosa's incredible cake, though I didn't get nearly enough of it. And I definitely remembered the wedding dress, which fit perfectly. Turned out the alterations lady had hand-delivered it when she heard I was in the hospital.

Funny, though. None of that mattered. After all of the planning, after all of the chaos, after everything everyone had done, only one thing mattered. D.J. Neeley and I were husband and wife. I was his, and he was mine.

In that moment, as I contemplated that vast and yet-unknown truth, I realized something. My work as a wedding planner was to offer assistance to the bride, of course. To keep things going so she wouldn't have to. But ultimately, I did what I did so that she could enjoy the one thing I couldn't do—fully devote herself not to the wedding but to her new life.

That day, wedding planning was the farthest thing from my mind. On Saturday, the 14th of February, I was fully a bride in every sense of the word. The cake could have toppled over, and I would have found it humorous. The programs could have been printed upside down, and I would have stood on my head to read them. The bridesmaids' dresses could have been hideous, and I would have found something wonderful to say about them. In short, none of that mattered. All that mattered—all that would ever matter—was watching God at work, joining a quirky Italian girl with a slow-drawlin' country boy. Watching two lives merge into one.

As D.J. and I shared our first dance, I finally had a chance to whisper a few things in his ear. I needed him to know how much the last few weeks and months had meant to me, and how excited I was about sharing the rest of my life with him.

317

The band played the first few notes of "Then," one of Brad Paisley's most poignant hits. It was a song that exemplified our love for each other in every way. D.J. and I took a spin around the dance floor with all of the people we loved looking on. In that moment, I wondered how I could possibly be any happier.

"How are you feeling today, Mrs. Neeley?" D.J. asked as he held me close.

"Never better, Mr. Neeley," I responded. "And I have all of you to thank for it."

"Oh?"

"Yes." I paused, pushing back the tears. "D.J., I'm so grateful to you. You planned this wedding, and it's everything I ever dreamed it would be and more."

"Well, if I'm going to be completely honest, I'd have to say the ladies did most of the planning. I was more on the sidelines."

"Not true. Mama told me you were right there in the thick of it. Guiding them every step of the way. You knew just what to tell Bonnie Sue about the programs. You oversaw the flowers and the food. You knew just what to tell Gordy about the music. I heard you even helped put the cake together. Sounds like you pretty much coordinated everything."

"Well, shoot," he drawled. "That was the easy part."

"Easy?" I gazed into his beautiful eyes, completely captivated.

"Well, sure, Bella." He kissed me on the cheek, and we continued to dance. "My only real job was to know you—and know you well. That way I could give the same instructions I knew you would have given. You've had your wedding planned since you were a little girl. All I did was listen."

"Well, you did a fine job, let me tell you that. And it means the world to me that you know me so well. Better than any-one."

"And I'm going to go on knowing you for the rest of my life." He waggled his brows, and I laughed, realizing he was talking about a differing kind of "knowing" now.

He pulled me into his arms and kissed me with both the tenderness of a gentleman and the forcefulness of a cowboy. Wowza! I heard the cheers of our families off in the distance and realized they were egging him on. Not that I minded. No, I would be happy kissing this cowboy . . . for the rest of my life.

# 30

## Thanks for the Memories

When I awoke in the hotel room the morning after my wedding, I rolled over in bed to catch a glimpse of my husband. The whole "I'm married now" thing still seemed surreal, especially the "waking up with a man in your bed" part.

As for the wedding night . . . well, there was really only one way to describe it: *bada-bing, bada-boom!* I finally understood all of the anticipation. There was something incredibly special about sharing your wedding night with a man who'd waited for you—in every sense of the word. I wouldn't trade that for anything.

For a moment, I lay still, just watching D.J. breathe. My thoughts drifted back to our first meeting—how I'd fallen for him as he ambled up the driveway in those boots of his. Now his boots would have a permanent residence in my home . . . and my heart.

After a few minutes, I woke my D.J.-turned-deejay cowboy

hubby. He yawned and pulled me into his arms, whispering, "Good morning, Mrs. Neeley."

"Good morning, Mr. Neeley." I kissed his cheek, and he responded by drawing me close. For a while we lay there cradled in each other's arms. So *this* was what it felt like to wake up next to the man you loved. I liked it. Very much. I had a feeling I would go on liking it for the rest of my life.

Unfortunately, we didn't get to relish this experience much longer. A glance at the clock told me it was time to get moving. We had to be at the airport in two hours. At least that's what D.J. had said last night. I still didn't know where we were going, though I had my suspicions. He'd planted a few clues along the way.

D.J. and I hit the road less than an hour later. With every mile north we headed on Interstate 45, my curiosity grew. Likely he was taking me to Cancun, I reasoned. Or Cozumel. Or Jamaica. Regardless, we would have the time of our lives, and all the more now that I got to wake up in his arms every morning.

The trip to the airport was spent in nervous chatter on my end. Just passing the time, of course. Secretly I was dying to know what he had up his sleeve.

We arrived at the airport, and D.J. parked in the extended stay parking. Then we boarded the shuttle, exiting at the international terminal. My antennae went up. Why the international terminal? Most flights to Mexico went out of one of the other terminals, right?

Hmm. I wasn't so sure. Only when we stepped into the line for Lufthansa did it hit me.

"We're going . . . to Europe?"

He grinned, looking quite proud of himself. "Maybe."

"Where?" My heart rate quickened, and for a moment

I thought I would faint, but I pushed that idea out of my head. There was no time for fainting today. We had a flight to catch!

"We're flying to Rome, then staying ten days in Italy, doing our own personal tour. Laz and Sal set me up with a map and all sorts of places to visit."

"No way."

"Way." He smiled. "There was never a doubt in my mind about where we should go, Bella. Your family is from Italy. Your roots are there. If I want to know you—if I want to know them—I have to go to the place you're from."

"That's the sweetest thing I've ever heard!" I paused, my eyes filling with tears.

"One day we'll go to Scotland," he said. "That's where my mom's grandparents came from. But for now, it's all things Italy. We're going to go boating on the Mediterranean and swim in the indigo waters."

"D.J. . . ." I shook my head, words failing me. "How can I ever thank you for this?"

"Well, actually, you can thank Francesca. At least in part."

"W-what?"

"She and Emilio have a country home outside of Napoli. When I told them about my plans, they gave me a key. We can stay there and use it as our hub. And anytime we get tired of driving, we'll just head back home to our Italian villa for a few days of rest and relaxation."

"Among other things," I teased.

His cheeks turned pink. "Well, that too." A mischievous smile lit his face.

The line inched forward, and we finally arrived at the ticket counter to drop off our luggage. Half an hour later, we were standing in line to board the plane. Once again, the languages of those nearby overlapped. English and Italian were predominant, but there were a few other unrecognizable ones as well. And talk about a crowd. Looked like everybody and their brother wanted to go to Italy!

Our turn finally arrived. We made our way down the ramp toward the plane. The flight attendant nodded and greeted us with a smile, which I returned. Then D.J. and I located our seats—the second row in the business section. D.J. put my carry-on in the overhead compartment, and we settled into our seats. I leaned over and gave my husband a kiss, then whispered, "I'm married to a cowboy."

"Yep." He extended his arm, and I cuddled up next to him. "You are married to a cowboy from Splendora."

"Who would have dreamed?" I giggled.

"Me," he said, suddenly looking quite serious. "You really are like a dream come true, Bella."

"In spite of my quirky family?"

"Not in spite of," he said. "They're part of you, Bella. They make you . . . you. Things just wouldn't be the same if I'd met you in Splendora. God took me out of my comfort zone, not just by moving me to Galveston, but by bringing me someone so different from myself. You balance me out, Bella. You're exotic and fun-loving and—"

"Wait. Exotic?" I had to laugh at that one. I'd pictured myself a great many things, but never exotic.

"Well, sure," he responded. "You're Italian. You've got the most wonderful voice in the world. I love listening to you talk."

"Wow." I paused to think about that. "That's so ironic, D.J., because your voice was the first thing that drew me to you. I fell in love with your voice over the telephone before I ever met you in person. That deep Texas drawl just did me in."

"Then I'll go on using it for the rest of my life."

"I'm counting on it." I gave him a little kiss on the end of his nose and giggled.

The flight attendant greeted us, offering smiles and all sorts of instructions on how to handle a plane crash, should we have to do that. I prayed we would not. If given the option, I'd rather fly all the way to Rome without seeing the Atlantic firsthand. Minutes later, the flight took off and I settled back, happy to see the movie playing overhead.

"Look, D.J. How ironic is that?" I pointed to the screen as *The Wedding Planner* came on.

"Totally bizarre." He laughed and reached for my hand. "I'd have to say that God has a sense of humor."

"No doubt about that." As Jennifer Lopez's larger-than-life persona filled the screen, I fumbled to get my earplugs fastened to the seat. Just about the time I started to slip them on, I heard a voice coming from first class, one that sounded all too familiar. "What in the world . . . ?" I looked at D.J., but it appeared he'd dozed off.

I strained to hear the woman's voice once more. If I didn't know any better, I'd have to say that sounded like . . .

No way. It couldn't be.

Though the "fasten seat belt" sign hadn't yet gone off, I unsnapped my belt and rose.

"What are you doing, Bella?" D.J. looked up, his brow wrinkled in concern.

"I'll be right back. I just have to . . ." I took a few steps forward, peering through the opening between business and first class. I almost tripped over my own feet as I saw my parents seated just a few rows up.

"Mama?"

My mother turned to me, her mouth opening wide as she took me in. "Bella? What in the world? I thought you and D.J. were going to Cancun!"

"I did too. It was a surprise."

"No way!" Mama laughed. "Well, speaking of surprises . . . you know how Pop and I have always said we were going to go on another European vacation?"

"Of course! You've been planning for it for years."

"Now that the wedding facility is in such good hands, I finally decided the time was right," my father said, giving me a wink. "Planned this trip as a surprise for your mother. Been working on it for weeks."

"Yes, but who's home manning the facility now?" I asked. "What if someone calls? And what about Sophia and Tony's big day? And Norah and Joey's? And Lilly and Gordy's? And Jenna and Bubba's? Who's—" I didn't get to say another word because D.J. cut me off.

"Bella?"

I looked back at him, seeing a stunned look on his face as he noticed my parents.

"Surprise!" Mama jumped up and threw her arms around D.J., who looked more than a little shell-shocked. To his credit, he gave her a warm hug and a convincing smile.

"Don't worry, Son," my father said with a nod. "We didn't plan this on purpose. And I promise you won't even see us or hear from us once this plane lands in Rome."

D.J. flashed a crooked grin. "I'm counting on that, sir."

Pop laughed so loud that it drew the attention of the flight attendant. She came our way with a look of warning on her face.

"I need you to take your seats, please."

"We're going." I waved good-bye to my parents—both physically and symbolically—then turned back toward my seat. As I did, I happened to glance down, noticing the boots on Mama's feet. Suddenly, I felt like laughing.

My, how far we had come. And we had a certain Splendora cowboy to thank for it all. Well, one cowboy and the Lord, who had clearly arranged all of this from the get-go. Why had he brought our two families together, merging D.J. and me into the first Tex-Italian duo in our family's history? Only one reason I could think of—to add a little spice to our lives.

But oh, mama mia! What a lovely spice!

# Sister Bonnie Sue's Top Ten Swing Dancing Tips

1. Make sure you're prayed up before choosing a partner. You never know what God might do!
2. Sign up for swing classes. They will keep you in shape and give you plenty of new friends.
3. Keep your dancing shoes nearby at all times. You never know when the music is going to begin.
4. Make sure your dancing shoes are comfortable but stylish. No point in cramping your toes . . . or your style.
5. Dancing is great exercise, so be prepared to drop a few pounds as you swing. You can always spend a little extra time at the buffet table to make up for it.
6. Memorizing the right steps isn't as important as having fun. Swing's the thing! It's meant to be enjoyed!
7. Keep swing CDs in your car. (Warning: It's difficult to dance while driving!)
8. God is the ultimate band director. Pay close attention, because you don't want to get ahead of him. Stick with

him in perfect time, and he will make a beautiful melody out of your life.

9. When you're facing a battle, remember Jehoshaphat and those Levites. Praise your way through it! (And don't be ashamed to tap your toes!)

10. Struggling to fill your dance card? Remember, the Lord wants to be your ultimate partner. He's the one who knows you best, after all.

# Acknowledgments

To my agent, Chip MacGregor: This quirky series would never have found its home if not for you. Thanks for not thinking I was crazy.

To my editor, Jennifer Leep: You have made me feel both welcomed and loved at Revell. How can I ever begin to thank you for falling in love with Bella and her family? I'm so thrilled that Rosa and Laz get to have their happily ever after!

To my copyeditor, Jessica Miles: Girl, you put a Texas spit shine on all three manuscripts, catching my errors and encouraging me every step of the way. I could never have done this without you.

To Michele Misiak: We're email buddies and so much more. You have been a constant source of encouragement and have worked so hard to get the word out. How can I ever thank you?

To the whole Revell team: You have blessed me beyond belief. I'm tickled you've taken this Texas gal under your wings.

To my critique partners: Bada-bing, bada-boom! Man,

you're fast! You buzzed through this series, adding your sparkle and shine. I'm so grateful.

To my Lord and Savior, Jesus Christ: You are not just *at* the heart of every story I write, you *are* the heart of every story I write. This one is no exception.

**Janice Thompson** is a Christian freelance author and a native Texan. She has four grown daughters, three beautiful granddaughters, a brand-new grandson, and two more grandbabies on the way. Bada-bing, bada-boom! She resides in the greater Houston area, where the heat and humidity tend to reign.

Janice started penning books at a young age and was blessed to have a screenplay produced in the early eighties. From there she went on to write several large-scale musical comedies for a Houston school of the arts. Currently, she has published over fifty novels and nonfiction books for the Christian market, most of them lighthearted and/or wedding themed.

Working with quirky characters and story ideas suits this fun-loving author. She particularly enjoys contemporary, first-person romantic comedies. Wedding-themed books come naturally to Janice, since she's coordinated nearly a dozen weddings, including recent ceremonies and receptions for her four daughters. She currently serves as the wedding coordinator for her church as well. Most of all, she loves sharing her faith with readers and hopes they will catch a glimpse of the real happily ever after as they laugh their way through her lighthearted, romantic tales.

# A Romantic Comedy That Will Have You Laughing All Day

Don't miss book 1 in the Weddings by Bella series!

When *Hollywood's* most eligible
bachelor sweeps into town,
will he cause trouble for *Bella*?

Don't miss book 2 in the Weddings by Bella series!